DESTINIES in MOTION

by Liliya V. Galitskaya

ACKNOWLEDGEMENTS

Conceived and written by   Liliya V. Galitskaya.

Illustrations drawn by   Liliya V. Galitskaya.

Reviewed and Edited by   Roderick J Rhodes. A.I.B. (Scot).

Original Manuscript typed by   Vitaly Galitsky.
Liliya's son.

CONTENTS

PREFACE

Dreams really are a mysterious phenomenon. Sometimes they are so light that they barely touch the surface of our consciousness and, in the morning, they leave no memory of themselves except a restful feeling. At other times they are heavier and come to entertain our minds with intricate plots. Fascinated, we try to remember them to share their stories and meanings with someone close. However, the last type of dream is usually recognized as a warning and, as such, it lies on the heart like a heavy stone and needs to be examined thoroughly to decode the secret message that is imprinted in its somber picture. This dream doesn't bring comfort or pleasure but mostly a troubled mood.

Lana's dream was of this latter kind and was definitely not a peaceful one. She woke up in terror, unable at first to understand where she was and by which means she had managed to escape being killed. A quick look across the room revealed to her that she was alone and, thankfully, safe. Apparently, the frightening images that still tumbled through her mind were just creations of a bad dream. She sat on the bed and took a deep breath, trying to take control of her shaking body and to slow down the fast beats of her heart.

A moment later she realized that she was crying. This discovery made her feel embarrassed because, only yesterday, she had been laughing at girls for being scared by the frightening stories that they had been telling each other around a table late at night. She admitted to herself that she could have spared herself a nightmare had she not stayed up until midnight to listen to them. Fortunately for her she hadn't screamed out and woken up the household as a consequence.

Lana moved to the edge of the bed, unable to sleep anymore. Wearing only her long nightshirt, she went to the window to let fresh air from the garden dry her wet eyes and cheeks whilst she looked at the blank face of the full moon that stood lonely in the dark sky. Her dream scared her this much because it was related to her current situation.

She remembered that she had been walking with a man whom she knew very well on a narrow pathway alongside the stone crenellations that crowned the city wall and had stopped for a moment to look down at the people who were busy with their casual business in the yard below. There was nothing frightening about this picture until she had taken her gaze away. When she had returned it to the same place she was surprised to see that the view had changed completely and realized that she now stood on the top of a grassy hill that threw a deep shadow down to a river flowing at its foot. As she turned her head towards her companion to ask him what had happened, instead of him she saw the figure of a horrific creature towering over her.

The narrow teeth of the monster were almost on the same level as her face. The quivering of the skin around his nose and on the upper jaw clearly showed that he was not in a good mood and had no intention of playing games with her. The creature's strange, artificial voice frightened her even more as he said to her. "Didn't I tell you that I would kill you if you came here?"

Lana's answer. "Yes!" was little more than a whisper.

"So why didn't you listen to me?" The beast suddenly roared, in a rude and angry manner, then mocked her with the question. "Where is your sword? Is this the weapon that's going to protect you against me?"

Lana looked down at her hand and discovered that, instead of a sword, she was holding a single red rose on a long stem.

"Run!" The monster ordered. "I don't like to be fed; I like to hunt!" His orange eye sparkled with cruel excitement as his mouth twisted into a sadistic smile.

Lana had wanted to run but she couldn't move her legs and, when the monster had thrown his heavy head in her direction to grab her, she had brought the rose close to her chest as a shield and closed her eyes, honestly believing that this would be enough to save her. The last thing that she had seen was a splash of red color under her eyelids.

Perhaps, for someone else, this dream may have seemed like a riddle but it wasn't for Lana. The man in her dream was actually a real person. He had warned her about the danger of her being killed by him should he turn into a monster and, because of this, he had begged her to stay away from him. But it was too late for her to avoid him now since she was already in love with him and the only thing that might help her to save herself was to find out the meaning of the rose in her dream.

No doubt her friend, who happened to be a wizard, would help her with this task. Approaching him, Lana had doubted that he would look at her story as seriously as she did. But the wizard had shared her concern and, in the end, had asked. "Do you intend to cancel your important event next week because of this dream?"

"No." She had replied. "I care about him so much that it would be easier for me to stay here and die at his hands than live in doubt as to whether or not he would kill me."

At this the wizard had nodded, understanding.

"Is there any possibility that this is only a dream?" The wizard had tactfully probed. "Is it possible that the frightening image of this beast came from the stories of your world and later, in your sleep, it molded together with the threat that you have received from the man that you described to me? Perhaps your nightmare has nothing to do with him or the events that have recently happened in your life."

"I wish you were right." She had responded, ruefully. "But the circumstances that brought me here started as an adventure, not as a horrible experience…"

Tod and Tac Viewing Pokerweild Village

CHAPTER 1:

TWO CAT'S LIVES

Tod and Tac were sitting at the side of the road.

Cool air and soft darkness hugged the overheated village of Pokerweild. At that moment the summer night was clear of clouds, allowing onlookers to enjoy the show of stars scattered on its dark blue canvas. From where they sat on the hill, the two saw the bright and low-hanging moon illuminate the open spaces of their village, leaving the rest in mysterious shadows.

The full moon always had a strange power over Tac's imagination. A game of light and shadow made places that he had seen many times before look different. His own neighborhood had become an unknown, frightening territory and at the same time he was tempted to look deeper into the dark shadows of the bushes, which grew at the side of the road, for possible predators or prey.

The place which Tac had chosen for his meeting with Tod was at the exact spot where the road made a sharp turn to the right and then sloped down towards a small stone bridge across a large creek, separating the village into two parts. The bridge and the sandy country road glimmered with small, silver sparks that were created by reflections of moonlight from the surface of countless bits of seashell that had not yet completed their transformation into sand. The road, exposed to the sun, was very hot close to midday and radiated soft waves of heat for many hours after dusk.

A few young village children, coming home late from a movie, were unable to resist the pleasure of walking along the road barefoot. Warm sand soothed and relaxed the tired muscles of their feet and made a nice playground. Usually one of the boys would start a game by stamping on the sand to make it spurt from between his toes like small explosions. This often made his friends laugh, then all of them would get busy trying to find more ways to play with the warm sand by kicking it, or chasing and knocking each other down onto the mat of the road. Eventually, their mothers' voices calling them would finish their fun.

Tac had selected near to midnight as the time for the meeting for good reason. He knew that the road would be empty at night and the view from the top of the hill would allow him to see the bridge and the road clearly if someone did appear unexpectedly.

Below the bridge, the road divided itself into two parts. One part branched to the left where the village continued with rows of bungalows built on both sides of the road. Cherry trees, planted on the front lawns, shaded the round, stone walls which were painted in pale blue and surrounded the properties. Instead of having lawns, some village women had preferred to decorate their front yards with great displays of flowers such as different types of marigold, some of which were reddish-brown with single petals in the form of stars whilst others were shaped like big, sunny orange blossoms. Clusters of mint topped with scented, oval flowers were mixed with irises and impatiens. Tall, white and yellow daisies stood in the background like big sisters watching over the children at play. But the night favored other flowers that preferred to bloom under the moonlight such as night stalks, flowering tobacco and a plant with dark green foliage and pink flowers resembling a carnation known in this village for its delightful fragrance. The second part of the road turned to the right and slid along the creek like a silver ribbon, eventually hiding itself behind an outgrowth of reeds.

Tac was looking in that direction. His eyes inspected the dark masses of reeds that were regularly visited by wild pigs which were looking for edible water plants or to drink water from the creek. Tac did not like it when Tod reminded him of the time when they actually met a pig face-to-face. He shook his head to chase away this memory. The narrow snout of the boar had appeared unexpectedly from the green wall of reeds. Its huge, yellow tusks had stuck out from both sides of its mouth and a wet, pink, nose moved in all directions sniffing the air. Little black eyes had examined both Tac and Tod with a clear, culinary interest. The boar had narrowed its eyes and grunted and this had been enough to make Tod and Tac disappear in a second, as if they had gone with the wind. They had stopped running only when they had reached their home and had found themselves to be safe at last.

Tod had chuckled and said. "What a couple of fools we are, to be afraid of a harmless animal."

"Harmless?" asked Tac. "That boar looked at me as if I was freshly roasted and was lying on a plate surrounded by green peas with a baked apple in my mouth."

This incident was the reason for Tac's negative feelings towards wildlife. He never again joined Tod in his night trips to explore the neighborhood, no matter how hard his friend had tried to re-ignite his interest in adventures. And, no matter how much Tod had exaggerated the stories of his success in studying the life of wild animals, Tac remained stubborn about his decision to stay close to home. He invented a hundred reasons to hide the truth that he was too scared to step outside the gate after midnight. His mind drew pictures of danger await-ing him behind every corner, such as the figure of a boar jumping out at him from nowhere or a wolf going after him.

So Tac preferred to sit near the porch, waiting patiently for Tod to come home with another of his hunter's stories, whilst the night entertained him with a symphony of sounds. Crickets played a background melody on their little violins while their songs harmonized with the solos of frogs living in the creek. Village dogs barked into the night sky for fun, or to share some important infor-mation with neighbors. Sometimes, the low and strong voice of a resting Heron came from the mass of rustling reeds and, naturally, this scared Tac and made him run for the protection of the house.

Now, allow me to introduce you to my two friends, Tac and Tod.

Tac's full name is Tacker but he doesn't mind when family simply call him Tac. He is a big and lazy, gray cat with dark stripes and a large bushy tail.

Toddeysh, or simply Tod, is an orange-brown dog with short fur and large ears. Whenever someone asks about his breed his Master, Nicholas, just shrugs his shoulders and answers. "Unknown." You might have seen a sign on the gate which reads "Guard Dog on Duty" but, if you promise to keep it a secret, I will tell you the truth; Toddeysh is the friendliest dog you could ever meet and he just does his job by barking at strangers.

Tac and Tod have lived in the house of farmer Nicholas since the seventh birthday of his daughter, Lana. She had been asking her parents to buy her a dog or a cat for at least a year. Lana had done everything that she could to be a good girl during the past year and had expected to receive a special gift this time. When the candles on the cake had been blown out, and the birthday girl had made her wish, she rushed into the corner where the boxes containing the presents were displayed.

"Darling, come and get your piece of birthday cake first." Her mother called her to the table but, instead, Lana quickly ripped the wrappings from the packages. She had been given another Barbie doll, a book with beautiful, bright pictures and a new dress. Her heart pumped fast as she opened the last box but saw that it only contained a new pair of shoes. She turned in the direction of her father and his smile faded away from his face as he saw that large, clear tears were quickly forming in the corners of her eyes.

"There is no dog or cat here!" Lana's lips trembled finely and lines of tears gushed down her face. Feeling guilty, Nicholas picked up his keys for the truck and disappeared without a word. He came home about an hour later, carrying a large cardboard box in front of him, to find Lana sitting on the couch and being hugged by her mother, Natalie, who rocked her daughter whilst stroking her hair gently.

"Look at what I have!" Nicholas smiled at her, but Lana only buried her face deeper into her mother's chest.

Suddenly, something alive scratched inside the box and made the sound of an unhappy, little creature. Excitement blew Lana off her mother's lap as Nicholas put the box on the floor and she looked inside it to see a little, orange puppy and a gray kitten. Lana brought her hands up to her chest and looked at her new pets, speechless with happiness. When the kitten made an attempt to climb out of the box she picked him up and scratched his ears, which made the kitten lie comfortably in her hands, purring.

"Let's see the other lad." Said Nicholas, taking the puppy out of the box to place him on the floor. At this, the orange puppy gathered his small body, shivering with fright, and a round pool of liquid appeared under his hind legs quickly expanding in all directions. Nicholas shook his head in dismay and, in a tone of voice that did not allow for any negotiation, said. "The cat can live in the house but a dog's place is outside in the doghouse." After a long discussion, the family decided that the puppy's name would be Toddeysh and the kitten would be called Tacker.

During the first night they both slept in a cardboard box on one of Nicholas's old shirts. But the next day Lana and her father drove to the pet store to buy everything that her new friends would need.

The contents of the store amazed her. The messages and pictures on the covers of the boxes and packages which lined the shelves encouraged the customers to buy all kind of things to spoil their pets.

One look at Lana's radiant face told Nicholas that this was exactly what she was planning to do. Money was tight at this time so Nicholas thoughtfully rubbed his chin, wondering how to stop the flow of things that she kept putting into the shopping cart without removing that expression of happiness from her face. He cleared his throat and, as diplomatically as he could, said. "Honey, if you buy all these things and throw them on these two poor animals, they will probably be more scared than happy. Imagine how you would feel if someone dumped a full shopping cart of food and toys on you? I assure you that you would be confused about what to do with all of these things. But if you buy this kitty-treat, in addition to Tacker's kitten food, I'm sure that he would really appreciate it. And, for Toddeysh, we will buy this bag of dry food and a milk bone so he can exercise his teeth on it instead of on our shoes and furniture. Then add to your shopping card a couple of squeaky rubber toys and this red ball for Toddeysh, a package of plump mice for Tacker, two soft beds and some plates for food and water and we're done with shopping." Adding, hopefully. "Darling, your pets are very young and probably will need some time to figure out how to play with the toys. When you notice that they are losing interest in their old toys you can always buy new ones to keep them in a healthy and happy mood." From his point of view it was a difficult task for a child to process this speech and he waited patiently in the hope that Lana would surrender at least a part of her choices.

The Chicken Chase

Lana's mouth turned into the shape of a puzzled letter 'O' and her eyes centered on the ceiling as she tried to make a decision. After some time, she nodded agreeably and started to unload things that had not been mentioned by her father. Nicholas sighed with relief, happy that the peaceful matter of shopping for pets had not turned into a spoiled day for both of them. Free from any worries, Lana pushed the shopping cart to the car while she balanced with one leg on the edge of its metal frame and kicked the ground with the other. She was very excited by the thought of showing everything she had bought to her mother.

Tac and Tod did not realize that they were different, being a cat and a dog, Instead, they simply thought they were brothers, despite their differences in size, color and the matter of one barking and the other one meowing. They understood each other perfectly and worked as a team when they played forbidden games.

Their favorite game was called 'chicken chase.' At first, Tac would quietly sneak into the chicken-coop where the hen would be sitting peacefully on her nest and scare her out. Then Tod would chase the hen along a wooden fence which separated the yard from the front lawn. The frightened bird would run in an effort to escape back into her coop or would make an attempt to sneak through the gate into the garden to seek the protection of her husband, the rooster. Except that Tac would stop her and send her back to Tod. The chase would continue until the hen realized that the only way for her to get rid of these two was to fly over the fence. A chicken after all is a bird. With frenzied squawking, the hen would finally manage to fly her heavy body over the fence and run into the arms of her family, continuously cursing the cat and the dog in her own bird language.

With looks of disappointment, Tac and Tod would follow the hen until she had reached her destination and then both of them would run back to dig in the garden.

Lana would lift and carry them to the washroom to clean their dirty paws. Neither troublemaker argued over this procedure and only Tac, who did not like water, made the low cry of a cat approaching the end of his life.

Nicholas, loyal to a farmer's practicality, wanted to make Tod and Tac useful in his household and, when they had reached the age of adults, he tried to train Tod as a guard dog but had very little success with it.

Apparently, when the dog jumped on somebody's chest and knocked him down with his weight, the only danger the person faced was an attack from Tod's big, wet tongue.

Tac, on the other hand, was told to keep rats away from the eggs in the chicken coop and mice from the wheat and vegetables in the storage area. The cat made an attempt to do it but faced a real challenge as a result. There was a jar of cream in the storage and, as everyone knows, a cat cannot resist the temptation to taste cream so he was caught by Natalie in the middle of his crime. He endured being placed on the bench and given a lecture about his dishonorable behavior.

After this, she forbade Tac to have any treats for a week. The cat took the punishment without complaining, fully understanding the fairness of it, but did not change his ways.

The cream-theft incident was repeated with steady regularity no matter how many times Tac was left without any treats. Nothing worked for the cat. Even Nicholas's threats to put Tac in a bag and take him to the forest, where he would be alone and would probably have a short meeting with a wolf, changed nothing.

Eventually, he broke the last of his family's patience. The situation that occurred was the worst yet and had happened on the day when Lana and her mother were baking a cake for her sixteenth birthday party. This day was important for her because, for the first time, her father had allowed Lana's boyfriend to be invited to their house.

Lana had been very busy with her housework, cleaning and cooking snacks but most of all she worried about the cake. She was continually looking through the glass window on the front of the stove to check on it until Natalie had sent her to bring a jar of cream from the refrigerator in the basement to make whipped cream. However, when she returned carrying a jar of cream in her hands, she found her mother removing the already-baked cake from the stove.

"It's ready?" She quickly put the jar onto the table and ran to help her. She knew that the cake was quite heavy and was worried that her mother would drop it on the floor.

"Now we need to let it cool before we can decorate it with the whipped cream and the strawberries." Natalie put the hot tray on the side table and removed her padded gloves.

Lana realized that she had completely forgotten about her cat who was sitting silently on a kitchen chair watching all this chaos with a gleam in his eyes. "Oh! The cream!" She shouted, but unfortunately she was too late to save the situation.

Predictably, Tac had not missed this opportunity and he was, by this time, already standing on the edge of the table with his head deep inside the jar, thinking. 'I am just going to try the cream to see if it is still good. I will take just a little bit and no one will even notice the difference. I want to have a taste of its smooth, sweet, buttery flavor in my mouth.'

"Tacker!" Yelled Lana, with her arms in the air. Tac jumped up in fright, knocking the jar onto the floor.

Nicholas rushed into the kitchen, following the sound of the broken dishes. He did not need to ask any questions since he saw the red spots of anger on Natalie's cheeks, Tac's crazy eyes and Lana's frozen and pale face. He lifted Tacker, holding him like a wet and dirty cloth, with the intention of taking him outside.

Natalie quickly recovered from the shock and said. "Killing Tacker will not save the situation and we can deal with him later. Just go to the neighbor and ask if we can borrow some cream from her."

But Nicholas was too furious to let Tac walk away unpunished for ruining his daughter's birthday mood and he threw Tac onto the passenger seat of his truck. Determined to end the cat's bad behavior forever, he drove him to the wood, about ten kilometers south west of the village, and left him there.

Tacker found himself to be completely abandoned and alone. At first he was afraid to even breathe but after some time he decided to find a safe place. He looked around and saw the remains of a tree destroyed by a storm. Carefully slinking through the tall grass, he reached the stump and then climbed onto it, thinking 'What am I going to do now? My Master was right when he told me that I would not survive here for even a day. If I had never touched that cream I would probably now be sitting safely at home on the couch and enjoying the party. Tod told me that he could find his way home by sniffing his own footprints so maybe I should do the same.'

At this, the cat stretched his neck out and sniffed the air to detect the specific smell of the rubber tires of Nicholas's car. But his nose registered only the smell of wild flowers and grass. Then he continued to think… 'Yes, my Master has an explosive temper but he is not a cruel person. After his anger has settled a little bit he will surely come back for me. He will start to think that the punishment is too severe for my case. Basically he has punished me for being a cat.'

Nicholas returned home with the cream just before the first guest arrived at the party and took on the responsibilities of a host whilst Lana finished off the cake. He saw that Lana was upset and not in the mood for partying and, although she blamed a headache for this, he knew that the real reason was that she was worried about Tacker.

The guests did not stay for long and, as soon as the last of them had left, Nicholas took a flashlight and said. "I'm going to go back to the wood to look for that brat. He's probably still sitting where I left him."

Natalie and Lana also took their jackets and flashlights and joined him in the search for Tac. But, no matter how hard the family looked everywhere and called out his name, they could not find him. Tacker had simply disappeared.

Upset by his loss, the family did not talk to each other for at least a couple of days. They completed everyday chores amidst a heavy silence until Nicholas, unable to stand it anymore, said. "That's enough, I'm sorry that Tac is missing and I hope that he is alive and somebody has found him."

Natalie then came to Nicholas and put her hand on his shoulder, saying to him. "Darling, nobody blames you because we were all angry at him but we love him, no matter how bad his behavior has been, and we will try to find him. We will go to the wood and look again." Lana did not say anything; she just placed her face on her father's chest and cried. Nicholas did not know what else to say to comfort her except "Don't cry sweetheart, we will find him!"

Tod did not know about the incident in the kitchen and, for him, Tac had just mysteriously disappeared. It had been almost a week since Tod had started to look for Tac everywhere he could think of, both in the garden and around the house. He stuck his head in the storage area and in the chicken coop and he even tried to climb Tac's favorite resting tree, thinking that Tac was playing hide and seek. Eventually, there was only one place where Tod had not looked and that was in the house itself. Desperate to see his friend, he spent hours sitting on the porch and looking at the door. Every time someone opened the door, whether they were coming in or leaving the house, Tod tried to squeeze his long, lean body inside. To his surprise, nobody yelled at him. He would simply be led back outside with a pat on the head and left without an explanation about Tac's disappearance.

At night he lay at the entrance to his dog house, crying out his pain and anguish, until someone would open the window to say. "Tod, stop it, we're depressed enough without having to listen to your crying as well." Feeling hurt, he climbed out of his house and ran to the road where no one could stop him from barking. Suddenly, out of the corner of his eye, he saw a movement and heard the rustle of the low branches of bushes at the side of the road. 'A rat?' Thought Tod, with satisfaction. But, when he turned in the direction of the noise, the figure of Tac appeared from the shadow of the branches. Tod broke his forward motion with all of his legs and dropped his bottom onto the ground. He just stared at Tac, as if he had seen a ghost. Tac, purring, ran to Tod and rubbed his head against the dog's body.

Once Tod had recovered from his surprise, he grabbed Tacker and gave him a series of happy dog's kisses.

"Stop, stop, my friend, remember I am a cat after all and I do not like to get wet and, in addition to this, I must remember the dignity of my current position." Tac laughed, carefully straightening his disheveled fur. "In my wood, I am a person of some importance." He added, leading Tod to their favorite place at the corner of the road.

"What?" Said a very puzzled Tod.

"I brought our Master to a rage and he took me to the wood, as he has promised to do many times, and left me there alone." Advised Tac. "I was told later by my new friends that humans had been searching for somebody, or something, in the wood but I was too busy at that moment with my own problems to respond. Only today have I found the time to come home to say that I am alive, fine and well. Is Master still angry with me or is it safe for me to come to visit all of them? What do you think?"

"First, tell me." Said Tod. "What did you do to make Master angry to the point that he decided to kick you out of the house and what do you mean by saying that you are visiting us? Are you not going to stay at home from now on?"

"Questions, questions." Laughed Tac. "I spoiled our Lana's birthday by leaving her without a cake, which she wanted so much. Believe me, it was just an unintentional accident." Suddenly he added. "How was the birthday?"

"Spoiled, thanks to you." Tod answered sarcastically. "She got her cake after all, but now I can understand why she was so upset. It was because she was worried about you, Fluffbrain. Can't you control yourself at least once in your life and not cause trouble?"

"You're right." Tac replied. "I deserve everything you said but it's in the past now and I am unable to change it, I'm afraid."

"Ok, let's talk about the present." Replied Tod. "Where are you going to live? Have you now joined a Gypsy tribe and are you intending to become a tramp?"

"No, my brother." Laughed Tac. "I am going to become a King!"

"What?" Exclaimed Tod, in complete surprise.

"Why! Every forest has a King, and somebody has to take this position when it's vacant, otherwise there would be chaos in the forest." Tac explained, while licking his paw, studiously.

"But you do not have royal blood in your veins." Tod pressed the issue.

"Blood?" Chuckled Tac "You do not need to have noble blood to become a King." He added with pride. "It's simply a matter of having a sharp brain and some luck, is it not? And if you want to hear all of this story you had better sit here and do not interrupt." Then Tod dutifully sat down and prepared his ears.

Tac began by saying. "Well, everything started that evening, when our Master left me alone at the edge of the forest from where only a scared fool like me was unable to find his way home. But, at that time I was only a helpless, scared cat with pictures of my own death in my mind. The edge of the wood has the shape of a horseshoe. Tall grass, weeds with bright yellow flowers and foxgloves of various colors, make a soft carpet outlined by bushes. The lines of pathways run in different directions, going deeper into the wood through a stand of tall, mature trees growing in the background. Some of them died a long time ago, perhaps broken by a storm, with their remains slowly decaying into the ground. Young ferns struggle to grow through cracks in the tree bark to reach the sunlight, fed by the nutritious soil below. But, for some reason, this peaceful landscape did not appeal to me.

By that time it was twilight between the thick stems of trees and the voices of birds, invisible from below, made my ears move nervously. Distracted by sounds coming from everywhere, I was unable to concentrate on my thoughts and all of them were spinning in circles in my head. I tried to find the way back home, but without success.

I chose a large tree stump and climbed up on the top of it, knowing that it would be safer to be above ground. I do not remember how long I sat on this stump before I noticed that some animal was stealthily creeping through the bushes, sniffing at something on the ground. Watching carefully, I realized that this animal was following my footprints but it was too late for me to run and I just waited for it to come closer. Looking down from above, I was trying to figure out what kind of animal I was dealing with. My possible opponent had a russet appearance and short legs covered with darker fur. In addition, it had a bushy tail with a white patch at its end and black-colored ears. Its long and narrow body was perfectly adapted to living in narrow spaces underground. This animal's confident moves convinced me that it had a great sense of smell and was definitely a skilled hunter. I remembered that it was called a fox.

The fox made a circle around the stump and quickly realized that its prey could only be on top of it and, as it raised its eyes, our gazes locked. I was scared stiff but instinct made me arch my back and lift my tail up to make me look bigger! Then I showed the fox all of my sharp teeth and hissed at it angrily. Interest twinkled in the eyes of the fox as it sat on its back legs wrapping its tail around them.

"Who are you?" Asked the fox. "I have lived in this wood for a long time and I have never seen an animal like you before."

'A predator never eats an unknown prey in case it may be poisonous.' Came into my mind. 'If I can prove to this fox that I am not worth eating and am difficult to get, or have powerful relatives that can become dangerous enemies afterwards, it may just leave me alone.' In desperation I prepared myself to lie, shamelessly. "I am a cat from a family of many cats!"

"And who is your family?" asked the fox, with a smile.

"My older cousin is a lion, King of the Savanna. Have you heard of him?" I responded. Judging by how fast the smile disappeared from the fox's face, I understood that this name was familiar to it. This realization lifted my spirits and I continued. "There are a lot of famous cats in my family. I am related to a tiger who is the King of the east, a puma who is the King of the mountains, a cheetah who belongs to a family of great sprinters and a bobcat who is the King of the swampland." I was prepared to add more names to this list, but the fox suddenly asked "What is your name?"

"Lord Tacker!" I answered proudly. "I was born in a castle many miles away from here. I am traveling today just for the fun of it and I stopped here for only a couple of minutes to rest but now I cannot find my car and my driver. Such bad luck!"

"Are you married?" Asked the fox, after a few minutes of thinking.

"No." I replied.

"It just happens that I am single too and my name is Alisa. Do you want to be my husband?" She asked suddenly.

I was stunned because I had never thought about marriage. But it's better to be married than eaten I decided and answered promptly. "Yes I would like to marry you."

"In this case, let's go home." The fox smoothly jumped over the stump and waited for me. "It's getting late and, by the way, I liked your story about a large, royal family. There are a lot of animals who are stronger than I but not one who is smarter. I am the most skilled trickster in this place so please, my dear, do not try to fool me! I have more respect for any animal that can find a way out of a difficult situation, using every weapon that they have, including falsifications like you did, than for those who give up and cry for mercy." Alisa then added, for effect. "Only someone like me, who has experience in detecting false stories, can pick up the trembling notes in your voice which betrayed you." Then she led me through the dark forest to her den. "Tomorrow we will add some more details to your story, polish your performance a little bit and, after this, you will be ready to meet your future opponents for the position of ruler of our forest. I am not Alisa if I cannot turn you into a winner, no matter how many obstacles you may meet on your way. Power will be in your paws." Then she quickly added ."In our paws."

Somehow, I had started to like her. With a wife like her, who was possessed of a sharp mind and was ambitious, I felt that I would have a chance to do something important with my life, rather than being just a house cat. I could use all of the knowledge that I had gained from the educational T.V. programs, which I had seen with my Master, to make the lives of the inhabitants of this forest more civilized and meaningful.

"We are almost home." She interrupted my thoughts.

I noticed that Alisa's den was on the south side of a small ridge. The sandy slope was free from any vegetation except for two big blackthorn bushes that camouflaged the entrance to the den. A small creek burbled its happy song between stones at the bottom of the ridge and gave support to a group of dogwoods and shrubs on the other side whilst a narrow, sandy pathway ran alongside it. Three tall firs were standing on the top of the hill like a line of guards. I followed Alisa through a narrow entrance in the rocky hill that eventually expanded into a big round cave. It was very quiet and unexpectedly warm inside the den. Tired, I lay down on a pile of straw covered with a blanket and instantly fell asleep.

When I woke up in the morning I found Alisa serving breakfast on a table which was just a large narrow stone sticking out from the wall. Two smaller, flat stones served as chairs.

A plastic bottle was hanging above the table on a curved string, one end of which was wrapped around the neck of the bottle with the other being tied to a hook on the ceiling. I noticed that some insects crawled around the inside of the bottle radiating a weak light which was just sufficient to light up this place slightly.

"Good morning, Alisa. How did you manage to cook? There is no fire in the stove."

"Good morning, Lord Tacker." She answered, with a smile. "I cooked in my other home because it's not safe to attract attention to this place by emitting smoke."

"Yes, you're right. If someone decides to attack us here we will have only one way to escape." I replied.

"One way?" Laughed Alisa. She went to the opposite wall decorated with a rectangular bright rug and lifted its corner. Underneath was a big round hole which served as an emergency exit. "And another is hidden behind the bed." She added.

'How prominent and smart she is.' I thought. Then Alisa returned to the table and lifted a lid from the pan which contained a big omelet and a sausage. Plastic cans with milk were standing in front of each of us. Breakfast was simple, not a fancy feast, but I was very hungry and could not complain. After we had finished eating, Alisa gathered the dirty dishes and put them in the basket.

"We need to wash the dishes in the creek, otherwise the smell will attract ants. I do not want them in my den." She shook her head, disgusted with the thought of having ants as tenants. It did not take her too much time to wash the dishes but I personally did not touch the water and I offered to carry the basket home as my fair share of the chore.

"I want to show you another entrance into the den." She murmured.

We walked for a couple of minutes along the creek to the foot of two large rocks which protruded from the side of the slope of the ridge. A large plant grew from the strip of soil separating the rocks and its branches almost hid the entrance that had the shape of an upside-down triangle. "I brought this plant from another place and it hides the entrance perfectly." Alisa exclaimed proudly, then moved the branches aside and entered a narrow tunnel. We turned left and, after wandering in darkness, I again found myself inside the den where Alisa had put the clean dishes back on the shelves. I noticed that everything she had in her house was simple and practical and would not take much time to pack in case she needed to leave this place.

'A practical wife is easier to please.' I admitted to myself.

"Now." Said Alisa. "Sit down on the chair. I want to tell you everything you need to know about our wood and its inhabitants. We live in the east of Pokerweild which is the lower, flatter and more habitable part of the wood. It became a chain of hills covered by grass on the west side leading up to the Cursed Forest which I have personally never visited." I opened my mouth to ask a question, but Alisa continued: "Nobody goes to the Cursed Forest anymore and stories about this place are very frightening. If you are curious, I will tell them to you at another time. Right now you need to know that a wise bear had ruled our forest for a long time but he died two years ago. The King's grandson, Bertrond, and the wolf named Alowsius, had to compete for the position of ruler. But neither of them had enough supporters to overcome their opponent. They had strong muscles but small brains, which is the reason why none of them were able to win the challenge that required intelligence.

The bear and the wolf were so busy with each other that a third applicant could easily have taken the Mace but there was no one else to challenge them. With my knowledge of the politics in our forest, you have a good chance of becoming that successful third person. You have to repeat the story about your Royal ancestors until you start to believe in it yourself to convince the residents that your noble blood gives you the higher claim to assume power. My part in this plot is to introduce you to everyone as a rightful candidate for the position of ruler. The most difficult part of my plan is to prove to your opponents that they must step back and accept you as their leader. You will need to give a speech to the forest Council to prove to them that, with your Royal blood, strength and wisdom, you will be able to protect our kingdom against any intruders. You must act like a lion to make the matter of your small size irrelevant to the issue."

"Do not tell me that I have to shave myself, leaving only a tuft of hair on my tail and a scrap of fur on my head?" I asked.

"We do not need to go to that extent." Alisa smiled. "You are a cat, from a cat's family, but you are the smallest member of this group which is working against you. Somehow you need to draw attention away from your size to your more valuable qualities. Convince everyone that you are a fighter who can stand up for himself and probably even scare Bertrond and Alowsius a little by pretending that you are a dangerous animal."

"Dangerous animal? A house cat?" I said. "Maybe I should growl at them scarily... Meow? "

Alisa ignored my remark and continued: "I need to think about how to move our affairs forward, step by step. First, I am going to introduce you to Bertrond and Alowsius and I already have a plan about when, and where, it's going to happen. I am going to leave you now to work on your speech while I go to make sure that the place which I have chosen will be a good background for your performance. This place has a lot of bushes to allow you to sneak up on the wolf and the bear without giving them time to take a good look at you. Then you will surprise them with your story and do not forget to mention to them that your cousin, the lion, is going to send an army to back you if you meet strong resistance from their side."

After she had left, I spent some time thinking about what I should say to the bear and to the wolf in order to convince them that I had more right to take the position of ruler than they had. The more I thought about it the more the whole idea looked completely hopeless. I had never considered taking on the responsibilities of caring for myself, let alone the whole forest. My Master had provided food and shelter for me, had taken me to the Doctor when I was unwell and, for all of this, I had never bothered to catch at least one mouse to show him my gratitude. I had lived like a spoiled aristocrat, doing nothing. 'Stop.' I thought. 'I think I have nobility but so far I am expressing just the negative part of it. Now I must find the positive side that will make me a King.'

First of all, I needed to improve my personality, starting with my fear of water. I walked closer to the rock and looked over its edge at a small fish which was hiding here from the sun, rhythmically moving its fins to counter the stream of water to ensure that it stayed under the protection of the rock. Patiently, I waited for the right moment and in one fast move dug my claws into its flesh. A second later it was lying on the stone in front of me flapping its tail under my paws. It was my first catch. "Meow." I cried, unable to keep my feelings under control.

"What happened?" Alisa's voice came from a distance. She came closer, carrying something feathery, and looked approvingly at my catch. "Nice! It will be our dinner and I have brought a chicken with me also. Let's go home."

After the dinner Alisa told me that I was going to meet Bertrond and Alowsius the next day, close to evening. She told me about her trip to the village to get the chicken, after which she had deliberately returned home by a pathway where she expected to meet the bear and the wolf.

As soon as Bertrond had seen her with a chicken tucked under her arm, he had demanded. "Fox, give me this chicken!"

Then the wolf's harsh voice had growled from behind the bear "You had better do it without a fight otherwise we might spoil your nice red fur!" He stepped forward next to his companion, glad to have a free meal.

Usually they would get what they wanted, but this time she hid the chicken behind her back and said. "No! If you dare to harm me, then I will complain to my husband who has been sent here by his cousin, the lion King, to be the new ruler in our forest. He will rip both of you into small pieces. He has a short temper and becomes vicious when someone angers him. Even I do not dare to argue with him."

Bertrond and Alowsius looked at each other in dismay and asked if they could have a meeting with this husband of hers.

"You two had better avoid seeing Lord Tacker because he has heard enough bad things about you from other animals to decide to kill you on the spot. But, if you agree to follow my instructions, I could find a way to show you my husband without his being able to see you. You, bear, bring a skinned bull and you, Alowsius, bring a sheep and leave them both out in the open. I will come early to hide you and then I will go home to invite Lord Tacker out for a walk. We will find your gifts by chance and, if he is pleased by them, I will call you and introduce you to him."

Since fear usually exaggerates things, Bertrond and Alowsius immediately drew in their minds the picture of a large and furious animal and scared themselves to the point that they agreed to do everything that she had told them to do.

"Now." Said Alisa, to me. "You need to finish what I have started in order to convince these two fools that you are Tacker the Great, the future King of Pokerweild."

Then, for the rest of the day, I listened to Alisa's stories about the funny episodes that occurred in the lives of the animals that lived in this wood.

The next morning we had a simple country breakfast, and Alisa called me to go for a hunt but I refused, wanting to think more about the future meeting. I sat on the rock where I had caught my first fish and tried to recollect all of the information about the bear and the wolf which I had learned from Alisa, musing. 'Bertrond is the biggest animal in the forest and the grandson of the previous ruler, which will give him a good chance of becoming an important person in the forest. However, he is so naïve and trustworthy that some of his so-called friends have selfishly used his strength for their own gain. This has often put the bear in difficult and stupid situations, giving a reason for the inhabitants of the forest to laugh at him behind his back.'

But the last incident had ruined his reputation completely. It had happened when Bertrond had decided to become a farmer and had taken a boar, named Boran, as a partner. The agreement between them was clear and simple. Working together, they were going to grow the crop and share the harvest in such a way that the bear was going to get everything that grew above the ground and the boar would receive the roots. When the ground was ready, Boran chose to plant potatoes and later on the field became a fine plantation of tall, dark-green plants topped with light purple flowers.

Bertrond had teased Boran, exclaiming. "Look at my part of the crop. If it continues to grow like this, then I will collect a full cart of leaves but you will only get this." He pulled out one of the plants to show the boar a bunch of roots with tiny potatoes attached to them.

"An agreement is an agreement." Answered Boran. "I cannot complain if I lose because it was my decision to take the roots." Time passed and the stems of the potato started to turn yellow. Bertrond, worrying, demanded that he be allowed to dig them out but Boran refused, answering. "It's not time yet." Only when autumn had started to paint the leaves with yellow and red, did Boran comment. "Tomorrow we will harvest our crop." After one day's hard work, all the plants had been pulled from the ground and the leafy tops were separated from the roots. Boran gathered all the potatoes into a pile, lit a fire and placed some of them into the hot ashes to bake until the potatoes were ready to eat. Seeing what the boar had done with his potatoes, the bear also decided to put his green tops into the fire but all that he got as a result was ashes.

"Let me try your roots." He requested from the Boar.

"Help yourself."

The bear had tried the potato and roared loudly. "Your potato is sweet and tasty but my tops are just dust!"

Thus, after this unfortunate climax to all his hard work, the bear stopped being partners with the boar. He fully understood that the boar had taken advantage of him and he wanted to keep it a secret, but soon the whole wood had learned about Bertrond's farming fiasco and laughed at him. His reputation was damaged so badly that the forest Council made the decision not to give him his grandfather's crown until he became smarter and proved that he was able to make decisions without looking like a fool. Alowsius, on the other hand, came from a family of common wolves. Leaving his family at an early age he learned how to stand on his own feet very quickly. The most important rule that he had convinced himself of was. 'Do not expect any sympathy from anyone and do not attach yourself to anyone.' A real gentleman of luck, he never missed an opportunity to misappropriate someone else's catch, punished everyone who dared to challenge his authority and kept all the neighbors in fear. His relationship with Bertrond had not been a friendship at all. He had simply found that he could do his bad deeds through Bertrond's hands and then just wait patiently to get more than his fair share of the profits.

I admitted to myself that Alisa's expectations for me were unrealistic because my opponents appeared to be too strong for me to handle and therefore this competition for the kingship could end badly for me. But I decided to put myself to the test, at least for the pleasure of seeing how a cat could scare both a wolf and a bear in order to earn their respect. After these thoughts, I returned to Alisa's den, my new home.

"Where have you been?" Alisa asked. "I am anxious to tell you how nicely I have prepared the stage which is waiting for you to give your best performance." And, to add to the point, Alisa bowed playfully.

Seeing her crafty smile and the ironic sparks in her eyes, I concluded that she had managed to wrap both males around her pretty, little paw and was very proud of herself as a result.

"Do not worry about Bertrond and Alowsius." She continued, showing me the way. "I have hid them in places where they cannot see you very clearly. You will need to behave like one of your big cousins, growling furiously, whilst eating the meat which they are going to prepare for you as a gift."

"And, after I have finished my performance, will I ask them to wrap-up the rest of the meat so that I can take it home?" I queried, sarcastically.

Alisa chuckled and said. "I am only trying to help."

"I understand. It's just that I have never eaten raw meat before. I must admit that even the thought of putting it into my mouth makes me feel sick."

"You just have to pretend that you enjoyed it." She sounded upset by my uncooperative mood.

"Ok. How far away is this place of my future suffering?" I surrendered, realizing that we had been walking for at least fifteen minutes into the depths of the wood.

"We are almost there." She responded, quickly.

I looked up through the branches of trees and noticed that the sun was preparing to leave the sky, lingering on the horizon just to check that everything had been prepared for its little sister, the moon, to have her turn at taking over the duty. A light evening wind played with the leaves on the top of the trees but, at ground level, the air was trapped between rough, brown tree trunks. We continued steadily walking through the wood, diving under the low-hanging branches of young ferns.

"There will be a glade appearing very soon." Alisa told me.

The woods opened onto a large clearing in which freshly cut grass had been gathered into a large pile. A few young trees stood close to the left of this pile but my attention was concentrated on the lifeless bodies of the bull and the sheep lying under it. Suddenly I realized that I had forgotten to ask Alisa where she had hidden Bertrond and Alowsius but it was now too late to make an enquiry about them.

"What should I do now?" I asked.

"Pretend that you are a lion." Alisa whispered.

I had seen a TV program about lions and have to say that the picture of these animals feeding on their prey had not appealed to me. But I made myself look as savage as I could, making wild eyes. Instead of a lion I pretended that I was a Samurai warrior, slashing at his enemies with a sword. "Yeeaa!" I cried and jumped on top of the bull, ripping it with my claws and screaming hysterically. "MeoOOww!" I do not think that anyone in this wood had ever seen anything like it and even Alisa seemed to be stunned. Can you imagine what kind of an effect I had made on the bear and the wolf?

Alowsius had been hidden by Alisa under the pile of grass but Bertrond, had chosen to climb up a tree and looked down at me from above. When he saw me, jumping wildly on top of the bull, the bear was unable to keep his feelings to himself and whispered down to the wolf. "Look at him, Alowsius, how small but how incredibly greedy he is! The meat that we have given him as a gift would be enough to feed us both for a week, but he is still yelling "More. More." What a horrible animal."

Alowsius, who was unable to see anything under the grass, started to move the straw aside. He wanted to see this furious Lord Tacker for himself. When I heard the sound of the moving straw I decided that there must be a mouse running under the grass and I wanted to show them a thing or two about hunting. So, continuing to play the role of a Samurai warrior and shouting "Bonsai", I jumped inside the pile. I was lucky enough to dig all of my claws right into the face of the wolf. Blinded, scared and yelling with pain, Alowsius shook his head and succeeded in throwing me aside. Afraid to even look behind him, the poor wolf ran straight home without a second of rest and it was only after he had closed the door of his house that he was able to take a full breath.

In the meantime, I was scared no less than him and was pushed by fear to find a safe refuge up the tree. Using my claws, I climbed up fast and eventually reached the bear who was sitting on one of the large branches. Not realizing that it was him, I continued to climb along the bear's back and now it was Bertrond's turn to yell out in pain. He released the branch, and we both fell down into the straw. Bertrond rolled up onto his feet and promptly ran off. Knowing that the bear's back had been injured with my claws, I had become so frightened by my mistake that I climbed back up the same tree to hide.

Alisa, laughing herself to tears, applauded my efforts and cheered me on, crying. "Bravo, Bravo!" I sat on the tree for at least another two hours until she eventually talked me into coming down, convincing me that my opponents were far away and that there was no danger anymore."

Tacker stopped for a moment and looked into the night, with the pictures of these adventures still going through his mind like a movie. But a sound behind him returned his attention to Tod whose body had been shaking strangely for at least five minutes. "What's that?" He asked, but was interrupted by Tod.

"Bo! Bo! Bo!" The dog laughed, holding his stomach with one paw whilst wiping away tears with another. "Oh." He finally managed to say. "I've never heard anything funnier. I do not know what is more amusing, this last episode of your life or the whole idea of your kingship! Imagine that Tacker, who was once afraid to show his nose behind the gate, now king of Pokerweild wood?" And he started to laugh again.

"People change, you know." Murmured Tacker, with some annoyance in his voice.

"People change?" Tod repeated. "But you are not a human, you are a cat and a quite spoiled one at that I may say. How are you going to make decisions regarding the life of wild animals when you know nothing about their wild life? You are a house cat, Tac, and you have become accustomed to having everything prepared for you by your human family."

"Do you think that the Council of the wood is stupid enough to give the power of making decisions to a stranger without any training?" Tac sounded irritated. "Then listen further. The news about how I saw off the bear and the wolf spread in the wood with the speed of wildfire and a lot of the animals cautiously approached Alisa's den to look at me. Remember this, Tod, I was the first one who had managed to scare and scratch-up Alowsius and Bertrond. In this circumstance, you will understand that I did not have any other choice but to go outside and greet everyone!"

A mature elk named Rainar, a member of the Council, invited me to a meeting to give me the opportunity of introducing myself. He explained to me that the Council makes all the decisions in the wood during the absence of the King. Walking slowly and gracefully, he led me to the hill where our meeting was about to take place. It was located on the biggest of the Western hills. Trees had been completely removed from all sides of the hill, leaving only a round line of them on its peak to give shade on a hot day. Nine stone chairs marked the places of each member of the Council in the shape of a circle. By the time we had arrived at the meeting place all the animals were sitting, or lying, at their designated places and only one large stone seat had been left empty. I realized that this was the place for a King. I walked without fear into the center of the circle to give everyone a good look at me. It was difficult to understand what kind of an opinion they had of me until some of the members started to walk closer to me. The eagle, Galibur, even made a circle around me to examine me from behind and then returned to his place with a strange gait.

"He is very small." He pointed at me.

"A small King requires less meat to eat." Cried a mouse called Mixie, in a squeaky voice.

"That's right." Replied a rabbit named Shustin. "Less of us are going to die for the privilege of having a King."

"You have nothing to worry about." I said to them. "I do not eat raw meat. My food is milk, cream, fish, and cats' food from the store, but sometimes I do not mind eating a piece of fried chicken. I hope that I am not hurting your feelings, Galibur?"

"Not at all, I like chicken myself." The eagle answered.

"The next thing that we need to discuss is the bloodline of the candidate." Rainar reminded the council and then addressed me. "We are not familiar with an animal like you. Who are you? You have stripes and a bushy tail like a raccoon but have a different shape of a body."

"I am a cat, from a cat's family."

"Secretary Roxal." Called Rainar. "Please bring me the book."

The raccoon brought a book and a folding table and put it in front of Rainar. The elk opened the book, found the right page, and invited all the members of the Council to look at the paragraph describing the family of cats.

"This family is very famous." Admitted Brown Bob who was a bear. "Lions, tigers, and pumas are all cats and therefore I think this question is now clarified." He looked around to see if anybody disagreed. Seeing none, he remarked. "The last question which I would like to address to the candidate is… how much experience does he have as a leader and what position did he occupy before arriving in our wood?"

"I must honestly say that I do not have any practical experience in politics but I have theoretical knowledge from my studies of humans whose affairs, from my point of view, are much more complicated than those of animals." I replied.

"You can leave now." Rainar responded. "We will convey our decision to you soon."

I spent long hours waiting before I was invited into the circle again to be informed that, by the decision of the Council, I had been added to the list of candidates for the position of King. After a further year had passed, the Council would decide who deserved the crown of the kingship of Pokerweild wood. Then the members of the Council, one by one, came to congratulate me. Clumsily walking towards me, Bertrond growled. "A year is a long time, stranger and you might decide to go back to where you came from."

Alowsius, in his turn, gave me an unfriendly look and said. "We shall see."

My mood dropped down after this but, looking at Alisa's happy face, I stopped thinking about this unpleasant incident."

"Well." Tod got up. "I see that you have made up your mind and talking against your decision is a waste of time, so I will not do it. But, if you find that you have made a mistake in deciding to live in the woods, I assure you that our Master will be happy to have you back. Let's go home and you can see for yourself."

It did not take much time for them to reach home which was on the same side of the road, the second house from the corner. Tac and Tod jumped over the fence where it had deliberately been constructed low to allow them freedom to come and go without disturbing the family. They crossed a long front yard, walked up the stairs onto the porch and stopped in front of the door.

Tod barked once, waiting for an answer, and then added a series of more barks until Natalie opened the door to ask. "Tod, what's wrong?" When she saw Tac on the porch, she opened the door wide and shouted to the inside of the house. "Lana, Nicholas, come quickly, Tacker has come home."

Tac had planned to enter the house by walking into the living room slowly and gracefully but Lana spoiled it. She lifted him up off the floor and turned him from side to side to check for any injury that he might have sustained.

Nicholas then took the cat from her hands and roughly rubbed his neck, saying. "You should have waited for me and we could have avoided all this worry."

But, Tac, with his green eyes half closed, only thought. 'I would have missed all the adventures if I had waited for you.'

Nicholas, surveying Tac critically, went on. "It looks as if someone has taken care of him; he's well-groomed and does not look like he's starved because he hasn't lost any weight." Finishing his inspection, he put Tac back down on the floor, whereupon the cat proceeded to the kitchen with a self-satisfied look on his face. He did not beg for food anymore, waiting for it to be placed in front of him. After the meal, he spent the rest of the evening with the family giving each person an equal share of his attention. Eventually, the cat walked to the door, showing that it was time for him to retire. Lana wanted to stop him but Tac jumped softly from her arms and looked at Nicholas, expressively.

"I think that Tac definitely wants to go out. I suspect that he has a new life and we must respect his wish. He knows his way home and will come and go as he pleases." Nicholas then opened the door to allow Tac to walk outside.

"How was your meeting with the family?" Tod asked, impatiently.

"Very nice, thank you! I am going to visit you as often as I can or send someone from the wood with a message."

"Tac, maybe I should walk with you. It's not safe to go to the wood alone."

"I am not alone." Tac smiled. "My bodyguard is waiting for me in the bushes."

At the sound of a brief cat's 'Mrrr' the figure of a raccoon appeared out of the dark shadows. Tod, who did not like a cheeky raccoon, showed his teeth and growled.

"Where are your good manners?" Queried Tac. "This is my new friend, Roxal. He is going to bring messages from me when I will be busy, so be nice to him."

Hearing this, Roxal looked at Tod with a frown but said nothing.

Tac visited his family, the Vladners, occasionally, knowing that his long absences would make them search for him in the neighborhood and in the wood again and, until his position in the wood's society had become more stable, he did not want to make his connection with the humans public. He busied himself with many tasks, one of which was to remodel Alisa's den transforming it into a nice little house. He did, of course, discuss this matter with Alisa, who looked at this renovation as a fanciful idea but did not want to upset her husband by refusing him this odd, but harmless, wish. Together they started to remove soil to prepare a foundation for a new bedroom to be separate from the kitchen, widening the living room and creating a separate space for storage. Tac wanted to put in new windows but Alisa rejected this idea, saying that she would not feel safe in the house with too many openings through which anyone could see inside. Tac thought a little bit about this and decided to abandon his idea because, after all, the house did belong to Alisa and he felt the need to respect her wishes.

Since he did not have much experience in construction work Tac hired a local builder, the beaver, Iver, to finish the work that he had started with Alisa. Iver promised to make new furniture for the bedroom, chairs for the living room and shelves for storage. Alisa liked her old granite table and decided to keep it and, in order to complement its color, the chairs were made from dark wood with woven backs and arms. Then the couple decided to add a few cabinets and a buffet to complete the living room. Tac looked around and said. "If this place had a window I would feel just like I was back at home."

Beaver scratched his ear and found a very simple way to satisfy the taste of both of his clients. He proposed making a false window in the shape of an oval bay, dressing it with trim and putting in a window ledge to make it look like a normal window. Later, a local artist drew images of wild flowers on the back panes of the window to complete the illusion.

Alisa was glad to find such a nice compromise for their differing tastes and admitted that Iver had done a good job, combining the dark cherry color of the furniture with the light beige paint on the walls. To color the walls of the bedroom, Alisa and Tac dipped their paws into a darker paint and covered the entire lower part of the wall with paw prints, as if they were playful cubs. The beading in the bedroom was made with animal prints to match the design on the walls and large baskets, filled with dry grasses, completed the room's decorations. The home of a common fox was transformed into the living quarters of a relative of the royal cats.

Alisa invited Roxal inside to observe his reactions to the changes and was pleased to see him carefully wiping his feet at the entrance and cautiously walking inside to avoid leaving dirty marks on the floor.

Besides the house renovations, Tac was busy learning about the life of the forest. A member of the Council, a rabbit named Shustin, became his guide and partner in the long trips to the different parts of the wood. After a while, Tac became very familiar with the south side of the wood where the ground was mostly flat and was cut by two deep ridges with creeks running at the bottom of them going east. Tall firs that grew between the ridges had very little undergrowth of grass alongside them. Only openings between the trees had grass mixed in with wild flowers of different colors. Some sunny clearings had bushes of wild raspberries growing right in the middle of them. Different types of bees, wasps and butterflies fluttered over the flowers but the cat was too tired to chase them.

Exhausted after half a day of running, he and Shustin took a short rest in the shade of raspberry branches. The sweet scent of ripe berries, mixed in with the smells of grasses and flowers, felt pleasant. By mutual agreement, they decided to return home by making a big half circle to explore the entire site of Lake Haidy. Firs here intermingled with tall, white-skinned birches and some poplar trees with dark green, shiny leaves having white, velvety undersides. The sandy soil under the trees was covered with a carpet of brown, dry needles and the air, full of the strong scent of pine, made the cat sneeze.

Shustin found an edible mushroom and stopped for a snack but Tac did not have any interest in eating mushrooms. He concentrated his interest on another specimen which had bright red tops covered in white dots and a funny, white, wrinkled skirt along the lower parts. Peacock-green insects that circled above the mushrooms amused Tac and he tried to catch at least one of them in his paw until Shustin called him to continue their walk home. Tac reached home close to dinner time, very tired, but full of valuable information for his work on a map.

Alisa was quick to advise Tac that she had prepared a dinner for both of them and, during the course of the meal, he talked to her about his discoveries. Occasionally he would jump up from the table and run to his little work-table to draw new images on his map with a sharp, bird's feather that had been dipped in ink. He had learned more about life during these couple of months of living in the wood than he had ever done before. He now understood that animals in the forest have very little pleasure as they struggle for survival and he had already started to think about ways in which he could improve their lives.

A question that bothered him, however, was whether or not the inhabitants of the forest would look favorably upon his ideas and whether they would agree to adjust their lives to go along with his suggestions. This prompted him to start making notes for his report to the Council which was due in the next month.

Another thing that concerned Tac was the strange secrecy that surrounded the western part of the wood. No matter how many animals Tac asked to guide him to the west, no one had agreed to go farther than the Council Hill. Only the raccoon, Roxal, had not refused to join Tac in his expedition to the western part of Pokerweild. Next morning, he came to Fox Hall carrying a few empty bags which Alisa started to load with fresh baked bread and dried meat, also adding a blanket and matches to allow them to make a fire to keep them warm at night. In one of the bags Alisa put a small bottle of alcohol and two narrow rolls of linen to treat any possible wounds that they might sustain on their journey.

"Even a scratch in this place can be dangerous. If you get injured, disinfect your wound in the alcohol and wrap it in bandages." She advised Tac.

"I do not like this idea of your visiting the Cursed Forest." Stated Roxal "But you will need to have someone to watch your back and help you to carry the supplies, although I assure you that you will not find anyone there. That place was abandoned by animals a long time ago. Rumors about a strange disease had reached the ears of the Council and the oldest member of the Council, Carfield the crow, had decided to fly to this distant part of the wood to make inquiries about the true situation. He reported the result of his observations to the Council and, after some discussion, they gave orders to all the inhabitants to leave this place. The banks of the Leehar creek marked the boundary of the infected forest and those who had not listened to the Council's advice, and decided to stay, had disappeared beside the creek without a trace. A family of beavers, that still lives on the safe side of Leehar, has told us that they have not seen anyone cross their bridge for many years."

"But it happened a long time ago and probably the infection has dissolved itself and disappeared." Replied Tac.

"Maybe." Mused Roxal. "But everyone has become so used to calling this place 'Cursed' and, being afraid of it, even migrating animals have been fearful of passing through."

"We are not Nomads, though." Tac corrected him. "We are not afraid to visit the abandoned forest, a place which is wrapped in mystery, in order to study it."

"For what?" Roxal queried.

"To find out the truth of what happened there and to unravel the mysteries of false stories." Tac replied, loading one of the backpacks onto his back.

"Some false stories! We will be lucky to return from that place alive." Roxal put his arms into the straps of his backpack and ran to catch up with Tac who was jogging with an easy heart and no worries. They followed Alisa's creek for a while and then turned left towards Council Hill, leaving the creek happily rolling its water towards Lake Haidy.

Tac and Roxal reached Council Hill around noon and made a camp under the shade of the trees growing at the foot of the hill. An hour later, after lunch, they resumed their walk towards Leehar creek through an open, grassy space between the south part of the forest and the river Woblar. Good weather followed their footsteps, brightening their day with sunshine. The bees and butterflies flew, carefree, from flower to flower whilst grasshoppers jumped up from under their feet, spreading their red and blue wings as they walked through the meadows. The voices of birds, coming from high above their heads, completed the picture of a perfect day. Even Roxal relaxed and stopped frowning and welcomed Tac's idea of making a stop just for the sake of enjoying the pleasure of a nice day out.

It was almost five o'clock in the evening when they reached the banks of the Leehar where Beaver, the owner of this part of the creek, invited them to share a dinner with his family. Tac did not have a taste for the branches of willow provided at the table. He started to think about the best way to turn down this invitation without hurting the feelings of their kind host. Beaver understood the expression on Tac's face perfectly and, with a short chuckle, he pointed with a paw in the direction of his wife who was swimming towards them carrying a big fish in her mouth.

This sight prompted the cat to say. "Certainly, we will be glad to join you." After finishing his share of the fish he asked the beaver about the forest which stood like a gloomy tower on the other side of the creek.

Beaver wiped his mouth with the back of his paw and said. "It's a strange place, this forest. It's really dead and there are neither songs of birds nor sounds of insects in it and I have not seen any animals come to the creek for a drink. My family is afraid to cross the creek to cut the trees on the other side of it and we end up dragging branches from the part where the creek bends, much farther away. It takes more time to store food for the family but this is a safer way for us to do our work. My brother went to the Cursed Forest once for supplies and never came back." Beaver shook his head sadly.

"I need to find out what's wrong with this forest and then find a way to destroy this danger." Replied Tac. "Protecting the forest and its inhabitants is my job if I want to be the King."

"You have found yourself a nice job." Chuckled Beaver. "I'd like to help you and that's why I want to show you a place where a dry creek cuts through the trees. In any situation where you might need to run, using this road may give you a better chance of escaping if someone were to attack you."

"Thank you, I will take your advice, Beaver." Tac got up from the table and gave Roxal a signal to follow him.

"Maybe you will want to wait until tomorrow?" Beaver looked in the direction of the darkening sky with concern.

"No." Tac answered. "If I wait, Roxal will lose the last drop of his courage and I will need to go to the forest alone, which would not work well for me because I count on his senses and instincts. Unfortunately, I lost mine living under the protection of humans." He added, with a wry smile.

It was getting late so Tac and Roxal put their backpacks on and followed Beaver, who preferred to swim along the creek as he showed them the way. Very soon Tac saw a place where the trees gave way to the stone stream that joined with the Leehar. Here, Beaver quickly put together a few chunks of wood and made a small raft to deliver Tac and Roxal to the other side of the creek without either of them getting their feet wet.

"Good luck!" Shouted the beaver after them and swam back to his house.

The day was almost finished. The sun was hanging low, drawing long shadows on the ground. "Let's go." Tac's voice was not so brave now. Both of them were scared by the dead silence and a complete lack of motion inside this strange forest. Fading light made the whole scene even more frightening. Thoughts about the possible mistake of his decision to come here late began to haunt Tac.

"What can we find in this darkness?" Complained Roxal. "Only a broken leg?"

Suddenly, an unusual sound made him stop to listen carefully. It sounded like a hissing whisper or a vibration in the air. Something that looked like a blanket of mist moved towards them in the shape of a half circle. The edges of this cloud were darker in color and they resembled many spread-out hands. Fear made Tac's fur rise up along his back. "Light, we need light!!" Cried the anxious voice of Roxal, prompting an idea to jump into Tac's head. It took him only a second to shake out all the contents of his backpack onto the ground. Selecting some bandages from the pile, he quickly wrapped them around a couple of branches lying right under his feet and wet them in alcohol. Realizing the urgency of their situation, he rushed to light the matches with shaking hands and, after a short struggle, the improvised torches lit up.

"Drop your backpack!" He yelled to Roxal, trying to stick one of the torches into his friend's paw whilst he himself waved with another.

The greedy hands of the approaching cloud tried to grab them but the fire burned them away.

Eventually, Roxal managed to shake off his fear and, allowing the backpack to slide from his shoulder, he grasped one of the torches from Tac. Together they burned and pushed back the menacing mist that was now colored raspberry red, probably from the unknown creature's rage. Running for their lives, they quickly reached the creek bank. For a second Tac stopped, being afraid of water, but Roxal pushed him with all his weight and they found themselves in the cold water swimming in panic towards the other side of the creek. Frantically mounting the bank of the creek, the terrified explorers ran until they reached Beaver's house.

Without asking any questions, Beaver wrapped them both in blankets and shouted for his wife to light the fire so that they could dry out their guests. He looked with alarm into the darkness surrounding his house but nothing had followed them. Very soon a piece of bread and a hot drink helped them to calm down and stopped Tac's teeth from rattling against the edge of the mug like small castanets. His fear settled down and was replaced by embarrassment for his stupid decision to go into the forest at night, which had almost cost them their lives. At the same time, he was afraid to look like a coward in front of Beaver.

"To run back here was the right decision." Beaver read Tac's thoughts. "What good would your bravery do for you if you end up dead?" After some silence he added. "I have seen eagles flying over the forest many times and they definitely have seen what has attacked you and might be able to help you understand its nature, but this is a business for another day. You have had enough worries to deal with so far and right now it's time for a rest."

In the morning, Tac and Roxal quickly swallowed their breakfast, anxious to leave this place as soon as possible. Even the bright sun was unable to wipe away the terror of what had happened to them yesterday. It was only after they had reached the Council Hill again that they were able to discuss the unknown attacker. Tac thought that it may have been some mutated animal, but Roxal described it as some pulsating cloud which constantly changed its shape. They agreed that it had been the killer of all the creatures who had lived inside the area formed by the mountain chain and the two creeks, Leehar and Trout, whose origin lay in the melting glaciers on Bogan Mountain.

Tac suddenly realized how lucky he had been that Alisa had thoughtfully put the supplies for torches into his backpack and this had truly saved their lives. He felt the need to see her to express his gratitude and, at the same time, he realized how badly he missed his home.

Even before Tac had returned to their den, he had made-up his mind not to discuss his discoveries with Alisa. This decision was motivated by the feeling that he needed to gather his thoughts before saying anything to her.

"Is it really a dangerous place?" Alisa was too curious to leave him alone.

"Yes, it is."

"Ok." Alisa nodded her head. "You don't want to talk about the Cursed Forest, but what about your map? Can we talk about that?"

"Of course we can."

"So what is wrong with it?" Continued Alisa, coming up behind Tac and looking at the map over his shoulder, which prompted Tac to explain:

"When I started working on my map, it looked like a simple business of just walking around and making notes to allow me to eventually know everything about this wood. But I can't do anything about this part." Tac pointed with his paw at the troubled area. "I can't leave my map with a big, white spot otherwise my work will be incomplete. And I have no one to ask for help except Roxal. But he will not go with me again."

Alisa looked at the map herself. "The eagle, Galibur, lives somewhere close to this place. If you can get his support, then you will be able to gather all the necessary information without walking into this dangerous place by yourself."

"It looks as if I do not have a choice but to listen to your advice." The cat sighed.

"What else worries you?" She asked again.

Getting up, he stretched his tired back and sighed. "Some smaller matters."

"Like what?"

"Like I have seen the squirrels burying their nuts in different places and they never find half of them again. What if we could build sheds in different parts of the wood to allow small animals to keep their supplies there to help them survive through the cold winter?"

"That will save them a lot of time. If you let somebody else work on your ideas, instead of trying to do it all yourself, you will also have much more time to do other very useful things." She added, teasingly. "Such as going for a run with me? I am tired of sitting at home all day. Ummm… the one who loses this race has to make the bed tomorrow! Agreed? "

Feigning surprise, Tac replied. "Are you trying to say that I am the one who is going to lose? Well, we shall see won't we?" He laughed.

They started their run from Tac's "fishing stone." A sandy pathway led them along the creek which, after a mile, crossed another pathway that ran upwards and disappeared over the top of the hill. After both of them had reached the highest point, Alisa remarked. "Look, there's a group of deer on the left!"

"Yes I see them." Answered Tac. "I think that the one with the crown of antlers is the elk, Rainar."

"Do you want to go that way to talk to him?" Alisa suggested.

"Yes." Tac responded, jogging to the place where Rainar had had his conversation with the deer family. He bowed politely, receiving a nod of the elk's head in response.

After greeting the elk, he repeated his conversation with Alisa to him, adding "I am hoping to get good advice from you. My wife told me that the small animals will not come to the sheds since they are afraid of being ambushed here. What if the Forest Council makes this place a sanctuary and forbids hunting in close proximity to them?" His voice ended on an uncertain note.

"I can see that you have thought about this idea from many angles." Rainar looked at him respectfully. "And it certainly would help to get support from the Council members, Shustin and Mixie. But the look on your face tells me that you have something else to discuss?"

"I really do. I have found from humans that it can be very helpful to have a map. It not only gives us knowledge about the place where we live but helps to plan rescue operations and protect territories against intruders. Believe me, a map has many purposes and it has great value. But, when I started my study of the western part of the woods, I encountered some very serious obstacles. I found that no one had any real knowledge about this area and all the things that I hear about it seem to be only extremely exaggerated stories. I did not believe them and decided to find out the truth for myself. Traveling from my house to the west, my helper Roxal and I eventually reached Leehar, studied a small part of it and then crossed the creek and went to the Cursed Forest."

"You went into the Cursed Forest?" Gasped Rainar, with fear in his voice. "You must be crazy. Do you not know know how lucky you are to have been able to return from this dangerous place alive?"

"I ran, fighting, to get away from something I could not name."

"You are incredibly brave and incredibly irresponsible." Rainar frowned. "You should have talked to the Council before going on such a dangerous journey. Why do you think the Council has forbidden animals to cross the Leehar and called the place Cursed? Just for the sake of scaring everyone?"

"Yes, you are right."

Rainar shook his head disapprovingly. "Next time, before doing something like that, please talk to me first. You are the only one from the competing candidates who is capable of producing ideas and I do not want you to die simply because there is no one to stop you from doing something thoughtless. The Council knows more about the Cursed Forest than they are willing to make public and they have good reason for it. I want to ask you not to create a panic amongst the animals with your story. I am sure that the Council will want to listen to everything you have to tell them about this place."

"I will try to give them an accurate story but, honestly, I know very little. Rainar, I need help from Galibur to get the information that will allow me to finish my map. Do you think he will do it?" Asked Tac.

"Galibur lives with his family on the side of the mountain and frequently flies over the Cursed Forest. I cannot see any reason why he would not help you. You have found out the secret of this place for yourself and your curiosity probably will help you to find out even more strange things."

"Does this forest keep more secrets?" Tac eagerly asked.

"One thing at a time." Laughed Rainar. "For the time being, I suggest that you wait patiently until a new adventure will find you. It appears that the next meeting will be arranged shortly, but do not be surprised if Bertrond and Alowsius will not be invited to attend it. In all probability it will be a secret meeting."

Returning to Alisa, Tac told her that the Council meeting would be set-up for at least two weeks hence and it would be a closed meeting.

"It will probably be better if you spend those two weeks with your friend, Tod, and your human family." Alisa advised. "Otherwise, there will be a lot of nosy neighbors who will want to talk to you, in the hope of dragging out of you at least some of the details of your trip."

"I had the same idea, but I was afraid to discuss it with you since I thought that you would not be happy about staying on your own for such a long time." He sighed.

Alisa smiled. "Do not worry, I was alone for a much longer time than that and I will be fine, thank you."

CHAPTER 2:

THE DATING CRISIS

Lana opened the door of her house.

"Is anybody home?" Only silence answered her.

"Perfect!"

The last thing that she wanted to do right now was to talk to her parents. Lana walked upstairs to her room, dropped her backpack on a chair and let out a long sigh. Thoughts of a hundred things that she still needed to do today filled her mind like a cloud of annoying flies, but she had no strength or desire to do anything. She had gone through a bad day, a really bad one. The chain of unpleasant events had started early in the morning when Lana had met her girlfriend, Maggie, in the corridor of the school where their lockers were located.

Maggie had given Lana that strange look that every girl recognizes as a warning. It meant that something was wrong with the makeup, or the clothes, or you had said something about someone else and your words had come back to you changed so much that you were not able to recognize your own story, and now you had to face the music of your own composition. It appeared as if Maggie was not looking at Lana but was studying the contours of her aura instead.

"What happened?" Asked Lana.

"Well, I told you that you needed to spend more time with Jeff instead of on your fancy lessons. I saw him in the movies with the blonde that I don't like, talking very animatedly." Maggie deliberately closed the door of her locker loudly to show how annoyed and irritated she was.

"Why are you so worried? Jeff is my boyfriend, not yours."

At this, Maggie turned to face Lana. "If you have so little interest in him why did you start dating him in the first place? If you had turned him down he would have dated me instead. I know he likes me but, because he sees me around you all the time, he probably thinks that I will be as cold to him as you are."

"I am not cold to him!" Lana was surprised by this unexpected attack from her most trusted friend and didn't know what to think yet.

"Really?" Maggie's lips stretched into a sarcastic smile. "So where were you yesterday when he was bored and needed company?" She didn't wait for an answer, only throwing Lana a cold look and walking away.

'Bloody, innocent lamb. She has never learned to stand up for herself, nor will she ever be able to keep her man.' Thought Maggie, frustrated that Lana had not picked up the fight, thus giving her a reason to say more. Part of her frustration was related to the necessity to keep her desire to have Jeff's company a secret.

She liked to think that she was making a big sacrifice of her own feelings for him for the benefit of Lana and, because of this, Maggie expected Lana to owe her a great deal. If Jeff started to date another girl, then all of her sacrifices would be meaningless and her carefully-nourished opinions of herself, as a generous and unselfish person, would be shattered. Maggie felt angry at Lana and wanted to smack her stubborn head for showing such neglect of both their interests.

Lana walked to class with aching feelings of emptiness and hurt inside of her. She still did not understand why Maggie blamed her for his decision to go to the movies with someone else. Maggie often tried to control and boss her around, but never before had she expressed her envy and sense of ownership of Lana so openly and undiplomatically.

She felt that, after this conversation, it would be difficult to continue their friendship and the realization of this brought sadness and a sense of loss to her. On the other hand she resolved to be the mistress of her own life. Weighing these different feelings on her mental scales, she soon decided that this change would be a positive event for her.

Right then her thoughts were interrupted by the Mathematics teacher who was walking between the tables, returning the results of their last test.

"Lana, what has happened to you? Are you not feeling well? Your last test surprised me and I was wondering whether you had studied for it?" He asked.

"I am fine, thank you." Lana felt embarrassed and scared at the same time.

"You are a good student, responsible and hardworking, that's why I am concerned about your progress. I don't want your final mark at the end of the year to become lower than it should be. If you need help I can find a tutor for you from one of my best students."

"I had a hard time with my other lessons and I had some problems at home. I was probably too busy thinking about them and not thinking enough about my test.' She responded. "I promise to do everything that I can to make sure this doesn't happen again."

"Are your parents well?" The teacher continued, with concern.

"No, it's not that." Lana replied. "Nothing is wrong with my parents; it's our cat that's been missing for almost a week."

"I am sorry and I believe that's a serious reason for a teenager to lose her concentration over her studies, but I hope that once the cat is found you will return to your usual self."

"Yes I will." Lana promised, still feeling that she was far from her normal self. 'Why am I so afraid to tell Maggie that I don't need her as a mentor?' She thought. 'Clearly, I allowed her to interfere in my life too much and press her opinions upon me too strongly. What I need to do is talk to Jeff personally and find out for myself whether or not this whole story is solely the result of Maggie's imagination. Perhaps he will just laugh at it and will say that there is nothing serious between him and that girl he went out with. He just did not want to go to the movies alone. Maggie was definitely right about one thing, I must spend more time with him.'

Lana looked for Jeff in the cafeteria during lunch time but, to her surprise, she didn't find him there. Searching for him at school would probably take her half an hour. Lana walked straight over to Jeff's buddies who were sitting at the table near the window. "Hi, guys. Do you know where Jeff is?"

They stopped laughing and turned towards her. "No." Said the closest boy. Another opened his mouth to say something but his neighbor gave him a nudge to make him stop.

"O.K." She shrugged. "See you later."

She only had five minutes before the beginning of her lesson and decided to give up her search and meet Jeff at his car after class, thinking that this way she would definitely not miss him. Waiting for him at the parking lot, Lana saw Jeff from a distance going over to his car with a girl hanging on his arm and talking as if her mouth would never run out of words. As soon as Jeff saw Lana he stopped and said to his companion. "I am sorry. You will need to go home alone since I have other business to attend to." She gave Lana a sharp look and walked off towards the bus stop.

"Hi Lana." Jeff didn't look pleased to see her. "I need to talk to you. Can we sit down here for a moment?" He sat on the bench and pointed to the spot next to him.

Unpleasant feelings tightened Lana's throat but she did not want to show them to him since she still had pride and well knew that crying would change nothing. A decision was written all over his tight and distant face. 'Oh! Oh!' She thought to herself, as she sat down on the bench. 'The faster we get through this the better.'

"Lana." Jeff paused, having difficulty finding his words.

Noticing his discomfort, she quickly responded. "Jeff, do you want to tell me that our relationship is finished? I think you want to date another girl and just be friends with me. I know that I am not exactly your type since you've told me before that you would appreciate it if I was less smart and more fun." She ended on a bitter note.

Jeff lifted his hand, wanting to say something, but Lana interrupted him. "No matter what you say it will not change the outcome. You want to break up with me. Am I right?" He only shrugged his shoulders, so Lana added. "You can therefore do what you want because I can't keep you in this relationship against your will. I hope you'll be happier with her." Then she got up and moved away, without seeing where she was going.

Jeff did not make any attempt to stop her or say anything. This hurt her most of all. After walking along not feeling or hearing anything, Lana eventually reached her home. She felt the need to cry, but tears wouldn't come and this only increased the pressure of the unfair situation that had befallen her suddenly and without the fault being hers. By the time that her parents had come home from work she had detached herself from her emotions, moving and talking automatically as if she was a machine instead of a living being. Only later, as she took a shower, did something change inside of her. Maybe it was the hot water that soothed her hurt, or something unexplainable had come to rescue her, but she succeeded in giving in to her tears. Lifting up her face, she mingled her sobbing and bitter complaints with the hot water until not only her body had become clean but most of her pain had left her. She didn't feel as if she had been healed completely, but the load on her shoulders became lighter.

Next morning she came down from her bedroom and told her father that she would not be going to school that day because she was not feeling well. Nicholas touched her forehead and wanted to say that it didn't feel hot but changed his mind after he looked at her pale, motionless face.

"Is something wrong Lana?"

"I broke up with my boyfriend." She didn't have the strength to lie.

"Sweetheart." Nicholas hugged her. "I'm so sorry. Of course it will be better for you to stay at home. Tomorrow is Saturday and a couple of days without seeing him can change everything. Maybe you'll decide that it's the right thing for you to do after all?"

"Maybe." Lana's voice was weak and tired.

"Did you sleep darling?" Asked Nicholas, concerned at the way she looked.

"Very little."

"Do you think that you should go to bed and try to sleep?" Suggested Nicholas.

"Dad, thanks for your concern, but I am going to be fine." She replied. However, seeing from the expression on his face how unconvinced he was, Lana lied. "I'm hungry and I had better find something to eat."

Nicholas, more satisfied, kissed her forehead and left for work. "Call me if you need to talk to me or to go anywhere. Call me if you need anything." He shouted from the doorway. "And don't worry about school. I will call your teacher."

"Thanks Dad." Lana whispered after him, going to her bedroom to avoid having the same conversation with her mother and to postpone answering all her questions until later. The first thing that she intended to do was to get control over her emotions. Breaking up is not easy, even if you are not madly in love but have started to develop feelings for another person. The loss of someone close to you hurts for at least some time, no matter what kind of relationship you have, a happy or an unhappy one. She cried a little again and then went to the washroom to splash some water on her face but she did not recognize the face that looked back at her from the mirror. A sleepless night had put light lavender circles under her eyes, making them look darker. The gentle skin of her face was pale, showing her exhaustion and making Lana look even more tender and defenseless than usual. She lifted up her long hair and rolled it into a design and teased her reflection 'You definitely look like a poor girl with a broken heart who has been left to cry alone, don't you?'

The girl in the mirror didn't answer and she returned to her bedroom, climbed onto her bed and wrapped herself in a blanket. She tried to replace the confusion of her thoughts with the memory of many happy hours that she had spent in this room in the past. She remembered how glad she had been when her father had allowed her to redecorate this room, transforming it from the pink bedroom of a little girl into the room of a young lady. Lana had struggled over the decision as to what color she should choose next. First, she wanted to repaint her bedroom in sunny yellow accented with blue bedding, then red with orange. This combination almost gave her mother a heart attack and Natalie called her husband in to rescue the bedroom from becoming a rainbow-colored disaster.

He had looked around and said. "I don't think that red is a good idea because all of the furniture in your bedroom has the color of dark cherry and this means that you need to choose a light color for the walls, otherwise it will be overpowering."

Lana had put strips of colored paper against her night stand and all of them agreed that a very light green would look the best. Natalie had helped Lana make a blue-green canopy for her bed to be accompanied by satin, beige bedding. Clusters of silken, deep-purple flowers had added a dramatic look to the bedroom. All sweet, comforting things that surrounded her now brought back these memories of happiness and returned peace back to her heart and mind.

She looked at the bookcase where her favorite books were displayed, all carefully aligned and cherished as best friends from her childhood. Her school books were standing separately, to make finding them easier, and their glossy sides reminded her that on Monday she would have to go back to school. This thought scared her. If she would have Maggie by her side no one would dare to show pity towards her, or make jokes. Her classmates would simply pretend that nothing untoward had happened. But now she must go through this difficult time by herself.

The First day of School for Lana and Maggie

She had known Maggie since she had started middle school. Her slim figure, topped by a cloud of red curls, had caught Lana's eye right away. Being easygoing and sociable, Lana had not hesitated to go over to her to introduce herself, saying. "I'm Lana Vladner."

Maggie's green eyes had critically looked at the plain jeans and T-shirt on her but, as her eyes had drifted over her soft and gentle face, brightened by an open and genuine smile, she could not resist smiling back.

"Are you an elf?" She asked, scared by the sudden change inside of herself.

"I think I'm a girl." Answered Lana, bending her head and examining her little body with curiosity.

"Well, that's interesting, but now it's time to go to class and, by the way, I'm Maggie O'Donnell." Was the rejoinder.

In time Lana's earlier empathy for Maggie had transformed into pity for her because she noticed that her exaggerated demands upon people had the effect of destroying her relationships. Great belief in the correctness of her actions separated her from the rest of the students. But, despite this trait in Maggie's character, Lana stayed friends with her hoping that eventually she would manage to soften her in order to make her more likeable.

Maggie, on the other hand, had accepted Lana as if she was a little puppy being handed to her for her birthday. She had decided that Lana needed her protection and guidance because, from her point of view, Lana did not have a strong character. So, for many years, Lana had been treated like an ugly duckling under the wing of the white swan, Maggie, the girl who came from a family with money. Her parents had encouraged their friendship and had decided that the company of a quiet and well-mannered girl, dressed in affordable clothes, would be better for her than the relationships with her other noisy girlfriends who were dressed fashionably but had limited interests.

When Lana came to visit Maggie for the first time she did not feel comfortable in her friend's big house. The grand design of it almost scared her by making her feel small and insignificant. This had happened for the first time in Lana's life and she did not like the feeling. She probably would never have come back to this home if she had not opened the door to the library by accident. Lana liked to read and had a bookcase full of books herself. But the number of books in the library of Maggie's father stunned her completely. She needed a good ten minutes to gather the courage to dare to take a couple of steps inside to take a better look at this treasure. Her big blue eyes reflected her delight. They were opened so wide that it looked as if there was nothing else on her face except two blue pools of excitement. Lana's happiness was boundless when she got permission from Mr. O'Donnell to take home any book she pleased if she promised to return it undamaged. For this, Lana was ready to overlook her friend's domineering character and the scornful looks from her wealthy girlfriends.

The house immediately shrank in size in her opinion and became just a good-sized box whose purpose was to keep the library safe because, to her, it was a precious possession. It was the place to which she quietly escaped every time that she found herself becoming tired of the empty talk and the noise from

Maggie's parties. Lana found that she wasn't the only one who preferred the silence of the library to the screaming music and the loud chatter coming from the living room. It was also a favorite place of refuge for Mr. O'Donnell when the hordes of teenagers led by his daughter occupied his house and consumed many trays of sandwiches and pop.

Lana and Mr. O'Donnell found a mutual interest in discussing books of famous writers and different aspects of history and science. They spent many pleasant hours talking together, interrupted sometimes by Maggie who had been looking everywhere for Lana to share some extremely exciting gossip with her or wishing to introduce her to a potential boyfriend.

The relationship between Lana and Jeff had started from one of these introductions. This time it had not been so easy for Maggie to get Lana out of the library since she refused to break her interesting conversation with Mr. O'Donnell. Maggie had no choice but to shrug her shoulders disapprovingly and leave her to herself. Desperate to get Lana out of the room, and having a plan for her, she used a trick to get what she wanted. She told her mother that her dad was testing his own scientific article on Lana and it would be an act of mercy to rescue her from the claws of this discussion.

Mrs. O'Donnell was very busy with her duties and did not have much time to argue with her husband. She simply turned off the lights in the library and kicked both Lana and Mr. O'Donnell out, saying. "The meeting is closed and both of you must now return to the world of normal people who, right now, are eating, drinking, and dancing." Then she turned to Lana. "I want you to meet a very nice man whose name is Jeff. You have probably seen him in school and I hope you'll have fun together."

Lana was the only girl at the party who did not have any interest in flirting with Jeff. She just mumbled "Hi" to him and, as soon as Mrs. O'Donnell had left them to return to her hostess duties, Lana excused herself and walked away, leaving Jeff with a deeply bruised ego. His interest in this strange girl was inflamed to the point that he went looking for Maggie to ask some questions about her. Maggie had watched how Jeff followed Lana with his eyes until she had disappeared into the kitchen and she decided that it was time to add a few more drops of fuel to the fire. She described Lana as an intelligent girl, having self-respect and a lot of talent, which was not an entirely exaggerated thing to say since Lana was indeed a girl like that.

"And what kinds of talents does she have?" Jeff's question sounded slightly sarcastic.

"She can dance solos beautifully and I think that I'll ask her to dance one for us." Retorted Maggie, then left Jeff to his opinion and went into the kitchen to talk to Lana. At first she refused to dance saying that the dance of her choice could be dangerous with so many people standing around and also that she did not have a costume to wear. Maggie made a face as if she was going to cry and said that she had already made public that Lana was going to dance and now everyone would laugh at her if she refused to do it.

Lana put her half-empty cup on the counter and said. "Please, before you make these kinds of promises, at least talk to me first. There is no need for you to put on this upset face because I will dance, but I still don't have a costume."

"We'll find something." Maggie ran to her mother, prompting Mrs. O'Donnell to immediately go upstairs to look for something appropriate for Lana to wear. She returned with a bright, beaded scarf and a box of jewelry while Maggie brought a sword from her father's office. Lana looked at everything critically, then chose some jewelry and gave both Maggie and her mother instructions as to how to prepare a place for a safe performance, reminding them that if any one of the guests did not behave properly she would stop dancing.

A minute later she heard the noise of moving chairs and the excited voices of the guests who were happy to have some entertainment. Lana had rolled up her black tank top, wrapped a scarf around her hips leaving the long tails hanging down her left leg and, as the music in the stereo was changed and the lights dimmed, she slowly moved towards the middle of the living room that had been cleared of all furniture to leave it solely as a stage. Lana carefully held the sword with both hands and slowly moved her body gracefully to the rhythm of the music, then turned the sword from her right side to the left whilst following it with her eyes. During the movement, she unexpectedly and quickly rotated her body holding the sword over her head, returning it back to a slow, flowing movement with arms stretched out in front of her, offering the sword to the guests. Jewelry on her arms, neck and hips intriguingly sparkled in the dim light and increased the feeling of mystery. Guests were almost hypnotized by the magic of the dance, whilst Lana's inspired face made her look like a priestess performing a secret ritual in a distant temple. No one was able to take their eyes off her, hardly breathing, while they silently watched her.

Maggie had chosen the dance correctly. Watching a woman dancing with a sword always has had a powerful effect on men, making them see her as an almost mystical creature, dangerous and desirable. By the time the dance had finished, and everyone had thanked Lana for such a beautiful performance, Jeff's doubts about her were extinguished as well. He knew for sure that Lana was a girl whom he wanted as his girlfriend.

He tried to talk to her but, again, she smoothly evaded him by saying that she needed to return to her normal appearance and therefore would have to leave him until later. Since Jeff was desperate to catch Lana's attention, he followed her into the kitchen where she was pouring herself a cup of coffee, having felt thirsty after dancing, and he deliberately stood close behind her back so that, if she were to turn round, she would spill the whole cup on him. This, of course, is exactly what happened.

"I am so sorry! I didn't see you standing there." Lana exclaimed, staring at Jeff who was pulling his T-shirt away from himself to prevent the hot coffee from burning his skin. "I am really clumsy." She continued, trying to wipe away the coffee with a paper towel.

"You don't need to apologize since it's my fault for being in your way." Replied Jeff, ruefully, allowing Lana to clean some of the stain off his clothing.

"I am sorry, Jeff, but I think your T-shirt is ruined."

"Yes! And how are you going to compensate me for this loss?" Asked Jeff, seriously, prompting Lana to give him a very puzzled look. "You owe me and, to make us even, you must go with me to a cafe so I can pour a cup of coffee on your T-shirt." The expression on her face made him laugh. After a few seconds, Lana joined him, being glad that his words were just a joke. The ice had been broken between them and the conversation flowed freely until Lana looked at her watch and said that it was time for her to go home. Jeff suggested that he could give her a ride home and showed her his car key. Lana was too tired to argue and, after saying goodbye to everyone, they left together.

Maggie was satisfied with her success as a matchmaker. If Jeff needed to date someone, before he realized that Maggie was his future destiny, it would be better if this girl would be Lana and, in due course, Maggie could put everything in its rightful place. Next day she caught up with Lana on the way to school and demanded a detailed accounting of everything that had happened later. However, Lana had not had much to say on this matter because the conversation between them had been about everything in general terms, but nothing personal.

She had not been in the mood to flirt and Jeff had been afraid to move closer without signs of obvious affection from her. She had kept the conversation going, but had not crossed the line between just being friendly and something more personal. So, Jeff decided to wait and not to force the issue until he could figure out what had been going on in her mind. He expected a goodnight kiss but Lana had not even made a move to hug him, let alone give him a kiss. Her behavior had made him feel even more interested, instead of being disappointed which he probably would have felt with another girl. He even forgot to ask her for a date, a thing which had never happened to him before.

"She placed me exactly where she wanted me to be." He admitted to himself, laughing.

Lana did not know what kind of an impression she had made on him. She had not been invited to spend time with him the next day and did not know what he thought about her.

Of course, Maggie was not pleased about this and let her feelings be known in her usual, undiplomatic way. To save herself from a lecture, Lana simply admitted her mistake, knowing that otherwise Maggie would be unstoppable.

Luckily, Jeff approached Lana at lunch time of the same day and invited her to share a cup of coffee with him after school. Lana, unintentionally, looked at her tank top but he understood her without words, made an innocent face and promised to behave himself.

"Thanks for your invitation. It will save me from listening to Maggie." She said.

Jeff lifted his eyebrow. "What is her problem?"

"She is playing my big, overly-attentive, sister." Lana advised him. "Were you a bad girl?" Asked Jeff, with a smile.

"I haven't even had a chance to be bad yet; but I am already tasting the fruits of my potential badness." She replied, with a sigh.

"Get used to this." Jeff suggested with a wink and then whispered into her ear. "Let's give her reason to be annoyed." Then he quickly kissed her on the lips.

Her face changed color, becoming pink. Grabbing her belongings, Lana ran from the cafeteria, followed by the astonished looks of the girls and smiles from the boys. Unable to concentrate on her studies, she gave up and waited for the end of the day so that she could find some peace in the safety of her bedroom to gather her thoughts. She refused to discuss Jeff's boyish actions with Maggie.

"I don't want to talk about him. I dislike being the subject of a stupid joke and, unless you want me to cancel our meeting at the café, please leave me alone." She warned her angrily. Personally, she did not feel right to characterize her future meeting with Jeff as a date without knowing the reason for his sudden invitation. She admitted to herself that Jeff was quite attractive and the fact that he was the captain of the school's basketball team made him irresistibly appealing to girls. However, being a sports star was not enough for her. She needed much more than that. She needed a person who would make her heart beat faster and who would bring something special into her life. Unfortunately, Jeff did not make her heart skip even a beat. He was a nice young man but dating him would make her feel as if she was taking advantage of him, without her having adequate feelings for him. She had agreed to see him again only to have an opportunity to explain her feelings to him fully.

"He is not stupid and will understand." She comforted herself, as she opened the door to the Cafe at the scheduled time. Deciding not to delay a difficult conversation, she immediately surprised Jeff by commencing to tell him her reasons for not deepening their relationship and explained to him why they could not be more than school friends. Unfortunately, Lana only succeeded in undermining his confidence because, before this meeting with her, Jeff had believed that he understood girls very well.

"What is she talking about?" He wondered. "Am I not playing the nice, uncomplicated game of love that all girls want? Am I not the big, strong, handsome, easy-going guy they are all looking for and is this not the reason why the girls always try to get my attention?" He had never committed his heart to anyone and had never demanded a commitment, so he was puzzled by Lana's strange behavior. He was ready to say to her that she was right and that their personalities were too different to continue together, wish her a good evening and walk away. However, a thought suddenly came into his mind that perhaps all this talk about feelings was just another girlish way to make him think that she was someone special and, by this means, be successful in attaching him to her.

"So, she wants to play this game? Very well, I am ready."

Jeff took Lana's hands into his, looked into her eyes and said how deeply she had touched his heart and how difficult it would be for him to be happy without her. He asked her to give him a chance to change her heart so that her present good feelings for him would transform into a deep love, but Lana was confused. She did not know what to say, having very little experience in matters of the heart. On the other hand, she did not have a reason to disbelieve him and chose her words carefully to avoid wounding him too deeply.

"Jeff, I need some time to get to know you better in order to make a decision."

"I will wait."

The emotional tension that had arisen between them at the beginning of the evening was no longer apparent and had been replaced by a pleasant and relaxed conversation that pleased both of them.

Next day Jeff waited for Lana at the front door of the school to say hello to her and have a quick exchange of smiles. At lunch time, he courted her politely and made her the subject of envy of the other girls. Then, after school, he took her home in his car, despite her worry that this would attract the attention of her school mates.

Even at home Lana did not achieve peace. Maggie had phoned her the very moment that she had crossed the doorway of her house, throwing question after question at her whilst screaming with excitement and not giving Lana any real chance to answer. She did not even want to hear about Lana's doubts concerning her blooming relationship with a school celebrity.

"He is the dream of every normal girl and I won't let you make the mistake of turning him down." She firmly stopped Lana's weak attempt to argue. "Jeff is the best man you can get and everyone will think that you are crazy if you let him go." She continued, emphatically.

As a result of all their arguments, Lana accepted the position of his girl-friend. This suited Maggie very well but, at the same time, she did not allow them to be alone. Instead, she acted like a chaperone from the olden days, being always under his feet, watching, interrupting and giving advice and, in the process, driving him mad. He even asked Lana why she allowed Maggie to pull her strings like a puppet.

Lana advised him. "It started a long time ago, probably because in every relationship one leads and the other one follows the leader, otherwise a friend-ship doesn't work. Maggie's character does not allow her to follow anyone so I had no choice but to accept my place as her follower. Unfortunately, she has often abused the position of a leader and made my life difficult."

"So why don't you tell Maggie to find someone else and stop seeing you?" asked Jeff.

"Ah!" She countered. "It's not as simple as that. No one leaves Maggie because she thinks that only she has the right to make such a decision and she's quite impossible to shake off if she doesn't want this to happen."

"So, she is stuck to you forever?" He frowned.

"Maggie doesn't have a lot of friends and I simply pity her. This is the rea-son why I don't want to push her away when she has no one else." She sighed.

"That is her problem, isn't it?"

"Yes. And maybe one day I will tell her to stop interfering so much in my affairs!" She agreed.

"You are too soft!"

"I know. But may we change the subject because I would prefer that we didn't talk about her all evening?"

He shook his head but said nothing further. Sometimes, when Jeff was in a good mood, he would invite both Lana and Maggie to the party or movies. This made Maggie feel very happy but Lana didn't like to be with both of them. She was irritated when Jeff paid most of his attention to Maggie and wished that she would find her own boyfriend. But this triangle perfectly suited Maggie and Lana's wish, therefore, never had a chance of coming true. However, Lana could not have predicted that in one day her whole life would change and she would find herself literally standing amidst the debris left over from her rela-tionships. Tired from her contemplations, she put her head on the pillow and wafted into the soothing depths of a dream. Waking up in the late afternoon, refreshed and hungry, she went downstairs to the kitchen.

"Lana, I thought you were at school?" Natalie stopped wiping the table, surprised to see her.

"I didn't feel well in the morning so dad allowed me to stay in bed. I man-aged to sleep almost half a day and now I feel that I can eat half a cow."

"I'm glad that you feel better." Remarked Natalie.

The telephone rang and startled both of them. Lana took some food from the fridge and waited for her mother to finish her conversation and return to the kitchen. "Dad called." She advised. "He told me what happened between you and Jeff."

"Mom, you don't need to worry, it doesn't feel so bad right now." Lana tried to look brave but her trembling lips betrayed her. "Oh, it's time to feed Tod!" And she grabbed the bag containing the dog's food and ran outside to escape further discussion. Watching her, Natalie wisely decided to leave her alone, thinking that time would be the best healer. Lana was absent much longer than was required to feed the dog and Natalie started to worry about her whereabouts. She even considered calling Nicholas, but the sound of the opening of the front door changed her mind.

"Mom, I took Todd for a walk and met my classmate, Stephany." Lana's voice reached Natalie before she could even see her daughter. "Do you remember that her father helped dad to change the tires on our truck?"

Lana looked much happier now and, seeing this, Natalie only remarked calmly. "Ah! He is our neighbor from across the street."

"Yes, Stephany and her brothers are planning to canoe along the river and cook fish on an open fire, if they are lucky to catch any. May I go?"

"Let's ask your father first." Natalie knew that Nicholas had just come home and could hear them through the open door.

He appeared in the doorframe and, with a gesture of approval, quipped. "Hi, girls, don't pretend that it is I who has to make this decision."

"In this case we need to prepare your backpack."

Then both mother and daughter got busy choosing and packing the things that would be needed for the weekend picnic and fishing trip.

"It will be very good for Lana to spend Sunday in the fresh air with teenagers her age." Said Nicholas, on his way to bed, to which Natalie responded. "Yes, I agree with you."

Saturday was the longest day in Lana's life and she was glad to see the end of it. Very early the next day, chilled by a cool breeze, she went to join Stephany who, along with her brother Steve, had almost finished loading the truck which belonged to her other brother, Mathew.

"Good morning Lana." Stephany greeted her. "I'm glad that you are here on time and I don't need to send Steve to wake you up. Please put your backpack in the truck and take a seat. We will be leaving in a few minutes, otherwise Mathew will be upset if we arrive at the river too late and his fishing will be spoiled."

"Lana, is this jacket all that you are going to wear?" Asked Stephany. Lana nodded. Turning towards her brother, Stephany shouted. "Steve, run to the house and get a jacket for Lana. If it's going to be too big for her then wearing this jacket will be her penalty for not having any idea of how to dress to go fishing."

Lana smiled and stood on the wheel to put her backpack into the back of the truck. Lifting the cover she discovered two canoes tied to the sides of the truck, surrounded by a cooler with drinks and food in it, fishing rods and backpacks packed with different things that they would need to have a good time at the river.

When Mathew and Steven finally came out of the house, the girls were already in the car with their seatbelts fastened. Mathew waited for the youngsters to make themselves comfortable, whilst chatting to each other like birds, and pushed the accelerator.

The village was still sleeping and even the dogs were too lazy to leave their warm beds to run out and bark at the car. Lana saw just a few vehicles on the road apart from theirs. She followed them with her eyes, resolving that she was going to enjoy this Sunday camping trip, no matter what the next day would bring to her.

Stephany touched her hand to get her attention. "I know what happened between you and Jeff and that's why I invited you to come with us. I went through a similar situation myself and I know how bad it feels. If you want to talk about this, then you have my ear to listen but if you wish to be silent you are free to do so. There is no formula on how to break up, it's like the 'flu and you need to go through a fever to recover from the effects."

"Does everyone know about us?" Lana gasped."

"Well, Lana, Jeff's relationship with girls always attracts attention and now the whole school is talking about your break-up. You made a mistake by not coming to school on Friday. Your absence created even more suspense."

"Do you think that it's my fault that our relationship is over?" Asked Lana, looking straight at her.

"I think that Jeff is a fool." Stephany's eyes had humorous sparks in them. "He had a pearl in his hands but, because he was not aware of its value, he decided that it was only a stone. He dropped it on the road but, if someone else will pick it up and place it into a beautiful ring, Jeff will be the first to be astonished by its beauty and will be very sorry in the future if somebody reminds him that it was once in his possession."

"So you think I'm a pearl?" Laughed Lana.

Stephany laughed with her and replied. "Like any other girl, all you need is a good goldsmith to fully understand and appreciate you and one day you'll meet him. So, keep your chin up high tomorrow and make Jeff wonder why you are not upset."

Their conversation on the back seat was interrupted by Mathew. "Wake up, sleeping beauty, we've arrived!" He yelled at his younger brother.

Lana left the truck and looked around her. They had parked on the sandy ground of the beach where patches of grass grew here and there and the gray water of the half-sleeping lake lazily rolled its waves to the shore and back, like a slowly-breathing large animal.

Mathew, an enthusiastic fisherman, couldn't wait to start his favorite activity and hurried everyone to unload the canoes from the truck so that he could go to his special place on the creek where the fish would be biting well.

"Lana, you'll sit in my canoe." He said. "I can't trust Steve to have you in his canoe unless you don't mind getting a cold bath."

"It happened only once!" Argued Steven, frowning, but Lana decided that it would be better for her to go with Mathew because she felt that he had more experience in paddling a canoe.

"Liar!" Stephany laughed at him, sitting down in the other canoe with Steven. "Just try overturning this canoe and I'll make you pay for it for a long time." She promised her brother.

"I'll go along the shore of the lake until we reach the river, then we'll go west to the place where I regularly feed the fish. I promise you that we will have a couple of good trout within five minutes." Mathew pushed the canoe away from the shore and started to paddle.

Very soon, Lana was lulled by the rhythmical movement of the canoe and the warmth of his old jacket which was probably five sizes too big for her. Her back rested comfortably on a couple of backpacks which made her half-asleep condition very enjoyable. Mathew did not want to disturb her, thinking that she probably needed the sleep, and he just coughed politely when his canoe had arrived at the spot where they needed to turn into the creek. This sound made Lana open her eyes and she was surprised to see the sun standing quite high on the horizon, painting the sky and the water with shades of pink. The absence of clouds promised a warm and sunny day which would be perfect for fishing and the picnic.

Mathew waited for Steven to come closer and then shouted to him. "Now, watch out for a big creek to your left, it's coming from the north-west and the water will be going quite fast. We'll enter the creek and go against the flow for approximately half a mile and then make camp on the left bank. There are a couple of large trees growing close to the water to which we can tie up our canoes so that the creek does not drag them back into the river."

"O.K." Steven shouted back to him. Following Mathew's lead, he turned into the creek and paddled along it to the northwest. The right side of the creek was clear of vegetation and had a sandy pathway along the shore which looked comfortable to walk upon but, well beyond that, the forest stood at some distance from the shore on a rather high slope. Trees in this area were tall and mature, growing tightly one against the other like a tall green hedge. For some reason the forest did not look inviting and gave Lana goose bumps on her flesh.

The left side had a narrow strip of rocks between the water and the forest. In some places, dense reeds grew along the outline of the shore which made docking impossible. Trees on this flat ground were scattered around but sometimes they combined into groups, leaving open spaces for weeds and flowers. It was only in the background of the clearances that Lana saw solid forest, similar to what was being revealed on the right side. Lana did not have time to figure out why the left side of the creek looked different to the other because Mathew had turned the canoe towards the rocks and let its nose run aground on top of the first line of them. He helped Lana to jump out of the canoe without getting her feet wet and started to unload it, followed by Steven who docked his canoe next to theirs. Half an hour later, Mathew and Steven took an empty canoe and went fishing, leaving Lana and Stephany to organize the camp and collect dry wood for a fire.

"I saw you in the cafeteria, sitting separately from Maggie. May I ask what happened between you two?" Asked Stephany, breaking small, dry branches off a bush.

Lana stopped her work and looked at the creek. "We had a fight over Jeff and she was unbelievably angry at me for losing him. Her behavior suggested to me that Jeff had become the meaning of my relationship with her and, without him, she didn't see any need to have a friendship with me."

"Ah!" Said Stephany. "I thought that Maggie was attracted to him. She always looked like soft butter around him, almost begging him. 'Eat me, eat me.'"

This made Lana lift her eyebrow as she tried to remember Maggie's face at times when she had been with her and Jeff and, eventually, she chuckled and replied. "You have a good eye." Then they returned to the collecting of branches and very soon each of them had brought a pile of wood to the camp to light the fire and put a kettle on it to make tea for the lunch break.

"You will need to keep yourself busy doing something to fill the time that you used to spend with Maggie and Jeff and later you will get accustomed to living without them." Stephany tried not to sound boring and patronizing.

"I can replace Maggie with books, but evenings I spent with Jeff. I don't think I want to go to the cafe by myself." Lana replied.

"What about working in the cafe?" Asked Stephany. "My manager is looking for two new girls to replace my teammates who have quit."

"Hmm, that's not a bad idea!" Lana realized that a couple of days ago she would have been able to do this only over Maggie's dead body. But now she was free to work anywhere and even to make money to buy herself a motor bike which was not advisable when Maggie and she were together since Maggie had no respect for bikers. "If your parents can't afford to buy you a car, it's better

for you to take a bus." She said, copying Maggie's voice perfectly. "I'm starting to like my new life." She continued in her normal voice and with a rather
pleased expression on her face.

"Bring your resume to me after school and I will try to convince my boss to
hire you." Replied Stephany, as she ripped a piece of paper from a cardboard box
and wrote the address of the café on it. "It's close to a bus stop and is not difficult
to find. We can try to get shifts together so that it won't be too boring going home
after work and your parents won't have to worry about your walking home alone."

"Do you think that it's time to call the boys back for tea?" Stephany asked
suddenly.

Lana looked inside the kettle and remarked that the water was boiling.
Hearing their calls, Mathew and Steve promptly paddled over to the campsite
and landed, holding four big trout in their knitted bag and some smaller fish in
a plastic bag.

Mathew called out excitedly. "I will put the larger fish on ice in the cooler,
but these smaller ones we'll cook right now." He took out a knife and quickly
cleaned and washed the fish, then baked them on the fire. Needless to say, the
trout had a wonderful taste and was eaten very quickly.

"Do you want to try to catch a trout for yourself?" Mathew asked Lana.

"I don't know how to do it." She replied.

"Don't worry." Commented Steven. "Mathew will teach you. It isn't that
difficult. You just need to wait patiently until the fish bites your fly and then
you simply pull him into the canoe."

"That's the big specialist talking." Laughed Matthew. "Really, Lana, come
with me and perhaps you will like fishing. I know many girls who like to do it."

"I don't know whether or not I am going to like it but I am willing to try."
Lana answered, delighted at the prospect of learning the sport.

At this, Mathew took a fishing rod for her out of the case and put it into
the canoe. Steven put his into the second canoe and turned to see Stephany
approaching him, also holding a rod in her hand.

"Are you going to go fishing too? Is it safe to leave all of our things unat-
tended?" asked a surprised Lana.

"There is no one around for miles. It's the bears that we must be afraid
of, but today I have not seen any of them nearby so I think it's safe." Mathew
assured her, pushing the canoe away from the shore and handing Lana her fishing rod.

She cast the fly onto the running water and prepared to wait for a fish to
jump at it. After about fifteen minutes of useless waiting, and no bites from
the fish, she decided that she definitely did not like fishing and, after another
unproductive fifteen minutes, she became bored.

"Mathew, I am a hopeless fishing student and my back is hurting. I don't mind if you take me to the shore and let me walk a little bit to get the blood circulating in my legs." She complained. Mathew examined both shores with his eyes and decided that if Lana wanted to walk he would need to take her to the right side of the creek. He then softly landed the canoe on the sand and allowed her to jump out of it.

"I'll go along the shore and then come back." Said Lana, noting that Mathew had pulled something from the pocket of his jacket.

"Here's a map and compass. Do you know how to use it?" He asked.

"Yes. I was taught that at school." She replied.

"If something happens, and you get lost, just look at the compass and find your position on the map. But the best thing to do is to walk along the creek because it will guide you back to us." Mathew was sure that nothing could happen to her on this empty shore.

Lana put the map and the compass into the pocket of her jacket and set-off, walking towards the unknown. The sun was high in the sky and warmed the air and, after a short time, she was forced to remove her jacket and carry it in her hands. She found that there was nothing to look at and, apparently, there was nothing alive around her. She continued to walk, sometimes looking at the forest, surprised by the absence of the voices of birds. Returning her attention to the water, she suddenly spotted something. As she got closer, she realized that it was a boat. Someone else was fishing too. Lana wanted to turn back but then changed her mind, thinking that she needed to check whether or not this fisherman was in some kind of trouble.

Coming closer to the boat, she saw a stranger who had been bending over some wood and trying to light a fire without any success. At the sound of her footsteps he straightened his back and called out "Hullo" to her. The fire gave off acrid smoke and died out.

"The wood is too wet." She remarked. "You will need to find some dry wood and then you won't have a problem."

Instead of following her advice, the man just gave up trying and turned his attention to her. "What are you doing here alone?"

"I'm not alone." She responded. "I'm with my friends who are fishing not too far from here."

"I still think that it's not a good idea for you to walk alone." The stranger stated, eyeing her with interest. "How would you protect yourself if a bear were to come to the shore out of the forest? I assume that you do not have a gun?"

"I will not kill any animal!"

"I didn't mean to kill the bear, but to scare him away with the gunfire." He went on. The last word reminded him of his problem with his attempt to light the fire and he sighed. "Let's make a deal. If you will help me to collect dry branches for my fire I will take you on my boat to your friends. How does that sound?"

"It's a deal!" Lana smiled at him.

The man then proceeded to take a piece of rope to tie the branches into a pile and they both walked towards the line of rocks, because the access to the forest from this side was easier than climbing up the high slope of the shore. Lana and the man, who introduced himself as Don, walked deeper into the openings between the trees, picking up the branches that had been lying on the ground. It took them some time to collect enough to make a nice pile.

"I'll carry it." Don told her. "Just give me a couple of minutes to rest in the shade. It's very hot and stuffy here and I'm not so young after all." And he left the pile in the middle of the opening and walked towards the shadows of the ferns. "If you are not tired, you can collect some flowers as girls like to do." He joked.

She looked around and thought to herself. "There are no flowers around here." She decided to join her companion but, suddenly seeing something white lying on the ground close to the edge of the trees, she changed her mind. Jumping from rock to rock, Lana reached this place and, to her surprise, it turned out to be the skeleton of a bear. 'What could have killed such a big animal?' She thought, walking around the skeleton. Suddenly she heard a terrible scream and looked in that direction. The picture that she saw scared her. Something unexplainable was completely wrapped around the figure of Don. His body was shaking and his eyes had an expression of suffering and fear in them. Suddenly the flesh, in the places which were not covered with his clothes, opened as if it had been cut by a knife and blood spurted out from his wounds. Lana actually saw how the drops of blood moved towards the far end of the cloud to form a fine design. The flesh of the poor man dried out and became tight around his bones until there was not even a drop of liquid left in his body, making him look like a mummy.

Lana's brain refused to accept what she was seeing as a reality. 'You're sleeping and having a nightmare.' A voice screamed inside her. 'Wake up, Lana, wake up!' She pinched her arm to test that everything that she had witnessed had really happened but, unfortunately, it was not a dream. The cloud gathered itself to digest the blood of its victim and, as this process continued, it changed from colorless to dark scarlet. Lana realized that, if it sensed her presence, she would be its next victim. Her common sense urged her to run away. But to where? Inside the forest, or towards the river? Lana now understood why she had found the skeleton of a bear lying there. The animal had wanted to escape too, but had been caught and this is what clearly would happen to her if she lingered in this place. She would die to satisfy the appetite of this terrifying life-form.

Suddenly, something grabbed her from behind, firmly covering her mouth and eyes, and she instantly fought back in an effort to rip this something from her face. Blind, she was only able to rely on her sense of touch and, to her relief, this something felt like a human hand. She tried to pull it away from her eyes with both of her hands to see who was holding her but was only pulled closer to the attacker. Crushed and powerless against him, she could feel that his body was tense and vibrating. She didn't know for how long this went on but was on the verge of fainting when the muscles of his body relaxed and the stranger eased his hold. Lana angrily ripped the hands off her and looked towards where she expected the cloud to be preparing itself for the next attack. She saw only a pile of gray dust lying on top of the rocks.

Turning round to deal with the other danger, she met the calm and curious look from the dark brown, almost black eyes of a stranger. "You scared me to death!" She cried out angrily. "I hope you are proud of yourself!"

The stranger said nothing and continued to study Lana with interest. Angrily she straightened her clothes and looked at the stranger for herself. His hair was as dark as his eyes, the face definitely needed shaving and his hands were not very clean. It appeared that he had spent a long time in the forest but he did not look like a forest Ranger.

Lana's curious eyes rested on his clothes, noticing that the shirt had lost its whiteness and did not look new but was made from good quality fabric. He was dressed more like a knight from past centuries than a modern man, with the sleeves, the collar and the front of his shirt being decorated with skillful embroidery. His pants and jacket had lost their color and were ripped in some places but had been properly repaired. She thought to herself. 'He has definitely seen better days, judging by the quality of the expensive fabric of his clothing, but now, for some reason, life has stopped favoring him and he must take good care of what remains. This man has somehow managed to destroy this horror and to save my life.'

"I am sorry that I was so terrified by what happened that I completely forgot to thank you for saving me." She looked into the eyes of the stranger, waiting for his response but not a single muscle moved on his face and she thought. 'What is wrong with him? Did he not understand me?'

"I am Lana. What is your name?" He did not answer but only continued to look at her with interest.

"Validar." He finally answered.

Lana heaved a sigh of relief, glad that she had managed to move the conversation forward at last. "What are we going to do now?" She asked.

Validar shrugged his shoulders, to show that he did not understand, and walked towards Don's dried-our corpse. He looked at it for some time, thinking, and then started to cover the remains with stones to make a grave. Lana, ignoring the sickness in her stomach, went over to help him finish the work while Validar cut a couple of branches of fir, joined them in the middle and inserted the long end between the gravestones. Then he froze, with a sorrowful look upon his face, and uttered a short prayer. Having finished praying, he looked in the direction of the forest and shouted something. Immediately a large, brown horse, with white spots on his forehead and around his hoofs, appeared from under the branches. Validar jumped into the saddle and reached his hand down inviting her to join him.

Validar, Lana, Lachin at Leehar creek

'Very well. Now I am going to be kidnapped.' She thought, but didn't appear to have any choice but to give her hand to Validar who lifted her up like a feather and placed her in front of him on his cloak which he had rolled up like a cushion for her comfort. He touched the horse with his heels and slowly moved the animal towards the river. As they approached the shore, Validar asked her something in his own language, pointing to the right and then to the left.

'He is probably asking for directions?' She mused, starting to search in her pocket for a map. She unrolled it over the neck of the horse and pointed at the place where she had stopped with her friends to camp. Validar looked at the map, then at the sun, nodded with his head and turned left. 'First, I was a character in a horror movie and now I am acting in a romance story, returning home in the hands of a mysterious knight whose language I don't know. What a day.'

Having good visibility from the back of the tall horse, she saw Stephany and her brothers before they were able to see her. She turned to Validar, showing with words and gestures that the people in the canoes were familiar to her.

Eventually Stephany, also recognizing her, stood up and waved with both hands, shouting "Lana, Lana!"

Mathew immediately turned his canoe towards the shore, his face showing his readiness to fight with the kidnapper. However, Validar stopped the horse and helped Lana to climb down to avoid a confrontation. He rode on some distance then suddenly changed his mind and came back towards her and, lifting something from under the collar of his shirt, he leaned forward and slipped a heavy chain over her head. Turning his horse again, he unexpectedly galloped off and disappeared, leaving Lana standing open-mouthed.

Mathew ran towards her and grabbed her shoulders. "Lana, what happened? Did he harm you?"

"No, Mathew, he just gave me a ride." She replied.

Stephany and Steven also ran over to her to ask what had happened and to tell her how worried they had been when she had not returned within half an hour. They were on the point of calling the police.

"Oh no, don't tell me that you did that, I am fine." Lana spread her arms and demonstrated that all the parts of her body were in place. "I was lost in the forest and Validar helped me to find my way back, that's all."

"Who is Validar?" asked Mathew, in a suspicious voice.

"Honestly, I don't know. He doesn't speak English."

"He doesn't speak English?" Repeated Stephany, surprised. "So how did you communicate with him?"

"I just showed him a spot on the map and he brought me here." She did not want to tell them the whole story, afraid that they would think that she had lost her mind. If it was not for the feeling of the coldness and the heavy weight of his gift around her neck, she herself would have thought that what had happened to her was just the workings of her imagination.

"What did he give you?" Asked Stephany, who had regained her curiosity.

In reply, Lana put a hand inside her shirt and pulled out a massive cross, hanging on a heavy chain.

"Wow!" exclaimed Stephany.

Lana studied the cross for herself. She could not say if the stones on the cross were worth anything, since she knew nothing about the value of precious stones, but she was amazed by its craftsmanship and color. The ends of the cross were pointed like arrow heads with a big, bright red, round stone placed right in the middle of it. Small pearls outlined the edges of the cross with some clear crystals sparkling in the spaces between the green and blue stones.

"You could easily pass it off as something made of real gold with gemstones if it was not for its weight and size." Remarked Stephany.

"So what? I'm going to keep it, even if this is a cheap imitation."

If Lana had known exactly into what kind of trouble this cross would eventually involve her then she probably would have changed her mind but, for now, life was perfect and the sun still shone…

Two canoes returned safely to the campground where the campers were having a late lunch. Packing everything didn't take too much time and very soon they were on their way back to the lake. Going along the shore of Lake Haidy, they quickly reached the place where they had left their truck and found that it had been surrounded by the vehicles of other people who came here on Sundays for the same reason – to have fun. The whole side of the lake was occupied by patches of colorful towels. People, clothed in shorts and bathing suits, were eating, reading and watching their children running around. The air was filled with the sounds of laughter, the yelling of children and the overpowering smell of hot dogs cooking on a barbeque.

'It looks like a normal, peaceful picture of a Sunday afternoon at the beach. She thought, touching the cross to check that it was still there.

Mathew loaded the canoes onto the truck, leaving the lighter pieces for the youngsters to load and, after they had finished packing, he checked that nothing had been left behind.

It was not quite dark when Lana arrived home from the trip. She patted Tod's head as they walked on the pathway leading up to the front porch of the house and opened the door, expecting her parents to be waiting for her to hear the stories of her adventures. However, it was very quiet in the house and, for some strange reason, nobody came to greet her. She found only Tacker, sleeping on the couch with his body stretched out to its full length. Lana had missed him very much, so she lifted him up with difficulty and cried out. "Tac, you're so heavy, you old fat cat. Did you come to visit us?" At this, Tac finally woke up and expressed his happiness at seeing Lana again by purring loudly and licking her ear with his rough tongue.

"Oh Tac, don't do that!" Laughed Lana. "I had a shower in the morning." The sound of a closing door prompted her to turn her head in that direction to see the figure of her dad walking from the bedroom with a tray full of empty plates and a cup.

"Ah!" Lana looked at him with humor. "You're spoiling yourself with dinner in bed, celebrating that I'm not at home and leaving Tac to guard your privacy. I have to tell you that your bodyguard was found asleep on duty!"

"Please, talk quietly, Lana." Said Nicholas, looking upstairs. "Mom has just fallen asleep. After you left, she suddenly felt unwell and I took her to the hospital where she spent almost the whole day."

"Is she sick?" Exclaimed Lana with fright in her voice, putting Tac down onto the floor.

"Well, sick is not the correct word for it but the doctor was concerned and suggested that your mother needs to have some tests done. Tomorrow she will go to see our family doctor to clarify the situation." He wanted to say something more but Lana rushed upstairs to look at Natalie through the half-open door. She discovered that her mother was not sleeping but was looking through the window with a light, gentle smile on her face that reminded Lana of the expression that she had often seen on her mother's face many years ago when she was very small.

"Mom." Lana entered the bedroom, followed by Tac. "Dad said that you're sick and he took you to the hospital." Then she sunk down on the edge of Natalie's bed.

"Lie down with me." Natalie invited her.

Tac decided not to wait for his Mistress to call him to join them and jumped onto the bed without an invitation.

"You have a visitor." Lana smiled, allowing the cat to lie between them.

Natalie rubbed Tac's head, saying, "My body isn't working correctly and I need to be under the doctor's care for some time to come. I'm a little too old for this, I'm afraid." Then she stopped, thinking about how to explain her condition to Lana in a better way.

"You are too old for what?" Asked Lana.

"Well, I know it's late in my life, but I'm going to have a baby."

"A baby, Mom!?"

"It happens."

"Is it safe?" Cried Lana, worrying about her mother, but already accepting the fact that their family would soon have a new member.

"If I listen to my doctor, and do everything that he recommends, then it will be difficult, but possible, and you will have a brother or a sister like you wanted many years ago." Natalie replied.

Lana put her head on her mother's shoulder, swept away by a stream of images from her early childhood when having a brother or a sister had been her most precious wish.

Nicholas found them both lying on the bed with happy smiles. "You woke mom up after all and I'm upset." He said, pretending to be angry.

"I told her the news." Replied Natalie.

"So now you know why I'm kicking you out of the bedroom. Mother needs her rest." And, at this, he gave Natalie a long look, to show his wife that he meant it, then gently moved Lana from the bedroom and went out himself.

"Are you leaving, Tac?" Asked Nicholas, but in reply Tac only rolled on his back, showing his striped stomach.

"Allow him to stay."

"I need to talk to you, dad." Lana remarked, as she started to walk downstairs.

"O.K., let's go into the living room." He replied.

When they were sitting comfortably on the couch, Lana said. "I am thinking of starting to work evenings in the cafe where Stephany is working. I want to deliver my resume to its owner tomorrow. What do you think about this dad?"

"Lana, your schedule is very busy without this. I do not want to have another patient on my hands."

"Dad, I am strong enough to work and now I'll have my evenings free since I have broken up with Jeff." Lana reminded him. "I need to fill them with something."

"I don't mind it as long as you do not exhaust yourself." Nicholas felt guilty for forgetting about Lana's problem.

"A couple of days ago I wanted to work just to buy myself a big, black motorbike, but right now I think I will work to help you and mom pay the bills so that mother can take time off and rest more."

Nicholas gathered Lana closer and kissed her head. "You have a good heart but you don't need to work and, by the way, I have an old motor bike in the garage which you can use instead of buying a new one. I will ask our neighbor, Stephany's dad, for his help to fix it. There are probably some parts that will need replacing but, eventually, we will be able to bring back an old Harley Davidson. Now I need to go upstairs to remove the cat from the bedroom. It appears that he's not planning to leave today. I wonder why?"

"He feels that mother isn't feeling well and is probably trying to heal her."

"He definitely does not have a license for it." Remarked Nicholas, jokingly.

"A cat doesn't need training in healing. He has an instinct to sense a troubled spot. Grandma once told me that, when she lay down with a headache or arthritis pain, her cat would always lie beside her to be close to the source of the pain and, after some time, the pain wouldn't be so hard to bear."

"This is quite a theory that you have. But anyway, how did your trip go?" He quizzed her.

"Wonderful." Lana's eyes flashed with excitement. "We caught four huge trout. Stephany's mom is going to cook them tomorrow by using some special recipe and give one of the fish to us."

"Stephany looks like a nice girl. Are you thinking of continuing to see her?" Queried Nicholas.

"Yes, dad, she is a farmer's daughter, as I am." Lana replied, leaving the couch. "I think I'll go to my bedroom so, goodnight, dad."

"Goodnight, darling." He had said this to her many times before but today his voice was especially soft.

Lana's viewpoint on life had changed so much that she was no longer afraid to meet Jeff or Maggie. The issue between them had become insignificant compared to her new responsibilities of becoming a big sister and, in addition to this, she needed to find Validar in order to return the cross to him.

One thought that bothered Lana in the morning, as she was getting ready to go to school, was what she should wear to hide the cross because she was afraid to leave it alone for some unknown reason. She found a black tank top and a vest to hide the cross, and decided to put on black pants to keep her clothes in some style. She put on a metal belt and was satisfied with her appearance. Lana made a point of not going to school earlier in the morning to avoid seeing her school mates, or later when most of them would be in class, but at the correct starting time. She walked jauntily on her high heels as if nothing worried her, with a calm expression on her face. Her whole being expressed carelessness and beauty.

Everyone who watching her was intrigued, expecting that Lana would try to sneak into the class like a mouse into a hole but, instead, they saw a Queen proceeding to her throne and carrying a bag over her shoulder.

"Stephany, how are you?" Asked Lana, with an open smile, taking Stephany's elbow and leading her towards the door. "I want to talk to you."

"I think there is someone else who wants to talk to you." Chuckled Stephany, walking away and giving her place to Jeff.

"Hi Lana, you look radiant." Jeff studied her face to understand why she looked so beautiful and fresh. "You have a wonderful color in your face today." He continued, without exaggerating even a word.

"I went camping with my friends on Sunday."

"Maybe you'd like to go camping with me sometime? We could have a lot of fun." He asked, hopefully.

Lana turned to him, anger pushing her to say something malicious but, at the last moment, she stopped herself, thinking. 'Jeff is heartless and selfish and he deserves to be put down but, if I let my anger speak for me and hurt him, then I will only confirm that I am no better than him.' She took a deep breath and said, politely. "Jeff, you definitely need to go and take a hike. You'd be able to put a good color in your face also."

Then she turned and entered the school door, leaving their school mates laughing at the clumsy Romeo.

CHAPTER 3:

THE VALLEY OF MONSTERS

Tac returned home on the eve of the Council meeting. Alisa had started to worry about Tac's absence, thinking that something had happened to him on the way home, and was glad to see him at last.

"I expected you to be back home yesterday. What happened, Tac?"

"My older Mistress was not well and I felt the need to stay with her until I could be convinced that her condition was more stable." Surprisingly, he didn't look overly concerned.

"I see you are smiling. Is there something funny about her illness?" Asked Alisa.

"Actually, yes! Her illness has a very happy explanation. She is expecting a baby and I am going to be an uncle." Tac gave her a wink and patted his whiskers. "How do you feel about taking the role of an aunty to a human kitten?"

"Ah." Gasped Alisa, stunned by the thought and trying to think of an answer. "I probably will like the baby just as much as I would like anyone else related to you, but I heard that human babies can be rough with animals. They can grab your ear or pull your tail." She hid her tail under her stomach in mock fear.

"Yes." Agreed Tac. "This is the danger. Sensibility grows slowly in their little minds and you must be patient not to scratch them back when they get hold of your tail."

"How did the rest of the family take the news?" Alisa queried.

"My Master and my younger Mistress, Lana, looked touchingly happy and concerned. Lana is even going to go to work to provide food for the family."

"Maybe we can help somehow?" She responded thoughtfully.

"Right now the best help is not to interfere and to just wait until the baby is born." Tac wisely replied.

Next morning Alisa woke Tac up with the news that the weather would not be good that day. The sun was hiding somewhere amongst the gray clouds which was sending drizzly, boring rain to the ground. The rain slowly soaked the vegetation and roads, making the pathways muddy and slippery.

"I hate to walk in weather like this. By the time I reach Council Hill I will look like a wet scarecrow all covered in mud." Wailed Tac, taking some milk for his breakfast.

"If you walk on the grass, avoiding the muddy pathways, you will be only a very wet cat." Joked Alisa.

Tac only flattened his ears in response, disgusted by this picture. But, to his delight, the weather improved. Close to early afternoon the wind succeeded in rescuing the sun from its trap and, when Tac looked through the door, he saw that the sun was sending weak smiles to the ground trying to dry out the damage.

"Alisa!" He shouted, inside his home that he proudly called Fox Hall. "I will have to leave in half an hour if I am going to make it to the meeting in time without getting wet.

"Wait for me! I will show you the shortest way." Her voice reached him from the kitchen.

When both of them arrived at the meeting place they found that Tac's report about his adventure was up next on the Council's agenda for discussion. Alisa was asked to wait at the bottom of the hill until Tac had finished his story. He and Roxal went up to the round opening on the hilltop and, after they had related the entire tale of horror whilst frequently interrupting and correcting each other, the Council Members remained silent. They needed some time to think over and compare the story they had just heard with the facts that they had already learned from different sources and, only after this, did they start to ask questions about the nature of this mysterious creature.

Roxal remembered nothing, except the fear that he had experienced, so Tac was left to answer the questions as best he could. "I cannot say whether it's an animal or a plant. I have mentioned that it can easily stretch itself to try to encircle you, or just as easily gather itself into a darker and more concentrated mass to resist the heat of my torch. One thing I can definitely confirm is that it was afraid of fire and having the torches in our paws saved our lives. This thing controlled the whole area of the Cursed Forest and avoided crossing the creek, according to the words of the beaver that lives there and knows the matter very well."

"Do you have more questions to discuss?" Rainar asked the cat.

"Yes." Tac replied and repeated to the Council his suggestion to build winter storage sheds.

Mixie the mouse said that there was a lot of common sense in Tac's ideas. But they needed to be thought over very carefully, and that the opinions of the different animals in the wood must be carefully considered, to avoid the making of a mistake that could cost the life of many rodents. The Council therefore agreed that every member would require to step forward with their remarks, after which the Council would make a decision on the matter.

"I know you have another project to introduce to the Council. Do you want to talk about it now?" Continued Rainar, prompting Tac to tell the Council about his desire to finish the work on his map. Upon hearing this, all the Council members looked at Galibur.

"I can help you in your quest if you will find a way to stay on my back during the flight." The eagle offered.

"With politeness, Galibur, may I ask you to carry a pillow on your back so that I can dig my claws into it instead of into your body?" Tac asked. "If I can have some form of support to hold onto, then I can stay on your back firmly."

"Yes, of course, but you will need to find some way to attach it to my body without its preventing my wings from flapping."

"I will ask Alisa to sew straps on the sides of the pillow and then we will cross them over your chest. I hope that both the pillow and I will not be too heavy for you?" Queried Tac.

"Not at all, I can easily carry a male goat in my claws so I will probably not even notice your weight. I will wait for you tomorrow afternoon by the fir tree that grows above your home to try out your invention. Thanks for your time, Lord Tacker." Galibur ended their discussion by stating. "Now, please leave us to so that we can discuss the next matter on our Agenda."

Tac went down the hill and said to Alisa that he was now free to go home.

"Are you satisfied with your conversation with the Council?" She asked.

"Yes, fully." Tac answered. On the way home he advised Alisa what kind of needlework he would require from her and she agreed to provide this much-needed assistance. The couple arrived home late in the afternoon, ate some leftovers from the previous day's dinner and both went to bed early, feeling very tired.

"It's easier for me to start making the seat for you first thing in the morning rather than doing it now when I am half asleep. Personally, I can no longer concentrate on any work." She yawned.

Tac had already wrapped himself into a circle and was fast asleep. But, early in the morning, he suddenly jumped from the bed with a question for his wife." What time is it now?"

Alisa looked outside through the open door and said. "It's still dark." She shook the bottle containing the insects in order to arouse them to make more light and started to search the shelves for her box which contained all her sewing materials.

"Here it is." She quickly cut straps from the backpack and stitched them to the corners of the small, blue pillow which had already been stuffed with wool. After examining her creation, Alisa added one more strap to the middle of the pillow to allow Tac to fasten himself to this improvised saddle for his very important flight on the eagle's back.

"Now you have nothing to worry about." Alisa crowed, lying on the bed and returning to her interrupted dream.

The second time they woke up they did the usual, lazy stretching and spending some time in grooming each other without any urgency and then had breakfast. Tac and Alisa had plenty of time to clean the house and left, climbing to the top of the ridge where Tac had planned to meet Galibur. Since the eagle had not yet arrived, Alisa persuaded Tac to go for a run from the old fir tree to a nearby pile of stones and back. After the runners had completed a circle and returned to the trees, they noticed that Galibur was already perched on a branch above them and watching their every move with his beady, and very observant, eagle's eye.

"Good afternoon, Galibur." Tac changed his run to the slow walk of an important person.

Galibur cocked his head and asked with amusement in his voice. "Did I interrupt some family fun?"

"No. Actually, we were exercising only to kill the time."

"Let's try out my work." Alisa lifted and held the pillow out in front of her. At this, Galibur turned his body towards her to allow the fox to close the straps on his chest and stomach. He then made a few powerful flaps with his large wings creating a whirlwind around them. With one push of his strong legs he soared upwards towards the sky and made a couple of wide circles around the top of the slope before returning to the same spot.

"Now you can sit on my back and in less than half an hour we will be above the area of the forest that interests you. Shout if you want me to make another circle."

"I will." The cat climbed into the pillow case and closed its strap which made him seem to be sitting inside a big pouch.

"Good luck." Waved Alisa, as the explorers rushed upwards trying to reach the rising waves of warm air to catch the wind and glide north-west towards the mountain chain named Turan Crest. Galibur tried to keep his back straight and avoid flying in places where the streams of air could lift him up rapidly, worrying that Tac might empty the contents of his stomach onto his feathers.

Actually, Tac had been very close to that experience more than once but he managed to keep control over the sickness and dizziness by swallowing the unpleasant taste in his mouth. The feeling of flying did not impress him and Tac hoped that it would be his first, and last, flight. But he also discovered that looking down at the Earth from high above gave an incredible view of the forest below, which lay in front of his eyes like a spread-out table cloth. At the same time, seeing the land from this perspective lifted up the fur on his back from fear. 'Ahh! There are the ruins of an old bridge slightly farther from the Council Hill. It needs to be fixed.' He thought. 'And another one that was made by a family of beavers can be widened and put into the forest service.'

"A nice field of grass behind the chain of hills can produce a lot of dry grass for winter, the only problem being the harvesting of it." Galibur shouted, turning his head and interrupting Tac's observations. "Can you see that place where the river makes a fork? Then make a note that, after it flows past that point, the river Woblar changes its name to Trout creek. The creek on the left is called the Leehar."

Upon hearing that dreaded name, Tac instantly dug his claws into the wool and pressed himself to the pillow, wishing that he was invisible. 'I hope that these horrible things cannot fly as high as an eagle.' He mused.

At that moment, Galibur turned left to make wide circles above the Cursed Forest which was armed with the sharp tops of fir trees. Tac opened his eyes as wide as he could to store in his memory as many images as he could. The ribbon of stones, where he had battled with the monster, was the third in the fork of creeks running into the Woblar River but now this creek was completely dry.

Galibur's next big circle covered the middle of the forest and Tac discovered that it hid some open space surrounded by low hills and fields of grass which were brightened by many wild flowers. The top of the largest hill showed the outlines of the remains of stone walls which had been buried under the luxurious branches of climbing plants, next to some structures that were scattered into shapeless heaps of stones.

Tac noticed an old stone road, hardly recognizable, that led in the direction of the dry creek and thought. 'What happened to the people who lived in this village?' He searched avidly with his eyes for some clue to their unexplained disappearance. 'Maybe they were killed by the cloud that attacked Roxal and me?' He wondered, as he examined the ruins, the groups of bushes, the forest and anything else that could possibly hide the creature. However, he only saw the lonely landscape of an abandoned place…

"In the northern part you will see nothing but trees. Do you want to go there?" Asked Galibur.

"Yes. Let's check this last area as well. I cannot find this living jelly anywhere."

"Are you talking about that killer cloud?" Asked Galibur. "I saw it many times crawling under the trees. Once I even saw it hunting a bear and this picture was the subject of my nightmares for a long time."

"When did it happen?" Tac queried.

"Approximately two years ago." Galibur circled above the area looking for the cloud himself. The next circle brought them almost to the foot of the biggest mountain in the Turan Crest, the Bogan. The forest, covered by valances of mist, climbed over the mountain in an uneven line until it stopped its progress just a few miles further on, leaving the rocks open to the wind. Galibur was forced by strong gusts of wind to lower his flight path and look even more carefully down below to counter the ever-present danger of being caught by surprise. Their attention was focused on the ground below and this was the reason why both of them did not see the danger that came from above.

From the corner of his eyes, Galibur saw the shape of something large dropping on top of them and suddenly changed the direction of his flight. This almost shook Tac out of his pouch and, as he prepared to ask what happened, he saw the huge flapping wing\ of the strange-looking bird that appeared above his head. The creature missed them by only a matter of feet, falling down almost to the top of the trees but quickly rose up again, frustrated by his unsuccessful attempt to intercept them. Now Tac had a chance to see this creature clearly and noticed that it looked like a giant in comparison with the eagle. It had the torso of a human with hands pressed tightly to the sides of its body to make its flight smoother and a normal human forehead and ears, but the lower part of its head was deformed and covered with dry, grayish skin. When it opened its mouth to produce a screeching sound of anger, Tac saw triangular-shaped teeth. This was indeed a special hybrid.A pair of colossal wings grew out of the back of its shoulders and the lower part of its body was bird like, with a feathery tail and strong legs ending in sharp claws. The man-bird did not need clothes since it was covered by white gray feathers that were soft and fine on the legs and grew bigger on the tail and wings. The chest was probably free from feathers since it was covered by a piece of animal skin tied around its waist. This unnatural creature scared Tac out of his wits.

'What a cursed place this forest is. One inhabitant looks scarier than the other.' He thought.

Galibur did not have time to study his opponent. As soon as he saw the first move of the big wings of the enemy, he dropped down like a stone, shouting to Tac. "Hold on!"

Tac & Galibur Fend off the Monster's Attack

Tac was again thrown out of the pouch, desperately digging his claws into the pillow but the fabric barely held his weight and started to give out so he pushed one of his free paws under the strap for support. His second paw ripped the fabric into shreds after his body was again thrown to the side. Since he was unable to do anything except hang-on to the cushion, the man-bird decided that the cat would be an easier target for his next attack and concentrated on him. The creature made a half circle and, before Galibur understood exactly what its intentions were, the wicked animal swooped down towards the rider and tried to grab him with a greedy hand. At the last second Galibur strongly flapped his right wing and, with this maneuver, saved Tac's life. Instead of ripping the cat from the eagle's back, the man-bird only managed to scratch his shoulder with its sharp claws. Pain first scared and then angered him to the point that he forgot that he was clinging-on in a very vulnerable position and his face turned into the mask of a cat in a rage, sending out menacing looks. Showing his small, but sharp, teeth he growled and hissed at the creature.

The monster stopped for a moment, surprised. His hesitation gave Tac enough time to make a fast attack, ripping the skin of the man-bird. It flew away screaming, losing speed and its dominating position in the battle.

Galibur used this opportunity to throw Tac back onto the pillow with a sudden move of his body and, quickly flapping his wings, he flew directly towards the mountain. He was looking for a cave in which he and Tac could hide but, at the same time, not big enough for the man-bird to be able follow them inside. Unfortunately, the rocky wall of the mountain did not show any caves. Suddenly Galibur's eyes noticed a small tree, growing on a ledge on the side of the mountain. Beaten and twisted by the wind, it had somehow managed to survive and produce a tight round ball of branches. Galibur decided to hide Tac inside the branches of this tree and then turn back to give the man-bird a fight to the death. At least one of them would have a chance to survive.

"Tac!" Yelled Galibur. "Jump on the tree and hide!" Tac quickly gathered himself ready to jump but unexpected circumstances scrambled all of their plans. A big section of the mountain suddenly started to vibrate and then disintegrated into a fine gray matter. At the same time, both Tac and Galibur felt that some force was sucking them inside of it. This fine substance did not stop them from breathing, only blinded them for a second. With their vision quickly returning to normal, the cat and the eagle saw themselves sliding through a pulsating tunnel towards a round eye of light in the middle of it. Small dots of light, separate from the source ran in straight lines towards the center.

"What is this?" Whispered Tac, too scared to talk aloud.

"I don't know."

They both moved closer and closer to the source of the light. Suddenly it flashed brightly, blinding them again. When Tac opened his eyes he found himself lying at the top of a slope which ran down at a sharp angle and, by now, it was already night. He rubbed his eyes and looked around, seeing very little in the darkness. Galibur was sitting silently right on the edge of this slope and looking downward. At the sound of Tac's steps he turned his head towards him.

"How is your shoulder? Still bleeding?" He asked.

Tac tried to examine his wound under the weak light of the moon and discovered that the fur around the wound had mysteriously been cleaned and the bleeding had stopped, but the shoulder still bothered him with a constant dull pain. "It does not look like it's infected or bleeding." He murmured. "I must say that it looks like someone has taken care of me."

"I got the same impression when I looked at you an hour ago." said Galibur.

"Why did you not wake me up?" Asked Tac.

"I did not want you to make a noise and spoil my mice hunting. But I kept one for you."

"You want me to eat a dead mouse?" Queried Tac, shocked by this proposal.

"What's wrong? It's fresh. I can even remove the skin for you if you're so picky." Replied Galibur, who then limped to the body of his prey and skinned it.

Tac, collapsed on his back, showing his dislike at seeing a skinned mouse.

"Tac!" Yelled Galibur, losing his patience. "You have lost a lot of blood and need to eat to gain strength, so you must eat the mouse at once!"

In surprise, Tac responded. "You mean that you want me to put this raw, possibly contaminated, animal into my mouth? Did you wash it?" He was hoping to reject Galibur's gift using this reason as an excuse.

"There is no water here, I did not wash it nor did I clean its teeth and maybe it's contaminated like you said. But this meat is all that we have to eat. We are in the middle of nowhere, have barely escaped the claws of an animal that is not supposed to exist in nature, and all that seems to worry you is that this meat is not to your taste. We shall probably be dead before morning because we do not know what happened to our feathery friend. It's possible that he is close by, looking for us."

"You are right. Everything that you have said is a truthful fact and I would be a fool to argue or deny it. It's not the time to be picky, so I will try to eat it."

Then, closing his nose with a paw, the cat swallowed the meat, chewing very little and afterwards he made an effort to ignore the desire of his stomach to eject it, afraid of offending Galibur who had gone to the trouble of finding the food. "Galibur, please go to sleep because you are a bird and your kind likes to sleep at this time. I will take the first watch but, when I start to feel sleepy, I will wake you up for the second shift. Frankly speaking, if someone were to decide to attack us here, there would be very little we could do without fire or weapons to defend ourselves and we would have no place to run." Tac sat on the edge of the slope and looked into the night.

Twilight, created by a full moon, allowed him to see some details of the land lying beneath their feet. The dark outline of the woods, and the sparks of moonlight reflecting from the water, suggested to Tac that there was a possibility that they were still on the ridge of Bogan and had a good chance of reaching Leehar in order to get home safely. He listened to the sounds of the night as long as he could but, when he caught himself uncontrollably slipping into a dream, he woke Galibur up.

The cat instantly fell asleep, being weak after his injury and exhausted from fighting his fear. Time had stopped for him and when Galibur had woken him up it had seemed as if he had closed his eyes for only a few seconds. "What happened?" He asked, without opening his eyes.

"Look around you!" Galibur intoned as he shook him...

The cat made an attempt to lift his heavy head and open one eye, losing his sleepiness instantly at the scene that lay before him. There was a lake and a forest in a valley spread out between the mountains. Instead of being round, like most lakes are, it had a very unusual shape. It looked like an invisible rope had pulled two shores together leaving a narrow line of shallow water between two circles. A big river flowed into the left circle carrying its dark water into the lake. The water in the right lake, which also had a small island in its middle, was clear. The thing that surprised Tac the most was that the color of the foliage in the forest showed an endless variation of autumn shades, from gentle beige to yellow, bright burgundy and rusty brown.

"I cannot understand these colors. I am pretty sure it was summer yesterday." He remarked.

"I have never seen pine trees with needles of this color before." Galibur agreed. "And the color of this tall, butter-yellow grass along the lake does not look real either."

"Where are we?" Asked Tac.

"I think I know where we are." Galibur looked at the sun and added. "According to the position of the sun we must be on the northern side of Bogan Mountain."

"But how did we get here?" Asked the confused cat.

"I assume that we were sucked inside the cave in a mountain by a strong wind and thrown out the other side." Responded Galibur. "And perhaps we should accept this explanation for now. I suggest that you sit in what is left of your pouch and I will fly us to the lake to get a drink and maybe I will catch a fish for breakfast. Then we will think about how to get back to our side of the mountain."

The magic of the word "fish" had its effect. Tac, without thinking about his fear of flying, climbed onto Galibur's back again with his mouth already watering at the prospect of eating his favorite food. A couple of powerful flaps of Galibur's wings ended in a smooth glide which brought them close to the water. After they had satisfied their thirst Tac lay down under a big patch of grass, resembling the long silver mane of a horse, which hid him under its soft strands completely. He had hidden himself because of the close proximity of a wide pathway that connected the lake with the wood. Its width suggested that this spot was visited by someone frequently and it would be safer for him to wait for Galibur's return, hidden away, rather than being caught out in the open ground.

The cat started to fall asleep, but was woken up by the sound of lapping water. Remembering the danger, he did not immediately jump out to run but, instead, he lightly moved the grass aside to take a look. The person who had made the noise was not Galibur but an unknown, short man. He was dragging his canoe onto the pebbles of the shore to hide it under the bushes. The stranger was dressed in a long shirt and had pants tucked into striped socks and his brown, curly hair stood up like a fan around his head. His face, with small dark eyes and a round nose, had an expression of careless happiness and benevolence about it. Tac had seen enough strange things during this day not to start trusting in the apparent harmlessness of anyone easily. So he still lay hidden, ready to run at any minute.

When the short man stepped onto the pathway, another type of feathery monster dropped from the sky and tried to attack him but the man did not show any sign of fear. It seemed to Tac that he was amused by this incident and laughed at the unsuccessful hunter. The new creature was different to the one that had attacked Tac and Galibur in so far as it had a lion's body and head with an eagle's beak. The feathers on its wings had a light beige color with darker stripes on the ends and a triangle of dark feathers ran along its back, starting at the widest part of his shoulders then narrowing down to its tail.

The creature hung above the man, trying to peck him with its beak, but missed its target every time. Teasing it, the man waved his hands under the monster's beak, saying. "You're the most stupid Griffin I have ever seen during the many centuries of my life. You probably hatched out of your egg only yesterday and your mother didn't tell you that I am the Master of this lake. This is fine, but I will have to teach you a lesson you will never forget." He then created a spark whilst chanting. "Missicota Chirpicatta!" Immediately the huge Griffin shrunk to the size of a sparrow. Surprised, it stopped flapping its wings, dropped to the ground, jumped around in panic and screeched out peculiar screams of fear. It pointed with its small wings at its body, chirping fast and pleadingly.

"Have you smartened up?" Asked the man, in a threatening voice, while putting his hands on his waist. The Griffin quickly nodded its head, jumping and chirping even faster.

"Well." Said the man. "In that case I will forgive you but, if I see you here again, you will end your life at this size."

The Griffin held its head with both of its wings, shaking it from side to side, showing how deeply sorry it was. At this, the man snapped his fingers again and the Griffin started to grow back to its normal size, taking up all the space on the pathway. At first it had doubts about its good fortune but, seeing that it had gone back to a normal appearance, it rushed upwards and flew away before the man could change his mind.

The short man, still laughing, walked towards the woods and disappeared behind a thicket of bushes whilst Tac congratulated himself for being smart enough not to have shown himself to this powerful and dangerous man. 'Who knows into what shape he might have turned me if he had not liked the look of me?' He gasped to himself, in great relief.

Half an hour later, Galibur came back to the place where he had left Tac, holding a big fish in each claw. The cat left his place of refuge, grabbed the fish and tore at it with his teeth.

"Do you need salt?" Exclaimed Galibur, watching him with interest.

"Muam, muam." Was Tac's reply, from out of a very full mouth.

"I am glad that I do not need to fry it." Galibur joined him, ripping pieces from his share of the fish with his sharp beak.

When these new friends were done with the fish, they completed their breakfast by drinking a generous amount of water. After satisfying his thirst, Tac told Galibur what had happened on this pathway not so long ago.

"Have you seen a Griffin before?" Asked Tac, noting that Galibur was not really surprised.

"If this beast has a long, naked tail with a tassel at the end of it, then I saw it this morning fishing at the lake. It is the reason why you waited for me almost till noon. I had no choice but to wait for it to satisfy its appetite and fly away before looking for fish myself. I must say that the Griffin is more skilled at flying than that excuse-for-a-bird that hunted us. We will have no chance of surviving if a Griffin decides to chase us." Sighed Galibur, with concern in his voice. "I think the quicker that we leave this strange place the better. I suggest that we wait in the forest until this evening and then fly to the mountain to look for a way home."

"I agree with you. But I am afraid to use the same pathway that the strange man used. Maybe we can go to the left and take another route to reach the group of large trees where we can take refuge in their branches." Suggested Tac.

Hiding in the tall grass, they eventually reached the place of their interest where trees with heart-shaped leaves stood at the top of a hill. The eagle easily reached their top branches and landed on one of them to wait for Tac to join him. Then they moved closer to the tree stem where both of them could sit comfortably without being seen, either from the ground or from the sky, and prepared to wait for the evening.

The cat and the eagle were not the only ones who had decided to choose this grove as a place to rest. A dozen white pigeons came from the far side of the lake and settled themselves on the branches of a tree closest to the water. Its nicely-shaped, beige leaves with brown red veins hid clusters of small orange berries. The pigeons pecked at the berries, jumped from branch to branch and chirped constantly.

"What do you think about catching a couple of them for dinner?" Enquired Galibur, watching the birds with increasing interest.

"If you start to hunt pigeons, they will make a lot of noise and this is not what we need." Tac whispered back to him. "I will crawl to the end of this branch to shake it a little bit and scare the flock without making them screech with fear."

He started to crawl to complete his plan, but the pigeons suddenly dropped to the ground and transformed themselves into twelve young and beautiful girls who were dressed in long, white, linen dresses decorated with silk ornaments and embroidery. Each girl had a silk headband and streaming, colorful ribbons attached to her braided hair.

Leubarta, her Handmaidens & Tac at the Lake

One of the girls, the most beautiful, was dressed in even more expensive clothing. Her dress was made from white silk, with precious stones sparkling on her neck, wristbands and along the embroidery running through the middle of her dress. On her head she wore a Princess's tiara, which had a large, sparkling, white stone embedded in it. Her sandy, blonde hair had only one braid, which differed from that of her friends who had two braids each. The tiara was fastened under the braid with a lock in the shape of a half-moon and accented by a fine veil.

"How did this happen?" Tac looked at the girls from his unstable look-out, afraid to make a move. The girls removed their dresses and went for a swim wearing only long, white undergarments. After swimming for a short period in the warm water, they returned to the shore. Some started to run, chasing each other and laughing happily, while others danced in a circle slowly and rhythmically, frequently changing the position of their hands. They sang a sad song about the misfortunes of love, waiting for their clothes to dry-out in the sun.

Tac's eyes were focused on the girl that wore the tiara, understanding that she was the most important person in the group. Another reason why he concentrated his attention on this girl was because of the expression of sadness on her face. She quietly left her friends and, deep in thought, sat alone on a stone looking at the girls who continued to enjoy the freedom of playing on an empty shore. He made a slight move on the tree to get a better view of the girl's face and revealed his presence with the creaking noise. The girl lifted her eyes and met the frightened gaze of his green eyes.

"Who are you?" She questioned, displeased that somebody had seen her not completely dressed. "How dare you spy on me! I will make you pay for this. Come here!"

Tac did not move, being frozen to the branch. The girl made a motion with her hand and he was lifted by force and transferred to the spot in front of her.

"Let's just see who you are, you shameless thing." She made a circle with her hands. "Ahh!" She smiled when nothing untoward happened. "You are a real animal, despite my suspicions that you were a human being. Sit with me, unknown animal."

"Fair Princess." Tac pleaded. "Do not turn me into something frightening because I did not mean to spy on you. I was simply hiding in this tree and waiting until the evening came so that I could go home without being chased by Griffins. Please do not punish me for this tiny fault."

"If you will help me in my business." The girl replied. "I will not only refrain from punishing you but I will reward you with something that you desire. And this will also apply to your friend, the eagle, who is sitting up there on the tree as well." She added, with a crafty smile.

"My lady. You can see-through living beings and things as if they are made of glass. For what do you need my help?"

"I have knowledge of magic." She replied, with a sad sigh. "And I can understand, and do, many things. But, when it's a matter of feelings, even a great wizard can find himself helpless, so do not be surprised that a girl like me can sometimes find herself without the power to solve a puzzle."

"Tell me what is making you sad and I will try to help you if I can." Responded Tac.

"My name is Leubarta." The girl replied. "I am the daughter of a powerful wizard. I don't remember my mother at all because she died when I was very little. My father was always busy with his books and experiments with different philosophical matters and material substances, like a wizard should, and left me in the care of my nannies. The old palace was a strange place for a little girl to grow up in; but it gave me plenty of freedom to play and learn, not only about life but various things about magic. My small body didn't need much space in which to hide and, very often, I was able to use this to my advantage to watch my father at work on his spells and transformations. On occasion, I even tried to improve his work by adding ingredients of my own design after he had left the laboratory to rest. Many times my efforts ended in disaster, or resulted in the creation of several frightening, or funny, creatures which sometimes managed to escape.

When this happened, my servants dropped their chores and, armed with pots and broomsticks, chased the poor victims of my experiments through the old palace throwing around clouds of dust whilst I followed them, laughing happily. Dad would often end our fun by disintegrating our prey completely. The servants returned to their work and I was obliged to follow my father to the library. I kept my hands placed behind my back, copying him, whilst I listened to a detailed list of all the bad things that I had done, including all the rules that I had broken. I was forgiven after promising that I would never do it again and pretending that I was sorry for my misbehavior. After this scolding, I was allowed to climb onto my father's lap and ask questions about the forces of nature, the qualities of different substances and magic transformations, which were very strange subjects for a girl of my age to discuss.

At that time, my father was willing to share his knowledge and even had a few students of his own. One of them, Ashtam, the most talented of my father's students, disappeared one day which upset my father deeply. We did not see him for almost three years, no matter how hard my father looked for him everywhere. Without warning, Ashtam re-appeared on the doorstep of our castle dressed in a long, black cloak looking pale and exhausted. He had become a stranger from whom one cold, penetrating look was enough to freeze my tongue and send me running away, looking for a place to hide.

He stayed in the palace for probably six months and this visit changed my father completely. Much later, when I was not a naive little girl, but a young woman who understood more about human nature, I realized that Ashtam had introduced my father to the dark side of magic and had succeeded in plunging his mind into the dangerous depths of it. The secret teachings, that were revealed to my father by his past student, poisoned his mind and seduced him with incredible, but evil possibilities but, in return, demanded a heavy price for this knowledge. Serving the forces of cruelty and madness had turned my father's heart into a black crystal, changed his personality and twisted his understanding of fairness.

So, I lost my influence over him completely and was left to watch him slide deeper and deeper into the abyss, leaving me crying out for a miracle. The desire to dominate the minds of the people of my country, and his increasing suspicion of the people who served him, pushed my father to look for an ally in the person of Aligarna, the Queen of Vanymar. Her mind was even more cold, calculating and versatile than the man who was no longer the father that I had known.

One day I was invited into my father's new palace to listen to his long speech about my responsibilities relating to the future and the priority of political interests over personal wishes.

He ended. "After a long discussion with Ashtam, we have decided that your marriage with the son of the Queen of the country of Vanymar would act as an unbreakable seal on the "Agreement of Mutual Support" which both the Queen and I will sign immediately after the marriage ceremony."

"Do you want to make a seal out of me?" I asked him, refusing to believe what I had heard. I was so angry that I made the mistake of saying. "If you need a strong guarantee for this ominous alliance, why do you not marry the Queen yourself? Apparently it is not enough for you to subjugate our poor country by spreading fear and unhappiness, but do you also need to do the same thing to your daughter? I will marry a man who will choose me, not for the profit that he might gain as a result of our union, but a man who will love me for my heart." My answer made him fly into a rage and he needed to walk around me to control his anger. Then he made an attempt to bribe me with descriptions of the luxurious lifestyle that I would have, should I agree to his proposal. However, he didn't get from me the result that he expected so he then tried to scare me with threats of punishments that would befall me if I continued with my stubbornness. One angry word followed another and the result was that we ended up shouting at each other.

The air, activated by our anger, spun around us like a whirlpool. Losing control over his feelings, my father placed a horrible spell upon me and ended his rant with the words. "If you want someone to love you for your heart I will give you what you want." After that, my mind was a blur and then a spinning black void moved closer and closer to envelop me. Finally, I found myself sitting on the floor in a room where everything was incredibly large compared to my size. Even my father now looked down at me from above. I had been turned into a frog during the daytime and only at night would I be able to return to my human from. I had been cursed to remain like this for three years but, if someone would fall in love with me during these three years, my father would lose his power over my future forever. At a later time my father did wish to undo his incantation, but he had put such a strong spell upon me that even his power had been insufficient to remove it.

I was sent into the swamp to wait until the end of my punishment but something unexpected happened. I met a man who married me in my frog's appearance and cared for me. At first I was only grateful to him for giving me a home, food and protection. But, after living in his house for almost a year, I discovered that he was a man of honor and dignity who was loved by everyone, from his servants to the rich and noble people of his country. I never heard him raise his voice to anyone, or demand something unfair from them, but I saw that his people respected him for his fine qualities.

He treated me with kindness, protecting me from the nasty jokes made by the wives of his brothers. After more than one unpleasant incident, he built a winter Garden with a little pond in it for me where no one except he was allowed to enter. He visited me there frequently, to entertain me with stories about events that happened outside my sanctuary and to check that I was supplied with enough food and had everything that I needed. Very soon we became friends. I knew this because my husband started to spend more and more time with me to share his worries and discuss the problems in his daily life and I spent many sleepless nights thinking about the transformation of our relationship. Finally I realized that I had fallen in love with him. He probably detected a change in me because he started to take me with him inside a specially-made little box and gave me a little crown so that his subjects could see that I was a special frog.

Some nights, when I was in my human form, I quietly tiptoed to his bedroom to whisper a deep dream to him and stayed by his side almost until morning. Looking at his relaxed face and gently touching his forehead, hearing him breath peacefully, became my deepest happiness. I dreamt of how amazed and happy he would become when the time of my curse had finally ended and I would be allowed to show my true human face. I felt that we were going to be happy together.

To fulfill this dream I needed to wait just three more days, but my plan was altered by an unexpected turn of events. Instead of waiting patiently, he had burned my frog's skin and by doing this he sent me back to my father's palace and all of my plans and dreams were postponed. Nevertheless, I did not abandon my marriage but escaped from my father's prison to reunite with my husband whom I missed very much. However, one of my trusted servant girls betrayed me and told my father about my whereabouts.

This resulted in my capture and I was promptly returned to the castle. Now I am under constant watch but this won't stop me because my life without him has become an unbearable anguish. At the moment, I can't do anything to free myself until I find out which of my girls betrayed me because I can't allow more of my friends to pay with their lives for helping me if I decide to run away again."

"I understand your concern." Tac frowned. "But I do not know how to recognize a spiteful heart under the lovely appearance of your girls."

He studied their faces while they were busy playing games. Suddenly the youngest of the girls said. "Let's play the game of 'hawks and chickens' now, but I don't want to be a hawk because it is he who separates the hen from her chicks." All of the girls gathered around her to discuss this new game. One thing they all agreed upon, however, was that none of them wanted to be a hawk.

"I will be a hawk." Proposed a tall, attractive girl with long, shiny, black hair falling like a waterfall over her shoulders. The rest of the girls allowed her selection and walked in a circle around her. The little girl who had chosen the game started singing and the others soon joined in. When the song was finished, all of the girls started to run in different directions, trying to confuse the hawk and distract her from catching the little player who had started the song.

The hawk robustly pushed them all aside, determined to get at her "prey" and, grabbing her shoulders, she threw her down onto the ground. Tac was surprised by the expression of cruel enjoyment that came over her pretty face, which revealed her evil nature. The change lasted only for a moment, but it was long enough for him to make up his mind about her.

"She betrayed you!" The cat shouted, following the impulse of his heart. "This is the traitor, since only a person who enjoys someone else's suffering could do such a thing."

"Come to me Rasalada." Leubarta called out curtly. "Did you betray me by telling my plan to my father? You now have a chance to explain yourself."

Rasalada's eyes filled with fear and shifted about restlessly.

"Look at me!" Ordered Leubarta, but Rasalada dropped to the ground instead, shaking and weeping.

"Do you know how many good people you have sent to a terrible death? No! You don't care! Your heart is cold and selfish so now turn into what your true nature is!"

Rasalada's body started to shake violently and suddenly a huge black centipede crawled out from inside her white shirt. All the girls jumped aside in fright and repulsion at the sight.

"Don't be afraid, girls." Leubarta cried out. "She will not hurt anyone ever again. I am still willing to give you the chance to earn forgiveness." She said to the centipede. "If you will learn how to love and care for someone, man or animal, and he will respond to your kindness with feelings similar to yours, then you will become a girl again. So be it!" Said Leubarta.

The Centipede drew herself up to her full length, swinging aggressively above the Princess, and shuttered her large teeth but was still afraid to attack her. It slithered in the direction of the trees and disappeared whilst everyone relaxed with a sigh.

"How can I reward you?" Asked Leubarta of Tac. "Do you want gold or silver, herds of horses and cows, or a castle?"

"No, no." He stopped her, shaking his head. "What would I do with all of this? I do not even have any pockets into which I can put your gifts. All I need is to find a way to get to the other side of this chain of mountains. Can you do it with your magic?"

"Unfortunately, my magic has power only inside the world which lies behind these lakes.""Lakes?" Queried Tac. "I thought that there was only one lake."

"You are not the only one who thinks this way. But the legend says that many years ago a star traveling from a distant world met our planet and, as their paths crossed, it fell down in the middle of these mountains which, together with all the surrounding territories, are now called Crestan. The impact of the explosion evaporated the water from the Middle Lake and created two, almost identical, craters. With the passage of time the river Karnest filled up the lake again. Underground creeks then found their way into the second crater, eventually filling it as well, and thus hid all of the evidence of the tragic event."

"But why is the water in the left and right side of the lake a different color?" Asked Tac. "On the right it's dark and muddy but, on the left, it is clear and slightly salty."

"The river brings down a lot of dirt making the color of the water dark but, at the same time, it is rich with life. On the other side the water is clear and you can see the rocky bed of the lake far away from the shore. However, I hear that monsters live on the bottom and sometimes come up to the surface from its depths." Answered Leubarta.

"Monsters?" Tac whispered in fear. "I wish I was home in my own wood without any monsters, dragons or Griffins to worry about. Now, after hearing your story, my world seems even more precious to me and so far away that I do not know if I will ever find my way back."

"If you came through the Gate of Running Light, I would suggest that you go back to the place where you originally found yourself and try to activate the Portal again. I hear that the gate works in both directions."

"But how can I activate this gate?" Asked Tac, nervously.

"You need to move aside all your memories about the things that you have experienced in this valley and concentrate only on pictures of your homeland, your family and friends. You must prove to the keeper of the gate that you are here only through a mistake or that you have a reason, or business, to be on the other side of it. I believe that if you are able to prove to the Force that you have rights to pass through the gate, then it will open for you, or you will need to stay nearby until someone else opens it and then you may be able to sneak through, beside him." Answered Leubarta.

"What if this 'somebody' discovers me and becomes unhappy about my spying on him?"

"You don't need to rush because the gate will still be open for a long time." She explained, patiently.

"How long will it remain open?" Asked Tac.

"This I don't know." Sighed Leubarta. "I am very sorry that I can't help you, but I wish you success in reaching your home. Unfortunately, I need to return to my father's castle because my time is running out. Every year I come here to swim in the waters of this lake which have very special powers."

"I suspected that there was something wrong with this water. Now I understand why the forest around this lake is dead."

"I assure you that you are wrong. The water is clean and the forest is healthy and alive." She answered him.

"So why does all vegetation have that dry, brown color?" He decided to investigate the matter to the end.

"I once heard from my father that the energy of the star is still present in this place." Leubarta replied, allowing one of her servant girls to slip a white dress over her body. "And it is slowly changing the plants, animals and even people into something different. The color and shape of their bodies also became deceptive and you must be very careful about approaching any of these creatures, even when they look harmless. Once, in the past, a wind brought rain clouds here which became trapped above the mountains and they stayed here long enough to be transformed into dangerous predators. Instead of supporting their own lives, by absorbing water only from the lake, they started to attack any life form which had water inside it, sucking the moisture out of it like a sponge and leaving behind only a petrified corpse. The clouds would have killed everyone in this valley if one man had not found a way to destroy them."

"Does this cloud look like a dark, shapeless mist with growths like hands on the outside of the mass?" Asked Tac, making a quick comparison of Leubarta's story with his own experience in the Cursed Forest.

"Yes, something like that. Did you see it?" She quickly replied.

"Yes, I did, but not in this valley. I saw it in my world. It killed all the inhabitants of a small forest completely. I need to find that man to ask him how he killed the cloud. Do you know his name and where I can find him?"

"I've never seen him myself. I was in the body of a frog when it happened, but I heard the story about him from one of my girls who was attacked by the cloud and was saved by this man."

"Gladana!" Leubarta called out. "Tell us how you met your savior?"

The girl named Gladana stepped forward and replied. "My Lady, during the three years that you were away from us we continued to fly to this lake for swimming so that we could keep our gift, of being able to turn into birds, intact. We arrived at our favorite place on the lake at the usual time before noon, took a swim and then started to play on the shore, waiting for our shirts to dry. I decided to collect the dresses, which the girls had dropped everywhere, to hang them on the branches of a tree so that they would not get wrinkled. As I was hanging up the last dress I heard a terrible scream. I turned in the direction of the sound and saw my companions turning into pigeons and leaving in a panic, forgetting about their clothes.

Two girls, who were sitting on the beach, did not have enough time to escape and they were sucked into a mist which suddenly came up from the lake. Pulsating ribbons of vapor wrapped around their bodies, squeezing and hurting them. I don't want to describe what happened next because the memories of that time are too painful to recall." Pausing and swallowing tears, she continued. "When life was taken from them, the cloud threw their bodies onto the ground like broken toys and turned in my direction. I don't think that I would have been able to escape because the distance between us was too short and I didn't hear the man coming up behind me. To be truthful, I don't think that he would have been able to scare me any more than I already had been at that moment.

Saying nothing, the man just stepped in front of me and blocked me from the cloud. I only saw his back but seeing even so little as that was enough for me to understand that this warrior was fighting for our lives. Suddenly the shape of the cloud started to change by shrinking and rolling inside of itself. Then the edges of it darkened and flashed with fire and, after a few minutes, this monster turned into a pile of dry ashes. The man turned to me and said. 'It is dead and now you have nothing to be afraid of.'

I was so relieved that I turned myself into a bird instantly and escaped without even thanking him" The girl put her head down, ashamed, and avoided looking into the eyes of anybody there.

"So, you do not know his name?" Tac sighed, disappointed.

"It's time to go home." Leubarta addressed her maidens. "Are you ready?" Immediately all the girls lowered themselves to the ground and took-off into the sky as birds.

"Goodbye, Tac." Leubarta stroked his head. "I want to advise you to leave this dangerous place. The creatures that live around the lake avoid the wood and prefer to live and battle each other on the hills and sides of the mountains. There are a lot of them that make their nests in caves and on slopes and have a habit of going to sleep at dawn. Wait inside the wood until the sun sets in the west and then go back to the place from where you entered our world."

Thereupon, Leubarta turned into a bird and shouted from the sky. "Try to activate the gate."

Tac didn't answer, distracted by the sound of the wings of another bird. "Did you hear what she said?" He asked Galibur.

"Every word. I agree with her and think that it would be much better for us to go as far from this place as we can. Perhaps another, not so nice, wizard will want to refresh his power in the water of this special lake too."

"It's time for me to again turn into Tac, the eagle rider." The cat joked, climbing onto Galibur's back. The eagle's two vigorous wings easily lifted them both from the ground and carried them off towards the trees. They both made the mistake of looking down at the water, to watch out for monsters, and missed the trouble approaching them fast from the side of the mountain in the shape of a big flying lizard.

When the dragon prepared to attack, hanging above them and stretching out his long neck in order to catch them, his attention was turned in the direction of a growling, thunderous scream coming from the lake. The figure of another dragon, smaller in body but looking much more aggressive, came from under the ribbon of mist which lay between the sky and the water. Instead of going hunting, he was forced to fight for his own safety and this gave them a chance to escape.

Galibur, skillfully maneuvering between the reptiles which were ripping at each other, waited for any mistake that either beast might make in their battle strategy.

The eagle would have been successful in his escape had Tac not annoyed the smaller of the two fighting adversaries by yelling out from his perch on his back. "Get him, get him, you little coward!" Hearing this cry, the smaller dragon used his sharp teeth to rip a big chunk of flesh from the shoulder of his opponent, wounding him badly, then turned his head and breathed a narrow stream of fire in the direction of the cat.

Galibur promptly folded his wings and dropped into the water like a heavy stone. Suffering belated regrets, Tac saw the orange flames and trailing black smoke touch the surface of the water above his head as he struggled to free himself from the pouch. Finally, he managed to push his body back up to the light on the surface but was horrified to see that the motionless body of Galibur was still slowly sinking down deeper into the water. In consternation, he dived downwards again and grabbed the pillow with his hind-leg claws and then, working fast with his front paws, he carried Galibur upwards.

The first thing that he saw when he came to the surface of the water was the wounded, larger dragon flapping with only one wing and trying to fly away. He had lost the desire to fight and only wanted to escape, moving slowly towards the mountains. His smaller opponent didn't pay any attention to them so Tac turned

Galibur's body around, to keep his head above the water, and dragged him to the shore whilst cursing his own stupidity. Fortunately, Galibur had not swallowed too much water and quickly recovered from his terrifying experience. When at last Tac's paws touched the sandy bottom of the lake shore, he only had enough strength to drag his friend's wet and heavy body out of the water and then they both collapsed into a copse of tall grass, completely exhausted.

Spreading out his wings, Galibur whispered to Tac. "We will leave this place as soon as my feathers are dry."

The cat, as the initiator of the trouble, assumed the duty of guarding them. He watched the smaller dragon make a couple of circles over the area and then finally disappear, probably to return to his nest. When Galibur had regained his strength, after their unwanted bath, they flew away to the forest. Tac was afraid to breathe during the whole of the flight and relaxed only when he found himself sitting on a branch of a tree beside the eagle.

He was not familiar with the type of tree on which they landed. It did not have a rough, hard bark but was dressed in a light, beige, thin skin. It's softly curved, oval leaves were just slightly darker than the skin of the tree but were also lined with bright green veins. Clusters of single, almost white, flowers hung on long, moss-green stems. And their centers reminded him of open eyes which had long eyelashes and bright yellow pupils inside. When Tac tried to touch one it quickly closed, hiding the pupil inside.

"Wow!" Said Tac, in surprise. "Galibur, I want to go down to explore this strange place and to see if I can find something to eat. I noticed that we passed a big creek on the way here and perhaps I can use my fishing skills to bring back some nice fish for us."

"Be careful." Responded Galibur, quite tactfully "Everything that we have learned so far about this place has taught us that you cannot relax here even for a moment, unless you are planning on becoming another animal's dinner."

"It's not dinner time yet." Laughed the cat, carefully climbing down the tree trunk. "But I will take your advice. I do not think that I could relax even if I wanted to." He stopped to look at the strange insects running under his legs, which looked as if they were dressed in bright, red uniforms crested by black epaulettes on the shoulders. They reminded him of soldiers in olden times and he silently mused. 'This place is bewitching.' Stepping carefully over the line of bugs, he walked towards a fir tree which had an unusual orange color and climbed up to the first branch. He then bit one of needles, expecting that it would be crunchy and dry like the dead needles which were lying under the trees in his wood. But, instead, the needles were moist, full of life and had a strong taste of pine.

'This is a really unexpected combination of taste and color.' He thought, as he climbed back down to the ground. His stomach grumbled, reminding him that it would be a good idea to find something to eat. So, deciding that the trees would not go anywhere and he would be able to continue his studies later, he ran in the direction of the creek and found it without a problem, probably led towards the water by instinct.

'Thank goodness! At least the water here is still normal.' He cautiously sipped it and found it to be cool and tasty. After satisfying his thirst, he walked along the creek looking for fish and made many attempts to get one but without success. Continuing to move along the creek, he soon found a group of small fish resting in the afternoon sun. So he tried again, but the fish could see him perfectly in the clear water and they swam away before he had managed to catch any. By the time that Tac had decided to give up, he had three small fish in his possession to feed two very hungry mouths-- his own and that of Galibur.

'There is nothing to share.' He thought to himself, looking at the fish. Then, heaving a sigh, he took his small catch to Galibur and pretended that he was not hungry.

"Did you get some for yourself?" Asked Galibur.

"Of course I did." Replied Tac, patting his stomach. "But I found it much easier to carry them in here."

'Do not even think of making that crying noise.' He silently addressed his empty stomach and, to make his suffering less painful, he lay on the grass with his eyes closed until Galibur had finished eating his lunch. 'I am just luggage on the back of the eagle.' He thought to himself. 'The lighter I am the better, but Galibur is an engine and needs to flap his wings for a long time before we reach home, so he must be fed first. When I have reached my house, Alisa will make pancakes and I will eat as many as I can.'

A rustling sound in the bushes made him jump and look intently in that direction, ready to climb a tree at any minute. Galibur, who had started to clean his feathers after the snack, did not wait and silently flew up on a high branch, feeling safer higher above the ground. Suddenly a wall of grass opened up and a huge pancake rolled out of it, obliging Tac to rub his eyes in disbelief. "This cannot be real." He remarked out loud. "This has to be an illusion resulting from my hunger."

"Who is an illusion?" Asked the pancake, rolling to a stop and turning to face Tac. Three small black eyes looked at him scornfully and a wide mouth formed into a petulant arch.

"No, this is too much for one day. I have just escaped the teeth of a dragon and probably have lost my mind or am hallucinating. Otherwise, how can I be talking to a pancake?"

"I am not a pancake, I am THE pancake." Said the strange object, blowing itself wide apart and then returning to its previous size. "Shmata baked me for lunch, put me on a window ledge to cool down and then forgot about me. I waited for him, became bored and decided to run away to become a famous explorer."

"Who is Shmata?" Asked Tac.

"Oh, he is not worth talking about." The pancake showed his contempt for this mysterious Shmata by waving a skinny hand that suddenly appeared out of its body. Tac's eyes widened in surprise but he decided to say nothing, waiting to see what would happen next.

"Shmata thinks that he is a big man but in reality he is only the size of a dwarf. He talks about himself as if he is the Master of this valley and thinks that his important position gives him the right to hurt my feeling by ignoring me."

"Ah!" Said Tac. "So he is that short Wizard whom I saw turning a Griffin into a sparrow?"

"Wizard?" Shouted the pancake, filled with indignation at Tac's statement. "He is only a fraud and probably stole a couple of tricks from someone to pretend that he was a wizard. I think that I am more important and original than he is. Just look at me." He continued, playfully, turning and showing one of his sides to Tac in order to give him a good view. "I am made from the best flour and mixed with cream."

It was a big mistake to remind a hungry cat of cream and Tac's stomach made a convulsive move towards the subject of its desire, so he had to hold it with both his paws. His eyes narrowed into a glowing slit as he calculated the possibility of success should he jump on the pancake immediately. However, deciding that his chances were not great, he continued the conversation simply to allow himself more time to move closer to it.

"I have seen many dangerous creatures running around this place and I think it's too dangerous for such a delicious pancake to travel alone without protection, is it not?" he purred in a sweet voice.

"Do not worry." Replied the pancake. "I have already met a few and managed to run away from them successfully."

"Tell me about this." Tac intoned in a level voice, taking a few steps closer to his target.

"The first creature that I met on the pathway was an old rooster with his hens. He was glad to see me and said to his wives. 'Dinner is served.'

'You cannot start to peck me without my introducing myself first.' I told the rooster.

'Well then, introduce yourself. The girls and I are ready to listen.'

'I am not some ordinary little pancake, but Pancake the Explorer, who is made from the best flour mixed with cream and have raisins in me and I am also buttered on both sides. I ran away from my Master, so do you think that I cannot escape from you? You are just old broth's meat.'

"Then I rolled myself away from the rooster like this." It demonstrated, by making a circle around Tac. "Going farther and farther along the pathway that brought me to the edge of the wood, where I met a rabbit who said to me. 'Pancake, I will eat you.'

'How dare you eat me before listening to my story?' I said to the bunny, making it sit on its tail and lift an ear to listen. Then I repeated the whole story to him that I had told to the rooster, adding at the end. 'If I could run away from my Master, and from the rooster and his hens, do you not think that I could run away from you? You are just a collar for a winter coat.'

"I then rolled away fast into the wood. The last creature that I met, not so far from here, was a hedgehog. He was too busy trying to pin a mushroom onto his back to see me. So I decided to play a joke on him and rolled myself into the shape of a hedgehog and approached him cautiously."

'Who are you?' Asked the hedgehog, sniffing the air with his small bead-shaped nose.

'I am a bald hedgehog.' I said. 'And who are you?' I asked him. 'An unshaved pancake?'

'A pancake?' Exclaimed the hedgehog, happy to recognize the source of the smell, 'Now I know what it was that smelled so good, I really want to eat a piece of tasty pancake.' And with these words he moved closer to me.

'How are you going to get me if even a rabbit cannot keep up with my speed?' I teased him, with an ironic smile. 'But what can you expect from a bunch of needles without a brain, you are just a loser!' I said, rolling farther back and away from him.

"What about you, do you want to eat me too?" The pancake suddenly asked Tac.

"Oh, no." Laughed Tac, waving his paw in denial. "I like your story and I think it's very funny but there is one problem. I am very old and I cannot hear very well. So, will you please come closer to repeat to me all of your wonderful stories into my left ear, which hears better than the other?"

The stupid dough was so happy to find a sympathetic listener that it rolled right into the trap. Bending over Tac, who was still lying on the ground, it repeated the stories, and stopped for a minute to think of what kind of an end it could make to this meeting with a cat, when Tac jumped on top of it and bit a big piece out of its side. Sparks of blue light flew from the injured pancake which fell flat on the ground and then turned into a regular pancake, with three raisins buried inside of it in the shape of a half circle which replaced the former three eyes.

Tac, swallowing a piece of the pancake, thought to himself. 'Maybe a rooster is old broth meat and a rabbit is nothing but a collar for a winter coat and, probably, a hedgehog is only needles without a brain, but you my friend have too big an opinion of your own intelligence. So I had no choice but to surprise you greatly.' And breaking his train of thought, he called out to his friend. "Galibur, where are you? Come and eat while it's still warm."

When the pancake had been eaten completely Tac licked his paws and said. "Now I am full."

"So you lied to me about having your share of fish?" Galibur queried, after they had both returned to the branch to enjoy the feeling of fullness in their stomachs.

"When you are in a difficult situation you start to think about priorities and responsibilities." The cat replied, lazily.

"And what does that mean?" Galibur looked at his companion with interest.

"By a priority I mean that I must try to keep you in good shape because it is my responsibility to return us home in one piece." Tac looked at Galibur and corrected himself with a laugh. "Sorry, I mean in two pieces of course."

"Ah!" Nodded Galibur, now understanding Tac's motives clearly.

Their peaceful conversation was interrupted by a strange-looking animal that came out of the bushes. It looked like a boar, only dressed in thick, heavy armor. Two teeth, like two menacing lances, protruded from its mouth. Its tail, instead of being rolled into a spiral, hung straight down with hard, bony thorns sticking out of it from both sides.

"What is this?" Started Tac but, receiving a peck from Galibur, went quiet.

The animal stopped for a second, listening, but heard nothing and turned back to sniffing the ground in the place where Tac and Galibur had eaten the pancake. The armed boar, finding nothing tasty on the ground, decided that the smell was coming from some eatable root, or who knows what he decided, but the boar started to dig, throwing earth and grass roots around himself. Very soon his back was entirely covered in dirt, which apparently did not bother him, and worked his way in deeper, like a digger. When the hole was deep enough to bury his front legs almost to his stomach the boar stopped digging, grunted in disappointment and, with one turn of his neck, threw something heavy out of the hole. The object that looked like a black pot hit the ground, broke into pieces and left a pile of small flat discs spread out on the grass. Tac looked down with increasing interest.

"The boar has found a treasure!" He whispered to Galibur.

"It does not look like he is going to leave this place soon." Galibur whispered back. "Look, he is chewing something, so he did find food after all. We need to leave this place quietly and move to the slope of the mountain before it gets too dark for us to find the place where we were thrown out of the tunnel."

"I cannot leave without seeing what he found." Tac moved towards the end of the branch. "Maybe I should have thrown something heavy on his head to scare him."

"Do not be ridiculous. You could throw a whole mountain on top of him but the boar would not even move an ear." Galibur jumped down, landing on the ground some distance from the wild animal, then spread his wings and yelled something at the boar in his own bird language. The boar decided that he was probably the subject of an insulting joke, lost control of his temper and chased the eagle thoughtlessly. After both of them had disappeared behind some nearby bushes, Tac quickly climbed down to reach the pile of discs now spread out in front of him.

"Money!" Tac touched the pile with his paws. Some of the coins were large, some small, some were made from yellow metal but some were silver in color. Tac's mind worked on the dilemma of which one was the most valuable and, therefore, which one should he take? After all, he could not put the whole pile on Galibur's back...

"Tac, get up a tree!" Galibur's voice floated down from above. "He is coming back."

The sound of crashing vegetation confirmed his words. Tac grabbed two yellow coins from the top, shoveled them into his mouth and climbed up the tree at the fastest speed allowed by his paws. Unfortunately, the boar had already seen him climbing the tree and, without stopping, hit it with its head which was protected by a hard helmet of bone. The cat almost fell down on top of the boar, producing screams of terror through his closed mouth. Galibur, seeing that Tac could not withstand a second hit like that, jumped on the back of the boar and pecked his head as if he was a woodpecker. His action did not hurt the boar but it did succeed in diverting his attention. While the boar turned round, trying to knock the rider from his back, the cat managed to climb up the tree to safety where the eagle soon joined him.

"Quickly." Galibur urgently shouted to the cat. "Climb on my back. We are leaving this place before this mad animal attracts the attention of another beast more dangerous than he is."

A scared Tac was very glad to follow his order. He pushed the coins inside his riding pouch and did not open his eyes until they had reached the mountain slope from whence their adventure had started. He examined the wall now in front of him and, realizing that the portal was closed, the cat became filled with the fear that he would not be able to get home. Losing control of his emotions, Tac hit the wall with his paws and screamed out plaintively. "I want to go home!"

"Easy, easy!" Galibur responded, in a calm voice, understanding Tac's feelings. "This is not working, so let us both relax and do what the Princess told us to do. Let us think about our homes, families and all the things that await us there to be completed, to try to open the Portal by this method. Should these actions not work for us, we will just have to fly over the mountains. It's our last chance."

Tac sat on the ground, embarrassed by his irrational impulse, and tried to calm his feelings as he visualized everything that had happened in his life during the last half year. Images floated into his mind, replacing one with another-Tod, Lana, Natalie, Nicholas, Alisa, Home and Natalie's baby. He was sure that he had found the right key to open the gate. 'My family is expecting a baby and I am sure that there cannot be any more important reason for me to be at home than this?'

Almost immediately he felt Galibur's touch on his shoulder. The eagle pointed at the wall which had started to pulsate to allow the Portal to open. The movements in the wall increased accompanied by an intense, rumbling sound and, as the pulsations completed their cycle, they felt the hair and the feathers on their bodies being ruffled by the Force. Both of them did not resist this time, allowing it to embrace their bodies and take them into the depth of the vortex. The second time it was not so terrifying because now they expected to see their green and habitable world again. One thing that they did not expect was that the injured dragon that had chased them on the lake, and fled from the battlefield, had taken refuge on a nearby slope. The shoulder of the dragon had continued to bleed so he had decided to give his body a rest on this ground and, by chance, he observed the disappearance of Tac and Galibur into the mountain.

The dragon felt a strong urge to follow them so he jumped down and glided on one wing to the wall. Anger made him forget about the danger of this action. Naturally, he was sucked into the gate too and moved towards the other exit, completely confused and disorientated. He arrived at the other side of the mountain at the same time as they did and, in his confusion, he had knocked them down from the little platform where they had felt themselves safe.

So, as it happened, Tac and Galibur fell down on the top of a small tree which grew right beneath the slope, while the dragon rushed over them trying to reach the top of the mountain where he expected to arrive at his home. When the creature could not find his nest in the usual place, he became even more scared. The pain of his wounds increased and he started looking for any place where he could rest and take time to think over his dilemma. His eyes caught a glimpse of a vertical crack on the mountain on the opposite side of the narrow valley and, since he was happy to have a place to hide, he squeezed into its tight entrance and found that it led to a spacious, but dark and silent, cave.

The Dragon's Temporary Refuge

The smell which was in the cave appealed to his senses. He quickly found a small pool of raw oil close to the wall, licked up all of it and then he lay down to rest. Living on the hard rocks of the mountain, he did not need any special bed and was used to sleeping on the open ground. Another strange quality that he had inherited from his ancestors was the gift of being able to hibernate for a long time and he decided to use it now. He put his heavy head on the floor of the cave and closed his eyes, enjoying the feeling of relaxation which gradually came over him. Slowing the beat of his heart, he concentrated all of his strength on the healing of his terrible wounds and slowly fell into a deep, long sleep.

Tac and Galibur, after the unpleasant experience of the free-fall, had landed on the sharp branches of a tree. "Now I know the purpose of a tree that grows in this place. It is placed here to catch unlucky travelers from a parallel world." Joked Tac, stretching out his hurt back.

"Why do you think we were knocked down?" Asked the eagle.

"I think it's more correct to ask who knocked us down." Responded the cat.

"I saw the shape of a big body flying above us before I concentrated my attention on your falling figure, thinking about whether I should grab you in my claws or let you grow wings before you had reached the ground." The skin around Galibur's round eyes closed into laughing lines.

"I am glad that I did not need to do it but, at one moment, the idea of growing wings appeared in my mind too." Tac admitted. "Do you think that we should stay here until morning and find out the identity of this mysterious shadow?"

"It's not a bad idea. The surprises I have endured will probably be enough for me for a year, so I prefer to know with whom we are dealing this time." Answered a thoughtful eagle.

"Do you think that it was the dragon that sneaked up behind our back from the valley?" Queried Tac.

Galibur only shrugged his shoulders and proposed that they both take a rest.

He woke Tac up the next morning at the first ray of sunlight. Circling over the area, Tac and Galibur searched for something that could be large enough to be their follower. They looked at the sky, then searched the sides of the mountains and on the ground, but could not find anything except a thick layer of ash spread over the rocks in the place named the Cursed Forest.

"What do you think this means?" The cat asked the eagle who was walking around the pile of ash.

"I feel we both think the same thing and that the dust we are seeing is the remnants of that bloodthirsty cloud. This means that we have two intruders in our world and we still do not know which one of them knocked us off the ledge yesterday." Observed Galibur.

"If this intruder is the man mentioned by Leubarta, then I do not think he can fly." Replied Tac. Finally, he finished. "I am sure about one thing; we cannot relax yet. Your fellow birds need to be recruited to do patrols in this area until we can find the answers to all of our questions. Who or what, is the shadowy intruder and where is the man who killed the cloud?"

CHAPTER 4:

THE ADVERSARY
THAT HE LOVES

It was night.

The flame of the barely-alive fire illuminated only a small circle of space around it and gave out a weak heat but, for the man who was sitting close to it, spending a night like this was not something new. He was partly lying on a blanket, comfortably supporting his back against the saddle. His brown horse walked around him, ate the vegetation of its choice and listened to the voices of the night. He was the best guard that a man could wish for, giving a signal of approaching danger as soon as he heard something.

Trusting his old friend, the man allowed himself to relax, smoking a pipe and half dreaming. He was the same man who had saved Lana from being killed. Validar was in his late twenties. His tall, well-proportioned body was strengthened by everyday exercises with a heavy sword and a crossbow and it had become adjusted to life in a military camp, having the minimum of comfort. After he had completed his training, he was not afraid to stay on guard or fight a group of enemies by himself. In other words, Validar was a self-sufficient, independent Ranger who was highly skilled, perfectly armed and noble. He was the only son of the King of Vanymar, inheriting from his father not only his royal blood but the same oval-shaped face, dark straight hair and dark eyes. From his mother he received her well-shaped nose and mouth.

He had never seen his father but, despite this, he imitated his father's mannerisms and personality traits in a remarkable manner. The way in which Validar bent his head to the side and looked intently into the eyes of another person when he was interested in the subject of their conversation, and the same manner of touching his chin when he was deep in thought, mirrored his father's movements almost to the letter. But the most valuable qualities that he had inherited from his father were his sharp mind and a cool head when danger threatened. From his mother, Validar had inherited a strong will, a gift of being able to make fast decisions and a hot temper. You can ask, rightfully surprised, what is a Prince doing in the forest alone, at night, far away from home? His past life from his birth to this date, and his interactions with his family, which were turbulent to say the least over this period, is a long story.

Approximately twenty-nine years ago his father, who was also named Validar, was killed in a frontier fight with the guards of his neighboring country, Rossana, ruled by King Farlaf. After making an inquiry about the incident, Farlaf swore on his honor that it was accidental. His guards had not recognized the King because he was not wearing any Royal regalia, otherwise they would not have dared to attack a King of a foreign country. In his letter to the widow, Queen Aligarna, he wrote that he was deeply sorry for this tragic mistake and wanted to extend his deepest sympathy to her for the loss of her husband and to the country for losing their leader. For his part, Farlaf promised to punish the guilty soldiers but he understood that this would not restore the life of King Validar. He therefore agreed to pay a heavy sum of money in compensation for the loss, which would help to keep Vanymar's economy stable until King Validar's unborn child would be of age to rule the country.

The frightening word "war" had hung in the air for a few months whilst the widow, devastated by the loss of her husband, took time to make a decision in the matter. Finally, she wrote an answer demanding that Rossana would lose the province where her King and husband had lost his life and also pay the money tribute for sixteen years. This was a heavy penalty, but the case was very serious. So Farlaf, after an unsuccessful attempt to bargain down the amount of the tribute, finally agreed to this demand. Both rulers signed the required documents and prevented the war. However, the relationship between the two countries was never the same again and the Ross's and the Vanadians were separated one from the other by a wall of mutual dislike and mistrust.

Prince Validar grew up surrounded by armed men and in no way did he enjoy the life of a spoilt King's son, being constantly reminded by his mother of his father's short, but glorious, life. He missed his father very much but the sadness of his feelings did not make him an unfair person since he had developed fine, balanced judgment as he grew up. Being unable to forgive his father's death, he never became friendly with the Ross's or trusted them but, at the same time, he never punished the small population of them that still lived in the territory of Vanymar's newly-acquired province. Part of the reason for this was that Validar's grandmother was the daughter of one of Rossana's rich merchants and had married the captain of his father's personal guards. The King had then subsequently married their only daughter, Aligarna, for her beauty and high position at the Royal Court.

Aligarna had all the qualities of a Queen, a taste for political games, intuition in business and the ability to manipulate friends and enemies. She never allowed her feelings to take control over her reasoning and, eventually, the country under her rule became rich, powerful and respected.

Validar admired his mother and, at the same time, pitied her for enduring loneliness on top of her success due to the fact that she never married again. That is why he did not try to replace her on the throne knowing that power, political intrigue, and her concern for her peoples' welfare, had become the only reason for her to live.

He found that being a Queen's son and the General of her army fully satisfied his ambitions and was glad that his mother liked to carry the weight of the crown, because this gave him freedom to pursue the pleasures of his adventures and a private life. This appealed to him more than his becoming just a figure in an atmosphere of boring palace ceremonies.

He liked the company of people who said things that they actually meant, laughed over things that they found funny and girls that did not try to ensnare him into the net of marriage. He also enjoyed simple food in taverns, smoking a pipe which he was not allowed to do in the palace and having an occasional glass of beer with his troops. In other words, he preferred the life of a soldier to that of an aristocrat.

At the same time, in his private life, he did not confine himself to simply learning the difficult art of making the right choices for the sake of his country.

Aligarna, his mother, knew the character of her son very well and, knowing that they both had a strong personality, did not allow sparks of disagreement between them to ever turn into explosions of argument. She always offered to him reasonable explanations for her decisions as a soothing element and thus managed to keep the peace between them. But now something had destroyed that fragile understanding between mother and son and their balanced relationship had become disturbed. It had ended in a verbal fight between them, after which Validar had left his mother's quarters by slamming the door loudly and refusing to obey her order to him to marry a foreign Princess whom he had never seen before.

He had told his mother's advisers that he needed to be alone to think and left the capital of Vanymar, riding in the direction of the Valley of the Star, with the intention of talking to the Oracle, not so much to look for guidance from him but as an opportunity to cool down his anger and to look at the problem from his mother's point of view.

He was surprised by the absence of his old friend but did not worry about him too much, knowing that nothing could harm that little man. He made a camp in their favorite place, near Shmata's house which allowed a good view of the mountains, both sides of the lake and the forest. Validar was sure that, when the wizard would see his campfire, he would come to him.

Half-way through the night the horse lifted its head and, with a low whinny, warned his Master of someone's approach. Validar grabbed his sword, waiting and listening, and relaxed only when he saw the short figure of Shmata appear out of the shadows of the night.

"Validar, how are you? I didn't expect to see you here." Shmata greeted him, sitting down close to the fire.

Validar returned to his previous, comfortable position and replied. "I didn't expect to be here either, but I needed to talk to someone whom I could trust." After this he became silent, taking a puff of his pipe.

"Validar, you can count on me. If you need to remove the burden of your troubled thoughts then I am ready to listen." Shmata studied his face.

Validar blew out a cloud of smoke and said. "I have had difficulty under-standing my mother over the last couple of months. She doesn't think and act like her usual self and this worries me. I can't approach her because she has built walls around herself and will not let me come inside them. Her decisions are unpredictable because they don't reflect her previously-expressed opinions, her usual care for me and concern for our people's welfare."

"Stop, stop!" Shmata raised his hands. "You talk to me in riddles, giving me just speculative conclusions. Tell me about all your problems, from the beginning."

"All right!" Responded Validar, shaking the ashes from his pipe and putting it into a bag on the saddle. He thought for a moment, puckering his eyebrows while searching his memory for a place to start. "I think that you will understand me better if I tell you who my mother was before last week's incident. I need to start from my father's death. Very few men were left from the detachment after the fight at the border and it was these loyal soldiers who brought the body of my father back home. My mother locked herself in her bedroom for six hours, obliging my father's cousin to start the preparations for the funeral ceremony on his own. When mother came out, dressed in a long black dress, in order to give the necessary orders to her servants and the army, her pale face showed traces of tears but she held her head high and no one dared to question her authority.

Being a half Ross herself, she became the Queen of Vanymar and, by sur-rounding herself with the right people, she took the power from my father's cousins without a fight. They just stood around complaining about the issue in the corridors for some time, but did nothing to intervene.

My birth, two months later, strengthened her position by making her the mother of a new King and brought hope for stability in the realm to the common people. Some hotheads blamed her for her sympathy towards Rossana and called the country to war, but they weren't supported by the majority of the army and the people. Most of them understood that, without a strong leader, Vanymar had little chance of winning the war.

Mother told me that she had had a long discussion with my father's advisers and Generals and most of them admitted to the danger of going to war when the spirit of the country had been damaged by the loss of a King. Mother was afraid to take the full responsibility of the decision solely on herself and therefore decided to share it with the Council. But it was the only instance that I can remember in which she allowed persons, other than herself, to place their signature on a treaty with a foreign country. Only to me did she admit that the main reason for her hesitation to go to war was that she was afraid that something adverse could happen to me, resulting from the unpredictability of war. She therefore wanted to ensure that I was given the best possible chance to grow up, strong in mind and body, in a secure country. She had hidden from everyone her desire that I avenge her husband's death at a time that I will choose."

"What a woman!" Shmata exclaimed, unable to keep his excitement in check, but Validar had lifted his eyebrows to silence him.

"My mother remained in Vanymar and disassociated herself from everything that had tied her to Rossana, including her family. I suspect that she never recovered from her loss and placed on herself a heavy burden of care for me and Vanymar.

From a country which was hardly able to feed itself, with a population from whom only the noble or wealthy could become educated, and an army so small and unskilled that gangs of robbers and bandits roamed at will and easily evaded capture, Vanymar became a country with adequate resources, a highly-developed structure, good defenses and strongly-enforced laws. It had no King but a dynamic Queen. All this was achieved with the help of the silver and wheat which formed part of the tribute that the King of Rossana had agreed to pay to us.

Mother increased the army and built forts to protect the territory of Vanymar from intruders and strengthened the country's economy and ensured that no person would now go to sleep hungry. In addition, she opened the first public school to teach everyone who was willing to learn how to read and write and generally improved the life of all residents and their children. In our capital, Gerumin, she planted the first public garden and gave the city our old family library as a gift so that everyone could study the scriptures of Vanymar's famous philosophers and scientists of the present and the past. I remember well her excited face when she held in her hands the first complete map of Vanymar and the surrounding countries.

She and I both understood that it was not yet perfect and needed a lot of work to complete since the country where we lived was big and varied. Geographically, it comprised the dry and windy red canyons in the south, the high mountains to the east, the prairies to the west and the cold sea to the north. It had become a proud country of hard-working people with cities that had beautiful buildings, gardens, roads and bridges.

Gerumin was completely rebuilt, with the chaos of small wooden cottages clustered together being transformed into streets of beautiful townhouses standing in straight lines. The city was protected by a strong stone wall so wide that horsemen could ride on top of it and, day and night, guards stood on the wall protecting the peace of the citizens who were busy going about their daily chores. Another wall, which was not as wide as the first one, but was well built with imposing towers situated at regular intervals along it, one of which contained a large city clock mounted on the inside, protected the palace of the Queen, the central church, the armory, the storehouse, the library and a hospital. It was also more generously decorated with cultured stone and wall paintings than the other rampart."

Validar stopped for a moment, looked at the fire and then continued. "Everything in the country was perfect, stable and working very well when I left Gerumin to travel for the purpose of studying the different Provinces of Vanymar, before the responsibilities of a King would curtail my freedom to do what I wanted. Since I didn't like being followed by my guards, I left them in a little village on the edge of the desert before sneaking into the Valley of the Star through a narrow strip of the Vanadians' territory between Rossana and a chain of red canyons. The old road led me through forests with massive, very old trees then along a wide river and eventually brought me to this place which is so full of unexplainable wonders of nature. Almost every year, since our first meeting six years ago, I have returned here attracted by its mystery and beauty as if some strange force has been dragging me back here, if you understand what I mean?"

"I understand." Shmata's face became lightened by a warm smile. "This place is its own master. It invites some people in to reveal all of its secrets to them but it also pushes away others by making them feel unwelcome and some intruders are never allowed to leave. I always worry when you ride close to the mountains against my advice, or enter some of the deep caves in these mountains, poking your nose into matters and places which should not concern you."

"Had I not poked my nose into your affair, relating to your not-too-friendly conversation with a monster several years ago, it would have ended badly for you." Replied Validar, getting up. Ignoring that his cloak had slid from his shoulders, he took a handful of wood and threw it on the fire, then sat back in the same place.

"Tash is not a monster; he is simply an old Being." Shmata's voice suddenly changed as if something else was on his mind. "What happened to your family cross?"

Validar touched the collar of his shirt and smiled.

"Aah! It must be a romantic story." Replied Shmata, rubbing his hands. "Then tell it to me." A shy expression on Validar's face gave the wizard a reason to tease his friend. "So the mighty Validar has got himself into trouble? I have a feeling that you would not have given it to somebody who meant nothing to you?"

Validar's face regained its serious expression. "This cross has a special meaning to my family. When the body of my father was burned in a purifying fire, the servants who collected his ashes for burial found it and brought it to my mother but she didn't recognize it. The priest washed the cross in holy water and then said that it was the flesh and bones of my father that had been transformed into stones to become a protective amulet for his son. When I had grown big enough to carry it, mother put it round my neck and I have always worn it after that. Once it did save my life when an arrow hit it right in its middle, throwing me back but leaving no scratch on either the cross or myself."

"Who is the present owner of the cross now?" Shmata looked intrigued.

"Her name is Lana and she is a lady whom I met when I hunted the cloud in the parallel world. I have spent a long time chasing this monster and burying the corpses of its victims. My absence could be viewed as neglect of my duties as the General of my mother's army, but I felt that I had no choice but follow it into the vortex. When I had been ejected out of the opposite side of the mountain, I found that my cloud had a twin there. Together they would have easily sucked the life out of all the inhabitants of the nearest mountains and forests had I not intervened. Regrettably, I came too late to save Lana's companion who was already dead and, since I didn't speak her language, I was unable to ask what she was doing in that distant part of the forest. She had other friends with her, otherwise I would have had to take her to her home and involve myself in unnecessary contact with the local inhabitants.

Believe me, leaving her was like cutting a finger from my hand. I have never had the same feeling for anyone else, other than my mother. I was attracted to her not only by her appearance, but by a deeper appeal. These strong feelings came from a strange belief that I already knew her. When I held her close to me on my saddle she felt like somebody who was right for this place. Something like this had happened to me before, but I had forgotten about this for some reason. I felt for her as if she was not a stranger but somebody important to me.

I couldn't stay in her world, nor could I take her into mine since she would suffer from the discomforts of my soldier's life, so I decided to leave her to find her own destiny, protected by my treasured family amulet.

It was only after I had come home to Gerumin that I realized how smart this decision had been." Validar stopped, thinking and rubbing his chin with his hand. "The Queen that I found in the palace did not sound like my mother at all. At first I thought that she was not feeling well and that that was the reason for her strange moods. But, with every new day that I spent at home, my worries grew greater and greater. All of mother's behavior, tastes and beliefs were changed to such an extent that the figure that I saw in front of me seemed to have become a completely different person. Was that not enough reason to be worried?" Validar asked Shmata.

"I believe so." The wizard frowned.

"I even talked to my old nanny who had looked after my father when he was a child. She had authority to interrupt family affairs and on my question, as to whether she had noticed any changes in my mother, Zlada said that she was concerned herself but did not dare to disturb my mother with questions and kept her worries to herself."

"Can you be a little bit more specific about the signs that worried you the most?" Shmata queried, carefully avoiding expressing an opinion.

Validar nodded his head and said. "The first sign was mother's decision to start a war with Rossana."

"What?"

"She wanted to start a war with Rossana." He repeated. "However, if my memory serves me correctly, she never supported the idea of a war with Rossana in the first place, seeing the negative aspects of it clearly. She told me that all the benefits of being a victor would not compensate for the loss of lives unless the fight was for freedom and we would also require to keep extra forces in the conquered territory to control it. In addition to this, the farmers and tradesmen of Rossana will only pretend to work, having no interest in making the invaders rich. Vanymar has enough good land to produce everything that we need. We even have access to the sea to profitably trade our products with other countries and all that we really need is stability and peace.

Another thing that did not make sense to me was her new desires. I knew her as a woman who didn't like to display her expensive jewelry or garments to show others her status. Imagine how surprised I was to come home to find my mother wearing a crown, which I didn't recall seeing on her except on special occasions, and dressed in some ridiculous dress. Only after we were alone did I speak. "Mother, are you trying to blind the sun?"

Her reaction to my joke was as strange as her new style of clothing. She threw a disapproving glance at my attire and talked to me as if she was not my mother, but someone else. "Validar." She replied. "I have neglected my duty to radiate the greatness of a Queen and, as a result, have set a bad example for my son."

"Mother, you did not care about impressing anyone with the fashion of your clothes before this day. You are the recipient of the love and respect of your people because you care more about the interests of your country than your own. What more can a Queen do?"

She walked away to postpone her answer, leaving me to wonder what had happened to her during my absence to have made such a change in her personality. Making a swishing noise with her golden dress, she returned to me to say. "I have a more important matter to discuss with you than fashion. The secret force that is known as Cofiat contacted me, promising supernatural powers if I would accept his offer and would make changes to confirm my consent. This, of course, requires some sacrifices from you as well. My son, nothing will remain the same around us; even the boundaries of the countries of Crestan are not permanent. Our country under my ruling will expand and flourish but others will disappear. Kings who prove to be stubborn and refuse to take the offered place in the new order, such as our neighbor King Farlaf who is usually unwilling to surrender his own views for any cause, will perish. I don't want our country to be destroyed in the firestorm of a future war and I decided to join the strongest side in the coming conflict, meaning the rulers of Narymout and Ulacar. I will send back all the refugees that we are hiding in our brewery to show with this gesture how interested we are in establishing a friendship with Ulacar."

"Do you hear yourself, mother?" In disbelief I grabbed her hands and turned her towards me to see her face. "It was you who taught me to have no fear and never to kneel down before cruel and greedy dictators like the wizard of Ulacar and the King of Narymout. They are both servants of black magic who, in their desire to control and dominate the world, have lost all of their human qualities. Was it not you that told me how the people of Ulacar have been suffering from the dictatorial regime of the wizard who mumbles his spells and forces people to become informers and hypocrites? Was it not you who secretly gave refuge to the hundreds of people from Ulacar? What's wrong with you, mother?"

"Nothing is wrong with me." She pulled her hands away in anger. "Now I can see the results of my foolishness in bringing into the country the germs of this disease called education. It has even affected my son after he has read the dangerous ideas of those so-called philosophers. This country needs to know only one philosophy which is to obey the orders of the Queen. And you, Validar, must remember that I have power over you, as I do over any other officer in my army, and if you forget your duty as an obedient son then I will find a way of reminding you of it."

"I no longer wanted to listen to her, feeling that I might lose my temper and say something that I might later regret, so I exited the room by slamming the door and left the palace. This place did not feel like my home anymore.

A short time later my horse carried me to a little town on the border of Vanymar. The strip of land along the river belonged to a tribe of Gypsies. This place did not have enough good soil to attract farmers since it was mostly woods and grassy hills but it was good enough for Gypsies who didn't build homes or farms. These free-spirited children of nature did not attach themselves to only one place, but preferred to roam from place to place and often visited the villages and cities of Vanymar. Their two-horse carts, covered with denim, looked like big, round barrows on wheels and served as their home. It takes Gypsies only half an hour to make a temporary village by putting their carts in a circle to create a protected camp where women could light a fire and cook meals.

It was a noisy place where children ran under the adults' feet, playing and yelling. Men lazily lounged around the fire smoking pipes and discussing the tribe's business. Teenagers were sitting on the back of the carts playing their guitars and waiting for the young beauties of the tribe to start to dance by waving their colorful skirts and eventually involving everyone in the singing and dancing. Even older women shimmied their shoulders, remembering the times in their past when they had spun in the fiery dances themselves.

The most valuable assets of Gypsies are their horses, the subject of their love and pride. You would be hard pressed to find anybody who could understand the spirit of a horse better than a Gypsy and steal horses more skillfully than them. Whenever a tribe of Gypsies would appear on the outskirts of a city, villagers hurried to hide their horses inside their barns and lock-up their beautiful daughters inside their homes, because Gypsy men would not hesitate to take away whatever appealed to their eyes, without asking permission from anyone.

But, at the same time, they would bring into the people's monotonous daily life the brightness of a holiday and for this they were welcomed and forgiven. Of course, Gypsies did not come to town to look for employment, even though most of them were skilled blacksmiths. Usually they would give a colorful show in a rich part of town in which almost the whole tribe was involved. Men played on guitars and violins, younger women and girls danced while bewitching audiences with the sparkle of the coins on their necklaces and the smiles on their red lips. Their sons and brothers walked between the spectators and stole their wallets when they were too distracted to guard them. Then older men would usually bring their pet bear to entertain the villagers with different tricks. Older women at this time would sell different herbs to anyone in need and give advice to women on how to keep the interest of men on them alone.

I had spent some time learning the life and customs of Gypsies and became quite friendly with some of them, especially with their leader, the Baron

Colader, for whom I was now searching. The need to talk to him was the reason why I spurred on my horse in the direction of Dolan, the closest city to the Gypsy land. I reached the outskirts of the town close to evening and looked for a resident to ask whether he had seen a Gypsy nearby, but the street was empty. Continuing to ride, I looked over fences hoping that I could find someone to assist me in my quest. Eventually I saw an old man leaving his house, carrying a bucket in his hand.

"Good evening," I said to him. "May I have a minute of your time?"

The man came closer and, putting his bucket down on the ground, greeted me. "Good evening, Master, you are probably looking for a tavern or a lodging house?"

"Actually I am looking for a Gypsy." I answered him.

"Shh!" The man raised his finger to his lips. "Do not say this word because my wife is still angry at them."

"What happened?" I asked, putting my elbow on the pommel of my saddle as I bent closer to the man so that he could speak in a whisper.

"Teenage gypsies stole my wife's striped stockings and put them on the legs of our pig and, while we were chasing the yelling animal trying to get the stockings off him, someone opened the door of the storage room and stole my wife's jam. When she discovered that the door had been opened, and her precious cans had disappeared, I could not tell who was yelling louder, the pig or my wife." The old man chuckled into his fist and cautiously looked over his shoulder in the direction of the house.

"And where are the Gypsies now?" I asked the man.

"Thank goodness they left town a good hour ago, otherwise I would have had trouble stopping my wife going out to look for the offenders."

"Thank you." I turned my horse and rode back to the main road. It was not difficult to find the tribe because they had stopped for a rest on a big opening at the side of the road. Five or six strong men stepped forward, asking what I was doing there.

"I want to talk to your elder." I stated, knowing that the tribe was actually a big family where everyone was related to each other on different levels.

The men led me inside the circle of carts where I saw an old man dressed in brown, velvet pants and an orange, silk shirt with embroidery on the front and tied with a belt. The man was smoking a long pipe and patting his expensive leather boots with a lash, the symbol of his leading position in the tribe. I came down from the horse and sat on the wooden log beside him, putting a sword on my knee. The old man asked nothing, but only gave a quick glance at my hands, weapon and face. At this time the younger Gypsies gathered around my horse, expressing their admiration of his perfect pedigree and trying to win his friendship with a bucket of oats. But Lachin only snored contentedly and walked over to me to rub his head against my shoulder. He turned his back on the Gypsy man showing that he would not hesitate to kick if his Master was threatened or shown to be not welcome here. The man understood his intentions and stepped back, admiring the intelligence and loyalty of the horse.

"What is a warrior like you doing in my camp?" Asked the Gypsy.

"I am looking for your Baron Colader." I replied and, to prevent more suspicious questions, I removed my dagger and drew on the log the secret sign that had been entrusted to me by the Baron in case I needed help from his people to find him. The leader of the Gypsies took a burning branch from the fire and, after carefully destroying my drawing, gave an order to his men and, within a moment, a couple of his followers jumped on their horses and prepared to lead me.

Baron Colader's tribe was hidden deep in the woods and, although nobody had stopped us on the way, his guards were probably hidden along the road. Seeing who my companions were, they decided not to show their presence and let us pass since they knew that I could go nowhere except to their camp where I would be expected to explain my reason for being there. Seeing lightweight fences made from tree branches, and a quickly-built forge, I understood that the baron was thinking of staying in this place for some time. The Baron had been informed that someone was coming because he was standing outside, definitely waiting for me. A big smile lit up his dark face when he recognized me.

"Prince Validar!" He shouted, spreading his arms. "Welcome to my camp. Have you come here for a personal visit or do you have some business to discuss?"

I jumped down to the ground and shook hands with him. "I am glad to see you are in good health, Colader. I would like to say that I came here only to see girls dancing and to get a card reading from their old grandmas but, instead, I need to ask you for a favor."

"You are not a man who asks for favors very often. Let's go inside my caravan." The Baron invited me to follow him with a gesture of his hand. When both of us were inside his home, he put a square bottle of whisky and two glasses on the table. Pouring a generous portion into each glass, he said. "Now tell me, Validar, what kind of favor do you need?"

I lifted the glass, took a sip and put it back on the table. "I know you well enough to tell you everything without a long explanation. I need to hide about three hundred refugees from Ulacar, men women and children, amongst your people. They look very similar to your own people except that they dress differently. If you are in agreement, you will only need to change their clothing and tell them not to talk. This way no one will notice the deception. I will pay you for this as much as you ask but I don't have any money with me right now. However, any big city has a money lender and I can get it for you shortly."

The Baron finished his glass in one gulp and put it on the table. "I was told that some people from Ulacar were allowed to cross the border into Vanymar without the usual documents and they were transported and guarded by a regular army, but I thought that it was your mother's business, not yours." He paused and then continued. "These people can't work so we will need to feed them and they will bring danger closer to my family so this favor will be worth some reward. I will give this matter my earnest consideration. You do not need to borrow money from a lender because he will charge you outrageous interest. I know you as a man of your word, who has always paid his debts without having to be reminded, so you don't need to pay me in a hurry. Do it when you find a fair banker. When are you thinking of bringing your people?"

"They are located in our personal brewery on the border of the free territory and it will take probably a week to transfer all of them here." I replied.

"A week is a long time. Too long!" Colader narrowed his eyes, thinking of the things that could go wrong during this time. "This isn't the work for one man and we will do it in the way of the Gypsy." He laughed.

"And what kind of way would that be?" I asked, being concerned about the people who had already tasted enough bitterness and fear.

"We will steal them. In this case no one will blame either the soldiers for failing to watch over them or the workers from the nearest farm for possibly being involved. No one will be harmed and no one will be able to explain what happened."

Baron Colader got up, patted my shoulder and said, smiling, "Validar, I promise you a show you will never forget and I will prove to you that my people are the best in the business of stealing something without a trace." He then called over to his side a group of his followers and discussed something with them in their strange, throaty language. The men listened carefully, nodded their heads and quickly disappeared, waking up the whole camp to assist in the operation. The horses were harnessed into more than half the available carts and almost all of the young men jumped onto their horses to follow the convoy. Older men stayed behind to look after the women and children who remained in the camp and were especially excited by this unexpected change in their lives.

The convoy of carts moved at night-time, making only unavoidable stops to give rest to their horses and hid in the forest during the day. Some men were sent ahead by Colader to check for safe passage through small villages and to warn their leader about other people who might also be traveling on the roads.

We managed to reach Fielden, a small town known as the producer of the best beer in the country. The biggest brewery, and almost all production of beer in this city, belonged entirely to my father and had passed into the possession of my mother after his death. This was the reason she did not need to explain to anyone why she had decided to hire so many foreigners. Knowing that her decision to bring strange-speaking, foreign workers into this small town would create competition for jobs, and there would be tension and aggression, the Queen sent a Corp of the Royal army to keep the peace.

Their tents were set on the territory of the brewery itself and, together with the small homes which they had built for the refugees, they turned a regular brewery into a town on the outskirts of Fielden.

Following the plan of Baron Colader, I changed my officer's clothes for the pants and shirt of a local farmer, hiding a dagger under the old cloak. I rode one of the Gypsy's horses in order to look for a tavern, hoping that I would meet an old man whose job was to deliver empty barrels to the brewery. I was glad to find his cart which was harnessed to a couple of strong horses with short-cut tails. The heavily-built animals were chewing oats from the denim bags attached to their heads, standing slightly aside from the saddle horses that were tied to a pole placed outside the tavern. I added my horse to the group patiently waiting for their Masters and walked up the three steps of the porch leading into the inn. Immediately, the smoke from the pipes pinched my eyes and the smell of the food made my mouth water but eating alone wasn't the only business that interested me…

I looked around, searching for old Urville. He was sitting at a table in the corner observing a line of empty beer mugs with a peaceful, drunk smile. I looked at the line too. The amount of beer that Urville had imbibed was enough for him to be unable to recognize his own mother, let alone an officer that he has last seen a year ago, but I decided to cover myself with the hood of my cloak to avoid being recognized by someone with a better memory. So I sat behind the table next to Urville and ordered beer and roasted lamb, with potatoes that were a specialty of the house. I paid in advance to allow me to leave when I was ready. A carafe of beer appeared on the table instantly, but to get food I needed to wait. I poured the beer into a mug then sipped it slowly, knowing that, after the amount of beer that Urville had drunk, he would want to talk. Finally he lifted his last mug of beer and sat down at my table.

"You are not local? Are you passing through town or have business here?" He asked.

At this time, the owner of the tavern appeared out of the clouds of smoke holding a big plate of food in one hand and a towel in another. He blew the crumbs from the table right onto the floor, put the plate in front of me and then turned to my companion. "Urville, you are in the right condition to go to sleep. Leave the Master to eat his meal in peace."

"Shoo, shoo!" He flapped the towel at the old man as if he was an annoying fly.

"Leave him, I rode alone for a long time and do not mind talking to somebody."

"Well." The fat owner of the tavern shook his head. "You asked for it." And then disappeared in the direction of the kitchen.

"I'm from the western province." I said, looking at my plate. "I came to buy beer from the Queen's brewery to sell it later in my own town. It's a lot of work but it pays-off well in the long run. Local Masters really know how to make good beer."

"That's right." Nodded Urville, joining me in drinking.

"I hear that the tavern has rooms. I am thinking of staying here until morning. The gates of the brewery are probably already closed and the guards won't let me inside." I probed.

With an unctuous expression on his face, Urville moved closer to me and blurted out. "Son, this is your lucky evening because with me you will be able to pass through the gate without a problem. The keeper of the brewery is my old friend and I will help you to get a better purchase price for your beer. The friendship of old Urville is worth something." He ended, proudly patting his chest with a fist.

"No, I won't risk riding to the brewery close to night-time." I tried to look frightened. "The road there goes through an old cemetery and it could be dangerous to be in that place when demons are angry at mortals, unless, of course, you are a wizard and can keep them at a distance with a spell. Are you a wizard, Urville?" I finished my dinner, pouring the last of the beer into my mug.

Urville put his mug on the table with a loud bang. "I have driven though this cemetery for thirty years and haven't seen any demons in there, only good Christians resting in peace."

To which I replied. "So you do not know what kinds of troubles have been brought on the heads of your townspeople by foolish strangers working at the Brewery? The Dev, who is one of the local bad demons, promised to block all the roads around the town until he could find and punish a man who angered him. I heard about this from an old woman who lives on the farm just on the edge of town."

"Nonsense." Urville interrupted me. "She probably just told you her dream. I can prove to you that the old road is safe today, the same as it was yesterday and thirty years before."

"Firstly, I want you to listen to what an old woman has told me before you say that it is nonsense. Last Friday she went into the woods to find some berries for cooking and witnessed how one of the foreign workers, a man with a short black beard, cheated and upset the Devs' little sons. They threatened to complain to their father about their embarrassment. Now the inhabitants of the town must give a very generous present to the chief of demons, otherwise he will order the angry spirits to threaten and disturb the people at night when the dark forces rule unchallenged. So what do you say now?" I asked him sarcastically.

"Rubbish." Said Urville. "I will laugh at this story when we are sitting in the cottage of my old friend, Merloe, the keeper of the brewery, with a good supper in our bellies accompanied by a good mug of fresh beer. Let us go, son. You will help me with the horses. For some reason they become very stubborn when I stay in this tavern for too long."

I helped Urville to secure the barrels, tied my horse's reins to the back of the cart and joined him on the narrow seat at the front. The rested horses ran animatedly along the road, shaking their heads playfully and swinging the cart from side to side. I took the reins from Urville's hands seeing that he was nodding his head and was about to fall sleep. When we came alongside the long stone wall adjoining the cemetery I smiled, knowing that Urville's peaceful dream would not last long. The left side of the cemetery was shaded by tall, silver birches and afforded a perfect opportunity for someone to stealthily approach us unnoticed. I expected that my friends would choose this side for the first part of their show.

Suddenly, a screeching noise awoke Urville and his half -asleep eyes instantly opened wide, reflecting the moonlight. He had reason to become scared. The wooden cross on the head of the grave suddenly bent aside, showing exactly the same cross behind it then both of them started to wave like the sails of a windmill. Suddenly a coffin emerged by itself from a heap of freshly dug soil, its top slowly opened and a skeleton jumped out. Urville pulled his head back into his shoulders, shaking from fear. He grabbed my hand and pointed in the direction of the skeleton, afraid to make a sound. At that moment I felt a great desire to burst out laughing, as I saw the dark shape of a body dressed in a black garment with a skeleton painted on top of it, but Urville's eyes only saw terrifying bones.

The horses were indifferent to this interruption and continued at their now slower pace. Then a shout in a foreign language, followed by a shrill whistle, made my horse pull the cart back and eventually the prancing horse ripped the reins off the cart and turned back towards the voice of his Master and ran off.

The last act of this bizarre show awaited us at the opposite end of the cemetery where it would be necessary for me to disappear from Urville's sight. I couldn't follow him to the brewery since the guards at the gate would recognize me and, to prevent this, it must appear as if I was being dragged away by evil spirits. I prepared to jump from the cart onto the road but stopped, in surprise. A tall figure wrapped in a dark cloak holding a long scythe appeared on the road moving slowly towards the cart. At the same time many other frightening characters, including some with horns and long skinny tails, jumped out at us from all directions. Some of them had pigs' faces with snouts and fierce, protruding teeth. Others had black, human faces with fiery circles around the eyes and noses. All of them were yelling and jumping around chaotically, followed by a group of skeletons dancing some wild dance at the side of the road. The black-robed figure, impersonating Death, raised his hand. At this, all of them became silent and breathless.

"Woooh!" Howled Death, whilst shaking his Scythe violently.

"Aaaahhh!" Squealed Urville, in a terrified, falsetto voice, grabbing the reins with shaking hands and pulling the horses' heads up. At the same time I was being dragged off the cart by the hands of nameless demons choking with laughter. Somebody had already opened one of the empty barrels and, giving me a sword, whispered to me. "This one is new. Jump inside quickly." I did not wait for a second invitation. The top of the barrel was fitted into place but I was able to open it from the inside and leave whenever I wanted. A demon with a pig's face slapped the horses and they bolted in the direction of the cemetery gate, almost removing a back wheel when it hit the corner of the gatepost. The horses did not stop running until they had reached the gates of the brewery, almost knocking down the guards who, however, finally managed to catch hold of the flying reins and stop the mad animals. One of the guards ran into the guardhouse to report the incident to his commander and the rest of them turned to Urville to seek an explanation, giving me a chance to leave my hiding place unseen. Crouching in the shade of a fence, I quickly ran away and successfully reached a group of townhomes where all the refugees lived, not comfortably, but safe.

The street was empty and I jumped over the small fence of the back yard of the leader of the community of Ulacar refugees, whose name was Rafiel, and soon found him having supper with his wife in the company of another family who shared the home with him. Rafiel pointed silently at the door of the bedroom before I even had a chance to say anything. Once we were alone, he shook my hand and greeted me warmly. He had changed from the last time that we had met and, although he had lost a lot of weight and looked tired, I was still able to see the aristocrat in him.

"It's not difficult to recognize an Ulacar diplomat even under the clothes of a Vanadian brewer." I said with a smile.

"And it's not difficult to see a Vanadian Prince under the clothes of a peasant." He replied.

I hardly had time to explain to him why I was here, dressed as a farmer, but I told him briefly about the shift in the Queen's political interests. I needed him to understand the seriousness of this situation. Even after losing his position as a diplomat, he still retained the trust of his people and his help was very important for the success of my mission. I finished my story by advising him of the Baron's plan and about the adventure at the graveyard. I also gave Rafiel suggestions as to what to tell Surren, the captain of the guards, when he came to him demanding explanations.

The sound of fists hitting the door interrupted us. Rafiel opened the door and, after a short conversation with the guards, he followed them, leaving me hidden in his bedroom. He needed to tell Urville's story to Captain Surren in order to induce him to send his soldiers to the road and not interfere in the escape of the refugees. By the time Rafiel had returned with another few men to assist in the carrying out of my orders, I was walking around restlessly in the small room.

"We must move quickly to transfer everyone to the woods where the Baron's people are waiting for us to escort you to safety. My mother may have decided to change her mind to help you, but I am going to keep my word to you on this matter. I ask you to co-operate with your new guardians and do everything that they will ask." I opened the window and looked outside.

At this moment, a head with black curly hair appeared with a question. "Are they ready? The soldiers at the gate are getting ready to leave to check the road. It does not look like they really want to do it." The Gypsy laughed. "And the captain is getting frustrated and angry at their time-wasting tactics, realizing that his men are scared to leave the protection of the wall and face the demons."

I turned to Rafiel. "Tell your family to leave everything behind and follow the Gypsy. Tell them that their lives depend on their secrecy and speed of movement." To my surprise I did not hear anyone complain and the little community left their houses in silence. Within half an hour the first family had reached the forest where the carts were waiting to take them farther into the gypsy land, where no one would expect to find them. We approached the last building where I saw Colader standing outside talking to a man carrying a large bag.

"What is this?" Asked Rafiel. "Something from our home?"

The Baron turned his smiling face to us. "This is a headache for the captain of the guards. How many people lived in this building?" He asked Rafiel.

Rafiel counted quickly. "Ten men on this side and another six next door."

"Did to you tell the captain that the Dev had promised to turn all of your people into rabbits?" He asked Rafiel.

Rafiel lifted his narrow, black eyebrow and chuckled. "Yes, I said everything that Validar told me and added some of my own thoughts."

The Baron smiled. "You will tell us your version of the tale but, right now, we need to finish the work before the officer comes back although we left him some entertainment on the side of the road, otherwise nothing would have kept him there long enough to allow us time to leave. We need to place in each house as many rabbits as there were people in these houses."

We waited until the rabbits had been released into the homes then, silently, like shadows, our group moved along the back yards towards the forest. We needed to cross the street to reach our destination or make a big circle. I stopped my party of men and looked through the bushes to see the figure of a soldier in full uniform standing in the middle of the street. Suddenly, the door of the house closest to him flew open and the massive body of Surren appeared on the doorstep.

"Where have all the workers disappeared to? Can someone tell me?" His little eyes searched for somebody on whom to take out his frustration.

"I sent people to check the other buildings." Mumbled someone behind his back.

At this moment two soldiers appeared from the door of the opposite house, each holding a rabbit in his hands. "There is nobody in this house, just the same as in all the previous houses, just rabbits!" Reported the soldier, showing his animal. The scared bunny started to kick him with his hind legs until it managed to free itself. The soldier, scared to be punished for his clumsiness, started to chase the rabbit until the hand of his captain grabbed his collar and lifted him like a kitten.

"I didn't tell you to chase rabbits, I told you to look for workers. What are we going to do with all these rabbits?" Asked the captain, angrily.

"We can eat them." Mumbled another soldier, looking at his rabbit with a stupid smile.

The captain dropped his victim and moved towards him. "No one under my command is going to eat a man, even if he is from Ulacar and even if he looks like a rabbit. Let them all go!" He screamed in a complete rage. "I want all of them out of my territory. Out!" And he walked to his quarters to have a glass of beer to calm down his nerves and think of what he was going to write in his report to the Queen.

His soldiers did not bother to catch the rabbits, only opened the doors and left, expecting the animals to run away of their own accord.

We reached the forest without seeing anyone in our way and mounted the horses that were waiting for us.

"I am surprised that Captain Surren didn't send his men into the town and into the forest to search for the workers who had mysteriously disappeared." The expression on Rafiel's face revealed puzzlement.

I replied. "Surren will fight someone made of flesh and blood, but not ghosts. He is superstitious and is afraid of bad spirits, demons and the Dev. That's why he is guarding a brewery instead of being an officer in the army. But his superstition turned out to be very useful for us. I can only imagine what kind of report he is going to send to the capital." Then, giving a wink to Colader, who was riding beside me, I asked Rafiel. "By the way, what kind of a story did you tell Surren?"

Rafiel's face showed his usual sad look. "By the time that I had arrived at the Captain's quarters many soldiers were already there, asking for the reason for such a commotion. Surren came out, dragging the shaking Urville, and made him repeat the whole story again. Then everyone looked at me, waiting for my reaction. I said that the Dev is a demon of a low position and I would not pay too much attention to his threat. Surren screamed that he was going to make a judgment for himself and ordered me to tell him everything about my confrontation with the Dev, hiding nothing.

I started from what you told me. That on Friday I went into the forest and met two young sons of the Dev. It was a good thing he did not ask me why I was there. Then I improved your story with a tale from our folklore, as follows:

"The Devs are quite charming creatures with wide noses, hooves, little horns and donkey tails. They had managed to steal a big circle of cheese from someone and decided to have lunch but faced a problem--there were two of them and only one circle of cheese. One of them said that, since he was older, he had more right to the cheese, but the other disagreed, saying that he was the one who had stolen the cheese and it belonged to him. So they continued to argue back and forth. After listening to them for some time, I decided to teach them a lesson about sharing. Therefore, I left the place where I was hiding and approached the demons, saying that by chance I had witnessed their problem and I could solve it for them."

"How can you help us, you bag of bones? Can you multiply the cheese?" Asked the older one."

"No." I said. "But I can divide it and each of you will get your share." The Devs were surprised by this simple solution. Their minds didn't work this way since they only understood full possession of something, but had no idea of the concept of sharing. I took the circle of cheese to cut it in two, deliberately making one piece much bigger than the other. The Devs looked at the pieces and started to argue about who would take the larger piece. I said that I would even-up the pieces and cut off a big chunk from the larger piece and placed it in my bag. They started to scream that the pieces were still not even so I cut them again, and again, and again until there were only two small pieces left, but they were exactly even!

"Here we are." I told the Devs. "They are now completely even." Then I left them, each holding a small piece of cheese and wondering where the rest of it was. I knew that, eventually, they would realize that I had played a joke on them and would be angry so I ran home through the field instead of going along the river as I usually did.

Had I known that their mother was close to this place all along, I would have thought twice about involving myself in such a dangerous business. I was in the middle of the beetroot field when I heard the sound of hooves. Turning towards the sound I saw a big black horse quickly moving in my direction. I had no chance of running away from it on the soft surface of the field so I decided to wait for the stranger to come closer, hiding a knife under the sleeve of my shirt. By the time that the rider was upon me, I realized that a knife would not help me because it was a female Dev riding the demonic-looking beast. She resembled her offspring in appearance with one different detail- she had a long braided beard, decorated with golden beads sparkling on the end of it. Her red eyes looked angrily from under her frowning eyebrows and she waved a large hand clenched into a fist, clearly threatening me.

"You will pay with your life for making fools of my children!" She yelled from the distance.

I saw that an easy way to heaven was open to me, but sought a way to cheat death. The Dev jumped from the horse and looked at my small body with contempt. She spoke. "I will kill you if you do not tell me what you have done with the cheese that you took away from my children. Give it to me!"

I covered the bag with my hand and stepped back a pace. "The cheese is mine. I have it because I was smarter than your dull-witted sons."

"It's not the smartest but the strongest one that gets everything and I am the strongest here!" She picked up a stone and threw it almost to the middle of the field.

"I can throw a stone too." I shrugged, having a plan how to fool her. "Let's see if you can lift this horse and carry it to the end of the field."

This Dev was not much brighter than her children so she put her shoulder under her horse and lifted him but, after a couple of shaky steps, she dropped the horse onto the ground. Whereupon, I said. "You could hardly lift the horse with both your hands, but I will do it without even touching the beast with mine." And with these words I jumped on the back of the black horse and hit his flank hard with my heels, making him run in the direction of the town with threats and curses ringing in my ears. Being close to town I dismounted the horse and let him find his own way back home."

By the time that Rafiel had finished telling the story we were all laughing, amused not only by the story itself but by the skill of the story-teller. Rafiel's soft voice, accompanied by an expression of sad innocence on his face, made everything even funnier. Without noticing it, we quickly reached the place where I needed to say goodbye to my friends and to turn back to the capital before my mother decided that she had given me enough time to think over our last conversation and would start looking for me.

The first person who came to greet me at my home was our old Bailiff, Nican. He promptly followed me to my room and talked about how happy he was that I had come home. He advised me that my mother had been asking about my whereabouts and, if I had not come home, it would have been his duty to go from tavern to tavern to find me. The Queen had been seriously concerned at my lengthy absence because she wanted to give me instructions on how to properly receive the recently-appointed Ambassador from Ulacar, who was due to arrive the following month. Upon hearing this news, I immediately changed my clothes and went to see her.

"My son!" She said in a cold voice, with no feelings of love behind it. I didn't show any surprise, even when she kissed me on the cheek since the affection also felt false to me. "I am glad to tell you that the new Ambassador, Shridor, is coming next month and I want you to be very polite and kind to him. Show him our capital, take him hunting and do whatever is necessary to create some amusement for him. And, by the way, when he arrives he will want to discuss the terms of your marriage with his country's Princess Leubarta. I heard that she is very beautiful, a real pearl in the crown of her father, so you do not need to frown my dear."

Validar stopped and, hearing a strange coughing sound from nearby, he turned round to watch his friend burst into laughter then remarked. "Very funny."

"I am sorry, please continue." Shmata wiped his eyes.

Validar then continued. "There is not much more to tell. Two weeks quickly passed in arranging the preparations for the visit of the Ambassador. I tried not to be under the feet of the maids and my mother who was very excited. From my point of view the most interesting thing that I observed was the Queen's reaction when she read the report about the disappearance of the workers at the brewery. She didn't show any concern, only saying that this was a disappointment and now she would need to look for another present for Lord Shukatan, the ruler of Ulacar."

"She didn't order any further investigation of this matter?" Shmata expressed surprise.

"She did, but with no real interest since she was more involved in choosing the menu for the dinner than in searching for the missing people. Shmata, I think that somebody has been controlling her mind. Is this possible?"

"Theoretically, it is possible but, it is difficult to achieve and I know only a few wizards in this world who can do such a thing. It can be done for only a short time and there is only one entity that is powerful enough to make a permanent transformation. But, hitherto, he has never had any interest in countries located far from his own kingdom, like Vanymar is. However, who knows, maybe the King of Narymout has changed his plans and has recently taken a greater interest in your country?"

"Shmata, I need to find out whether or not my mother is making these decisions of her own free will or somebody is controlling her and trying to destroy our lives through her. I want you to talk to your Master Amer, to seek guidance and advice for me in this matter."

"Amer has not talked to anyone since he separated himself from the world that he created and indulges himself by devoting all of his time to deep thoughts. I am sorry, my friend, but I don't think that I am clever enough to find the right words to adequately express your concerns in order to wake up his interest and encourage him to become involved. Thus, you will need to do it for yourself. But I must warn you that talking to Amer is a very dangerous thing to do. His way of thinking is different from yours and mine and he may not necessarily answer all, or any, of your questions. He may choose to tell you something that you may not even expect him to talk about. After talking to the Thinker, you might never feel as if you are the same person again, nor ever feel free from his attention in the future. I would suggest that instead we look for another way to determine whether or not somebody has put a spell on your mother."

"Shmata, you did your duty as a friend to warn me but I must go to talk to him. I can't stand by and watch her moving farther and farther away from the woman whom I love and call my mother."

"If your decision is as strong as that, then I will say nothing more." Replied Shmata. "It will be better for you to have a good rest because we will leave this place early in the morning."

Validar wrapped himself in the blanket and instantly fell asleep, leaving Shmata, who did not need to sleep, to sit by the fire alone with his thoughts.

Shmata woke up Validar by touching his shoulder. "It is time to get up and we will leave as soon as you are ready."

Validar got up, quickly rolled up his blanket and attached it to the saddle. The cool morning air seeped into his clothing, urging him to move fast in order to keep himself warm. He jumped on his horse and led him to the lake to allow him to drink before the journey. The remains of fading stars still covered the dark blue sky, slowly melting away together with the milky white image of the moon.

He lowered his head almost to the horse's neck to avoid the low branches of trees, resuming a normal position only when the trees were suddenly replaced by tall shrubs. A single voice above made him raise his head to look for its owner, but the bird was still in its nest just asking her neighbors. "Is it time? Is it time?" The only movement that he saw was an owl crossing the space above him, returning home from its night hunt.

Usually Validar liked to watch the sun rise up over the horizon. But, today, his mind was busy and he only splashed a handful of water on his face while waiting for his horse to satisfy his thirst. A piece of bread and water made up his simple breakfast and, shortly after this, he left his horse at the camp and commenced paddling one of Shmata's small canoes to the island that was the residence of the Master Amer. Shmata helped him to paddle, sitting closer to the bow of the canoe.

The Lake Guard Observing Shmata & Validar

When they had managed to get two thirds of the way over to the island, the water around the canoe suddenly came alive. Streams of bubbles came up to the surface from the depths below followed by the large head of a lake creature emerging from the water dangerously close to them. Validar froze in surprise but Shmata stood up to watch the monster. The creature studied them, turning its dragon-like head from side to side, then stretched its neck out in the direction of Validar trying to sniff him.

Shmata stepped forward and hit the lake guard on the nose with his paddle and cried out. "Have you become blind, Lammess, it is me, Shmata, and he is none of your business?" In response, the creature shook its head and immediately dived under the water.

"Oh." Validar started to paddle more quickly to avoid another situation like this. "He could easily have swallowed me if I had been alone!"

The ground of the island which they had finally reached looked like solid rock rising up from the depths of the lake. It was composed of black granite, with a dull silvery-shine in some places, that unexpectedly flashed brightly in cracks along the walls where tiny crystals of different minerals reflected the light off their sides to make a display of colors.

"Don't touch anything." Shmata warned him, taking a pathway that climbed up towards a narrow tunnel between granite walls. Walking along it, they eventually entered a cavern open to the sky with a waterfall flowing out of the crack on the top of the wall and disappearing under the flat stone at its feet. Validar spent only a moment thinking about the phenomenon of water flowing steadily without having any obvious source to it and then focused his attention upon another wonder. It was a small, black pedestal topped with a sphere of fire which constantly pulsated and changed its form. A veil of a milky-white substance, surrounded by sparks of light, slowly rotated around this sphere.

Suddenly Validar dropped down to his knees shaking slightly. Shmata didn't look concerned, patiently waiting for what would happen next. After being in this condition for some time, Validar just as suddenly returned to his normal self, but not before he had taken two desperate gulps of air. Seeing a question in the eyes of his friend, he tried to explain. "It felt like something had grabbed me here." He pointed at his solar plexus. "And pulled out a part of me to somewhere outside my body, stretching my being to the limit. Eventually I found myself in another round space, similar to where we are now, except that I was surrounded by walls of steel air. It felt like something, or somebody, was viewing me with indifferent interest and was trying to determine the level of goodness or badness in me before making its final assessment of my qualities and character."

"Were you scared?" Queried Shmata, with interest.

"No, I did not sense any aggression from this Force and neither was it friendly to me, simply being neutral. In addition to my complete belief that I was safe here, some inner voice also whispered to me that there was no need for me to resist. It's a strange place indeed!" He mused, shrugging his shoulders. "I felt that everything that existed in this space was absolutely complete and perfect and that all life came from here and returned here after completing its cycle. Past, present and future became one reality, like an endless "now", affording me the opportunity to receive answers to any of my questions. I could obtain any information at all that I wanted by simply asking for it".

"Did you ask something?" Asked Shmata.

"Unfortunately, I forgot to do this. Countless stars looked down at me through a solid wall of air. Fascinated, I couldn't take my eyes away from them until it became too late for me to ask anything since, by then, the intelligent Force had finished scanning me and had thrown me back into my body. However, before I found myself back here, I saw more strange images."

"What kind of images?" Shmata was intrigued.

"The first picture was quite unclear but I think I saw running water, or it was dark blonde hair flowing in the running water. I am not sure. The second image was clearer and it depicted a sphere of light which was coming in my direction. When it had stopped, in close proximity to me, I touched it and the sphere exploded, leaving a key in my hand."

"Look in your pocket." Demanded Shmata.

Validar's immediate reaction was to say that he had nothing in his pocket but, resisting this impulse, he decided to check it before commenting. After the Prince had removed his hand from his pocket he showed a red key to Shmata and both of them looked at the strange object in surprise. Shmata said nothing, only making a clicking sound with his tongue.

"What does this mean?" Asked Validar.

"I think it will be best if we leave this place right now." Replied Shmata, nervously and promptly disappeared into the passageway leading them out from the enclosure. After wending their way back to the shore, they swiftly jumped into their canoe. As they started to paddle back to the shore from whence they had come, an unknown force softly moved their canoe with increasing speed and carried them to their destination while they helplessly looked on at the waves rushing past them.

Even after they had pulled their canoe up the bank of the shore, Shmata still looked at the lake nervously but didn't offer Validar any explanation for his strange behavior except. "You can ask me about all of this later." He allowed himself to relax after they had reached the camp where Validar had left his horse. "Let's go home." He prompted the Prince in his usual happy way, taking the reins of his horse. His little cottage was located at the point where the surface of the lakes almost touched each other and joined together. Both sides of the channel between them were clear of vegetation as if the woods had deliberately stepped back to give Shmata a good view of the lake. With humor, he had called the side with the dark water 'midnight' and the opposite side 'midday' for its clear color. Protected from the wind by the chain of high mountains, the water of the lake was motionless and mirrored the images of the white mountain tops and the woods growing on their sides.

Known as a wizard and a prophet, Shmata had lived here for centuries, falling in love with the peace and beauty of this place. The people from outside of his valley were afraid of him because of his close relationship with the Force, seen by Validar on the island, named Amer. They explained his mysterious longevity as witchcraft, which was very close to the truth.

In the beginning, Shmata's cottage had been a temporary home for loggers who visited this forest searching for the rare, orange pine. This species of wood was resistant to decay, to the point that boats made from it served for a long time without sustaining damage from penetrating moisture. Everything that had been made from the scraps of wood remaining after the construction of a ship also possessed the same qualities and was valued highly. When the orange pine was on the edge of extinction Shmata scared away the loggers, furious at their greed, and occupied their home. He had added a small kitchen that had many purposes, being a sitting room and also a dining room when he had guests. He transformed the rest of the house into four large bedrooms which mostly stood empty unless he needed the space to take care of an injured animal, or if Validar came to stay with Shmata for a few weeks. No one knew by which means all of the furniture had been delivered there, but it was comfortable and functional. Wooden shelves, full of books of different shapes and sizes, drew attention to Shmata's interests in various aspects of science, philosophy and mystery.

The door of the cottage had a lock on it but Shmata didn't bother to use it. He had pets as loyal guards of his property to scare away unwelcome visitors with their unusual, and sometimes frightening, appearance.

When Shmata and Validar approached the open space of the front yard with its mowed carpet of grass, of which the owner was especially proud, and walked between flowering bushes, one of Shmata's four-legged friends came out from the garden house to greet them. At this, Validar patted the head of something that looked like a dog. Most of its body was covered by a rough gray skin with only the top of its head and back being covered with reddish fur. Two naked, gray ears stood straight up on its head, followed by a line of sharp needles attached to its neck by strips of gray skin. At that time, these spikes lay flat along its back but were ready at any moment to be raised up to seriously injure an opponent who might challenge the dog. It flattened its ears and waved its body in an ecstasy of happiness at seeing Validar, wagging its naked, gray tail which had a black brush of fur at its end.

"Riston, you still remember me?" Validar scratched the animal's head and entered the cottage.

Shmata put the kettle on the stove, lit the fire with a snap of his fingers and quickly served a plate of bacon and eggs and then poured tea into two cups.

Validar took the key from his pocket and put it on the table, saying nothing.

Shmata looked sideways at it and, after taking a sip of tea, remarked. "A long time ago your father came here, in the same way that you have done. Only he was not moved by a concern for somebody's well-being, as you were, but rather was determined to obtain a sword which was one of the magical objects produced by Amer a long time ago when he had faith in the goodness of people.

I took him to the same place to which I also took you and let him talk to the Master. However, the King didn't receive a sword that could increase the strength of its owner many times. Instead, Amer gave your father a cross. I was about to say to your father something like this… "The Spirit could sense that your motives to possess it were not correct and he decided that you are not ready for such things as a sword of light since, in your present state, it could harm you. Rather than doing you this questionable favor, he has given you a special cross to protect you from your dangerous desires. You must seek the strength inside of yourself first."

However, I never had a chance to open my mouth, terrified by what happened next. Your father threw the cross onto the stone floor, near the black pedestal, and shouted that he didn't need a useless toy but had asked for a weapon to protect his country.

The next moment a transformation happened in front of our eyes. Slowly the cross started to change its shape. All four sides of it lengthened and bent in the same direction, becoming sharp blades. The cross rose from the floor, as if it was alive, and the spinning blades flew in the direction of your father. Only quick reflexes saved him from losing his left arm which, instead, only received a deep cut. I ripped the sleeve of my shirt and applied it to the wound to stop the bleeding and I kept an eye on the mad blades. To my great satisfaction it didn't make any attempt to attack again. By the time that I had managed to dress the wound properly, the cross had returned to its original shape and size. The King was now afraid to even look at it and left the cross lying on the ground so I picked it up and put it in my pocket. After losing a lot of blood, your father needed to hold onto the wall to reach the canoe.

In addition to all our troubles, the weather had changed and a sunny day had turned into a nasty storm. Large waves threatened to overturn our canoe as I paddled to safety. I was glad that your father slept, exhausted by the difficult walk between the rocks, and didn't see the giants circling around us. When the canoe finally landed on shore, I was ready to jump out and kiss the ground.

Dragging the heavy body of your father to my home didn't appear to me to be a difficult task after viewing the frightening faces of the guards so close to me during the return journey to the shore. You can't understand how scared I was seeing that the same events had occurred again and I desperately wanted to leave the island before you could do, or say, anything just as stupid to anger Amer again. Believe me, this time he would not be kind enough to allow you to leave. He had been disappointed by people whom he had trusted and had looked upon as his students. After he had surrendered a part of himself to them, together with great knowledge and power, he had expected that they would protect the world that he had created so lovingly. Disappointed, he probably does not know what to think about us anymore, but the things that he gave you have given me hope that he recognized that we are not all bad."

Shmata's story changed Validar's skeptical attitude towards the gift. He looked at it curiously then moving the key towards Shmata, he remarked. "So Amer decided that my father was not ready for the test of power and needed to strengthen his spirit? For what reason did he give me this?"

"The key is designed to open a door." Replied Shmata, sipping his tea. "There are many doors. Perhaps it's the door to your heart, or to someone else's heart, or it's a door to another world, I do not know yet. It has a specific design to it so the lock must be specific as well. Unless…?" Shmata paused, thinking.

"Unless what?"

"Unless you hold in your hand a magical key that can open any door and this means that Amer has decided to put the heavy burden of being its keeper upon your shoulders, Validar. I have a few magical objects myself!"

"Shmata, do you think that having a magical object is dangerous? If they are unsafe I will need to request that the girl, Lana, to whom I gave my talisman, returns it to me." Validar got up as if he was about to rush off to find her immediately.

"You don't need to worry." Shmata assured him. "The cross will not initiate evil deeds. It's one of the strongest amulets that one can use to counter evil and this makes it worthless for practicing black magic. As a matter of fact the person who engages in this activity will not even touch it. Only one with a pure heart will benefit from wearing it. Your girl is not in any danger." Upon hearing this, Validar relaxed back into his chair and commented. "Unfortunately, I am not good as a protector these days. I can't even save my own mother."

"Validar, I suggest you go home and receive the Ambassador of Ulacar. Please listen to what he has to say and read between the lines to assess anything that he may not reveal, whilst carefully observing your mother's reactions at all times. She still respects your opinions, otherwise she wouldn't have bothered to seek you out to discuss your direct involvements with him. She needs you right now, more than ever, without even knowing it. Should negotiations between Vanymar and Ulacar falter, due to a bad decision on her part, the Queen will require to take the blame and you can't tell everyone that she was controlled by a bad wizard. She might lose the trust of her own people and, to prevent this, you must be close to her and supportive. Apart from this, your enemy may make a mistake and expose his true intentions. I, for my part, will look into my books to seek information about the functions of the magical key which was given to you by Amer and to refresh my memory about the rest of the secret objects which my Master had given to his former students. Some of the objects have already been destroyed, some have been stolen or lost and some continue to be kept in secret. However, at all costs, please do not allow her to start a war.

With the long road back to the palace awaiting him, Validar thanked Shmata for his hospitality and left. His ride carried him along the land that belonged to the three sisters all named "Thoughts." He would usually stop here to have a glass of water and make small talk about the weather, or to help them. One day, at their request, he had put a large sign above their gate that read "Rancher of Thoughts" and, as a result, had become a welcome guest at any time. But today he didn't have time to stop so he patted the neck of his horse, sensing its disappointment. "Unfortunately, Lachin, we must forget about refreshment and rest and continue our journey back to the capital. Show me that you are a real brother of the wind." Immediately, the horse shook his mane and increased his pace.

Reaching the palace, Validar barely had time to remove the harness and saddle from his horse before being assailed by a stream of words coming from the same old Bailiff.

"My lord, I am so glad that you have come home. I have already prepared your clothes for the meeting with the Ambassador and for hunting, and the maids have washed and cleaned everything in your room. In addition, all your weapons have been cleaned too."

"Did the maidens clean my swords?"

"Oh no!" The old man shook his head, missing the sparks of humor in Validar's eyes. "I asked the men from the armory to do it."

"Good." Said Validar, walking to his quarters.

"My lord." Continued Nican, walking briskly to catch up with Validar's steps. "The Ambassador has already arrived and the reception will start in one hour. I have prepared a bath for you."

"Do you think that I am not fresh enough?" Validar stopped for a moment.

"Honestly, the horse smell which is coming from you is too strong." The Bailiff sniffed, covering his nose with a hand which made Validar laugh.

By the time that the reception had begun, Validar was clean, shaved and was wearing his best clothes which were fastened at the waist by a belt embedded with golden ornaments and precious stones. His dagger had been decorated with as many rare stones as the goldsmith was able to put onto it without overpowering its design. Validar had chosen not to wear a crown, but everyone could see his father's ring on his finger and the sections of heavy gold chain on his neck.

The Prince of Vanymar quickly walked to the golden chair, next to that of his mother who was already seated in hers and who looked beautiful from head to toe. The color of her dress was similar to that of Validar's dark blue tunic, with the exception that her dress was made from a shiny silk which had been embroidered from the hem to the waist. The white sleeves of her dress, almost touching the ground, were cut on the front allowing the sleeves of the under-shirt to be exposed. The sleeves of both her garments and the hem of the dress had been finished in blue fur, precious stones and embroidery. The wide border lay around her neck almost to the shoulders and dropped down to the hem. A pearl choker, carrying a large sapphire in the middle, was placed around her neck. One thick, blonde braid flowed over her right shoulder almost to the waist which, together with her sparkling crown set in the shape of an open flower with narrow petals, served only to add to the beauty of her appearance.

Noting that Validar had been late in arriving, Queen Aligarna gave her son a warning look under her long lashes which contained a promise that she intended to talk to him later about his tardiness. She then turned her head in the direction of the open door at the opposite side of the room through which the Ambassador was expected to appear. All of the members of the Queen's Court, who were dressed in colorful clothes matching the importance of this special occasion, took their allotted positions on both sides of the reception area.

When Ambassador Shridor entered the room, Aligarna met him with one of her charming smiles. His officials and servants entered behind him, carrying boxes and packages containing gifts for the presentation to the Queen. He didn't rush to approach the golden chair of the Queen, taking time to look around. His deep-set, dark eyes roved around, memorizing every detail of the palace. He made a note to mention to his own Master, the Lord Shukatan, the fine work of the large tapestry showing an intricate landscape and figures of mystical animals which served as a background to the Queen Aligarna and her son. Nor did he intend to forget a beautiful, round window in the middle of the ceiling made of exquisite, colored glass formed in the shape of a daisy, or the lines of slim columns on both sides of the room which had been decorated with lovely images of flowers and birds. He saw many things that appealed to him, such as the candle-holders wrought with amazing workmanship and the strange uniforms of the palace guards which had hard, golden collars rising up almost to their ears, topped by tall, white fur hats. He was, however, keenly aware that his immediate duty was to deliver a message from his Master to the Queen and to please Aligarna with gifts.

Ambassador Shridor saluted the Queen in accordance with the customs of Ulacar by touching his forehead with his fingers then transferring them to his heart and finally bowing. After this, he told her that he wanted to present her with greetings from his Master and offered a small porcelain box which he then opened to reveal a fine, shimmering, green powder. Taking a pinch of the powder he threw it into the air, whereupon it transformed into a sparkling cloud that quickly expanded into the shape of a sphere. The face of the wizard, Shukatan, slowly appeared inside of it. He was busy studying some substance in his retort but, sensing that someone was calling him, he moved it aside and, raising his eyes to Queen Aligarna, addressed her.

"Your Majesty, I am glad to have the opportunity of finally greeting you in person. Our countries have never been enemies in the past but neither have they been friends. We have had our differences, but there is one thing which we do have in common. We both desire to get more from life than is currently coming our way. If we were to combine our forces, we would not only consolidate our current power but would increase it to a point where other States could not ignore us at any time. Queen Aligarna, Ambassador Shridor has my approval to discuss the details of our proposed economic and political partnership. You may call upon me if you wish to talk to me privately and you can easily accomplish this by the use of my gift." With a gesture he ended his address to Aligarna and his image vanished.

The Ambassador bowed to the Queen again, confirming the words of his Master and, at the same time, indicating his willingness to be at her disposal for discussions. "The message that I have is only for you, your Majesty. Meanwhile, I will be honored to show you the gifts that my Master has selected for you to prove his sincere respect for a Queen and her country." He then ordered his servants to put the boxes and packages on the carpet in front of her.

Aligarna got up, moved by curiosity, and lifted her hand to wait for Validar to take it. The Prince didn't have any interest in looking at the gifts but he took his mother's hand to lead her to the display of treasures, followed by the Court.

"We are pleased with all these wonderful fabrics, carpets and jewelry." Aligarna lifted the porcelain box with the intention of taking it with her. "I will personally thank your Master, Ambassador."

Hearing this, he only bowed silently.

"According to the customs of our country, the guests first have to be fed and allowed to have rest and only after this can we involve them in conversation. Following this custom, I am inviting you to share a special feast with our Court in honor of your Master, Lord Shukatan, and you." The Queen, with Validar by her side, and the Ambassador on the other, proceeded to the door which was opened by the guards into another large room, prepared for dining. After Aligarna, her son and the Ambassador had sat at the head of the table, the rest of the guests took their seats according to their rank and position at the Court. Aligarna took the role of the hostess, introducing the Ambassador to the food that was new to him. In return, Shridor described some of the exotic dishes from Ulacar's kitchen and the customs of his country.

After dinner Validar personally showed Ambassador Shridor his quarters, saying to him. "I think you will find that everything has been prepared for your comfort but, if you need anything at all, please call our Bailiff, Nican."

"I appreciate your concern for me, Lord Validar. I think that your servants know their job very well." Shridor, studying the face of Validar, was thinking deeply. 'He was probably told to be a kind host but he cannot hide his dislike of me. Validar looks like his father and this has drawn the hearts of many to him. He is also a General, respected by most of the army, and that is why he must be our ally, otherwise the Prince will make a dangerous enemy since we know that he is helping the rebels by hiding them somewhere. Of course, he is a mortal and a mortal can die suddenly, but that would be such a waste.' He took a long, speculative look at the tall and strong figure of the Prince who, by then, was already walking away.

Validar passed along the corridor that led to his room but continued to walk in the direction of that part of the palace that was occupied by his mother. He knocked on her door and entered her room. Aligarna was sitting in front of a big table looking at a paper that awaited her decision to sign it.

"I thought that the life of a Queen would be very enjoyable and I didn't expect that I would have to sit for hours looking over piles of letters, orders and reports with which I am required to deal." She did not attempt to hide the fact that she was glad to use Validar's visit as an excuse to escape her necessary, but tedious, tasks.

"Ahh!" Aligarna stretched her stiff shoulders. "Did you take good care of our guest?"

"Yes, I did. When do you intend to talk to the Ambassador about the real reason that brought him here? I do not believe even for a moment that his search for friendship is genuine. He is hiding his plans for us and is trying to charm us with this story about a partnership. There can't be a friendship between the Eagle and the Wolf." Validar was referring to the emblems of the two countries. "I want to join you in the discussion and find out what that crafty fox is trying to steal from us, skillfully lying and promising to send stars to us from the sky!"

"My son, I intend to talk to Shridor privately. I think that he will be more open and honest with me alone and I forbid you to harass the Ambassador with your groundless suspicions."

"Why?" He became angry because of her undiplomatic and sharp words. "Am I not intelligent enough to discuss politics with him?"

"Validar, most of the time you are busy with your army and you don't understand the fine matter of politics."

"In that case, I had better return to the army and do the business that I know best, which is to protect the peace of my country." He retorted, angrily.

He left the Queen, the palace and Gerumin to return to his Division which was located to the north of the capital. His intention was to warn the loyal officers about the possibility of war and make a plan of action in case of it. The officers that had gathered in Validar's tent were not fair-weather friends who were willing to help him spend his money when times were good but would desert him when circumstances went against him. Hiding nothing, he told them all about the Queen's new plans for Vanymar.

"Yes, it's not merry news you have brought to us from the merry capital." Muttered one of his senior officers. "If you decide to take the crown from the Queen, to prevent war occurring, then a part of the army will be loyal to her and this might start a confrontation between Vanadians."

"So, we need to find another way to stop my mother's plans." Validar's eyes moved from face to face to see if anyone hesitated. "I am going to return to the capital to see what I can do to prevent a disaster from happening and I am asking you to be constantly on guard. Someone needs to send messages to trusted officers in other Divisions and all must await my further orders before taking any action."

The officers agreed that patience would be the best course of action in this difficult situation and, one by one, they left his tent. Validar changed the clothes that he had worn at the palace reception into a linen shirt and a long jacket but, after giving the matter some thought, he decided to put on a coat of fine chain mail. He removed his father's sword and dagger from his portable armory and wrapped himself in an old cloak. A soldier appeared at the opening of the tent and cautiously whispered.

"My lord, your horse is ready and I have put some food in your saddle."

"You are taking good care of me." He felt guilty for the conspiracy that had now started to affect the people around him. "I hope that I may be able to return the favor in the future."

The Prince returned to Gerumin in the late evening. The guards at the gate saluted him, then stepped back and allowed him to pass unhindered. He didn't want to talk to anyone so, after entering the city, he moved the hood of his cloak to cover his face, throwing it back only when he was behind the doors of the palace. The servants did not look at him since they were busy cleaning the rooms for the next day.

"Where is mother?" Validar asked Zlada, who was examining tablecloths and napkins for the next day's dining.

"Validar, you scared me!" The old woman put her hand on her rapidly-beating heart and shook her head. "You often did that when you were a child, playing your boyish games. You liked to jump at me from behind my back but, at that time, I was much younger."

"I am sorry. I only wanted to ask if you knew where my mother was." He got a chair for her.

"Of course, I know where she is." Said the old nanny, wiping her hands nervously on a white apron. "She is busy dragging that Ambassador about with her everywhere, showing him the palace and the city. Now they are behind a locked door, speaking for hours."

"And you don't like it?" He queried, wanting to know more.

"I am not the only one who doesn't like these secrets behind closed doors. An important advisor has arrived from Ulacar to teach her; but the Queen has plenty of her own advisers, whose suggestions have always been made with the good of our country in mind, so why does she need some foreigner?" Nanny paused, her face expressing disapproval and then continued. "I will not trust a single word from him. One word is on his tongue, another is crawling in his mind and the third is spying at you through his eyes. Honey drips from his mouth but, if you were to taste it, you would soon find that it is snake's venom!" Exhausted by her anger, she sighed. "Oh! What's the matter with me, I am sure that you have better things to do than to listen to a grumpy, old nanny? Your mother gave orders to the staff to place torches around the new marble fountain in the garden because she wants to show it to the visitor in the moonlight. What an odd idea, do you not agree?"

"Thanks, nanny Zlada, I will look for her." He walked through a dark and empty side gallery, used by their Court for a pleasure walk in the daytime when it was lit by the sun, and entered the garden through arched, glass doors. The trees and bushes of the garden were resting in the soft light of the moon as Validar walked along a pathway, breathing the scent of flowers that open only at night. They were planted for the purpose of enhancing the solitude of people who love to walk with a companion, enjoying conversations under the moon.

The next two steps brought him to the corner of a flower bed where another pathway crossed his way. He followed it until he saw the part of the fountain which had been surrounded by a line of brass torches burning oil. The Prince walked faster, hoping to see his mother, but the garden was empty and only a family of bats flew above his head, hunting insects attracted by the light. He intended to wait for her and sat on the bench opposite the fountain.

He had never seen the fountain in the dark and was surprised to discover that the marble that had been used to construct it contained other minerals that glowed in the darkness. Validar had only started to enjoy the view, and thought about the nature of the phenomenon, when a white pigeon suddenly arrived on the edge of the fountain, walked along it and cooed, obliging Validar to think. "What a strange event! A bird must sleep at this time. Perhaps it has been scared from its nest by a wildcat?" He turned his head to look for an intruder but, finding none, he returned his gaze to the bird and was shocked to see a girl standing on the edge of the fountain instead of a pigeon. She jumped to the ground and moved towards him, prompting him to get up from the bench.

"I am looking for the Prince Validar." She spoke to him almost in a singing voice. The sweetness of it didn't sound pleasant to Validar's ears because he had negative feelings towards witches and wizards, especially when witchcraft applied to his mother.

"I am Prince Validar." His voice was as cold as the expression in his eyes.

"I am glad that I have found you." The smile that she gave him was gentle and genuine. "I am a daughter of the wizard, Shukatan, ruler of Ulacar, and my name is Leubarta."

"Very well." He thought. "In addition to being the daughter of the worst dictator that I have ever known, my future wife is a witch." But he said nothing, wanting to listen to what she had to say first.

"I have decided to come to you because I think it will be unfair for you not to know the whole truth about me. I have very little time to soften it for you, so please forgive me if I hurt your feelings." Leubarta looked at Validar, expecting him to respond with some questions that would help her to continue, but he remained silent. So she took a deep breath and said. "I will not marry you." Then lowered her eyes and added "Because I can't!"

"This is interesting." Validar produced a sarcastic smile. "You are turning me down without even giving me a chance to give you a marriage proposal. I heard this idea about our union from my mother, but I didn't have the chance to listen to what Ambassador Shridor, the trusted servant of your father, had to say about this."

"Oh!" Said Leubarta, embarrassed by this awkward situation. The expression on her face was so childish and so naive that Validar, without even noticing it, started to relax his heart towards her, especially when Leubarta's cheek turned pink.

Lifting her head stubbornly, she firmly replied. "I can't be your wife because I am already married."

"Do you want to tell me, my Lady, that my kingdom is not large enough for you and you have therefore found a wealthier husband, or somebody who fits in better with your ambitious plans other than me?" joked Validar.

"You are sarcastic, my lord, and that means that I have hurt your feelings. Believe me, I have no idea how rich my husband is and I have only one ambitious plan and that is to be with him, even if my father will not be pleased with my choice or if he will punish me, casting me out of my home. But I don't want anyone else to be hurt except myself, nor to make a fool of you, Validar, and that is why I escaped my guards and came here to ask you not to call for my hand in marriage."

"If I understand you correctly, you are ready to go against your father's decision, and even get punished, for some man you have known for only a short time. Why?"

"Because he accepted me for who I am, married me without a dowry and because I love him." Leubarta smiled again, looking even more fragile and young.

"This is enough for me to know, Leubarta. I am never going to be your husband but I will always be your friend." And Validar gave her his hand.

"Friends and allies!" Leubarta affirmed, squeezing his hand firmly. "If you ever meet my husband, please be a friend to him also. His name is Ruslan."

"If I ever meet a man with this name I will take him under my protection." Responded Validar, gallantly.

Their conversation was interrupted by sounds coming from the direction of the pathway which had brought the Prince here not so long ago.

"I don't want anyone to see me here." Whispered Leubarta.

"Then, let us hide behind this bush." He replied, helping her to find a way through the branches. As he had expected, it was Queen Aligarna in the company of Ulacar's diplomat.

The Queen was dressed in a long, white coat decorated with fur on the front which was protecting her from the cool evening air. She had removed her crown and wore only a silver tiara inlaid with turquoise stones.

The long robe of the Ambassador, made from a bright fabric, was also lined with dark fur on the sleeves and the collar. They continued the conversation that they had started a long time before they had reached the fountain. When the Queen and the Ambassador stopped, a short distance from the hidden Leubarta and Validar, the diplomat said. "Your majesty has surprised me again. I did not expect to see such an impressive fountain in your gardens and I would like to offer you another gift which will complement this. Please allow me to bring a marble bathing house, which my skilled tradesmen will install in your palace. It may be extremely useful in your cold climate to protect the beauty of your Majesty's skin."

"You are flattering me, Ambassador, using the common knowledge that beauty is important for a woman." Aligarna looked pleased.

"I know how to keep your beauty intact forever." His voice sounded secretive. "You need only to identify yourself as a supporter of a new Force, as powerful as a God."

Aligarna turned to the Ambassador, laughing." Your Master is thinking of himself as a God?"

"Oh no, I am not talking about my Master Shukatan, but about someone who came a longtime ago from the dark depths of space whose name was known only to wizards. I am talking about Cofiat. He is going to give new meaning to the word "power." He promises absolute power and eternal life to those of us who will agree to surrender everything to him. From the dark waters of his desires a newborn Servant will arise to rule and dominate the weak. Will you join us, Queen Aligarna? Do you want to be one of the chosen few?"

By the time that Shridor had finished his speech, the face of the Queen had turned into a white mask and only her eyes still looked alive in her face.

"If Cofiat is so powerful why does he need Shukatan and me?" She asked.

"My Master, Cofiat, needs somebody to fight a war on his behalf in order to take power from his opponent, Amer, who is just as powerful as he is. High Beings cannot fight each other because that will destroy the entire planet and, at the end, there would be nothing left to rule and dominate. That is why they use mortals to fight for them. As a result, Cofiat chooses to give orders through us. He wants to be recognized and worshipped from afar, without coming in contact with many people. Like a General in battle, he only makes strategic plans but obliges others to carry them out. Since stability around him is necessary and important for the success of his plans, he preserves the lives of his faithful servants and rewards them with material goods and more land. For himself, he desires only power over nations. My Lord Cofiat sent a messenger to King Farlaf also, but he foolishly refused his offer, bringing death to himself and his family. What is your decision on this vital matter, Queen Aligarna?"

Aligarna touched her dry lips with her tongue to moisten them and said. "Unconditional power and eternal life appeals to me and, if Lord Cofiat can prove that he is capable of giving me such things, I will fight this war on his behalf."

"It is done, my Queen, your life is under the protection of Cofiat. Give me your hand." When Aligarna stretched out her hand, Shridor cut it deeply with a dagger that he had removed from under his belt. Aligarna screamed and looked at her hand in terror as the blood that ran from the wound was sucked back into her hand and the wound closed, leaving no mark. "Is that enough proof for you?" Asked Shridor.

The Queen only nodded, looking at the hand which had been healed so miraculously. "Now it's your turn to prove your loyalty to my Master. You must conquer Rossana and eliminate King Farlaf and his sons." Ended Ambassador Shridor.

"I have planned to invade Rossana for some time myself and only the stubbornness of my son was the reason why my army did not cross Rossana's boundary. After this night I will take away some of his freedom. He will no longer have the luxury of deciding whether he is going to be an honorable knight, with scruples and moral principles, or to marry the Princess. He must be the General of my army under my control and unite Vanymar and Ulacar or, alternatively, he will become a prisoner in one of the cells under the city tower.

"We don't need to go that far." Reasoned Shridor. "He is a gifted warrior and we can use him." He removed something from his pocket and a closer look revealed it to be a small box.

Aligarna opened the box and removed something from it." What is this?"

"This is a gift from Cofiat, a magical thing. Pin this on Validar's clothes, say on the collar of his shirt, and the Prince will forget everything that has happened to him before and become an obedient instrument in your hands."

"No more arguments, no questions?" Aligarna's eyes narrowed.

"He will follow your orders, no matter how much they will harm and hurt anyone."

Pleased, Aligarna put the pin back in the box and cried." I will see my darling son immediately and will enjoy seeing him turn into the most reviled man in Vanymar." Sudden hatred turned her hands into fists. "But, for the time being, I am going to play the role of a loving mother." She then relaxed her hands and walked back to the palace.

Leubarta and Validar stood silent in shock, even after Aligarna and Shridor had disappeared into the distance.

"You are in great danger, Validar. You need to leave Gerumin immediately or you will not be yourself anymore." Leubarta touched his hand and, breaking the chain of his troubled thoughts, prompted him to say to her.

"Now I understand what happened to your father and I know how terrible you must feel, being a helpless witness to the slow degradation of someone so close to your heart. You have seen how his actions changed the world around him, making you feel more and more as if you were being dragged into the web of a giant spider, except that my situation is different. I have a sword to cut through this web and free all who may become prisoners of it." Validar squeezed the scabbard of his sword, looking in the direction of the palace.

"Not all who serve Cofiat were forced to do it by circumstances in which they had no choice. Some chose to become his supporters because of their own nature--the evil inside their own hearts answered the call. Knowing that people of this kind live among us makes me feel frightened. You can free those who were too weak to resist evil but what are you going to do with the other half who freely gave themselves over to it?" Leubarta asked the Prince.

"I assume that you mean my mother? Before this evening, I thought that she was under the influence of your father but now I do not know what to think." He shrugged.

"I know one person who can help you to clarify this situation. She will tell you whether someone is controlling the Queen or whether she is making her own decisions and, if so, what are you going to do about it?"

"First things first. Where can I find this person who can answer my questions?"

"Seek out my old friend, Snodia. You can find her in the forest of Four Seasons."

"I have heard about this place from a friend who lived in the valley of the Star, but I thought that it was only a fairytale." He responded.

"So, in this valley, you must have seen a cottage on the hill?" She suggested happily.

"I know the sisters Thought who live there. The oldest is named Candice, the youngest is called Funny and the middle sister is Nasty. Their names are very close to their personalities and suit them very well. And there is somebody else living with them, but he is always in hiding." Validar paused, laughing.

"Validar, did you notice an old road leading off to the right?"

"Yes. I have stopped and looked at that road many times. But Shmata advised me not to go there, telling me that the inhabitants of that place do not want to be disturbed without a reason."

"Now you have a reason!" She said. "Go along this road until you reach a big stone at the point where the road splits into three ways and then follow the sign written on the stone which says… "If you go this way you will lose your heart."

"A very promising sign." The Prince laughed, but Leubarta continued.

"This road will lead you to the forest of Four Seasons where I hope you will find the answers to your questions. As for myself, I need to return home before my absence is noticed by someone."

And, with these words, Leubarta again turned into a white pigeon and flew away.

CHAPTER 5:

THE QUEST FOR A
SMALL FORTUNE

It had been four hours since Tac had returned home after his adventures. The news about the return of the missing explorers had spread in the forest like wildfire and had reached the Council members. They had decided that, instead of calling for the cat to attend their meeting, they would go to visit him since they expected to hear an unbelievable story which would be worth the long walk from their homes to Tac's doorstep.

Tac had just finished his dinner, surprising Alisa with his appetite, and then had drunk a large glass of milk to wash it down. So it was understandable that, when someone had knocked on the door of their home, the cat was reluctant to get up from his chair to answer the door.

"I should ask Leubarta to teach me how to become invisible." Complained Tac, walking to the door to see who it was. He had not expected to see almost the whole Council waiting outside and he even started to stutter in surprise.

"What? How did you learn that I had returned home?"

"On the way home, Galibur had decided to stop at Carfield's nest and you know how loud this old crow can be. Then the birds who had overheard their conversation spread the news in the forest until it had reached us from the branches above." Shustin advised. "We started to worry about you as soon as

Alisa had told us that you and Galibur had not come back from your flight of exploration over the Leehar."

"If all of us were not so afraid of that place then the Council would probably have sent somebody to search for you." Mixie added.

"What is the reason for your delay in arriving home? It has been two days since you mysteriously disappeared?" Queried Woodan, the wolf, usually simply referred to as Woo.

Tac let out a sigh, understanding that he must now forget about a nap, and took a step outside. "I cannot invite you into my home because Rainar's body will not fit into the tunnel. It will be better if we go down to the creek because the story is going to be long but, before we go, I want to show you something." And he disappeared inside Fox Hall, coming back with two round objects that he put on the ground in front of everyone.

"What is this?" Asked Shustin, who was closest to them.

"The people with whom I lived before I came to the wood called these flat, round things coins and, according to my observations of their habits, the largest ring with a face on it is valued the most. In exchange for this you can get whatever you want."

"What things can we get?" Asked Woo.

"Food!" Tac shrugged. "We can get much food. For example, meat that was grown on the farm. This means that you do not need to chase and kill the animals in the forest."

Woo touched the coins with his paw, still not convinced of their value.

"Where did you get this?" Queried Mixie.

Tac replied to this question by saying. "Be patient, Mixie. The episode about the origin of these coins will be included in the story about the adventures of me and Galibur." Then, turning to his wife, he asked her. "Alisa, will you please do me a favor and hide them inside?" All the animals, already intrigued, followed him to the creek while Alisa picked up the coins and disappeared with them into the house.

The next day he got up early, planning to visit Carfield, who had been the only one absent from the hastily-called meeting at the creek the day before, not counting Galibur who did not need to attend since he already knew the full story.

Carfield lived alone, almost at the top of the tall fir tree that enhanced one of the many hills of the Pokerweild Woods. Lightning had struck this tree when it was young, splitting the stem in half. The injured tree had healed itself by covering its wounds with layers of bark and had continued to grow both of its tops equally. In due course it became a strangely-shaped forest giant. It was not difficult to find Carfield's nest, but it was not exactly easy to get there. He climbed the trunk of the fir tree using his claws and rested from time to time on a branch to view the forest from his high vantage point. When he had eventually reached the spot where the tree trunk formed a fork, he admitted that Carfield had made a good choice for the location of his home. It offered not only a beautiful view but also some comfort due to the size of his nest. Made from branches of different trees and shrubs, the nest rose higher and higher every year, becoming wider at the top until it took the shape of its current form, a four-story apartment nest, separated by wooden floors with each having its own entry door.

Tac looked inside the first floor and found that it was only used as storage for nuts and dried berries. He assumed that Carfield's living quarters were probably on the fourth floor, where the increasing distance between the two forked trunks had allowed him to make a spacious platform.

"Carfield, are you home?"

The big round door that looked like the bottom of a wooden keg opened wide with a creaking noise and the head of an old crow popped out from it, saying. "There is a door on the top of my house and it will be easier for you to enter my home through that."

So Tac climbed to the level of the flat roof and, walking carefully, reached another doorway, also shaped like a barrel, which Carfield slowly opened up invitingly. After climbing down a rope which hung from the trapdoor, the cat jumped onto the floor and let out a sigh of relief.

"I have water here, would you like some?" Carfield looked at him, sympathetically, cocking his head to the side.

"I would be grateful for some water right now." Tac felt thirsty after the exercise.

A spacious room contained wooden boxes that served as a table and chairs. 'To bring such objects up to this height was probably just as difficult as building a pyramid in the desert.' He thought, looking at everything with respect.

"You have a nice place, Carfield." He praised, as he drank from an old porcelain cup which had a broken handle.

"Yes." Carfield admitted proudly. "It took me some time to settle everything so that it would be exactly the way that I wanted. As you know, crows are long-lived and have lots of time to do things. By the way, about time, I have heard your entire story from Galibur and you do not need to waste your energy by explaining everything again."

"In this case, you already know that the woods around Leehar are now safe."

"I am feeling very satisfied that the place has been cleared." Carfield looked sheepish. "I sadly admit that it was me who must take the blame for inviting the cloud into our woods in the first place."

"You?" Tac was deeply surprised. "I will not move from this spot until you tell me everything about this past event, despite the fact that I am not a member of the Council." He reclined into the chair to show that he was serious in his decision to stay.

"Well, if you promise not to tell anyone about the things that I am going to tell you, I will be fully satisfied." Sighed the crow.

"I assure you that I will be discreet." Tac' eyes flashed with interest, sensing that he was about to hear something very unusual.

"It happened a long time ago when my clan owned part of the forest close to the mountains. I must say that it was not the best location for living. It was difficult to find food here and I was constantly hungry, always searching for something to eat. That is how I got myself into the same trouble as you and Galibur. Thrown through the Portal to the other side of the mountain, I found myself inside an unfamiliar environment which looked exactly like what you described in your story. This surprised me and I flew on to see more of this strange valley.

Searching above the forest I spotted a cottage on the ground, shaded by tall fir trees. It was not the cottage that attracted my attention but the yellowing stems of corn close by that encouraged me to land in this place. Impatiently, I pulled the layers of thin covers from the corn and pecked at the juicy, golden squares with the speed of a peeling machine, gorging myself. I might even have killed myself with greed if a frightening creature had not come close to me and growled.

Day after day I flew over the fields, fattening myself with free corn. This annoyed the farmer so much that he tried all kinds of tricks to keep me off his field. My free meals ended when the owner, disappointed at his failure to protect his property, hired a hawk to sit on a tall post and look in all directions. I returned to the forest with an empty stomach to look for some other food, trying this and that. Eventually, I found a creek, the banks of which were covered by low-growing bushes carrying frosty blue berries. Having tried one, I found it to be sweet and juicy but was cautious about eating many because there was no evidence around that other birds had been there. The next day I did not experience any symptoms of sickness and allowed myself to eat more of the berries and then made it a habit to add them to my diet. However, one day, instead of my normal speech, I heard unusual sounds coming from my throat and when I tried to say "caw" I heard these strange words instead. "What's the problem with me?" This almost made me fall off the branch in fright.

Still puzzled by this incident, I thought I heard someone else nearby and looked around. I was alone. I closed my eyes and concentrated on speaking. "Caw! Caw!" It came out with the sound of a harsh foreign accent and, at the same time, I came to realize that I had no clue as to what this "Caw! Caw!"

meant. I understood with terror that I was actually thinking in human words, instead of the language of my own kind."

The cat tried to be polite by not showing how much he was amused by this story, but lost the battle with his good manners and burst into laughter.

"I do not blame you." Carfield ruffled his feathers, with sparks of humor in his small, black eyes and continued. "Now I can laugh at this situation myself. But at that time I was thinking that I had contracted a dangerous virus and had even started to check my feathers to see if they had started to fall out of my body. I looked at my reflection in the water of the creek, saying to myself. "Start to caw again, freak! How are you going to marry and have chicks if you will not be able to understand your own family when they speak? You will need to look for lessons in the course of C.S.L., "Caw as a Second Language", if you are ever able to manage to find a teacher, that is!"

"Ohhh." Tac rolled on the floor with laughter. "Carfield, enough! You had better tell me how you managed to find your way back."

"I was advised on this matter by a very smart bird. He might even be my distant relative who has lived a very long life and knows much about this world." Carfield respectfully intoned. "I believe he calls himself Felix."

"Do you not mean Phoenix?" Tac moved closer to the crow.

"Yes! Phoenix." The crow tasted the sound of the word. "That is correct. I met him when I was looking for something to eat. In addition to this, I was searching for some local crows in the hope that I could relearn my native language from them. Suddenly, I saw a large bird carrying something in its claws and the word "food" immediately came to my mind. Hiding carefully, I followed it to the side of the mountain where the bird had its nest inside a big crack in the wall. At first I thought that the bird was some kind of large eagle, but it was much larger and brighter than any other I had ever seen. As soon as the bird had left it, I sneaked into the dark opening of the narrow tunnel but, instead of food, I saw many small cotton bags which were filled with a substance too fine to be seeds. I pulled the string that was tied around one of the bags and found a grayish powder inside it that made me sneeze violently.

The bird was probably close enough to hear me because very soon the flapping sound of large wings told me that it was coming back. I moved away from the entrance, hoping to find a hole through which to escape. There were none and I was faced with no choice but to find my way out of this place by confronting the owner of the nest. As I turned in the direction of the entrance, to my horror I discovered a pair of fiery, red eyes fixed upon me. The light that was radiating from the feathers of the bird scared me so much that I could only think of saying. "If you want to kill me for trespassing on your territory and breaking into your home, do it quickly. My life has had no value to me after I ate some poison berries and started to talk like a man. There is no bird that now understands me when I talk and, if I am ever able to make it back home, I do not want to live the life of a refugee, rejected by everyone. It would be better for you to kill me and have me for dinner. At least my existence will have had some value."

My adversary lowered its wings and, closing its beak, looked at me in a different way. "So, you are new to our world? Animals and birds come here through the gate from time to time, but usually they go deeper into the land. Why did you stay in the Valley of the Star? Is there something wrong with your wings?"

"I am fine, thank you. I am Carfield and I came from another world, searching for a way to get back home. We crows are social birds and, after I became separated from my family, I got homesick and will probably die from loneliness. When I have all my brothers around me we have a tendency to fight amongst ourselves and sometimes I hate them. But, when I find myself alone, I realize how badly I am attached to them and miss all my noisy relatives."

"And you really want to return to them?" Asked the Phoenix, in a softer voice.

"I would give everything to go through that gate again, only I have nothing to give in payment." I moaned.

"Do not worry, I will help you." The Phoenix comforted me. "And I do not need any payment."

"I take it that you do not have any interest in eating me and, therefore, may I ask whether or not this grayish powder in the bag, whose drawstring I have just opened, is your food?"

"Oh no." Laughed the Phoenix. This powder is called the spice. Every five hundred years I need to collect enough spice to make a fire and burn myself in it."

"Do you kill yourself?" I asked, incredulously.

"Yes! After all of my body has turned into ashes, I arise from the last flame of my being, becoming a young bird again for the next five hundred years. The time of my transformation is imminent and I now have all the spice that I need for my resurrection." He informed me.

"I am glad that you do not eat this spice because it smells toxic. I hope we can leave this place before I get a headache." I responded.

"Unfortunately, we will need to wait until the rain that has just started will cease and this is actually the reason why I have returned myself."

"Oh! Are you afraid of getting your feathers wet?" I asked.

"Of course not." Said the Phoenix. "But it is dangerous to fly when the sun is dim. These mountains hide many vicious creatures and the dragons are not the most dangerous by any means. The cloud with the dark, almost purple, edges is the worst enemy and even I will run away from it without looking back. Although it appears to be a harmless rain cloud, in reality it's a cold-blooded hunter. Most of them were destroyed by the Ranger, Validar, but some are still hiding in the mountains and, when it is a rainy day like it is today, they come out looking for someone to attack. We will leave this place as soon as the sun has returned. Its presence will force all the evil clouds that may be circling around to go back to the snowy mountains, afraid to dry out in the heat of the sun."

"Phoenix, you mentioned another animal that I have never heard about before, the dragon. What does it look like?"

"From my point of view." The Phoenix explained. "A dragon is a wicked combination of a snake, a lizard and a bat. Its body is protected by a thick hide that is harder than anything in this world. Having a short temper, dragons will fight with any creature without a reason to do so. I suggest that you do not go close to the lake, which is the place where they choose to rest, and do not have anything on you that is made from gold. This way, you will be safe."

"Are these dragons attracted to gold?" I asked the Phoenix.

"Yes, very much so. I do not honestly know why these dragons need it, because I am not friendly with them, but I have heard rumors that the caves in the mountains are full of golden things which have been stolen by dragons. Perhaps the shine of the gold attracts them."

"Oh, I can understand this, since my family also makes the effort to fly to the city to take shiny objects from people." I was too shy to mention to him that I had my own collection, built-up from their trophies.

"It seems to me that the rain has finished, but let me check." Exclaimed the Phoenix, ignoring my last comment and starting to back-up towards the entrance. Then I heard his voice calling me from the outside. "Carfield, the sun is back and the clouds have gone. That means we are now free to go."

When I went outside, he said. "I am going to return to the Castle of Folding-Time where I serve my lord, the Master of Dreams, but I suggest that you keep closer to the slope of the mountain where the gate is located. It can open at any time for the new guest of this world and, when this happens, you must be ready to quickly sneak through the open door before it closes again. I will say my goodbye to you now and I hope that you may be able to join your family shortly!" With these parting words, the Phoenix jumped clumsily into the air and, rising higher and higher into the sky, finally disappeared over the horizon.

Listening to his advice, I found the slope from where I had seen the Valley of the Star the first time and had placed a broken branch into the ground to make it easier for me to find this place later. Sitting and waiting at the Portal Gate, on the off-chance that good fortune might bring someone careless to it, was a boring business. At the same time, thoughts about pieces of gold that might be lying around somewhere for the taking, had fired my desire to look for the hidden treasure for quite some time. Having nothing better to do, I decided to set off on my search.

Remembering what the Phoenix had told me about the lake, I decided to visit it first, expecting that this would be the place where I would definitely find the dragon. However, if I had known that he would be so huge and frightening, I would not have listened to my greedy thoughts. I am sitting and talking to you today only because the dragon that I encountered did not have any interest in anyone and was merely enjoying bathing in the lake. His large wings made him a bad swimmer and, for the most part, he only jumped about in the water splashing it around him and creating large waves. Then he made a couple of wide circles in the water and returned to shore, dragging his massive tail behind him. Shaking off the water, he spread his wings out to dry and the sheen of his wet body sparkled like dark metal in the sun.

After blowing-out a narrow stream of fire to clear his throat, he tried-out his wings and finally rose up off the ground. I quickly followed him, making sure that I was some distance away, but stayed directly behind him. Knowing nothing about my presence, the dragon guided me to the flat rocky top of one of the mountains and landed on it. He opened his mouth wide and roared with a thunderous, metallic sound which knocked me down to the ground in total fright. His call prompted another dragon to immediately appear from behind the sharp edge of the mountain. The second dragon was smaller and looked like a female. The expression on her face made it clear that she was determined to protect her territory against any intruder, but my dragon did not want to fight. He made a playful move, inviting her to join him in a contact game, but his moves made her only angrier and she hissed at him like a snake, pushing him away. Disappointed by his lack of success, the larger dragon retired but I did not follow him.

While the dragons were wrestling, I found the big opening of the cave where the female was living and I did not need the Romeo anymore to show me around. She came back to her cave but did not enter it. Instead, she wheeled away and flew up into the sky to make sure that the annoying intruder had left her space. After she had disappeared completely, I sneaked into the dark cave and went towards a weak source of light coming from a big opening on the left side which brought me into a large chamber.

A picture from my most precious dreams opened up in front of me as I saw a mass of sparkling gold lying on the podium, highlighted by the fire which burned in the narrow channel. I was afraid of the orange flames, but the desire to see the shiny metal was stronger than my fear and I flew over the fire to get a better view. It is impossible to fully describe the number of golden things which lay there in front of my enraptured eyes. I needed to have at least one piece of gold but, unfortunately, crowns and tiaras were too heavy for me to carry and round coins easily slipped from my claws.

I searched desperately through the treasures for something that I could take with me until I finally spotted something flat and narrow that was almost hidden under sections of a massive chain. I pulled it free to note that I was holding a narrow box which was relatively light and showed a picture of a bird on its flat top. The desire to have this box ended my search. Holding onto it tightly, I flew back over the fire and finally left this cavern, carrying my trophy. When I was quite a distance away from the entrance, I started to wonder why the dragon had left her home for such a long time. The answer came to me after I had reached the valley. I almost stumbled against her and noted that, for some reason, she was sending long angry streams of red fire in the direction of a low-hanging cloud. Avoiding being seen, I moved aside, desperately looking for a place to hide. The line of high rocks behind me could offer a sanctuary but it could also become a trap if she decided to come after me.

Meanwhile the dragon was fully preoccupied, constantly spitting fire at the opponent. The small forest to my left was already consumed by flames, filling the air with black smoke and making my escape impossible. At the same time I got the disturbing feeling that I was being watched. Looking up, I discovered another cloud standing above me, but it did not attack me because the situation on the battlefield had suddenly changed. The fiery beast had failed to recharge her fire quickly enough and this had given the cloud a perfect opportunity to attack her, tearing a large chunk of flesh from her shoulder. In turn, she had succeeded in burning the arm of the cloud before the increasing pain of her own injury made it impossible for her to continue the fight. Shaking the ground with her roar, the dragon crawled away to leave behind the pulsating cloud that was gathering itself together again. Presented with a sudden opportunity to kill a larger prey, the cloud above me changed its intention to hunt me and followed the dragon instead. I used this change of circumstance to reach the lake where I found a tree to push my box into a deep crack and then collapsed into my temporary nest.

A week later, I was cautiously walking to the lake when the sound of a human voice stopped me in my tracks.

"Ah, you poor, stupid kid. You've got yourself into trouble and have brought your mother with you. Is that it?"

The young goat answered him with a thin, bleating sound.

"You're very lucky that it was me, Shmata, who found you. Hurry up to my cottage, little one, because the wind is changing and it will bring rain shortly. The rain is not a good thing in this valley because another cloud has come over from the mountain and it will take some time for my friend to arrive in order to destroy it. Meantime, you and your mother will spend the night in my barn and tomorrow, if the weather is good, I will send you back home through the gate."

The last phrase I barely picked up, but it was the most important part of the whole conversation. I realized that finally the gate had been opened and I was anxious to seize this opportunity to return home. The weather had changed rapidly, just like this man had warned, and had turned into a dull and annoying rain. The wet bark of the tree, in which I had hidden my treasure, had expanded and become slippery and forced me to fight to get my box out. By the time that I was able to eventually reach the mountains where the gate was hidden, it was pouring rain. I had almost made it to my destination when I noticed something attached to a tree and flapping like a flag. I went away from it, but the cloud saw me and unwrapped itself surprisingly quickly to go after me. The speed at which I approached the Gate was too fast for a safe landing but the wall had softly bent itself inside and pushed me back, vibrating even faster. Nevertheless, the impact made me drop my box to the ground. Dragging my injured wing, I managed to find it and crawled to the edge of the gate. The Force lifted me softly to transfer me to the other side and, in memory of this event, I planted a small tree in this spot."

"I owe you my gratitude for doing this because I did not break any bones, being caught by the branches of your tree instead of landing on rocks." Tac interrupted the crow.

Carfield only nodded his head, accepting it. "Let me continue my story. My clan greeted me happily but I no longer felt that I fitted into their lives. A stranger to my family, I decided to live alone, observing the lives of the forest inhabitants from this high point and learning how to become a normal crow again."

"Why do you blame yourself for inviting the cloud?" Asked Tac.

"I assume that the cloud had some level of intelligence and eventually found its own way through the gate, craving my blood. Instead, it took the lives of the living creatures around Leehar and it remained here but never crossed the creek, avoiding coming closer to the water. This obliged the Council to call all the animals out of this area and put the responsibility of guarding it on the shoulders of the beavers."

"I think the Council can open up this territory again." Said Tac. "The Ranger did kill the cloud and I know this myself because I saw its remains lying on the ground."

"I do not agree, Tac. I hear from Galibur that another dangerous visitor came through the gate and, if he is the dragon that I saw, we can be in even more danger."

"I hope that all this talk about him proves to be only our suspicions." The cat had grown tired from the stories about dangerous creatures and decided to change the topic onto something less tense, asking. "May I see the box?"

"Of course." Carfield opened the trapdoor in the floor of his room and jumped down, then came back up with a narrow, golden box in which Tac found a small, boney pin adorned at each end with the figure of a bird carved on it.

"Do you know what this is used for?" Tac asked.

"No." Carfield spread his wings apart. "I think that the artist who created the box tried to make it functional. He decided to put something inside of it to give the box a purpose and made another fine toy to fill the space. Did you notice, Tac, that one of the carved birds is sleeping when the other is dancing?"

"Yes." Tac returned the box to its owner. "Very interesting, but it has no use. I know how to use my find in a very practical way."

"I am all ears to find out how you can use pieces of metal in a very practical way." Carfield spread the ends of his wings around his head as if they were donkey's ears.

"I am thinking of selling them for many dollars to buy much food for all of us." Replied Tac.

"Sell?" Carfield sounded astonished. "Who needs them?"

"These coins must be old and have great value. I know that some people buy old things and are willing to pay a lot of money for what they call antiques. All that I need now is to find a store that can sell these coins for me."

"Tac!" Said Carfield, excitedly. "You have come to the right crow to talk about this business. I already have an idea of how to find a store for you. Give me two days to transform my thoughts into a plan of action."

"In that case." Tac got up. "Thank you for the conversation and for showing me your treasure, but now I need to go. It will take me some time to climb down the tree and Alisa will worry if I miss dinner. Goodbye, my friend." Then he took leave of Carfield's nest.

Some three days later, a knock at the door made the cat open it to find a crow with a folded paper tied to his beak on his doorstep.

Carfield mumbled unclear greetings and, moving Tac aside, entered his home and went straight to the table where he unloaded the paper. "Tac, I have found a store that will sell your coins. I have even called the owner and arranged an appointment for next week!"

"What?" Tac looked incredulous. "How did you manage to talk to the owner?"

"It has taken me some time to learn how to talk like a crow again, but I did not forget the human language. I borrowed a big silver coin from my old friend, Willy, and called from the telephone across the street to avoid the possibility of my call being traced by the police." Carfield was apparently very proud of himself.

"Who taught you this?" Responded a surprised cat.

"My favorite character, Sherlock Holmes."

"Who is he?" Asked the cat.

"Tac." Carfield gave him a penetrating look. "You call yourself a modern cat? I need to educate you a little bit. Sherlock Holmes was a most famous detective and criminal scientist and possibly even the father of police science. I have a theory that he only pretended to be human in order to camouflage his identity but in reality he was a crow, skillfully masquerading as a man to bring logic and justice into the irrational world of people. In my opinion, only a crow could possess such a brilliant mind and such order in his thoughts. I owe my discovery of him to my curiosity.

Onc day, I was sitting on a fence of somebody's back yard and listening to the weather forecast coming from a square box called a radio, when somebody sneaked up on me from behind and caught me in a pillow case. I found myself in a large cage in the role of a prisoner of a boy called Jimmy. But I did not complain because, by closing the gate of the cage, he opened up another door for me into the world of education when he brought me to school as the pet of the week.

At school, I managed to charm the teacher by repeating some simple words and stayed at that school for a whole year on free meals and paid nothing to learn to read. Yes, my illiterate friend, not only can I speak like I am a human but I can also read their words. I have even tried to write these words but that is very difficult to do with my claws. I learned how to open the cage more quickly, then learned to read with ease and started to escape into the school library every night to read everything that I found interesting. The story about Sherlock Holmes fascinated me and from then on I became his fan. Only one problem bothered me; that the school library did not contain all the books that had been written about him. Therefore I decided to quit being a pet and exchanged my comfortable life for the freedom of continuing my research about this remarkable person. Rest assured, Tac, that I stuck my beak into any book that I could find, without success, until one blessed day I noticed an open window in Willy's rancher. Entering his home I discovered his large collection of books that included some with the famous name Sherlock Holmes printed in gold leaf on their hard covers. My surprise was even greater after I found Willy's driver's license in the name of William Holmes, whereupon I immediately became a secret patron of him and his library. Now, let's go back to my plan." Carfield continued, unrolling the paper that he had brought with him.

The first page was a list from the telephone book that showed the numbers and addresses of stores that bought and sold antiques. One in particular had been circled in red ink to draw Tac's attention and the other page was a map.

Carfield started off by saying. "This store, which I had marked on the map, belongs to a man named Jeff Tompkins who is interested in your gold. He wanted me to describe the design on the coins but I have never seen them and promised to bring him the coins for evaluation next Thursday at noon. I picked up a map from the gas station and found his store on page sixteen." Carfield turned the pages and looked for the right place. "Here it is." He said, pointing with his foot to the bright dot on the map. "I also made a trip to the city to study the location around it, looking for the best ways to escape in case of emergency."

Tac was too perplexed to say anything and only looked at the paper. When he had told Carfield about the idea of selling the gold, he had not expected him to become so involved. He had wanted to spend some time to think about the way of selling it but now felt a little frustrated about having entrusted his idea to this crazy bird who had taken complete control over the whole operation. Tac ignored the irritation that he had started to feel, blaming himself for having given out the raw idea without having carefully thought it through. 'What a lesson for you!' He said to himself. 'Do not open your mouth without having anything to say.' He then made a decision to co-operate instead of fighting for the ownership of the enterprise. Tac moved the map closer to himself, pleased that he was familiar with reading it too.

"The store where we are going to sell the gold is located on Sunbluff Street that stretches along the river Pontrov in an old part of the city of Murraydale." Carfield pointed to the place on the map.

"Not a good choice." Tac shook his head. "My family often goes there for Sunday fun and, according to them, it's the busiest street in the summer. The cottages that were built there by the first settlers have slowly disappeared and been transformed into straight lines of shops, restaurants and cafes of all kinds. The road alongside the stores has been bordered by wide concrete walkways stretching to the edge of the slope which drops towards the river adjacent to a three-step terrace. The slope itself was transformed into an endless garden, cut into sections with lines of steps that led to the wooden embankment, with benches for rest and platforms protruding into the water for the pretense of fishing, or to just hold a fishing rod. The People of Murraydale often use this street for gift shopping, meeting with friends, family fun and just for slow walks to enhance their health. The appearance of a cat, in the company of a crow, will attract the attention of everyone, from children who will try to pet us to adults who will question such a strange companionship. Of course, the fact that the meeting is scheduled for a Thursday will take some of the pressure off, but we will still attract no less attention than a bleeding finger on a child."

"I did not think about this." Carfield admitted, his mood drooping. Both Tac and Carfield became silent and only looked at the map, trying to think of a better way to present the gold to the store owner.

"Carfield!" Exclaimed Tac, suddenly inspired by an idea. "You said that your favorite character impersonated a man."

"Who?" Asked Carfield, allowing the question to pass through his mind."

"That famous detective." He was reminded.

"Sherlock Holmes?" His attention suddenly awakened. "What about him?"

"You told me that he only looks like he is human. What if we look like we are human also?"

"Tac, that really is a good idea!" Responded Carfield, excitedly. "We will both dress in a man's clothing."

"No!"Asserted Tac, thinking…'This is not going to work because, if you are going to use your legs for walking, where will we get hands from?'

"You need to work together." Said Alisa, coming in from the other room. "You, Tac, are going to be the legs and Carfield will have to stand on your shoulders and be the rest of the body."

"But, even if Carfield is going to stand on my shoulders, he still lacks hands."

"Yes." Alisa added suddenly. "Then you clearly need a third person to work the legs. You, Tac, will have to act as the shoulders, arms and hands and Carfield will have to forget about his wings and will have to become the talking head so that, altogether, you will be tall enough to look like you are a human being."

"Thanks, Alisa, this is a brilliant idea. Who do you think we can let into our plan as the legs?" Carfield asked both Tac and Alisa.

"I think the best candidate for the position of the legs is our good companion Woo. Firstly, he is a Council member and can keep secrets and, secondly, he is a wolf that is able to scare away any unexpected witness. He can help to carry the costume and guard our gold on the way to the store, not to mention all the money that we are going to deliver to the woods." Muttered the cat.

"Yes, you are right, he is a good candidate. But, as you said before, he is a wolf and people will start to panic when they see him." The crow pointed out.

Tac scratched his head with his hind leg as if he had been bitten by a flea and then relaxed, smiling. "We will need to dress Woo in the uniform of a special-care dog to stop them from thinking that Woo is a wolf and will view him just as if he is nothing more than a big, gray dog that only looks a little bit like a wolf.

"Why are you worried so much about Woo? He is going to be the legs and all that you need to do is dress him in pants?" Alisa reminded them.

"I am going to see Roxal and ask him to help me bring home some of my Master's old clothes. He always wanted to make a real scarecrow out of them but, with all the worry about the coming baby, I do not think that he will bother with it now. After seeing Roxal, I am going to do a detour and visit Woo in his new home between the rocks and try to talk him into participating in our business." Then he asked the crow.

"Carfield, I saw a brown hat, adorned with a red poppy, hanging on the wall of your house as a decoration. Do you think it would be possible to cut off that poppy and make it look more like a man's hat?"

"Of course, and I also have a pair of black glasses to wear with it so that I will really look like a detective." Whispered Carfield, with meaning.

"Carfield, you are not going to be a detective but only an average Old Joe who was lucky to find a treasure and wants to sell it so that he can have a happy retirement. You do not need to wear glasses."

"Are you saying that I have the eyes of an Old Joe?" Asked Carfield, feeling really insulted.

Tac looked at him attentively and, after deep thought, admitted. "No, you have tiny crows' eyes which will give away your identity completely so it will be better if you wear those glasses but, remember, no detective tricks because you are still an average Joe. We have only five days to prepare everything for the show, so I suggest that we meet tomorrow at my home to try on the costume and practice walking as a human."

"Agreed." Said Carfield.

Next morning, Carfield approached Tac's home from the air, bringing a young crow with him who was carrying a hat. He croaked out an order to his helper to drop the hat on the ground and return home. "Cannot trust the young generation in anything. It's a good thing that I gave him only a hat because if it were glasses he would have broken them a long time before we came here. He cannot hold anything in his claws and he has dropped that hat probably ten times already." Then, addressing Tac, he said moodily. "Where is Woo? Did you talk to him?"

"I am expecting him to come to my home soon." Tac chuckled, covering his mouth with a paw. "He did not even want to hear about joining us at first, saying that he was too busy with Council affairs. But he has a big family to feed and I exchanged a few words with his wife who came over to our side and, after that, it was not so difficult to change his mind."

"Shh!" Said Carfield, whose sharp bird's eyes had caught a glimpse of the figure of the wolf coming towards them as soon as he had appeared over the edge of the slope.

Woo slid down the slope, braking his impetus with all four legs, and finally stopped on the pathway. "Good afternoon to both of you." He greeted them. "Let's be quick about trying-on this costume of yours. I need to bath my youngsters and take them for a stroll so that mother can get some rest and stop growling at me."

"Alisa." Shouted Tac, into the house. "We need your help with scissors. I have no idea how to operate them."

He then touched his forehead. "Before I forget, last night, when I went out with Roxal to pick up the old clothes, I found something that we can use to make our Old Joe look more real." He disappeared for a moment to drag an old Halloween mask out of the house and both Woo and Carfield were so scared that they came close to running away. "This is only the mask of an old guy." He laughed, shaking it and showing them an empty rubber bubble then instructed the crow. "You may put it on yourself and look through these two eyeholes." And ended. "This big nose will be a perfect place to hide your beak and then we will put a hat on you." Then he placed the mask on Carfield's head.

"I wish it were a little shorter." The hollow-sounding voice of Carfield came from inside the mask.

"We can shorten the neck." Alisa proposed, coming over with a pair of scissors to trim the rubber on the bottom of the mask, which now looked even more awkward with black crows' feet sticking out of the edge of the neck of the oversized mask.

"I am a walking head!!" Sang Carfield, running in a circle around the assembled company.

"O. K. You have made your entrance." Tac caught him before the crow could bring the wolf to a state of panic. "Woo, now it's your turn." He helped the wolf to dress in Nicholas's old jeans which had already been trimmed by Alisa. The waist on the jeans was too wide for Woo and the pants dropped onto the ground as soon as he took his paws off them.

"We need a piece of cord to secure the jeans." Alisa commented, looking at the disaster. She slid the ends of the cord through the back loop, putting them across Woo's shoulders, then stretched them through the side loops and finally tightened the ends into a knot at the front.

"The jeans are still a little too long, but we can fold them. I have also found a pair of human shoes, forgotten by someone at the lake, which we can use to complete his costume." She showed the party a pair of runners. Everyone looked at Woo's gray-haired feet, with his black claws sticking out from the edge of the jeans, and they agreed that it would be a good idea to cover them.

After all the actors, who were playing the roles of the different parts of the human body, had dressed, Alisa helped Tac to put on Nicholas's shirt and stand on Woo's shoulders. Carfield then landed on Tac's shoulders and put the mask over himself. To judge the realism of this strange figure, Alisa took a couple of steps back. The cat wiggled in the middle, trying to find his balance, and the rubber mask containing the crow moved up and down. Seeing this, Alisa became frightened.

"Stop moving, all of you." She ordered. The actors froze and the figure looked like a frightening old man. "Good! Now try to walk."

Woo took three hesitant steps and tripped in the shoes that were too big for him. The head, the torso and the legs all fell onto the ground, rolling around separately. Alisa could not help laughing.

"I cannot see anything under this fabric." Woo tried to justify himself.

Carfield, in turn, pulled the mask from himself to interject. "The store to which we are going is located right at the corner of the block. There is a narrow, dark alley, which separates the side of the shop from the restaurant across from it, that is only wide enough for a small garbage truck to squeeze through to pick up garbage containers .We can hide our costume behind a pile of empty wooden boxes from the antique store and dress up there. Let's give our old man a walker to support his image."

"If we use a walker then everyone will see my paw." Mused Tac.

"We can dress the figure in a light coat to hide Tac's paws inside its sleeves." Said Alisa.

"This might work." Her husband agreed.

"I have a better idea." Carfield interrupted. "My friend, Willy Holmes, has a scooter. He can walk perfectly but he prefers to drive the scooter to the store. It saves him car expenses and the ladies in the store treat him with kindness, thinking that he is disabled. We will borrow the scooter from him and then return it to him later."

"Is it easy to drive a scooter?" Asked Tac.

"Yes! Very easy! You just press a button." Carfield reassured him.

"I will look through an opening in the shirt and drive the scooter and Carfield will speak so that Woo will not require to do anything except sit quietly on the seat." Tac agreed to this plan gladly.

"Very well." Replied Woo, shaking himself out of the pants. "It looks like we have discussed everything so I can run home now?"

"One second Woo." Tac halted him. "Do not forget that we need to meet each other at midnight at my house to deliver our costume to Willie's place. Carfield, how far is Willie's home from Sunbluff Street?"

"Carfield!" Tac called again, because the crow had not listened, nor answered, and was drawing signs on the ground with his claw.

"Ahh!" Replied Carfield. "I am sorry. I was thinking about the future operation and here is my proposition. I will draw a simple plan which will show you how to get to Willie's home where I will await you and Woo. I am not fond of night flights and I think it will be easier for you to run without continually looking-out for a black crow in the dark sky. Willie keeps his scooter in the small garden house that he has turned into a storage place for the scooter, old furniture and other useless items that he should get rid of but is too lazy to do it. We can comfortably sit there and wait until the late morning when Willie retires to his bedroom for a nap, which he does regularly before having a late lunch. As soon as he starts to snore we will ride the scooter out of his driveway. Willie's home is located on Riverside, four blocks from Sunbluff. We then need to turn left and go another two blocks to reach the store. There is a fast-food cafe on the corner of the next block and its bright red sign will be a perfect checkpoint for you, Tac. When we reach the store we will need to improvise because none of us can predict the future. Agreed?"

"Agreed! Can I run now?" Woo looked at them questionably, his body already turned in the direction of his home.

"O.K." Tac laughed, watching him run off.

They met after midnight as agreed and, without hurrying, ran side by side through the sleeping forest to Murraydale, taking a highway that led them to the city without even needing to look at Carfield's drawings. Both of them carried a backpack containing clothes in preparation for tomorrow's meeting with the owner of the antique store. The wide highway was mostly empty at this time, giving the runners a chance to cover a lengthy portion of the road before the glimmering lights of an oncoming car interrupted their progress. As the car came closer, they dived under the branches of the bushes that were growing alongside the road to avoid being detected.

Finally, the midnight runners reached the outskirts of the city after one or two more interruptions by cars. Tac stopped under a street light and unrolled the homemade map in order to count the number of blocks to the next turn. "Eight blocks in a straight line, then four blocks to the left to avoid the hospital and shopping mall where we could meet late walkers. After that, we will take another twelve blocks in a straight line through the empty streets and, after again turning left, we will be at the front of Willie's home." He advised the wolf sitting next to him. Woo did not reply.He simply left.

No one stopped them with boring questions about what they were doing out at night on the street and no one spoiled their steady pace to the goal, a white wooden fence along Willie's yard where the crow had been sitting on the post waiting for them. By the time Tac and Woo had cautiously approached the brightly-illuminated corner of the street, the crow had fallen into a sleep.

"Carfield!" Whispered Tac. But even this light sound was enough to scare him and he struggled to keep his balance on the post.

"I am not sleeping!" Carfield defended himself, landing on the ground and showing the way to the storage house that was standing deep inside the yard. The light above the door welcomed the gang and the door of the shed opened without a sound when he pushed it with his shoulder. The friends entered a past hobby shop which was now just a dumpster for broken furniture, kitchen appliances, clothes and broken lamps. Tac unloaded his backpack on the old couch but Woo dropped his onto the floor, sniffing everything curiously.

"Be careful!" Carfield warned him. "Do not drop anything on the floor to reveal our presence. Usually, Willie does his shopping on a Sunday and after this he does not need the scooter until the Wednesday when he always plays cards with his friends, so we are pretty safe here." Then, addressing Tac, he remarked. "You can find clean water in the bucket under the chair and I have brought some food, but first of all let me introduce you to the beauty". Whereupon he jumped on top of something which was lovingly covered with a plastic cover and unwrapped it to expose a dark cherry-colored scooter with black wheels, chair and panel. It sparkled mysteriously in the moonlight that was coming through the small window and waited to be driven.

"How am I going to operate this since I have no idea what these buttons mean?" Cried Tac.

"Do not worry, I have seen Willie driving this machine and I can explain it to you. The starter is here and this is the steering wheel. Here is the button to stop the scooter and you need to press here to accelerate it. Finally, this is the brake pedal. Now you know where all the controls are, you can drive off!" And Carfield showed how to do this with a sliding forward motion of his wing.

"I have a bad feeling about this venture." Woo looked at the scooter with some concern.

"I can give you a driving lesson if you will help me to roll it out. This thing is actually very light and silent." The crow opened the door to allow Woo and Tac to push out the scooter.

"Pay attention to me, again." Said Carfield to the cat who was sitting in the driver's seat. "Press this button." He pointed to the starter.

"Brake!" He screamed, falling on his back when the scooter suddenly went backwards, barely missing the frightened wolf. Carfield managed to get the scooter into the proper forward gear and it immediately changed direction, rolling towards the street.

"Let me help you to do the driving, before you kill Woo." Cried the crow. "Just hold the steering wheel and keep the vehicle going straight. There is a little park, not so far from here, where you can practice until you gain some experience."

The cat was almost lying on top of the steering wheel with eyes that were wide open in panic. He managed to turn into the park by balancing on two wheels, but his present skill in maneuvering the scooter almost gave the crow a heart attack.

"Cut the speed while you're turning." Opined Instructor Carfield and, after ten minutes of careful manipulation on the pathway of Quelth Park, Tac developed some knowledge about the use of the buttons and driving technique and actually did quite well. Now he was sitting relaxed in the driver's seat but Woo was still afraid of this crazy chunk of metal and sat at a safe distance, watching the novice driver as he practiced his new-found skills.

Unfortunately, he was not the only one whose attention had been attracted to the scooter. The police car that patrolled this district was passing along the road beside the park and, by pure chance, had seen the scooter from the corner of the block. It was rolling on the pathway, brightened by moonlight and easily noticeable. Intrigued by the question of what a disabled person could be doing in the park at this time of night, the officers stopped the car and turned their heads in the direction of the scooter to follow it with their eyes.

"Kim, I think I know this scooter." Said the driver. "It belongs to Willie, an old guy who lives not far from my house, but the driver of the scooter is definitely not him. It seems to be a child dressed in a black, hooded jacket. Maybe he took Willie's scooter for a ride."

"Welson, drive to the park quickly and we will catch him." The police car then dimmed its lights and moved slowly, like a crawling cat, towards the scooter. But the mouse that it was hunting had two heads, those of Tac and Carfield, and as soon as one of them got a glimpse of the police car, Tac turned the scooter away from the road to prevent it from being cut-off by the car. He had no doubt that his slower vehicle had no chance of running away from the police and he needed to take unexpected action. The group of bushes which were standing on the carefully-trimmed grass offered him a very dangerous way to escape.

"Carfield, fly away. If they arrest me, you will easily find somebody else to replace me." Shouted Tac, as the scooter plunged into the branches. However, he did not drive through the whole grove but turned the scooter almost immediately, luckily missing some tree trunks, and jumped out of the vegetation onto the open space of the pathway instead. He tried to reach the entrance of the park before the following officers understood his intentions and resumed the chase. As he expected, they lost sight of him and spent time looking around. Returning to the pathway, they saw that the scooter had already turned onto the main road.

"Drive back to Willie's place." Cried Carfield, staying with Tac on the scooter only by a miracle.

Being in a hurry, Tac had missed the road that led to Willie's house and instead had turned into a narrow alley which was partially blocked by garbage cans that belonged to residents. It was easier for a small scooter to maneuver in the chaos of the things standing in its way than a full-sized police car. It hit a few, full plastic cans scattering garbage all over the road and onto its own windshield. Losing visibility, the driver slowed the car down and gave Tac the necessary time to go round the corner of the last back yard, reaching Willie's driveway before them.

Officers Kim and Welson left their vehicle and walked through Willie's property to look at the scooter that still had a warm engine. At this moment, Woo had decided to look for Tac at Willie's place, feeling lost without him. The wolf jumped over the fence and landed on a pop can, making a banging noise. The officers instantly reached for their guns. Tac was afraid that the policemen would shoot the wolf so he walked towards the danger with an innocent "meow" and with his tail up.

Welson, being a woman, adored cats and was the first to lower her gun. "It's a cat, Kim. Come here, kitty, kitty!" She called out. The cat, purring melodiously, brushed himself against her and caught her leg with the hook of his tail. "Kim, look inside the shed while I walk around the house." Welson, followed by Tac, searched the yard but did not find anyone.

"He must have left." Said Kim. "We need to report this incident and investigate it further to see whether or not any local kid fits the description of the suspect."

"Goodbye, kitty!" She stroked Tac before leaving.

Woo, silently appearing from behind the corner, startled Tac. "Where is the crow?"

"I'm here." Said Carfield, who had been only one step behind Tac all the time, hidden in the darkness of the corner.

"Let's put the scooter into the shed and get some sleep. I do not know about you but I will never forget this driving lesson." The cat yawned, exhausted.

The next morning Carfield had risen first to wake up his friends, when an old, but still working, clock in the corner showed that it was already eleven o'clock. They had slept together on the couch to share the warmth of each other's bodies after their busy night. Stretching well, they had eaten their breakfast which consisted of Willie's supplies hidden by Carfield in advance. "Get dressed while I go and check on Willie." He remarked. Upon his return he found Woo was wearing jeans and runners whilst Tac was dressed in a shirt accented with a pair of white doctor's gloves on his paws.

"I think this way it looks better. I put some cotton inside the fingers to make them look more real." He added proudly.

"It's safe to leave now." Murmured Carfield. "I have checked out the street to make sure that it is empty." Then he placed the mask on the top of the box and dressed it in a brown hat and glasses.

"Carfield." Moaned a surprised cat. "You have still not dropped that idea?"

"Old people like to wear black glasses. If, by chance, someone should look through their windows, they would not pay much attention to the skinny figure of an old man leaving the driveway on a cherry-black scooter, except perhaps to note that he was wearing rubber gloves and a scarf wrapped around his neck in the summer."

Old Joe reached the antique store without any interruptions but was then faced with the problem of how to open the door of the store. A kind old lady, seeing his problem and feeling sorry for him, opened the door.

"Thanks." Said Carfield, entering a small store that had a musty smell of old paper and artifacts.

"Good afternoon, how may I help you?" Asked the short, half bald, middle-aged man removing his old-fashioned glasses.

"I have an appointment with Mr. Tompkins." Carfield coughed, deliberately trying to keep the man at a distance.

"I am Jeff Tompkins." The man replied, jumping up from his chair which was placed behind the display counter. "Are you the gentleman who wants to sell the golden coins?" He queried, rubbing his hands nervously.

"Yes." The crow kicked Tac to stop his peering through the hole in the shirt and instead put the handkerchief filled with coins onto the counter.

The store owner took a magnifying glass and started to study each coin very carefully. "These are very old Roman coins that exist only in low numbers and, if they are real, it will be a very exciting discovery for collectors. Do you mind if I do a test?" He asked, in an excited voice.

"Do what you need to do!"

Mr. Tompkins transformed the counter top into a portable laboratory in a matter of minutes. After taking a small sample from a coin to process it, he congratulated his new client on being the owner of a treasure trove and carefully replaced the coins into the handkerchief with shaking hands.

"I don't have enough money to buy such a valuable collection as this and I will need to have at least a week to make several phone calls to find a buyer for your coins. However, this will not be difficult. May I take a couple of pictures of your coins to show them to potential buyers?" "Yes of course!" Stuttered Carfield.

Mr. Tompkins ran around the counter and, fussing with pictures, said to the crow. "You can telephone me later, Mr. ...?" Suddenly he stopped and said in a diffident voice. "I am sorry; I was so excited that I forgot to ask you for your name?"

"Joe." Replied Carfield, adding. "Joe Holmes." Which made Tac moan through his teeth again.

"Mr. Holmes, you can call me next Thursday and I will tell you the result of my inquiries. My commission will not empty your wallet because the amount of this sale will be high."

"Thanks, Mr. Tompkins. So far it's been a pleasure doing business with you."

"Oh, the pleasure is all mine!" The store owner promptly ran to open the door for such a special client.

Tac found that the drive back to Willie's home was more difficult than when they had first arrived here. The sidewalks were full of wandering shoppers crossing the road in front of the scooter, sometimes without even bothering to look for hazards before stepping off the pavement. "With such carelessness, I am surprised that they are still alive." Tac grumbled at the pedestrians, maneuvering between them until he reached the corner where he turned onto the almost empty, parallel street. Finally he reached the familiar shed, emotionally exhausted. After clearing out all the evidence of their presence, and hiding their clothes under the rubbish, Tac placed a blind-dog's harness upon Woo and they both sneaked through the alley deciding that, for the most part, it would be safer to go this way. In some places they crossed open streets which, of course, attracted the attention of passers-by who followed the progress of a striped-gray cat, running in the company of a large wolf-like dog, with an expression of amusement in their eyes.

The next couple of days seemed to Tac to be an endless, boring existence and he was desperate to find something to do. He went to visit Carfield, hoping that the crow had found out something about the stranger that had followed him and Galibur through the gate. But the intruder that had pushed them over the slope had disappeared without even a trace. Then he tried to continue his work on the map but could not concentrate his thoughts on it long enough to produce even an inch of it.

Alisa, having watched Tac for some time, decided to put an end to his suffering and gave him a box of raspberries, saying. "This is for Natalie. Go and visit your human family. Perhaps they might have an invasion of mice in their barn and this will give you a chance to become a hero, saving the country from starvation by protecting the wheat. Life is given to us not to wait for the next big adventure but to enjoy small events like visiting your family. Go and find this truth for yourself." She watched him disappear round the corner on his way to see the Vladners.

Tac had reached his former home without any incident. He had jumped down from the stone wall that separated Nicholas's property from that of his neighbor. Tod's first intention was to 'get that cheeky street cat', thinking that he probably intended to steal food from the dog's bowl. But, after recognizing that the imaginary thief was in fact Tac, Tod started to jump like a puppy and buried his wet nose in the long fur of Tac's neck, sniffing excitedly. "What kept you from coming to see us for so long?" He enquired, after he had finished welcoming home his old companion.

"I will tell you everything later, but first I want to put Alisa's gift in the kitchen." Replied Tac, sliding through the animal's trap door. Natalie gave Tac a good rubbing when he joined her on the couch where she was resting, covered to the waist with a warm blanket. Tac noticed with sadness that Natalie was very pale and had dark circles under her eyes. He was able to comfort her only with his loud purring and walked carefully around her swollen stomach until he had found a spot close to his Mistress where he could lie down beside her without causing her discomfort. A thought that Tac looked like a sphinx guarding her mother drifted into Lana's mind as soon as she saw them together.

"Tac!" Said Lana, lifting him up. "It's nice of you to keep mother company. How do you feel mom?" She was scared to be alone in this situation and hoped that her father would come home soon to bring her a sense of security. Trying to hide her worry and pity for her mother, she made casual conversation. "Do you need something? I saw a full basket of raspberries on the counter and I will bring you some. By the way, Mom, I've started to work in the restaurant and Maggie almost fainted upon hearing the news that I'm going to work with Stephany, who is a good girl no matter what kind of opinion Maggie has of her."

"Lana, you need to concentrate on your studies to finish school successfully." Natalie reminded Lana with concern.

"I will, mom, don't worry! I am strong." And to prove it she bent her arm. "We need money to put you in a good clinic."

Natalie didn't argue, saving her strength to keep her constant sickness hidden from her family. "Darling, you need a dress for your graduation." She said, changing the subject. "Ask Maggie to go shopping with you."

"I don't need to worry about the dress. Maggie suffered a guilt attack when I told her that I can't afford a gown with a Designer's name on it and probably would not be able to go to the Promenade. She gave me an old one that didn't fit her anymore. Do you want to see it mom?"

Natalie nodded and sat up on the couch.

Lana, jumping around like a little girl, ran into the kitchen where she had dropped her backpack and a travelling bag containing the dress. She brought what appeared to be a sunny, yellow cloud into the living room, shook the dress to straighten it and showed it off in delight to her most notorious critics, her mother and Tac.

"It needs a wash." Natalie suggested. "But the color of the fabric is good."

"I don't really like these little gatherings all over the skirt. It makes the dress look like an old lampshade." Sighed Lana, wrinkling up her nose in dislike.

"Why don't we change it?" Asked Natalie.

"Mom, it's a big job to re-do it."

"I have plenty of time and you can help me undo the stitches. I hope the gathering has been stitched without the fabric having been trimmed." Natalie lifted the first skirt to discover a second layer underneath. This was made from a slightly lighter, yellow fabric which was weaved into a gentle, silk design that started from almost nothing at the waist then flared out into a wide border at the bottom.

"Who made the decision to cover this beauty with a tasteless cover?" Exclaimed a surprised Natalie. "Daughter, we need the scissors."

Tac prudently decided to leave, to avoid being under their feet and to stay away from scissors. So he went outside to find Tod. The simple life of the farmer's family soothed his disturbed mind and diverted his attention from dragons and treasures. He thought about visiting the barn to remind the mice that he was still the cat of the house but, as soon as he had stepped outside, his intention was altered. His adventurous life presented him with another challenge, this time in the figure of Carfield, who dropped down on the ground in front of him. Tac noted that the crow's beady eyes were sparkling with excitement.

"I found out from Alisa where you were and rushed over here to bring you the news." Croaked Carfield. "Tompkins has found a buyer for the gold. Can we find a safe place to discuss the business?"

Upon hearing this, Tac immediately let go of all plans that he may have had for this Sunday, sensing that his short vacation was now over. "O.K." He said, when they were at a safe distance from the house, sitting together on the pathway that ran through the garden. "What did you find?"

Carfield looked around suspiciously to ensure that the coast was clear and then replied. "Tompkins said that he showed the pictures of the coins to several collectors, one of whom was very interested in purchasing them and said that he was ready to pay three hundred thousand dollars for each coin." Knowing nothing about their value, he queried. "Do you think that is a lot of money?"

"It's a lot of money. If I were a man I would probably be able to double this figure, but I am a cat and have no way to do it. Carfield, I think we need to accept this price. Did Tompkins say when we can get the money if we decide to accept his price?"

"He mentioned something about a cheque, but we did not discuss a specific date for us to receive it."

"Then you need to call Mr. Tompkins to tell him that his client will get the gold on condition that he pays in cash." Said Tac.

"Why do you think that we will have a problem with a cheque?" Queried Carfield, counting the distance to the house in bird steps. "We can cash it at any bank, can we not?"

Tac stopped and looked at the crow, with a critical gaze. "We cannot go to the bank, Carfield. Have you been pecking at those mad berries again and, as a result, now think that you are a man? To get the money from the bank you must have a document that verifies your identity. Do you have any? No! You cannot even prove that you are a crow."

"My black feathers and beak prove better than any document that I am a crow." He huffily replied.

"Carfield." Answered Tac, patiently. "After applying modern science to myself, even I can grow black feathers on my tail and it's not difficult for a surgeon to put a beak on the face of those who desire it." With this statement he ended the argument.

Sneaking through the trap-door into the house, they tiptoed to the kitchen without disturbing Natalie and picked up the telephone.

"Hullo, Mr. Holmes, how are you? I wanted to call you myself but I forgot to ask for your number." Said the happy voice of Mr. Tompkins on the other end. Tac rolled his eyes expressing, with this grimace, his true feelings about the very expressive personality of the store owner. Carfield turned his back on Tac, to talk into the receiver.

"I have thought about the figure that was offered to me by the potential buyer and I am prepared to sell my coins for this price if the buyer will come with cash, instead of a cheque."

"But, Mr. Holmes, six hundred thousand dollars is a lot of money to carry in a case. It will be much easier and more secure for you to receive a cheque and then put it into your bank account or, if you wish, I can transfer the money electronically directly into your account." Mr. Tompkins blustered, in a some-what surprised tone.

"I want cash!" Carfield cut him off. "And, if you want your commission, make sure that I get my money in full or the deal with fall through."

"Ok, Mr. Holmes, I'll talk to the buyer, but I must say that your request is very unusual. May I have your phone number please?"

"I will call you myself." Replied Carfield, putting the phone down.

Walking with the crow out of the house, Tac said. "We need to take care of the last problem. Tompkins is right that it is dangerous to carry money in the briefcase through the city. That is why we need two mountain eagles with strong wings to carry the money to my house. Carfield, you will need to ask Galibur to help us deliver the money to the wood."

"The Mountains are the exact places where I am going to go to now." The crow rose into the sky and turned in the direction of the peaks.

A week later, everyone who was involved in the secret operation, that Tac called "Lucky Joe", met in Fox Hall.

The cat unrolled the map on the table. "The first part of the operation will be accomplished by a group under the name "The Brotherhood of the Disability Scooter." And then he continued. "The members of this group are going to be Carfield, Woo and I. The last visit to the city was completely successful and that is why I do not think that we need to change anything in our procedures." He followed this up by recounting the short story of their bold run through the city to the rest of the group. "This time our target will be different. Not only do we need to bring something into the city but, most importantly, we need to deliver two very heavy cases from the city back into the woods, and all in broad daylight. Doing it on the ground could be very dangerous because we may be chased by the police, or the animal control which could be even worse. In this case we will all end up in cages.

This thought is the reason why I invited my friend from our previous adventures, Galibur, and his oldest son, Glidden, to be a member of the second part of our group to be named "The Delivery Birds." Our eagles will patrol above the block until Joe leaves the store and turns round the corner. As soon as he does this, the delivery group will glide down into the narrow space between the buildings, take the cases and fly with them into the woods. After Joe will be freed from the burden of his money, he will change from being a cash-cow target into that of a hardly-noticeable old goat and will be able to drive safely back to the garage. I have thought about a way to make him completely unappealing to overly-curious bystanders or to uncontrollable youngsters. In addition, Joe will have a secret weapon with him!"

A knock on the door redirected the attention of the company from the cat to the door.

"I think this is him, our secret weapon." Tac ran to open the door and greet the stranger. "Please come in, I will introduce you to the group."

"Ahh!" Everyone shuddered as soon as they saw the white and black-striped skunk.

"Do not be scared." Said Tac to his guest, after the skunk had stopped for a moment, thinking of running away. "Lady and gentlemen, let me introduce you to our secret weapon, Stewy."

"Mr. Skunk." Alisa spoke sternly. "You had better behave around my furniture."

"Now you all see how powerful this weapon is." Her husband proudly asserted. "He does not need to do anything at all to make everyone move out of his way."

"I have nothing against him." Woo lifted his beige eyebrows. "So long as he promises not to spray on me. Otherwise I will be a divorced wolf."

The shy skunk nodded and smiled.

"Take your place, Stewy." Tac offered a chair. "Tomorrow will be the day that will afford us the opportunity of having a better life. I want to make sure that everyone understands their own place in the whole act and, to accomplish this, please allow me to go over the plan again. I will start with The Brotherhood who will have Stewy, our secret weapon, as a new member, finishing up with my review of the challenge involved in getting everyone back to their homes safely." Tac was pleased that he had managed to form a fellowship with so many different members of the forest community without the arguments and mistrust associated with some past incidents between them.

The scooter shed, where Tac and company had taken refuge, was familiar to everyone but Stewy. He made a few turns around it to sniff the dusty boxes containing potatoes and onions and sneezed after examining the last one.

"Stewy, stop it!" Carfield hissed, watching Willie who was outside, limping between two lines of the tomatoes and looking for the last available red spheres.

"I know there must be more of them here." Mumbled Willie. "If only the crows haven't yet got to the tomatoes before me. No, they haven't! Good! Here they are, my last ones." The company heard his happy voice and the sound of his uneven steps turning in the direction of the house.

"That's it, Willie is going for his nap and the scooter is now ours." Carfield jumped down from the window ledge and pulled the cover from the scooter.

The Brotherhood of the Disability Scooter put on their costumes and formed the body of old Joe, who this time was dressed in one of Willie's light coats to hide Stewy under the folds. Tac, as the driver of the scooter, carefully kept a steady pace and drove through the familiar streets of Sunbluff, worrying only about the question of how to open the door of the antique store. But the door flew open before he had managed to reach it to reveal the store owner, Mr. Tompkins, anxiously awaiting their arrival.

"Mr. Holmes, I have been waiting for you, please come inside." Tompkins stepped aside, allowing space for the scooter to enter safely. He locked the door behind his client and turned the sign over so that it showed "closed."

Tac drove up to the counter, which was occupied by a stranger, presumably the buyer. He had a companion who was a big, unfriendly-looking man standing behind his back. "I have cancelled all my meetings and I hope that you will not disappoint me. You had better make sure that this transaction will be sufficiently worthwhile for me to have come here." The buyer arrogantly asserted. His voice may have been calm but the meaning behind his words was quite clear.

In response, Tac brought out a handkerchief filled with coins and put it on the table, making the man behind the countertop raise one of his eyebrows. But, when Mr. Tompkins helped to unroll this unclean piece of fabric, the old golden coins sparkled with a dull sheen and attracted the close attention of everyone.

"Yes!!" Exclaimed the collector, taking the coins from the handkerchief without worrying about its lack of cleanliness anymore. "I've dreamt about having at least one coin like this and now I am going to have two. Mr. Holmes, you've made me happy, very happy! Brad, show the cases to Mr. Holmes." This prompted the bodyguard with the expressionless face to put two briefcases on the counter-top and open them, turning each one to face Holmes. "Six hundred thousand, like we agreed."

"The coins are yours." Carfield replied quickly, feeling nervous in this strange world of humans.

Tompkins closed the first briefcase, with a shrug of his shoulders at the strangeness of the situation, and put the case on Joe's knee. "Mr. Holmes, do you mind if I take my commission in cash too?" He asked with a small, apologetic smile.

"Take what is yours."

At this, Tompkins took out some of the bank notes and handed the case back to Old Joe with the words. "Now that everyone has received what they desire, shall we have a glass of champagne?"

"Thanks, but my health does not allow me to take alcohol." Carfield coughed like an old man. "I wish you all a good day and ask you to forgive my bad manners at leaving you now."

"Oh, Mr. Holmes, there is no need to apologize, it was a pleasure doing business with you." Tompkins ran like a rubber ball to the door to open it.

Tac, following the plan, rounded the corner and drove down the alley. To save time he turned the scooter to face the street and waited until the sound of large, flapping wings alerted him that the eagles were on their way.

"Good luck to all of us." Said Galibur, taking up the first briefcase. His son, Glidden, picked up another and both eagles rose up into the sky with their burdens.

"Half of the business is now done." Tac admitted to his friends with relief. "Let's go to the shed to get rid of our clothes."

"I feel myself trapped and vulnerable in this costume." Woo agreed, in support.

When Tac drove the scooter along Sunbluff Street to return home, he was caught up in a group of slow-moving pedestrians and adjusted his speed accordingly to avoid the possibility of creating an incident.

"Nice day today." Said a voice from the side.

"Yes. Nice." Carfield was abrupt.

"But when you become old you feel the cold even on a summer's day." Continued the same voice, noticing Old Joe's coat. "I saw you leave the antique store, probably to sell something and get a bit of money."

"Sold some old junk. Did not get much for it, but it's still money." Carfield answered grumpily, hoping that the persistent older man would leave him alone.

"I wish that I had something to sell, but no such luck. It is true that I've had my good moments, a well-paid job and a wife and son, but life has stopped being good to me. The first time it hit me hard was when my son died in an accident. He had just graduated from University and had gone out to celebrate with friends. Unfortunately, on the way home, his motorbike was hit by a drunk driver and he died instantly."

"I am very sorry for your loss." Intoned Carfield, in a softer voice. The sad notes in the voice of the man, when he had talked about his son, had touched Tac's heart and he slowed the pace of the scooter to adjust to the walk of the man, interested in his story.

"The second time it finished the job, destroying my life when my wife got very sick because she was devastated by the loss of her own son. I spent all my savings and re- mortgaged our house, but everything was in vain. Cancer took her and I started to drink and then I lost my job and my home. I don't know what would have happened to me if my old friend, who was the owner of a traveling amusement park, had not taken me with him and given me a home, a job and new meaning in my life. I have been traveling with him since then, fixing everything that was broken, making some modifications to the equipment and guarding his property at night. But, two months ago, he also died and the new owner, his nephew, threw me out of my trailer, which I had occupied for ten years, onto the street. He has decided to sell the amusement park because his girlfriend does not want to travel from city to city."

"Ask how much he wants for the park!" Whispered Tac to Carfield.

"How much do you think the amusement park is worth?" Asked the crow.

"Hmm! The rides are old and not worth much, but the rest of the equipment is in good condition. Probably three to four hundred thousand dollars." He speculated. "Why are you asking about the price?" The stranger suddenly asked.

"I know somebody who may have an interest in purchasing your amusement park and, if you can give me the telephone number of the owner, then I do not mind giving it to my friend. You will probably be able to keep your job too, because my friend will need to have a good mechanic and guard."

"Are you serious?" The stranger asked, hopefully.

"I am not joking. Are you going to give me the telephone number of your new boss or not?" Demanded an irritated Carfield.

What followed were the scratching sounds of a pen and the voice of the stranger. "My name is Carl Mayer and the name of the owner of the park is Leo Festrada. This is his telephone number and the address of the current location of the park where your friend can view all the equipment of this business. Tell your friend that I really need this job."

"Do not worry, I will tell him. Goodbye and thank you, Carl."

Tac, trying to control his impatience, rolled his scooter to the corner intending to return to Willie's home. However, he had a strange feeling of agitation, familiar to many who may have experienced an unfriendly stare from someone behind them. Tac's intuition had not played a trick on him and the danger was very real. Viewing the amount of money that had changed hands in the store could affect the mind of even a relatively good person, never mind the stained and bruised consciousness of the self-same bodyguard that Old Joe had already seen in Tompkins' store.

The clean, well-paid job of a bodyguard did not change the fact that Brad's mind was a nest of ever-hungry passions that required a lot of money to feed. "For what did this living corpse with a dead face need so much money?" Thought Brad, getting more and more angry every time he thought about Old Joe. Tempting pictures of the possible life that he could lead with this money continually ran through his mind until it finally resolved into a plan to rob him. Brad knew that, without signing papers, Joe could not prove that he had ever had the money in the first place. He waited until his boss was sitting inside his car and then told him that he had left his cell phone inside the store and needed to go back to pick it up.

"We don't have much time." The new owner of the rare coins reminded him, pressed by his urgent desire to hide his treasure inside his safe. "Hurry up! The plane is waiting for me at the airport."

Brad walked quickly to mix in with the crowd, pretending that he was going to the store when in reality he was searching with his eyes for the scooter. After seeing it turn the corner, and drive towards the quiet parallel street, he quickened his pace. This was a perfect place to intercept Old Joe.

Tac received a real fright when Brad unexpectedly jumped on him from the side street. The cat was lucky that he had poor visibility through the hole in his shirt and didn't see the gun which was pointed at him, or he probably would have jumped from the scooter and left his friends without a leader.

"Where is the money, old skunk? Give it all to me or I will shoot you." Hissed Brad, disappointed that the cases had disappeared from Joe's lap.

This reminded Tac of his secret weapon, the skunk. "Stewy!!" He yelled, opening the coat. The skunk reacted immediately by turning his back to Brad and spraying the entire amount of his foul smelling, bodily liquid into his face.

The guard lost his balance, ejecting the contents of his stomach onto the concrete of the sidewalk while hearing the sound of the scooter leaving. The sudden ringing of his cell phone made him swear when the voice of his boss said. "When you find your cell phone don't forget to check this message. Brad, you are fired!"

Tac rode the scooter at top speed, almost knocking-over Lana who was walking to the Sunny Side Cafe where she had started to work not so long ago.

"Watch where you're going!" She screamed angrily.

Suddenly coming across her had scared Tac even more than Brad's attack and his hands became numb and the scooter almost hit a tree. Making two fast swerves, he managed to return the scooter to the walkway and drove even faster away from Lana. The old coat was now flapping behind him like a flag, complemented by a skunk's tail waving in the wind.

Lana stopped, looked in the direction of the strange rider, and watched as the next twist of the scooter knocked the hat from the top of his head. She ran to the spot, picked up the hat from the ground and, waving it, screamed, "Heyy!" Receiving no response, she ran after them. The scooter reached Willie's driveway, turned into it with a screeching noise and disappeared from her eyes. When Lana reached the same driveway, she saw the clothes of the old man, who had almost hit her, now strewn all over the ground. She looked in disbelief at the strange scene - a crow trying to push a bank note with his beak into the crack in the panel of the scooter.

Turning his head, Carfield discovered that he was being watched by the girl that Tac called "Mistress." He dropped the money on the steering wheel and flew into the back yard. His friends jumped over the fence, appearing for only a moment before her eyes, but even this short moment was enough time for Lana to recognize her cat.

"Tac, Tac, come here!" Called Lana, but the whole group disappeared behind the fence. It was Willie that came to Lana's call instead of Tac.

"What happened, young lady?" He asked. "Why are you screaming?"

"This scooter almost hit me, driving on a walkway at high speed. When I almost caught the speeder he turned into a crow which left this." And Lana showed Willie the thousand dollar bill lying on the steering wheel. Willie took the bank note, rubbed it in his fingers to listen to the sound and then smiled sweetly.

"Sir, you have to call the police." Said Lana, destroying the beautiful picture he had already formed in his mind of spending some of the money with his friends.

"For what, miss? I see you are unharmed and my scooter is okay."

"But the crow?" Lana reminded him.

"What crow? A creature that brings a thousand dollars is called an Angel." Joked Willie.

"Angel?" She argued, not appreciating the fact that Willie didn't appear to be taking her seriously. "But it was black!"

"Probably this Angel had seen one of your girlfriends wearing a top from a bathing suit, instead of a blouse, in a public place. On viewing this apparent impropriety he had fainted into one of those dirty puddles that the city has not bothered to fix and stained himself. But even the dirt of the road had obviously not changed his loving nature and his desire to help me, a person in need. Go girl, your boyfriend is waiting for you."

Lana only exhaled her breath in anger and turned on her heels, resolving to have a "nice talk" with Tac soon.

CHAPTER 6:

THE KINGDOM OF FIRE

The branching design of the lightning which flashed across the sky inspired Validar to raise his head in surprise and wonder when the rest of the show would arrive. Only a few seconds later, the rolling sound of thunder hit his ears and the air seemed to be filled with the fresh smell of ozone. 'This is great.' He thought, when the first drops of rain reached his face. 'Just what I needed.' The droplets of water increased in their frequency and heaviness with every passing minute, becoming stripes of water blocking out the view around him. Validar moved his horse closer to the stone mentioned by Leubarta at their meeting in Aligarna's garden, barely seeing the letters on it behind the darkness caused by the rain. Eventually, he managed to read all of the signs with arrows on them and selected the direction to the road which he wanted.

The first sign read. "Go this way and you will lose your horse." With the arrow pointing to the right. The next sign warned. "If you will go this way you will lose your life." With the arrow pointing in the direction of the middle road. The last sign promised. "Follow this road and you will lose your heart." Pointing with the arrow to the left road. 'At least I don't need to worry about this trouble.' Thought Validar, with a smile and turned his horse to the left. The sound of the rain covered an unpleasant giggle coming from behind the stone and helped its owner to remain undetected. The Prince pulled his cloak more tightly around his body and moved along the road. The open spaces on both sides of it quickly filled-in with dark masses of bushes and soon Validar found himself crossing an old forest.

'So this is the Forest of Four Seasons?' He looked at the trunks of ancient fir trees growing along the side of the road. Rain did not reach the undergrowth here, having been stopped by dense tree branches, revealing itself elsewhere by the sound of dripping water. He did not stop to light a fire to dry his wet clothes, relying on the future hospitality of Leubarta's friend to accomplish this. His horse, glad to escape the cold rain, increased his speed, probably thinking of shelter also.

To their disappointment, the forest suddenly ended and the road now meandered through what looked like a giant opening which Validar urged his steed to cross faster, expecting to find cover from the rain on the other side. When he was two thirds of the way across it, a sudden gust of wind hit his chest and almost knocked him from his saddle. He definitely heard the sound of a whistle with it. The wind was so strong that his horse, Lachin, was unable to take even a step against it and bent his neck almost to his hooves, fighting to overcome it. Validar slid down from his saddle, holding onto it and shouted through the wind. "Down, Lachin, lie down!" When the horse was lying on the ground, Validar turned his body so that he could cut through it with his shoulder and advanced through the chaos of wind and rain. The closer he was to the other side the stronger the wind became, forcing him to lower himself to the ground. Suddenly the wind stopped but, as soon as he got up, it hit him again.

It seemed to him that during this short lull he saw a figure on the other side of the road. Since he was already on the ground, he rolled off the road and crawled away to the far edge of the forest. Ultimately, he found that the farther away he was from the road the easier it became for him to move. With great difficulty he reached his destination and, hiding behind the trees, was able to return to the road but this time from the opposite side. He crept up behind the stranger, who was sitting on the stone with his back to him, without giving away his presence.

Both of the man's hands were attached to his mouth, helping him to direct the incredible power of the whistle in the direction of the road.

'So this is the source of all my troubles.' Thought Validar, angrily, hitting the stranger with the full strength of his fury. The man rolled over and, before he had a chance to get up, Validar had grabbed him by his collar and shook him like a cat who had misbehaved. "Who are you and why are you trying to hurt me?" He asked the strange man.

"I am Roswan, the whistling bandit. I am famous for blowing drunken farmers off their horses and keeping their animals like trophies, that's all. Unfortunately, now only a few horsemen come this way and I get very bored sitting on this stone, waiting for an opportunity to use my talent to create a wind with my whistle. Since you have finished off my career, by knocking out my whistling tooth, I must now go to the village to look for employment in a tavern and forget about getting free beer from my fans because no one will ever look at me with respect again." After this, he lifted up his shoulders, walked towards the rainy road and disappeared behind the curtain of rain.

Validar followed the whistler with his eyes and suddenly burst out laughing. 'After he tried to rob me, then forced me to crawl in the mud, the tramp has managed to make me feel guilty for stopping him.' Shaking his head, Validar called Lachin and continued his way along the road.

A full hour's riding later, he noticed that the forest had changed. The trees became thinner, no longer giving the same amount of protection from the weather. To his advantage, the rain had ended suddenly. The Prince mentioned that the road made a gradual turn to cut through a grass field, at which point he stopped to look around.

'It doesn't appear that this is the forest that I am seeking.' He said to himself, raising himself in the stirrups to see farther into the distance. Hearing a noise, he turned in that direction. The sound became stronger and reminded him of the cry of a child, prompting Validar to jump from his horse and run to look under the trunks of two fallen trees.

Under their limbs he noticed a safe space which was hiding a small person, but the creature who was sitting there was definitely not a child. Not the child of a man, at least, but a strange creature about four feet tall with a delicate, thin body. The color of his skin was almost gray and covered by a slightly darker design of lines that twisted and crossed each other. In some places they were outlined by a dark, red color. Narrow eyes, placed at an angle, looked at Validar with an expression of emptiness. When the warrior moved closer to the creature, it made an attempt to pull back. A tear of a gray, violet substance slid from his eye which was half covered with overhanging hair resembling dry grass. His narrow face, accented by a small triangular chin and long ears, drooped forward onto his chest. The color of his skin sparkled for a moment and then faded.

'A salamander! What's he doing here? They live in a fire?' Suddenly he understood that this one, having been removed from his natural environment, was dying in front of his eyes. He had only seconds to think before he ran to his horse and pulled a book from the saddle and quickly returned to throw it under the feet of the little creature. The dry paper of the book was ignited by one of the sparks of the fire which he immediately produced. It gave off enough energy to allow him to slide into the fire and wrap the flames around his body like a blanket. The appearance of his skin, covered with flames, regained a healthy color and his hair straightened up again with sparks of light at their ends.

The salamander showed his gratitude with one expressive look of his strangely-shaped eyes. But the book was burning fast and, to keep the flame alive, Validar added some dry branches.

"My name is Validar. I am only passing through the Forest of Four Seasons, looking for a friend of a friend of mine. I don't want to leave you alone in this condition, but I have business to take care of. Do you know of somebody here who can help you get home?"

The salamander shook his head and said wearily. "I don't know anyone in this forest and you are mistaken in thinking that this place is the Forest of Four Seasons. I was walking there to see my relatives who live in the caves at the foot of the mountain. Taking the road through the forest would have reduced the time of my trip to the cave, except that I got lost and ended up here. I went almost to the end of the road but did not find any mountains so this means that we both got lost, or somebody misplaced the signs. And, by the way, my name is SanFar."

"All right. We need to return to the stone and look for directions again. Maybe we both didn't read the arrows correctly." Validar advised.

The salamander looked at Validar sadly "Unfortunately, the long walk and the rain have undermined the strength of the fire inside of me. This small source of energy that you have given to me will prolong my life, but the outcome will be the same. I will die here."

"I can carry you on my horse but at the moment you are too hot to hold. We need to find something that can protect my horse from your heat."

"I can cool down my skin, keeping the fire only inside. This is very close to the condition that you people call falling asleep. I will be completely motion-less, but still alive."

"That will work." Responded Validar, bringing a blanket and holding it for the salamander until he had risen out of the cooling ashes.

"You have lost your property just to help me?" SanFar asked, in a sleepy voice.

"Yes! Shmata, who is the owner of the book, will probably be mad at me but saving somebody's life is worth losing a book." The skin of the salamander continued to be warm, but not hot enough to set the blanket on fire. Applying magical force, he easily tore off a small piece of the blanket and put it into his mouth, muttering. "I need to sustain my fire. I will eat it very slowly."

"Do not worry. Help yourself." Validar placed the little body comfortably in front of him on the saddle and protected his face from the wind by a fold of the blanket. After about two hours of riding, he was back at the crossroads. He stopped at the stone, looked at the signs again and thought over the mystery. 'If Leubarta has given me the right direction, and the sign has pointed towards it, where's the forest? Something is wrong with this stone or somebody has been playing games with me.' Following an angry impulse, he picked up a rock and hit the stone with it. The thin layer of a magical substance on the surface of the stone broke into small pieces, accompanied by the sound of shattering glass, to expose an original text. Validar barely had time to recover from the first surprise when he became witness to another wonder. A small figure covered with soft, dark-brown fur with horns on its head and a donkey's tail, rolled from under the vibrating stone and ran away in a zigzag pattern waving its arms in the air.

"I don't think this is funny." Validar shouted after him." Your joke almost cost someone his life."

Not in the best of moods, Validar mounted his horse and sent him in the right direction prompting SanFar to open his heavy eyelids and whisper. "When you pass a bridge over the river into the season of spring, find a pathway to the right that will bring you to the mountains." After this he again fell into a limp state, exhausted even by this small speech.

The Prince said with concern. "We need to rush, otherwise I'll lose you." He secured the barely-warm body with his hand and sent the horse bounding forward. Lachin was almost flying, barely touching the road with his hooves and sending spirals of wind behind him. All that Validar was able to see were blurred stripes of color on both sides of them. He slowed Lachin down when his ear caught a change in the sound of the flying hooves as they ran over a wooden bridge to stop on the other side of it.

The wide pathway, that started right from the end of the bridge, was easy to find. It took Validar another hour to reach the farthest end where the wide view of the hills, crowned with granite rocks, suddenly opened up a panoramic vista before him. The massive mountains standing in the background were forested along their sides. He rode in a straight line towards the closest mountain, searching with his eyes for a cave. Coming closer to the weathered rocks, he spotted a dark, wide opening. Leaving his horse at the entrance to the cave, he carried the body of the barely-alive salamander inside but, as soon as he had stepped into the darkness, a narrow line of fire appeared in front of him as a warning. He did not have time for fear so he stepped over the fire and walked inside to discover a door, made from glowing gray metal.

"Put your hand on the door and call for the fire in your heart." Said the weak voice of SanFar.

The door was hot to the touch but Validar ignored the challenge of the searing metal and did as SanFar had bid him. The door shuddered slightly and opened in the middle to reveal a veritable kingdom of fire to his amazed eyes. The fire flowed down from the walls becoming shrubs and flowers at his feet and everything around him was made from this flowing, blue-violet substance. From many vantage points around the cave, salamanders of different ages gazed at Validar with their strange, narrow eyes that didn't blink. Opening the folds of the half-burned blanket away from the face of his exhausted companion, Validar lowered him to the ground. The four biggest salamanders moved in to pick up the body of their relative. The drink from a cup, handed to him by one of the women, brought some color back into his pale skin and he started to look much better than when he had first entered the cave.

"He saved me." Said SanFar to the others, worried for the safety of his companion. "Validar sacrificed his personal, valuable property to keep me alive." He added, showing them the missing piece on the burned blanket.

"Don't worry about the blanket and the book, SanFar, they are replaceable." Interjected Validar.

Upon hearing this, the creatures exchanged understanding looks and one of them stepped forward. "I am Perrune. In your world you would call my position King. A human is not allowed to cross our threshold but a friend of my nephew is a welcome guest." The chief then showed the way to his home, followed by a group of relatives who carried the exhausted SanFar.

Validar entered the quarters of the ruler, adjacent to one of the stone walls. They were made of a milky-white substance which was slightly warm to the touch. "What is the nature of this material?" He asked.

"This is a kind of plastic. We make it from a mixture of the energy of fire and minerals and it can withstand a very high temperature."

"Yes, it's warm in here." Validar removed his cloak and leather shirt. The salamanders who were present in this room exchanged quick comments in their own language.

"Master Validar. Stay with us in our cave until tomorrow. We cannot return your destroyed things, but we can make armor for you that will not just protect you from swords and arrows but even from the fiery breath of the dragon." Perrune moved aside a curtain of fire to show Validar a room suitable for him.

"I have important business to do but, without food and sleep, it won't be long before I'll be in the same condition as SanFar. I will accept your hospitality." He was thinking that if he were to turn down this proposition, worrying about lost time, he would possibly lose new friends who might be able to help him in the future.

After all the salamanders had exited the room, leaving Validar with their King, Validar remarked. "I need to take care of my horse which I've left at the entrance."

"You can bring him inside." Perrune agreed. "I know that animals of his kind eat dry grass. We keep some of it as toys for children to burn and play with living fire. I will ask my people to bring all that they have."

By the time that Validar had returned, leading the nervous Lachin inside, a big pile of grass had been prepared for him in a secure place.

Seeing that Validar had opened his saddle bag to look for his food supplies, Perrune said. "Keep your food for another time and share our dinner."

"Do you think I can eat your food?" Asked Validar, intrigued by the idea.

"Oh yes! We had human visitors in the past who shared our food. It's just that it was a long, long time ago."

Taking his place between the dining salamanders, Validar found that the dishes were made from the same milky white plastic. He looked inside the cup standing in front of him to discover that it was almost full with a pulsating blue fire which was the same fire that was burning steadily inside the big round plate. Validar looked at Perrune with a questioning gaze.

The King smiled. "This is the energy of the fire that we collect and carefully purify. It is similar to the energy that your body produces in the process of digesting your food."

"Does it have any taste?" Queried Validar, taking the cup.

"You can create any taste that you want with your mind. Simply transmute the fire into any food that you desire. Think about the texture of it, the color and taste in your mouth. Try it!"

"It will be an interesting experiment." Laughed Validar, surrounded by the encouraging smiles of his companions at the table. He closed his eyes and concentrated, trying to follow the advice of the King. After a minute of working on this he looked inside the cup to find that, instead of fire, his cup was full of milk. Validar sipped it and lifted his eyebrows, showing that it had a good taste, whereupon the attending salamanders lifted their cups and cheered. He transferred the remaining energy into bread, cheese and honey to create a quite adequate supper.

Faysar, Perrune's wife, waited until he had finished eating and took him back to his room which contained a large bed already prepared for him. He pulled a light, but warm, blanket over himself and fell asleep right away which was natural after the very difficult day that he had just experienced. Next morning, he not only managed to clean himself using the same fire energy but also to shave with a narrow plastic knife. Feeling refreshed, Validar returned to the big room where he had had supper before. Breakfast was already on the table and Perrune and SanFar were waiting for him. The young salamander did not show any sign of sickness or fatigue and had a good appetite.

"Validar." Said SanFar, watching his new friend eating a big piece of apple pie. "I owe you my life. You could easily have walked away from me, or watched me die out of curiosity, but you did not do either! And you did not hesitate to sacrifice what little you had in your possession, so I feel obligated to do the same for you. I have a gift from my family which I want to give to you."

He put a ring on the table which had the shape of a dragon whose eyes were a ruby, red color and was swallowing its own tail.

"It's very well done." Replied Validar, taking the ring and studying it. "I can't reject something that comes from the heart." And he put the ring on his finger. It was tight at first, made probably for the smaller fingers of a salamander, but suddenly it widened and easily slid into place.

"You have fire in your heart, that's why the ring accepted you!" Remarked Perrune, pleased. "This ring is not just a beautiful toy, it has power. Whenever you are cold, put it on the ground and give it an order. You do not even need to say it, just think about it and it will be a warming fire under your feet, or a circle of angry flames around you, to protect you from attacking animals. When you do not need that anymore, give it an order to become a ring again and it will obey." Hearing this, Validar looked at the ring with greater interest.

"Is it one of the magical things that are known in the world?" He asked.

"As a matter of fact, it is. Magical things must be used from time to time by somebody who can renew their power."

"In this case I will keep it safe until you decide that it's time for me to return it." Validar looked at the King.

"I am glad that you have understood us correctly." Perrune smiled.

"I'd like to stay longer and learn more about your world but I have important business and time is pressing in on me." Admitted Validar, with a sigh.

"I understand." Perrune rose from the table and called out to a group of salamanders to bring a set of brand new armor, made to fit the Prince.

"We combine metal with plastic to make armor unbreakable and fire-proof. Try it on!" Said one of the Blacksmiths, helping Validar to put the chain mail on. It fitted perfectly.

"You can make it shorter." The master gathered a few of the sections and lifted the hem just below his waist. "Or pull it down to its full length and it will stay the way you want it."

"This is fine work." Validar admitted, touching the sections. "And it's so light."

"Plastic is a very light material and that's why it has less weight than your own armor." He remarked, also giving him a matching full-length helmet and gloves.

"And the last part of the armor!" - With these words, the master rolled out a shield from behind his helpers, too big for salamanders but the right size for Validar.

"This is really a King's present." Replied Validar, touched.

At this moment the side door flew open and Faysar came out, holding Validar's cloak. "Our women cleaned it for you." She offered it to him. "And they tried to fix it up as well as they were able, but it is still badly ripped in places so we decided to attach a lining to it to strengthen the fabric." Of course, the lining was made from the same plastic material as everything else in this world. This meant that, in the places where the fabric was missing, it glimmered like the stars in a dark, velvety sky.

"Looks like new!" Validar smiled in gratitude, but hid his concern over the practicality of this improvement. He said nothing, not wanting to upset his generous hostess.

"We also checked your horse's hooves and replaced all of his shoes."

"I hope he didn't bite anyone in gratitude." Validar laughed.

"I will escort you to the bridge." Said SanFar.

"Don't you think that it's a little early for you to go so far? You were almost dying yesterday." Validar expressed surprise.

"Who told you that I am going to walk?" Laughed SanFar. "You mount your horse and I will go and get mine."

Validar exchanged good wishes with the inhabitants of the village of fire and crossed the threshold which separated the cave from the outside world. He turned his horse towards the incoming daylight and, at that very moment, a fiery creature flew over his head in the same direction.

'What was that?' He thought, touching the sides of his horse with his heels to send him forward. The first thing that he saw outside the cave was a giant fiery Moth carrying his friend, SanFar, who was sitting between its wings. The movements of its giant wings did not copy the pattern of its smaller relative, but flowed like a valance accompanied by gentle changes of colors from pale pink to deep violet. The Moth, following the orders of the rider, came close to Validar.

"Nice horse!" Validar nodded, approvingly.

They rode together side by side, Validar on the ground and SanFar in the air. When he turned his horse onto the pathway that led to the bridge, SanFar turned to the gap between the trees to maneuver between them. Reaching the roadway first, he waited until the Moth had landed on the sand and spread its wings wide.

SanFar nodded in the direction of the Moth and said. "Now you can understand why I am only able to follow you to this point. On the way back, when you finish your business in the Forest of Four Seasons, stop at Perrune's palace and we can go back home together. My family lives in Rossana but my home looks different. We do not have the same large cave as my uncle does. The palace was built underground by Gnomes hired by my father."

"I had never seen any salamanders or Gnomes until I met you." Mused Validar. "I thought that these ancient creatures existed only in children's stories, but now nothing will surprise me. If my plans don't change I will be glad to take you home. I can't go to Rossana but I promise you a safe passage through Vanymar. If we go together then the way back will be shorter for both of us." He saluted his new friend before riding off.

Very soon Validar understood why this place was called the Forest of Four Seasons. A large part of the forest that commenced from the bridge had only started to open its spring buds on the trees. But, farther on, the forest appeared to be in the middle of summer and continued until it was replaced by the richness of the colors of autumn. After another two hours of riding, Lachin stopped on the edge of a snowfield, breathing white clouds of mist through his nostrils. Everything in front of him was covered with a white, fluffy blanket of snow.

'Hmm!' He thought. 'I've just promised SanFar that I wouldn't be surprised at anything, but now it seems that it was a good thing that we didn't make bets on it.'

As he crossed the white edge of the snow bank, the warrior noted that somebody had regularly cleaned the road by pushing the snow aside but, in the design of the footprints of the different animals which he saw in the snow, he didn't find any that looked like the steps of a man. Surprised, he eased his hold on the horse's bridle. Following his mood, Lachin changed his pace to that of a walk.

The view was worth stopping for a while. The tree branches, covered by a silvery crust of frost and snow, bent low and crossed each other to create sparkling arches on the dark green background of ferns. In some places, bushes were brightened with clusters of red berries. This place, with its brightness and whiteness, felt like an everlasting holiday. Combined together, the white, the green and the red reminded him of the happiness of his past Christmases. His worries were replaced by happy memories and, with an easy heart, he reached a big opening in the forest. There he spotted a nicely-built, two-level log house which was brightened by light coming through the windows.

Validar rode through an arched bridge across a frozen river and entered the gate of the silent front yard, moving in the direction of the porch. His attention was immediately drawn to the sound of a door being opened. Two girls, dressed in similar coats, appeared from behind the corner of the house and ran towards him. He dismounted from his horse and prepared to ask questions, but the girls were the first to speak.

"Welcome stranger!" One of them invited him to enter the cottage. The other girl took his horse into the stable that was made in the same style as the house, a log home. Validar walked in the direction of the porch, noting that it was supported by two round columns. The top of the triangular-shaped roof above the porch was decorated with two roosters made from wood. Carvings of snowflakes adorned the window ledges and the same wintry pattern enhanced the wooden door which opened up in front of him as soon as he went up the front steps, exposing a large part of the foyer to his eyes. A line of mirrors on both walls reflected the figures of two brown bears that stood upright beside the open doors. Now alert, Validar entered the cottage after the girl.

"Upstairs please." She motioned, then stepped aside and disappeared through the side door. Tall glass doors at the end of the foyer offered access to staircases that went up on both sides. Validar chose the left staircase and went upstairs. A plush carpet allowed him to enter a room silently so that he would not disturb the hard-working group in the room. A girl, in a sleeveless, long dress and a white blouse with ruffles at the wrist, was spinning wool. She pulled the woolen thread from a big cloud, secured on the top of a tall, painted wooden holder, by means of a small spindle which danced at her feet. A gray rabbit sat at her side on the small work table and reeled a thread from a skein which was held in place by a white rabbit that was sitting on the floor.

A squirrel, nervously shaking her tail, collected nuts from the table and opened them, placing an eatable part on a deep plate for her Mistress. A couple of small birds hopped around the squirrel, picking up tiny bits of nut from the table. When the assembled company noticed that a stranger had entered the room, all the helpers instantly ran away to hide under the furniture.

The girl stopped her work too and rose up from her workbench to greet him. "Welcome into my home, unexpected guest. We haven't seen anyone new in this place for a long time. Are you sure that you didn't make a mistake by coming here, despite the warning written on the stone?" She asked, with a light smile.

"I assume that you are Snodia?" Replied Validar, looking at the face of the girl and realizing the real meaning behind the smile. Snodia was a real beauty. The shape of her face was perfect, combining a porcelain-white skin with clear blue eyes which were almost like the sky on a winter's day. Charming, but a little cold.

'Too perfect!' Validar thought to himself. 'Too immaculate to be human.' The girl looked more like a Goddess who lived in her own world, separating herself from mere mortals. Her raven black, waist-long hair was supported by a thin silver tiara which confirmed his opinion about her nature even more. 'A little less perfection, a little shorter and a little more fire in her blood and she would...' Validar stopped at this thought, realizing that he was drawing a portrait of another girl with dark hair that he had once met.

Snodia had been watching the changing expressions on his face and, understanding his thoughts, she said with a smile. "I was worried for no reason. You cannot lose your heart to me because you already have somebody to keep it safe."

Surprised, but choosing to ignore her remark, Validar blurted out. "By personal circumstance I became a friend of Ulacar's Princess, Leubarta, and became a keeper of her heart's secrets. She told me that you have a gift to see any trouble in a person's thoughts by just looking at him, or her, and that you can tell whether any influence from someone else's mind is present."

"Why is this so important to you?"

"My country is balanced on the edge of an unnecessary war and I believe that somebody applied an unfriendly hand to this developing situation. I wouldn't be surprised if this evil person had planned to take advantage of both countries, Rossana and Vanymar, which have been weakened by war. I therefore want to find out who this person is, so that I can pull him out from the shadow where he is hiding into the light and, in the process, free the mind of my mother, the Queen of Vanymar, from his influence. I don't believe, Snodia, that a mother can plan to kill her own son to please someone else simply by her own desire. I just do not believe this."

"I don't possess the skill to read the minds and thoughts of people. But I will try to help you." Now she was sympathetic to his problem.

"I will be grateful to you for this." Responded Validar.

"Do you have anything that belongs to your mother or something that has been touched by her?" Snodia queried.

Validar thought for a moment and then smiled. "My mother stitched one of my buttons onto my shirt herself after she had noticed that I had lost the original. Will this work?"

The Princess nodded her head and immediately Validar put his hand under his armor and ripped the button off his shirt to hand it to her.

"Follow me." She instructed, holding the button in her hand. Thus, they left the cottage and went towards the same frozen river that Validar had crossed over to ride here not so long ago.

"You must be cold." He took off his cloak, trying to put it on Snodia.

She stopped him by saying. "The cold cannot harm me. It's true that my mother is Spring but my father is the Northern wind. This environment is normal for me."

When she had reached the icy shore she dropped the button given to her by Validar onto the ice and said. "Frozen water, take my gift and in return give to me what I need. Show me the Queen of Vanymar."

And at that moment the ice started to melt around the button until it had disappeared inside a small pool of ripples which soon calmed to form still surface, reflecting images so fast that Validar was unable to understand them. Snodia was looking at the pictures intensely and then made a pass with her hand to end the phenomenon.

"I do not know what to say to you, Validar. My water reflects all people who live in this world but I cannot find your mother. Let's go back to my home and I will try other magic to find her." Snodia and Validar then returned to the same room where they had met.

"I need my box." She said to her companions, whereupon all the animals rushed around   looking for it. Snodia took the box from them and removed a plate and a small golden apple from it. Putting the apple on the edge of the plate, she incanted. "Golden apple, roll around the silver edge of the plate and show me the Queen of Vanymar." The apple made a turn and a half around the plate and its center became a screen, showing the running water of a fast river.

"What a strange thing!" Validar exclaimed. "I have seen a picture similar to this before."

"I am sorry, Validar, but my gift cannot help you with your problem. However, I can tell you who might be able to help. You need to see my mother's older sister, Summersenda. She is married to Somme, the Master of Dreams. All people have dreams, no matter who they are, and perhaps Somme will find out what has happened to your mother by examining her dreams. Take the plate and the apple to use it to find your way, or search for your missing friend. You can send it back to me when you no longer have a use for it."

Folding the plate into a piece of fabric, Snodia continued. "To find your way to Summersenda's castle you will need to return to the stone again and this time take the middle road. Since this will take you through the desert, you will need to ensure that you have enough water to last you until the end of your journey. Ignore any pictures that you may see in front of you in glimmering heat and always stay on the road because it's extremely dangerous to walk on the sand dunes, even a few steps. Sandy dunes are a habitat for snake-like, desert creatures, freely moving under the surface and hunting everything above them. Giant spiders and sand lions also roam the dunes but, apart from them, there is a danger even more terrifying. It lives in the ruins of an abandoned city, the walls of which will appear on your way. You must cross these ruins in the daytime, when the inhabitants are hiding in the deep labyrinths below. I beg you to ignore the voice inside your head that will encourage you to explore the white stone palace which you will be able to view from the road. Just continue your way along the road and, in due course, the sandy desert will be replaced by a stony prairie which is crossed by a river.

The river feeds the forest around the Castle of Dreams. There you can take a rest and replenish your supply of water. Summersenda has a kind heart and you can rely on her hospitality. Besides, she will be happy to see a human face, a real human face, because travelers across this land are very rare. Most avoid this place, being unable to cross this dry and harsh land."

"Thank you for your gift, advice and help."

He left the house of the Snow Princess and rode towards the bridge covered by snow. 'I'm glad that there are only three roads from which to choose, otherwise I would have been circling this place forever.' He muttered to himself, returning by the same winter road that had brought him here.

For a strange reason, the way out of the winter forest became longer to traverse. He was struck by the realization that he was lost. He didn't remember the bridge made of logs now lying in front of him. Surely he would have remembered the sound of running water under it. Alert, he stopped at the edge of the ravine to look around, saving himself with this from being buried under the large fir tree that was falling upon him. Reacting instantly, he sent his horse forward to escape a trap.

Scared, Lachin jumped onto the bridge only to lose his balance on its slippery surface. The logs under his hooves rolled aside and both Validar and his horse fell into the running water below. They were lucky that the bed of the creek in this place did not have any sharp stones and the water softened their fall, saving them from serious injuries. Since Validar was busy helping Lachin to get up on his legs and keep his balance on the wet stones, he did not at first pay much attention to the sound that came from above his head. However, soon realizing that he was not alone, he quickly climbed up the side of the ravine using the thick roots of a tree as support. When his head rose above the edge of the ravine he saw a strange creature. The little devil was jumping up and down excitedly and was kicking the snow around in his pleasure at having watched Validar's fall.

Perhaps, in the eyes of someone else, the creature may have looked like a mischievous child but Validar did not view him this way. He was wet, cold and angry. So, when the creature turned at the sound of squeaking snow behind him to face Validar, the devil became scared. The expression on the Ranger's face clearly showed that he was about to shake out the brat from his brown fur. The creature jumped away, screaming, with his donkey's tail flying up in the air. He did not wait until Validar could reach him but jumped into a pile of snow on the side of the road, digging into its mass like a mole. Only a moving and waving line on the surface of the snow revealed the direction of his fearful progress.

Validar wanted to chase him, but the noise of Lachin's whinnying brought his attention back to more important things. He returned to his horse and helped Lachin to get back onto the road. They both needed fire to heat and dry themselves and, in order to do this, Validar removed the Fire Ring from his finger and put it on the ground. Obeying his order, the flames jumped from the middle of the ring then formed into a widening circle and danced in the center of it in a lovely, even pattern.

The Prince silently thanked the salamanders for their thoughtful gift and sat down close to the ring of fire to dry out his clothes which had already started to freeze. When all of his belongings had dried out, he put the cloak back on and thought about how he should extinguish the fire. Following his thoughts, the flames were sucked inside the ring and disappeared. When Validar lifted the ring from the burned circle in the snow, and put it on his finger again, it was just slightly warm.

He easily found the place where the fake road had taken him aside from the correct way.

The forest of winter changed into the forest of autumn and then the forest of summer treated Validar with ripe berries until he had reached the forest of spring where he stopped in front of the bridge. Honoring his promise, he turned off to the pathway, determined to see SanFar in his uncle's cave.

The salamanders recognized him and allowed the guest to ride to the residence of Perrune and soon a curious crowd of them had gathered along the fences to look at him. SanFar stepped from the crowd of his relatives and greeted Validar. "Did you get your answers?"

"Unfortunately I need to search farther for answers." Validar related the story of the strange forest, Snodia the winter Princess and the incident at the bridge to SanFar and his uncle.

The young salamander added his own thoughts to the conversation by saying. "At first I thought that it was only I who was the target of this strange animal, but now I have no doubt that it was actually trying to harm you for some reason. I think, my friend, that I will definitely accompany you. The creature will think twice before attacking you in a densely populated part of Vanymar, but you will have to make a considerable part of your journey through the desert where you will be on your own. Do you think that it will be a good idea to see where he is now and what he is doing?"

Following his advice, Validar then removed the plate and the apple from his pouch and, putting the apple on the edge of the plate, he ordered. "Golden apple, roll around the silver rim and show me a small creature with horns and a donkey's tail." Immediately the apple made a turn and a half on the edge of the plate and the middle of it showed a wicked face that slightly resembled a human being, except that it was covered with fine, shiny, brown fur and instead of a nose he had the snout of a pig.

"Bessa!" Exclaimed Perrune. "I know him and his Mistress. Rumor has it that she is a cruel witch. She has a habit of eating the people whom she captures, especially children."

"In that case, I need to talk to this Bessa and find the reason for his interest in me." Validar again turned his attention to the plate. "Golden apple, show me the place where he is." The image inside the plate changed, showing a panoramic view of the area surrounding Bessa. Validar tried to recognize anything familiar and eventually saw a part of the river that triggered his memory. "I know this place." He cried out. "He's on the way to Vanymar. Unfortunately, I need to go alone because the little Bessa is far ahead of me and I have to ride fast. If you were a man I could put you on my horse, but you are a salamander and would probably fry poor Lachin." Validar smiled, sadly.

"I have thought about this myself and see what I have found?" SanFar ran into the other room, leaving Validar and Perrune to exchange puzzled looks. He returned with his face beaming, wearing a smaller replica of his friend's clothing. Validar put his hand on SanFar's shoulder and found out that the fabric perfectly insulated the heat radiating from the salamander.

"And I asked Fierton to make me a small sword and a shield." The young salamander added, with a happy smile on his face.

Validar spread his hands wide and said. "I have caught myself in my own trap. I have no arguments left. Go and get your weapons and we'll leave immediately."

"Wait for a second." Said Perrune. He went to the trunk, used by his family as a seat, opened it and removed a helmet from it for SanFar which was made from a clear, crystal material and whose pointed top was crowned with a white silky tail. "Now you are both fully equipped for this dangerous adventure."

"My friend, I am saying goodbye to you against my wish to stay in your palace longer. I hope we'll see each other again." Validar put a hand on his chest and bowed to the King.

Lachin, playfully shaking his head, carried the Prince, and SanFar who was sitting behind him on the saddle, towards the end of the old stone road which had been damaged by time and was now completely neglected. The forest hid them within itself for some time but finally opened-up in front of them and released the riders into the grassy hills, kept fresh by wind, from whence they eventually reached the boundary of Vanymar.

The land here was cut into manageable-sized fields, carefully cultivated and protected by the strips of trees and bushes growing alongside them. However, Validar's way lay only along the outer edges of these fields and then turned towards a chain of mountains. His destination was a small lake lying right in the middle of the valley between them. Tracks that had been carelessly left by Bessa confirmed that they were going in the right direction. When Validar and SanFar reached the pathway that led to the lake, it was late evening. Validar dismounted his horse and walked, bending low, looking for footprints left by Bessa's large, fur-covered feet. Lachin, well-trained for situations like this, stepped almost silently. The movement of Validar's small group slowed down and very soon even he could not see anything on the ground due to the falling darkness.

"We're done for today. Let's go to the lake to allow Lachin to drink and to fill my bottle. After this, we'll need to find a spot for the night and sleep by turns until it will be bright enough to look for Bessa." Validar remarked as he remounted his horse.

A narrow pathway gradually became a wide opening where the ground was embedded with small stones which had been brought here by the creek that had disappeared a long time ago. SanFar started to fall asleep behind his back but was woken up by the hand of the Ranger shaking him. "SanFar, SanFar. Look! A falling star."

The salamander looked upwards to see a star flashing across the dark sky. It looked like a bright, moving dot of light, dragging a long tail behind it. The star did not fall to the ground but was hanging above the water, dropping beams of twilight on the lake and the landscape around it.

Bessa and The Star

"What is happening?" Whispered SanFar, bewitched by the intriguing beauty of the light.

"I don't know yet." Validar dismounted his horse and crept towards the edge of the opening to get closer to the light. He stopped, hiding behind the tree nearest to the water, and saw that the star continued to move slowly towards the shore, hanging low above the water. Its dull, blue light gradually came closer and closer until the first beam touched the sand, blazed up brightly for a moment and then dimmed down. Only, instead of seeing a star, Validar and his friend saw a figure resembling a fuzzy, human shape. Slowly it came into focus in the form of a woman's body, dressed in a very long dress adorned with narrow, long sleeves. Both of the spectators felt that the clothes were not just dressed on the figure but were an integral part of it. They did not see any line between the clothes and the skin, in just the same way as the hem of the dress did not show any feet. The girl was just floating above the ground, dragging a long train of light behind her. A long shawl, composed of a fine thread of light, draped from her shoulders and appeared to be kept up only with her bent elbows. Silence followed her until the dark figure of Bessa jumped out from somewhere and plucked at the edge of her shawl, stopping the animated star that now looked in innocent surprise at the creature that had caught her.

"I have got you!" Shouted Bessa, triumphantly. "I will give this shawl to my Mistress and she will forgive me for my failure to fulfill my task." And he pulled harder on the shawl but the star decided to protect her belonging and held onto it firmly. "No, I will bring you to her to make a good lamp-post in her yard." Bessa cried out.

No one knows how this would have ended had Validar not quietly come up behind Bessa and caught him by the horns. Surprised and scared, Bessa dropped the shawl whilst he tried to free his horns from somebody's hands, kicking the attacker with his feet. Coming to help, SanFar managed to tie his feet together with a rope and, lying on the ground like a rock, Bessa whimpered." Celebrate your dishonest victory, jumping together at a poor, unprepared demon."

"Don't pretend that you are an innocent victim. I have had enough trouble from you already." Said the Prince, firmly. Then, turning to the frightened and motionless star, he spoke to her softly. "Brightness of the night, we won't harm you nor try to capture you. The steady light of your sister moon has helped me to find my way in the darkness of the night many times and I feel obligated to secure your safety as long as you want to stay here."

"Thank you, Validar, for your kindness." He heard from the moonbeam. "Take this piece of my shawl and if you ever need help from me, or from the Moon, remove it and say. 'Mistress of the night, show your round face and brighten my way.' And she will come to you. But now I think it will be safer for me to return to the sky." With these words, the shimmering light forming her body folded into one dot and rose up to become a small star in the sky again.

"I will talk to you tomorrow." Said Validar, lifting Bessa onto his shoulder, and carrying him to the edge of the forest where he found a suitable place to camp. After he had made a fire, using the ring, Bessa started to regard him with much more respect and even fear. Validar did not enjoy seeing anyone in discomfort, so he took his promise not to escape and cut the rope binding his limbs. The creature recovered and wrapped himself into a ball like a cat and fell asleep under the constant watch of the Prince who took the first turn, smoking a pipe and listening for danger.

In the morning, SanFar, who had taken the second watch, made a pot of tea and woke up everyone with a noise. Validar called his prisoner over to him to share his breakfast. Bessa took bread with cheese but turned his face away from the tea, saying. "Ugh! Dirty water!"

When both had finished their food, Validar placed Bessa on the log. "Now, I want to know why you are trying to injure or even kill me. Look into my eyes and do not even think of lying." His straight, heavy look pinned Bessa to the spot. The hairy liar tried to make Validar pity him by putting an expression of suffering innocence on his face and crying, but it did not work. "Don't try to pretend that you do not understand my question." Validar sternly rebuked him. "You set a trap for me twice. When you mixed up the signs on the stone, I thought that it was just a tasteless joke. I thought that it was just a coincidence that I had become the subject of it but, after you had spent time faking the road and building a false bridge, I had no doubt that it was me whom you were deter-mined to kill. And now I want to know why?"

Bessa squeezed out another of his liar's tears, mumbling. "Do not harm me, I am not a killer, I am only a petty wretch. This is the specialty of my whole family. I was trained how to silently open the door of the storage area to allow the cat to damage his Mistress's cream, spread gossip around to make good friends become enemies, steal toys from children to upset them and get them to fight each other, but that's all. Killing is not my business. I told this to my Mistress but she only beat me with a broom and told me not to come back until I had done something really bad. My family kicked me out too, saying that I was just an embarrassment because I was unable to keep my employment. I was in despair and decided to try something new, relying on luck since I had heard that it is sometimes merciful to fools, but even luck turned on me. Please do not kill me for my trying!!" He begged.

Validar frowned, disgusted by the thought of tarnishing the blade of his sword with the blood of this miserable creature. "Tell me who your Mistress is and why she is attempting to kill me?"

"My Mistress is a really bad witch. She is friendly with all the evil spirits, burglars and wicked creatures of Vanymar and even abroad. Her name is Erash. She does not like living in one place for any length of time, which is why I was in a hurry to return home before she had moved her cottage to some other place. I planned to lie to her that I had seriously injured you and you were only one step away from your grave. I do not know the reason why she is so angry at you. She does not give any explanations to her servants. If I dared to question her she would probably boot me out from the warm closet." Bessa started to cry this time in genuine sorrow.

"I want you to show me the way to the house of your Mistress, so that I can ask her questions for myself."

"Do not kill my Mistress!" Cried Bessa, jumping up from the log and rolling his eyes in a pleading way. "Where will I find another place to live if you kill her?"

"I give you my word that, if she gives me answers, I will leave your Mistress alive even if I don't like the things that I may hear."

Bessa looked sadly at Validar and, seeing no other way to satisfy him, nodded in agreement. "We will find her home on a flat platform on the third mountain of the chain named Vipract."

It took them four full days of riding through the forested valley to reach the small spot on the side of the mountain which was open to the sun. A wooden log cabin, surrounded by small fields, could be seen from a distance. Validar stopped the horse and said to Lachin. "Wait for us here." And then proceeded the rest of the way to the house on foot. Bessa found a narrow pathway that took them through tall stems of corn to the open space situated between the cornfield and a huge water barrel. They stopped at the edge of the corn to look around cautiously, but only saw that hens were wandering around and pecking at something on the ground.

"Bessa, go to the house and see if anybody is at home." Validar pushed him slightly.

Bessa, adopting an uncaring attitude and posture, pulled a wild daisy from the ground and walked towards the porch waving the flower. He knocked on the door once, then twice and, receiving no answer, walked around the house to look in the window. The house was silent. He returned to Validar, not knowing what else to do and advised him. "Erash is not at home. She is sometimes absent, collecting herbs for her medicine."

"Can you open the door so that we can wait for her in her home?" Asked Validar.

"To open the door you need to say a spell, otherwise it will not open." Bessa made a sour face.

"Don't tell me that you don't know it. Go and open the door!" Replied Validar, turning Bessa towards the house.

"Okay, okay! But remember, I told you that the Mistress does not like intruders." And he walked up the stairs again, put his lips right up to the crack between the door and the wall and whispered the spell. What happened next made Validar and SanFar back off a few steps. The log cottage suddenly stood up, revealing a giant pair of chicken legs attached to its underside. It bent itself on an angle, shaking poor Bessa from the porch, and gave him a powerful kick that made him roll over his head.

Chicken Legs Log House

"Run!!" Screamed Bessa, getting up and running away himself. All the unlucky visitors started to run towards the cornfield, followed by the log house that was trying to catch Bessa to give him another kick. The log house lacked a head, at least one from a chicken, and was only capable of keeping its attention on one person at a time. Apparently it was only chasing Bessa who was running around in intricate circles like a hunted rabbit and maneuvering between objects lying on the grass at random. At the same time, the chicken legs completely ignored Validar and SanFar as if they were invisible.

Validar, understanding what was occurring, stated knowingly. "After Bessa's first unsuccessful attempt on my life, the old witch has definitely expected that her appointed assassin would sneak back into her home while she was away and instructed the headless house to keep the door closed to thwart his intentions."

"Do you think that you and I can stop running now?" Shouted SanFar between breaths.

"No, we still need Bessa. He isn't a good runner and is losing speed fast because he is getting tired. If the house can get to him it might injure him seriously."

Proving that Validar's concerns were well-founded, Bessa duly made the mistake of looking for safety behind a tall fence that simply turned out to be an enclosure. He was trapped inside it and his attempts to climb over the top of the fence were unsuccessful. The yellow feet of the log house knocked him to the ground with the flick of its three toes, as if he were a bug, and towered over him with the intention of stamping on him. However, Bessa quickly rolled aside to escape being pressed into a fluffed up mat and jumped up at one of the chicken legs, hugging onto it for dear life.

By the time that Validar and SanFar were close enough to help Bessa, the house was standing on one leg and trying to shake him off. Validar picked up a long wooden feeder for animals and shouted to him "Jump from the leg and climb the fence!" But he was too scared to make any movement other than simply hanging onto the leg, leaving the rescue team with no alternative but to pull him down by force. Seeing that SanFar had caught his legs, and they had both fallen on the grass, Validar hit the chicken leg with the feeder.

This was enough to turn the attention of the house towards him, except that Validar was not an easy target like Bessa. He pulled out his long sword showing the blade to the house. His action made the headless chicken legs stand still, indecisively. Apparently, it had no instructions from its Mistress about how to deal with warriors. It made a decision that Validar was a person who would be better left alone. So, after stumbling for a moment on its long legs, the house turned away and walked towards the big square spot of open ground that marked the place where it had been standing before the disturbance.

"Bessa, go and talk to the gray figure that is hiding behind the carriage and find out where the witch is." Ordered Validar.

Bessa, still shaking from fear, went without arguing. He brought back the news that Erash had taken her broom and had flown off to Rossana to harvest herbs and minerals for her needs.

"I know that place!" SanFar cried out. "Our women also go there to collect some minerals that make strong dyes for their clothing and hair. It will take us months to travel there on the ground, unless you agree to ride the Fire Moth. You can leave Lachin here under the care of Bessa. I don't think that the house will attack him unless Bessa tries to open the door again. Otherwise it will be better for all of us to wait for Erash here."

"I don't have the luxury of waiting here. How fast can you get your Moth?"

SanFar produced a small flame and transformed it into a spark of light that disappeared in a moment. "I have sent a message." He said, amused by Validar's puzzled face. "The Moth will be here within an hour. Meantime, let's have something to eat and take the harness off your horse. You can leave him here on the slope of the mountain."

"I will look after him. Lachin can stay in the barn for the night if you are unable to return soon." Agreed Bessa.

"Let me look at that barn." Validar prompted the whole company to go to the recently-constructed barn on the edge of the grass field. The hot aroma of freshly dried grasses and herbs wafted past their faces as soon as he had opened the door of the barn and a family of sparrows, that had made their nests on a wooden beam that held up the roof, immediately flew out through the opening. The barn served a number of purposes: it was storage for drying herbs that were tied in bunches and hung on hooks along the beam and it protected the dry grass which lay on a heap in one of the corners. It also provided shelter for the goats that grazed in the section separated by a small fence.

"Lachin do you like it here?" Validar asked his horse, as he removed the heavy saddle from his back to put it on the bench. Lachin nodded his head approvingly and tasted some grass by pulling it through the gap in the wooden fence, whilst SanFar picked up some for himself, lighting it and swallowing the fire. "Nice!" He admitted.

Validar took food from the bag, gave some to Bessa and sat on the log to eat his share. Their rest was short-lived, interrupted by the appearance of a moving spot on the sky that soon took the form of the Fire Moth. The huge insect landed on the ground, turning its antennae in different directions. Validar and SanFar took only their weapons and two pieces of rope and sat down between its large wings. The Moth lifted them into the sky without the slightest effort.

It was Validar's first flight. A picture of the land below him looked like a drawing in a children's' book but with one difference -- it was spread out as far as the eye could see. Then his attention was intrigued by the Moth's wings and the lines of dots running under its smooth and warm skin. It was choosing directions for itself, without correction from SanFar who was having a nap, lulled by the steady movement of its wings. Validar, too curious to sleep, sat on his knees and surveyed the landscape of Rossana that he had never seen before. It resembled his own country and he saw the squares of fields looking like patches on a child's clothing, the buildings in the villages separated by masses of forest, silver threads of rivers and the tiny figures of horses, cows and sheep that were walking on open grass prairies.

The edge of the sea sparkled to the left, but the Moth made a turn flying towards the line of high mountains. Very soon they reached a strange place where the tops of naked masses of rock rose up wearing dirty stripes of snow, whilst sulphurous smoke streamed through a multitude of cracks in the sides of the slopes filling the air with an acrid stench. The whole valley between these mountains looked like a land that had sustained a disaster. Pools of liquid mud boiled lazily here and there and pushed up ugly bubbles. They exploded with a splash, to drop mud at the edges of pools etched with white-orange crystals. The boiling water flew down into dry stone pans to disappear inside cracks and, from time to time, high streams of hot water jets unexpectedly shot into the sky.

The air was full of the sounds of bubbling water and the low, sighing noises of plopping mud. Yellow, green and blue strips of a crystallized substance were surrounded by patches of strange-looking plants, serving as proof that life can exist even in places like this.

As soon as Validar had stepped onto the ground he found out that it was vibrating slightly. "Is this the place where your family lives?" He asked, looking around.

"No, this land attracts terrible storms. Lightning bolts hit this valley one after another, destroying any structure that may have been built here. Only fast-growing plants survive on these rocks. The ground cannot be trusted either since it can easily collapse under your feet into deep chasms. So, be careful and watch where you step!" Answered SanFar, giving Validar one of the ropes. "If Erash is looking for plants here, we will find her behind this rocky ridge. Put on your gloves because many of these plants can be dangerous to your skin."

Validar followed the advice and started to climb up the high, almost vertical, cliff. When they had reached the top and stopped for a moment to rest, he looked down and was surprised to see a small, round lake in the middle of the lifeless stony bowl. Water in the lake was neither hot nor acidic, proven by the wide circle of green vegetation that was growing around it. Helping each other, Validar and SanFar lowered themselves downward, using cracks on the rocks as steps.

From a distance, Validar saw that a simple tent made from a piece of colorful fabric, supported by a few sticks to give shade, had been set up by the lakeside. The tent shaded a carefully-laid-out pile of plants from the sun. Erash's broom was lying on the grass but they could not see any sign of her.

"I'll go left and you take the right side." The Prince suggested. "Let's try to find her."

To his satisfaction, he found a few places where the weeds had been cut with a sharp knife without destroying the roots. Inspired by his findings, Validar moved faster but broke into a run when the ground under his feet shook rapidly, accompanied by a loud, rumbling noise. This noise, followed by a cloud of dust, marked the place where the ground had collapsed into an underground void. Moving forward, he reached the edge of the hole and looked downward. Its sides were not smooth but stuck out, making good steps for his feet. Before jumping down, he decided to check whether or not anyone had fallen into the chasm and needed help. "Hey! Is there anybody down there?" He shouted.

The weak, distant voice of an old woman answered him. "Please help me, kind Master, I can't move. My leg is probably broken."

Upon hearing her plaintive cry, he promptly took up his sword to drive the blade deep into the ground and then wrapped the rope around its hilt. Using this improvised ladder, and the protruding stone plates of the slope, he reached the bottom of the crack quickly and found an old woman lying on a platform buried under a pile of small rocks and soil almost to her waist. The matter of rescuing Erash was quite difficult because the stone plate that held her weight had already cracked and was bending down dangerously. At the same time, the angled position of the plate was the reason why Erash had not been buried under the fallen ground completely. Validar therefore removed his dagger and carefully pushed the soil down until he discovered a piece of dirty fabric.

Attempting to gently free the witch's legs, he said to her in a comforting voice. "I know that you are badly hurt, but you have to move to the edge of the platform and hold onto my shoulder because I need to have my hands free to lift both of us up to the surface."

"Take my bag first." Erash moved the leather pouch towards Validar.

"This isn't the time to worry about your magic stuff. The platform can collapse at any moment."

"Without my bag I won't move from here." The stubborn, old woman cried.

Seeing that by arguing he would gain nothing he took the bag and, after a few powerful swings, he managed to throw it out of the hole. "Are you pleased now?" He asked, holding his temper in check.

Ignoring his remark, Erash slowly moved close enough to hold on to his shoulders. At this moment the stone platform cracked completely and fell into the narrower opening below. Validar did not make any nasty comments, thinking that the woman would probably be scared enough already. He started to lift her up steadily towards the sunlight. Reaching the hilt of the sword with his hand, he pulled them both to the surface with one last move. Erash screamed from the pain and rolled away from him onto the grass.

"Why are you helping me before even checking your own scratches?" She asked, surprised, when he went down on one knee to examine her broken leg.

He replied. "I am a soldier and have become used to scratches but you, mother, really need good care. You were right, your left leg is broken and the other one is badly bruised. Those two wooden sticks that are supporting your tent will make good braces for your legs. It isn't safe to leave you here alone to wait for me in this dangerous place and, for that reason, I will carry you to the tent." Validar wiped the blade with his cloak and placed it back into its scabbard.

"I will not go without my bag. Where is it?" Erash tried to rise up on her elbows.

Prince Validar walked back to her camp, carrying the old woman and her heavy bag on his shoulder. First, he dismantled the tent and folded all the plants into the fabric for ease of transport. Then he splinted the broken leg between the wooden sticks and secured it with the rope.

He was puzzled as to why she tried to get up until she screamed. "Demon! A Demon is coming towards us!"

Validar turned in the direction of her shaking finger and saw SanFar running towards them. "This is not a Demon. This is a salamander and he is my friend. He just looks a little different."

"What happened?" Asked SanFar, breathing heavily. "I began to worry when I did not meet you on the other side of the lake and ran here. I saw that hole in the ground and thought that you were injured."

"Not me, SanFar, but this lady is. She needs our help to get home."

"Lady?" Giggled Erash, flattered by this name. "No one calls me this."

Sanfar studied her with his strange eyes for a moment and then whispered to Validar, who was collecting Erash's belongings. "Validar, I know why women become witches. It is because they have been neglected by somebody who was supposed to love them and they did not receive enough attention and kind words."

In response to this, the Prince stopped for a moment to think. "You're right. It is frustration that makes them witches."

SanFar, having a good heart, came to Erash to see if she was comfortable. "I am sorry about your injury. You can stay at my home until your leg heals."

"Thanks for your kindness, Master." She replied. "But I must go home because my servants will be lost without me."

"In that case, I feel obligated to give my place on the Moth to you, an injured woman, and I will ride your broom for you." SanFar looked with great interest at this wonder of magical technology.

"That will be very nice of you." She sighed." I'll show you how to use my broom and, after my instructions, you won't have any difficulty in operating it."

The golden thread of the day had almost ended, already embroidered into the fabric of time, and the sun was on the way to its resting place, having almost finished its job for the day. Its light was fading when the whole company left the Valley of the Streams.

The Moth was carrying Validar and Erash who was wrapped in his warm cloak. SanFar was riding the broom which kicked, from time to time, like a moody horse that sensed the presence of a stranger on its back. This challenged the patience of the salamander who was tempted by the thought of taking off his gloves to burn the broom slightly, just to show this smart bundle of twigs who was really in charge. Validar and Erash were talking, enjoying the steady flight and watching SanFar who, fighting with the broom for control, was suddenly disappearing far ahead and just as suddenly coming back.

"Erash, I don't need any payment for your rescue. Just tell me who ordered you to send Bessa to kill me?" Validar asked.

"You're using the right word when you say ordered." Erash admitted. "I was ordered to injure, and possibly kill, you by the woman who is standing in a much higher position than I in the world of magic. She has never shown her face, always hiding it behind masks. Her name is never spoken, leaving me to call her 'Mistress of the Mask.' I have a strange feeling about her. The presence of this lady always chills my blood with fear because I sense the presence of a strong, dark power around her. She might have a beautiful face but it's only a camouflage.

For me she resembles a snake that can be attractive with a colorful design on its skin but, at the same time, it can be deadly for anyone who may stand close to it. I have had her as a customer for a long time and, according to the ingredients that she buys from me, I suspect that she practices terrible and forbidden rituals. I must admit that I was too scared to refuse to give her what she wanted. Now I am glad that Bessa turned out to be useless in the business of setting traps for people. I agreed to do her bidding against you only because I thought you were a spoiled, cold-hearted snob whose time was taken up with worries only about your own self and affairs. However, a person like this would not jump into a hole to save a stranger. Now I feel sympathy towards you and that's why I want to warn you against forces that are gathering like dark rain clouds above your head.

Look at the sky, Validar. The night is presently trying to push away the day to have this world to itself. The same thing happens sometimes between powerful forces. They challenge each other, struggling for control over this world. One chooses to be the light and another becomes the darkness. The light fights battles with honor whilst the other uses any methods, good or bad, to achieve the goal. And one educates chosen people with the knowledge of natural laws and wisdom whilst the other teaches witchcraft and cruelty. For millions of years they've been battling against each other, sapping their own strength without anyone becoming victorious. Then they discovered us, whom they had overlooked.

In time, more people became involved with these entities, picking up bits of knowledge from their Masters and using it, as they grew in magical power, to become Lords over nations. Thus they spread either light or darkness to widen their individual God's habitat. I hear that hundreds of years ago our whole world was under the influence of Amer and the worshippers of Cofiat were so small in number that you could count them on the fingers of one hand. But, now, the leaders of large countries like Narymout and Ulacar, and also many small tribes, are under Cofiat's complete control and even bring him human sacrifices. Only Rossana and Vanymar, and probably some other small kingdoms, still remain loyal to Amer whom they address by different names.

Prince Validar, somehow you crossed the path of the "Mistress of the Mask" and this powerful witch looked for the right person to stab you in the back, wishing you dead before you grew strong enough to challenge her power."

"You are probably right." Reflected Validar. "Maybe it's she who has succeeded in spoiling my relationship with my mother and is trying to push Vanymar into a war with Rossana and is planning to take advantage of both countries."

"Exactly!" She agreed.

"It looks as if I need to return home to protect my mother and to prepare myself for a possible confrontation with the witch." Validar's words were primarily directed at himself.

"Validar, what can a person, even a very skilled warrior with courage in his heart, do to overcome magic? If you confront the witch then you and your supporters will die a terrible death. For your own safety, I urge you to leave this world by going far away over the sea to find a new land where you can build your own kingdom with the people that you trust."

"Do you want me to sit in my new kingdom like a coward, waiting in a cold sweat for my enemies to forget about me? When they eventually come looking for me, as they will do, what should I do then? Run farther away? Vanymar is my kingdom and my home and, if my destiny is to die young, like my father, I would rather do so protecting my land and my people."

The anger in Validar's voice made Erash go silent and the vibrations of anger were still present between them for some time, until the voice of Erash broke the tension. "Maybe you are right. Perhaps it is I who is thinking like a coward? I live by magic and it has a power over me. My whole life depends on spells and magical substances from which I draw my power. But you rely only on the strength of your body and mind and that is why magic has no power over you. It will not make you tremble in panic and oblige you to surrender. You will still look for ways to win the fight, even if the possibility of achieving victory is very small, and I know how to increase your chances of becoming the victor! Listen, warrior! At the same time as the entities, known among the small circle of Wizards as Amer and Cofiat, arrived at this place a little nation called Kickquar lived around the lake in Rossana. They found a piece of a star that had fallen from the sky and started to worship it. One day the precious rock disappeared from the temple together with the lower level priest, named Quat. By the time that the thief had been found, the artifact, which consisted mainly of unknown metal, had already been melted, purified and forged into a sword by a dwarf.

To all persons from Kickquar who blamed him, the blacksmith answered that he hadn't known the value of the metal and was simply hired to give form to it. From his point of view, it was appropriate to forge metal with such rare qualities into a sword and therefore the nation of Kickquar had no choice but to accept their relic in a new shape.

Later, the sword was stolen and, having been used in many wars, it changed hands quite often or remained hidden for many years but suddenly re-appeared from time to time. To become its true owner, the recipient needed to have a pure heart and all deeds accomplished with it needed to result from good thoughts.

If you became the owner of this rare sword, and succeeded in unleashing its power, you would be able to destroy any leader who ruled by black magic and hatred. Only this sword would be capable of killing Ashtam, the present King of Narymout and the Servant of Cofiat."

"Where can I find this sword and who is its owner right now?" Validar asked.

"I don't know." Answered Erash. "I've only heard stories about the sword from a suspicious-looking creature in a tavern in Ulacar, where I was selling ingredients for spells to more wealthy and successful wizards who didn't want to climb the mountain themselves to search for them. The other patrons of the tavern were laughing at the storyteller and he angrily left soon after. You have my assurance that, as soon as I'll be able to move, I will fly to Fahrash, the capital of Ulacar and the city of magic and wizards, to try to find the storyteller to ask him if he knows who now owns the sword."

CHAPTER 7:

THE FROG PRINCESS

V alidar was not the only man who had worries connected to a woman. He did not know about the matter of having a brother in trouble - Ruslan, the Prince of Rossana, who was also thinking about his woman while twisting a wedding band around his finger and looking into his untouched mug of beer. Ruslan felt too upset and lonely to drink so, surrendering to his mood, he moved the mug aside and got up to leave the Orchard Palace. He had built it for his wife to give her privacy by keeping the nosy and annoying servants at some distance from her. The sound of running water in a little pond in the middle of the winter garden drove him mad with the desire to crush everything around him. Without her, this palace had no purpose and neither did his life.

He left his home and walked towards the old wooden palace where many generations of Rossana's Kings had lived happily before they died, gladdening the hearts of their successors. The face of Ruslan, the youngest son of Rossana's King Farlaf, did not express gladness. One look at it made the servants and the guards change the direction of their walks to avoid crossing his path, no matter how much people respected him. He found his father in the working room which was full of war trophies and family relics. They were kept here, as reminders of both the successful and the disastrous events in the history of the country, to help the King find a correct decision for any problem that may beset him. When Ruslan entered the room, Farlaf was busy studying old scriptures.

"Ah Ruslan, come in!" He greeted him, interrupting his business.

"Father, I want to go to look for my wife. My thoughtless actions are the reasons for her leaving me. I don't know where my mind was at that moment when I did the most stupid thing that I now regret."

"Ruslan, you must always be very careful when you deal with magic, but it's too late now to give you a lecture. Instead I wish to help you, but..." And King Farlaf spread his hands, displaying helplessness.

"I will find her for myself. I cast her away and it's my business to bring her back. I am leaving immediately."

"No, son!" Farlaf came closer to put his hand on Ruslan's shoulder. "It's either the influence of your impatient heart or a sense of guilt that is pushing you to act, without thinking first. Let's leave emotions aside and think logically. From whence can this beautiful and graceful Princess come to our palace?"

"She is not from one of our own big cities because, if she had been, the rumors about her beauty and talents would have spread far and wide and would already have reached our place before I would have found her."

"You are right." Farlaf laughed. "Were she from Rossana, you would have had a step-mother a long time ago!"

"Maybe she lived with her parents on a farm somewhere, far away from the eyes of envious gossipers?" Ruslan chose to ignore his father's joke.

"Her manners, skill in dance, harp playing and her knowledge relating to household matters and of handicrafts all tell me that the girl has lived in a wealthy family." The King went on. "She has had considerable luck in the securing of good teachers and is definitely a Princess or the daughter of a nobleman. The only question is, from whence did she come? She is a blonde and her skin is too fair to be someone from a northern country where most of the people have dark skin and hair. I am glad that you don't need to search for her in such dangerous kingdoms as Narymout and Ulacar. Remind me of her name again."

"Leubarta." Said Ruslan, quietly.

"Leubarta?" Repeated Farlaf, analyzing the sound.

"Very similar to the names given to Vanadian women, but Queen Aligarna doesn't have a daughter. On the other hand, your wife could be her niece or a more distant relative. It appears that your way could lie in Vanymar." He finished, removing the map of Vanymar from a shelf.

"Vanymar?" Ruslan reflected, as he unrolled the map and let his eyes run over the names of the cities, rivers and mountains.

"This country is so close and yet so distant. So unfriendly to us." Muttered his father. "You'll need to change your name and we'll find you Vanadian clothes and armor."

"I don't care much about the fashion of my clothes but I prefer to have my sword if I need to fight for my life."

"Hmm! In this case it will be natural for you to tell everyone that you are from Berrystani, the Province that we gave to Vanymar a long time ago. Half of its population is Ross. They are still armed with grandfather's straight and heavy sword instead of the lighter and curved swords of Vanadians. In this situation, the combination of our sword with Vanadian clothes won't surprise anyone. We have a round shield somewhere in our armory that will serve you better if you intend to fight on your horse against their cavalry. We use the large, oval Rossa shield to fight on the ground."

Ruslan raised his eyes from the map. "I will follow your advice but I want to leave as soon as everything can be made ready."

To this, Farlaf nodded agreeably.

Ruslan was almost at the door when he turned and said. "And I am thinking, father, that I will really need to find a better horse."

"Look in the stables and take any horse that you want."

Ruslan expressed his gratitude with a movement of his hand and then left. To his disappointment, the choice of clothes and armor was much easier than the choosing of a horse that was suitable for his journey. He inspected all the stables around and did not find any that he liked. In the evening, when the whole family and their friends had gathered around a long table for supper, raising toasts in honor of Ruslan, he was the only one who did not drink the honey-brown, bubbling beer and laugh. He preferred to sit deep in thought.

"Ruslan, why do you deny yourself a last drink with your family before taking the long road?" Questioned Farlaf. "Don't allow heavy thoughts to make your face sad."

"I am sorry if my expression has spoiled your party, father, but I can't think about enjoying myself. It's time for me to leave and I still haven't found a horse for myself."

Ruslan's older brothers were in a humorous mood, after having partaken of a few tall mugs of beer, and had started to make jokes about the pickiness of their younger brother in his choice of a horse and a wife. But Farlaf stopped them.

"Pay no attention to the foolish words of your brothers which are fuelled by alcohol, Ruslan." Remarked an irritated King. Then, turning to his older son, Ratmir, he continued. "Put your mug aside. You've had enough to drink already. I have business for you to carry out so don't expect to sleep it off during the whole afternoon."

"What kind of business do you want me to do father? I thought you wanted me to spend every last minute being with Ruslan before he departs, because no one knows when we will see him again." Ratmir replied, sheepishly.

"Don't try to fool me, Ratmir, since I know that you would rather spend time with a wine bottle than worrying about your brother. A messenger came today from the border carrying a letter from the Steward of our province of Roslava. It was a report of sudden trouble that has arisen there. Somebody, or something - he emphasized the last word and looked at the faces of his guests to observe their reaction - has started to methodically ruin our wheat fields. No matter how many guards the Steward have sent to protect them, the fields have been found in the morning covered with strange imprints. Most of the wheat stems have been broken and trampled, but the guards have sworn that they haven't seen anyone, nor did they hear any suspicious noises coming from the wheat field. Unable to sort out this mystery the Steward, Slavver, has asked for my help. I think it's time for you, Ratmir, being the eldest son, to prove that you will make a good King of Rossana and will be capable of protecting it from any trouble. You will start your service by catching this intruder. I don't like it when somebody thinks that he can play a joke on me and get away with it." The King pronounced these last words with fervor to reflect his boiling rage.

The guests stopped laughing, eating and drinking. Some of them even stopped breathing, scared by the heavy silence that filled the room. Ratmir became sober instantly knowing that, when his father was in this mood, it would be better for him to be as far away as possible from the King. He jumped up from the bench and looked around for his servant to order him to start packing for the journey before his father might decide to hand him an even more difficult task.

Feeling pity for his brother, Ruslan rose from his seat and said. "Father, I have decided to go to Roslava to enter Vanymar from its border. Perhaps I can help Ratmir to catch the disturber of our fields and, if we ride together, it will shorten the journey to the palace of the Steward for both of us."

Farlaf didn't argue. He offered his guests a last toast and wished his sons a safe trip and success in their tasks. Without worrying too much about being polite, he kicked out the guests telling them that the party was now over because his sons had to leave their home early in the morning. The house Bailiff exchanged meaningful looks with his helpers, knowing that all of them would probably not be able to get any sleep until the next day, due to the work involved in preparing everything for the sudden trip.

Time is indifferent to everything that exists within it and it was now approaching midnight, regardless of the fact that Ruslan had still not been able to relax. He was sitting at the table and looking at the circle of light drawn by the flame of the lonely candle attached to a flat holder. His attention was focused on a tiny, golden crown which lay in front of him that had been specially made for his wife, the Princess Frog, as everyone called her. Without making any effort, his memory roved back in time to that day, a year ago, when his father had called all three sons to his working room.

"I don't expect anything good to come from this call." Moaned Ratibor, the middle brother. "Did you do something to anger father again?" He asked Ruslan. "I suppose he has decided not to waste his time by yelling at each of us separately, but to finish his parental duty all at once by gathering us here together?"

"I arrived back home only two days ago after an inspection of our border forts at sea." Replied Ruslan. "You were supposed to carry out this task, Ratibor, except that you were so sick after partying with your friends that we needed to call a healer to your bedside! I had no time to do anything improper except hunt ducks with my dog. But I don't think that that is the reason why father has decided to discipline all of us. Rather, he has discovered that you, Ratmir, have again started to drink and I must say that this would have been very easy for him to discover. You reek of alcohol as if you were a beer barrel!"

"Really?" Retorted his older brother, bouncing up like a rubber ball. "I will shake my money back from the old witch who told me that her brew would kill the smell completely. I turned down a nice glass of wine from a keg delivered to our palace from overseas because of her, thinking that her medicine would work only on beer."

Ruslan only shook his head, disapprovingly.

The brothers stopped for a second, looking at the door and arguing who would enter first. Ruslan, as usual, was the one who finally opened the door, taking their father's anger upon himself.

Farlaf dismissed the first spark of irritation that he felt as he viewed the familiar formation of his sons entering the room, blaming himself for this. He should have married again, after he had finished mourning for his wife, and given the children at least a stepmother to look after them.

So the King examined his sons critically. His eldest son, Ratmir, had become a drinker. His middle son, Ratibor, was getting fatter and fatter, better known for his victories in eating contests rather than for his prowess on the battlefield. And the youngest, Ruslan, probably had no character at all because he always allowed his brothers to use him for their own benefit. But this was not the real reason for the King's anger. When his wife had died, twenty years ago, her bitterest sorrow had been that she would never be able to see any of her grandchildren and his own worries now mirrored hers as he mumbled under his breath. "If I don't do something about this, then probably I won't see them for myself either."

"I have called you all together to tell you my Will." The King's voice was rough. "I am tired of waiting for you to grow up and start your adult life by marrying a nice girl and having a family. This palace has forgotten what children's laughter sounds like! I want to see my grandchildren running around these empty corridors, playing like you did when you were children. All three of you are irresponsible, ignoring your duty to give Rossana the next generation of Royal blood. Since you appear to think that it's not as important as your parties, or your passion for hunting, and you cannot find the time to find a wife, I have decided to do it for you. By the use of an old Rossana custom, the wife will be chosen by the will of God."

The brothers looked at each other with the same question arising in their minds. "Is he joking?"

"Father, this custom hasn't been used in Rossana for a long time." Ruslan hoped that he could turn the trouble away from them.

"I know, and I have therefore decided that it's time to bring it back. Tomorrow morning I'll wait for you in the courtyard. Don't forget to bring your bows and arrows and I won't accept any excuses. Now you are free to leave." Farlaf's tone of voice did not allow for any disagreement.

Early in the morning, Ruslan waited patiently for his brothers, kicking stones with the toe of his boot and hiding a smile. Having to get up at an early hour was punishment enough in itself for his brother, Ratmir, because he liked to stay in bed almost to noon.

The King eventually became chilled by the fresh morning wind that blew inward from the river and became indignant at the absence of his two older sons, saying angrily. "Where are these loafers? I don't intend to wait for them until lunch time!" He wanted to go and wake them up himself but the figures of both Princes, straightening their clothes on the way, appeared at the distant corner of the yard to the relief of the guards and servants who now ran behind their masters carrying their bows and arrows.

"Finally their Highness's have decided to make us happy with their presence!" Remarked Farlaf, sarcastically.

"Good morning father." Mumbled both of them, bowing clumsily.

"Ratmir, you are the eldest and the future King, so you will shoot your arrow first."

Ratmir took a bow and, placing an arrow in the string, he pulled it back to his limit. His position as the first archer gave him the advantage over the rest of his brothers in choosing the direction in which to shoot.

The palace stood on the top of a hill, with its massive stone body rising above the city, proudly displaying greatness and wealth. Arislad, the capital of Rossana, was built around the palace taking upon itself the blows of attacks during numerous wars with the Narymout tribes. It had been destroyed many times and then rebuilt again until it had taken the present shape of an almost unreachable and impregnable fortress. The moat that surrounded the castle had been built in the time of Farlaf's grandfather and had turned the palace into an island. Shortly before his death, the old King had completed the second channel and then filled it in with water, which made it almost impossible for enemies to reach the palace that had become the stone heart of Arislad. King Farlaf had just added some décor to the buildings, to give the palace some beauty, and built stone galleries and gardens which he filled with the most beautiful trees, shrubs and flowers that he could find in Rossana as a present to his wife who was in love with nature.

Thus, choosing to shoot with the wind, Ratmir sent his arrow in the direction of a rich part of the city knowing that, according to the old tradition of the Ross's, he must take as a wife a girl from the house in which his arrow would land. The citizens, warned by the flag raised in the sky, had hidden inside their homes and waited until it would be safe to search for the arrow to report its location to the guards. It did not take a lot of time to discover that Ratmir's arrow had hit the window ledge of one of Farlaf's Councilors. The daughter of the Councilor then duly wrapped her trophy in a silk scarf, as proof of her engagement with the King's older son, Ratmir.

Ratibor was told to choose any other direction in which to shoot his arrow. He turned to the right and took his shot to find out what was in store for him. His arrow hit the yard of the house of a rich merchant and his daughter pulled the arrow from the soil and brought it to her father.

Ruslan did not have any choice but to shoot his arrow to the left. When he did this, a strange thing happened. A sudden strong wind lifted his arrow and carried it away from the town. Knowing that Ruslan could not try a second shot until it was found, everyone searched for it, but without success. Realizing that to wait any longer would just be a waste of time, Ruslan said to his father. "I need to take my horse and ride from the city to find my arrow."

"Take all the guards with you since it will be difficult to find the arrow in the grass. We will probably even need to get volunteers to help in the search. I think that some kind of a reward will persuade them to participate gladly." The King interjected, dryly.

"Father, I'll do it alone." Cried Ruslan. "Something tells me that it was not just the wind that took my arrow and this means that the task is mine, solely. Otherwise, the initiator of this situation will not allow the arrow to be found."

"Then do what you think is right." He agreed.

Using his permission, Ruslan rode out of the city and stopped beside the last gate. 'This wind blew at the will of somebody, of that I am sure.' He thought.

"Lead me." He shouted, removing a feather from his pocket and throwing it into the air. His suspicion was correct. Instead of dropping to the ground, the feather was lifted softly and carried along the road, farther and farther from Arislad. Ruslan followed it through open grass fields, up hills, over the river and finally entered the forest on the opposite side of it. There was no movement in the air between the trees but the feather continued to fly as if propelled by some miracle. Eventually, Ruslan saw an oval lake surrounded by white and yellow Lilies. The feather dropped into the water and sank, its task fulfilled. He looked around and spotted the white, feathery end of his arrow rising up from the mass of leaves and flowers. The water in this place barely reached up to his waist, but masses of stems attached to the bottom of the lake made his walk towards the arrow a very slow one. The view from a closer distance revealed to Ruslan that his arrow was not alone on the pierced leaf. A big frog was sitting next to it, looking at Ruslan without fear. When he stretched out a hand to remove the arrow, to his surprise the frog caught the narrow body of the arrow in a green hand, claiming ownership of it.

The Prince stopped, puzzled by the meaning of it, and at this time the frog said in human language. "Your arrow has hit my home and, according to the rule, you must take me as your wife."

Not even a shade of the thought to cheat the old tradition appeared in Ruslan's mind. If his fate was to marry a frog, so be it! He therefore removed a handkerchief from his pocket, wet it in the water and wrapped the frog in it. He decided to leave it to his father to make the decision upon this matter.

However, Ruslan's choice to take the frog from the pond, where she had lived peacefully until their meeting, apparently did not fit in with the plans of some force that had kept her there. As soon as he was on dry ground again, part of the soil in front of him rose up like a terrifying giant with no face. Water plants grew from the skin on four muscular arms of the Monster whilst a black paste of swamp mud slid down his body and gave off the unpleasant smell of decay. It attacked Ruslan and tried to knock him down with the hit of a fist before he could recover from his surprise. The Prince reacted instantly, removing the heavy sword and cutting off the hand. A new one grew out from the fresh cut like a bubble of swamp gas and took the shape of a hand. Ruslan backed-up, having the feeling that the fight with this creature would not be an easy one to win. He watched every move of his opponent, trying to predict its next attack. The creature, in its turn, chose to change its tactics. It tried to hit Ruslan in the chest with its heavy fist and, at the same time, grab him with the second one. But Ruslan twisted his body to escape the trap and cut off its hands. This fat piece of swamp mud, apparently not feeling any pain, grew another hand with which it attacked his face but he managed to put his forearm up to ward off the blow. The impact sent him in the direction of the lake, revealing the great strength of the creature. The surface of the water, covered with soft vegetation, eased his fall but forced him to drop his sword into the lake.

Retrieval of Ruslan's Arrow

The creature did not bother to wait until his hands were able to grow back completely and again moved clumsily towards the enemy, making the ground shake in the process. Ruslan desperately searched for his sword under the carpet of plants, while keeping his eyes on the creature. Finally, he found the missing sword and raised it to block the next attack. In his peripheral vision he caught some movement in the shrubs and now expected a simultaneous attack from both directions. Concerned, he decided to reach the dry surface where he could move more easily, but the creature continued to push him even deeper into the water, careless of the fact that his opponent could cut off all of his hands at will.

The situation changed to the warrior's advantage only when a burning torch suddenly flew in his direction, thrown from the bushes. The Prince managed to catch the handle of the torch before it touched the surface of the water. Following an impulse, he thrust the burning torch into the place where the creature's face was supposed to be. It backed off immediately, followed by an excited Ruslan who realized that he had found a weakness in his enemy after all. The creature made a sudden jump to the side, breaking its body against the shore with a splash of dirt. Ruslan stopped, puzzled, and looked under his feet for the enemy but a rustle in the bushes made him turn to see a line of flaming torches stuck into the ground. 'Somebody must be trying to stop me from escaping into the forest.' He thought to himself.

A dirty line of wet plants, that grew between the lake and the forest, bubbled and moved slowly, gathering into a pile. Spinning fast, a clump of soil, mixed with vegetation and the branches of broken bushes, transformed into an even more repulsive form. This had a reptilian body with heads placed on two long necks. When Ruslan slowly retreated to the line of the torches in order to take one of them, the monster decided that the man must be scared and started to follow him to catch the running prey. It stretched out its long neck to bite him, but he cut off one of its heads with his sword.

The swaying, headless neck showed a large swelling coming out from the cut. Suddenly two heads jumped out of it, wailing loudly, and then all three attacked Ruslan in an effort to wear him out. But the Prince launched an attack and cut off another one. The creature made a sudden turn and the torch entered the place where the head was missing, burning the cut. It continued to attack him without showing any loss of strength but this time his body remained unaltered.

Ruslan was now very tired and his clothes had been ripped and stained with blood in many places. Using his last strength he chopped and burned off all of its heads, leaving the body to fall to the ground where it disintegrated into pieces.

Several small figures, with wide feet, shuffled forward and approached him, ignoring the alert and aggressive posture of his body. One of them spoke in an unusually-vibrating voice. "We don't intend to fight you. We are part of the Kickquar Nation and we have been sent here to serve the frog that you have hidden in your pocket. We want to warn you that if you take her from this lake you will involve yourself in many severe challenges because she is not a normal frog."

"I know!" Ruslan wiped his forehead with his sleeve "She can speak my language."

"You don't understand, warrior!" The little man continued. "This frog is not some pet that's trained to do unusual tricks, but a victim of terrible circumstances that can affect everyone who is connected to her. Leave the frog here under our care, then forget about everything that has happened and you will live a peaceful and happy life. Take her and the chain of trouble which you are presently experiencing will continue to follow you."

"I will take that chance."

At this, the man stepped aside to give way to him, seeing that the stubbornness of Man was unyielding. "Keep in secret that your frog can speak and perhaps adversity may pass you by." He added, thoughtfully.

Ruslan, carrying the Frog Princess in his pocket, reached the palace late and postponed his conversation with his father until the next day. He made his future wife comfortable in a big wooden plate, which he had filled with water surrounded by Lilies, before he retired for the night.

The next day he carefully wrapped the frog in the same handkerchief and again put her in his pocket to carry her to his father's quarters. When he entered the large hall it was full of people of differing status. Nobles, with self-importance showing on their faces, sat separately from merchants. Common people whispered excitedly, pleased by the unusual invitation to the palace. The Royal family gathered on both sides of the King's chair which was placed on a special podium. Two girls, each with an arrow on their lap, sat separately from the crowd with downcast eyes, clearly not yet accustomed to being the center of attention of so many people.

"Ruslan, I see you have found your arrow. You can repeat your shot right now because I want to have all three weddings on the same day." The king got up from his chair, expecting his son to follow him outside.

"Father, it is impossible for me to make a second shot since I have already found my destiny." Ruslan had a strange, sad smile upon his face. He proceeded to tell everyone the story of how he had found the arrow and then removed the handkerchief and showed the frog to everyone.

Farlaf was very upset by this unexpected problem. He turned to his Councilors to look for advice. Knowledgeable in the rules and regulations of the law, the King's advisors searched in their books for a way to cancel the undesired result of Ruslan's shot, but were unable to find any honest way. The code of behavior was simple. The Word is the Word and must be kept.

Farlaf felt upset for a little while, blaming himself for the fact that his youngest son must now marry a frog, but found an excuse not to worry about Ruslan's marriage choice. The King reminded himself that Ruslan was the third son and had no chance of becoming the King and, even if he never had any children, this would not hurt the interests of the kingdom too much. The second thought that came to him was that the frog would not live for many years and this made him forget his sadness completely.

All three weddings therefore took place on the same day in Arislad's most beautiful church. The brides, dressed in beautiful, flowing gowns, stood beside their grooms who held burning candles. The frog sat upon a small pillow carried by a boy who stood beside Ruslan.

No one in the church dared to laugh, seeing the tight muscles of the face of the third Prince and feeling sorry for him. No one would dare to make jokes about this bride at the wedding reception, with the exception of his own brothers.

After having been served one or two glasses of wine at the wedding feast, they started to tease Ruslan by asking him where he had found such a beautiful bride and whether he had searched the whole swamp for such a beauty. "Bring your bride to the wedding table. We would like to dance with her?" They pestered him.

Unable to stand this anymore, Ruslan left with a heavy heart. When he arrived at his cottage, which was set apart from the palace, Ruslan found his wifely frog awaiting him with a simple supper placed on the table in front of him.

Seeing his sad and tired face, she pleaded. "Let the hard feelings go away and don't hold onto anger against your brothers. Eat the supper that I have made for you and go to sleep. By the morning your sad thoughts will be transformed into happy ones."

Ruslan, who had eaten nothing at the wedding table, suddenly felt very hungry. He tried the food and found it very tasty. 'At least my wife is a good cook.' He comforted himself, before falling sleep. He did not see that the frog had removed her skin and had turned into a girl who was so beautiful that, if he were to compare her with any other woman, he would not be able to find any better.

The girl cleaned the dishes, folded Ruslan's clothes, tucked a blanket around him and left the room, taking her skin with her. She cut five roses in the garden and put them into a vase on the table. What remained of the night she used to fix his clothes and sorted things in their home into their proper places. At dawn, when the first bird tried out its voice to greet a new day with a song, she donned her skin and turned into a frog again. The Prince woke up in the morning to find his home clean and beautifully arranged. A yawning servant girl served breakfast to him. "Did you cook?" Ruslan asked her.

"No Master, I only heated it for you."

'This arrow has transformed my whole life.' Thought Ruslan, looking at the changes around him. After a week, he admitted to himself that his life had become more comfortable and, after a month had passed, he found that he enjoyed being married to his wife, the frog, and did not feel himself a victim of unfair circumstances at all.

One day, Farlaf decided to find out which of his daughters-in-law was the best at baking. He therefore called his sons together and told them that he wanted his new daughters to bake bread for the next day's breakfast and that whoever's bread he would find the best would receive a gift from him - a ring inset with a ruby. Ruslan came home with concern written on his face. How would he be able to tell his frog about his father's request and how would this small creature be able to bake bread for his father's breakfast?

Sensing that something unpleasant had happened to her husband, the frog jumped onto the table in front of him. Concerned, she asked. "What has happened, Ruslan, why are you so quiet?" He did not want to upset her, by telling her the truth, but she would not leave him alone until she had pulled out of him everything about the baking contest.

"That's it?" Laughed the frog. "Do not worry; I will not let your brothers humiliate you again. Go to sleep, my husband, and by the morning all your worries will have faded away."

"You are probably right. I had better go to sleep." Ruslan replied, suddenly feeling very sleepy.

As soon as he had lain down on the bed and had fallen asleep, the frog removed her skin and turned into a girl again. She straightened Ruslan's blanket and kissed his forehead and then went off into the kitchen. 'Where is my cookery book?' She mused, touching her lips with a finger. 'Ahh! I know.' Then, with a laugh, she ran to the table where a big, leather-covered book appeared out of nowhere and dropped onto the table, opening itself to the correct page. The girl became silent for a moment, reading the recipes, then thought. 'It's not so difficult. I think I'll add some walnuts or hazelnuts to the original recipe.'

By the time that she had finished reading, all the ingredients that she needed stood on the table. They had appeared in the same way as the book had, completely out of nowhere. 'And I think I'll need a helper.' She continued, after inspecting all the supplies that were laid out in front of her. Responding to a sudden knock at the door, she opened it to find the white heron that she expected.

"Come in Mr. Hin-U. I need to make bread for the King but I must complete my task by morning and that is why I need your help."

The heron lifted his skinny leg and walked into her kitchen. He looked at all the ingredients for making bread then bent his head and made a crackling noise of impatience with his long beak. The girl ran to the bench, where she had prepared a pot for the dough, while Mr. Hin-U mixed in it all of the necessary ingredients, working his legs like a mixer. When he had finished, the girl wrapped the pot containing the dough in one of Ruslan's old winter coats to keep it warm and cleaned the table for the most important part of the work that would make the bread light and fluffy. 'The dough requires to be kneaded for one hour at least and no one can do it better than Mr. Hin-U.' She thought.

While the heron was busy at his task, the Princess frog decided to look at the old clay stove that had not been used for a long time. But what she saw inside of it made her wrinkle her pretty nose in disgust. The lazy servant, using the excuse that Ruslan usually ate at his father's table, had not cleaned the inside of the stove and had allowed a family of spiders to build a personal castle inside of it. While Mr. Hin-U worked hard at the table, the girl cleaned the stove and allowed the heron to put the prepared dough onto the wooden paddle, leaving the final touch to herself. She made decorations on the top of the bread in the shape of two pigeons surrounded by a border of hazel nuts and leaves and continued by sprinkling crushed nuts on the wings and tails of the pigeons. To finish it all off, she dabbed egg wash on the bread to make it shine. Mr. Hin-U helped her to put the bread in the stove and, with a funny bow of his crooked neck, retired.

When Ruslan woke up in the morning he found that a white cotton towel had been stretched on the table with a big, round loaf lying on top of it, filling the room with the smell of freshly-baked bread that made his mouth water. "Thanks." He said to the frog, gladly, and took the bread to the palace where King Farlaf had been waiting to try out the different breads from his daughters-in-law in order to pick a winner.

The King tried the bread from Ratmir's wife first. This girl had never done anything with her hands and was too lazy to knead the dough thoroughly. Therefore, her bread was flat and so hard that Farlaf could not even cut off a piece of it. "Give it to the pigs." He ordered, tired of stabbing it with a knife.

The second daughter-in-law liked to look at herself in the mirror and forgot to watch her bread, made from whole wheat, which had burned to a dark brown color.

"Maybe the servants can eat it?" Suggested King Farlaf, after looking at the bread.

"Show me what you've brought to me." He turned to Ruslan, disappointed by everything he had seen thus far. "According to its size, it appears that you're carrying a rock." He continued, sarcastically.

Prince Ruslan put the bread in front of him and opened the folds of the towel. A tasty smell filled the air with the fragrance of a harvest, reminding everyone of the time when carriages with new wheat would frequently arrive from distant provinces to fill the King's storage bins. Farlaf closed his eyes, nodding as if in tune with the singing inside his head, and smiled. Everyone who was in the Hall moved closer, studying the artistic work on the top of the bread with great curiosity. Farlaf lifted the loaf. "Light as a feather. I can't force myself to cut this beauty." He pinched a piece from the side and bit into it, murmuring with pleasure. "Melts in the mouth. Everyone must try it." And his eyes filled with the glint of happiness. As many hands stretched out to take a piece, he pulled the bread to himself and removed the pigeons, saying. "The birds are mine, the rest you can eat."

Of course, Ruslan tried it too, admitting that his father was right. He had never tasted a better loaf of bread. His brothers tried to spoil the moment, saying that he had simply bought it from somebody, but Farlaf shooed them away and happily granted the ring to the frog.

'What is my wife, a frog, going to do with it?' Ruslan asked himself and, instead of the ring, he gave her a tiny crown which was decorated with diamonds attached to the ends of its points. She wore it on her head from that moment on, giving the servants a reason to call her the Princess Frog, first as a joke, but shortly afterwards it became her name. The second challenge came into the life of the Princess Frog after Farlaf had bought a rare, wool carpet from a traveling merchant. It had a bright design on it and it looked much more beautiful than the simple, striped rugs that Rossana's women had made for the floor.

"Let's see how skilled my new daughters are at knitting?" Said the King, ordering the young wives to each make a carpet for him in three weeks. Ruslan came home, upset, and did not even want to eat.

"What happened this time to upset you?" The frog asked him with concern. "You're wearing a stranger's face, instead of that of my Ruslan. I hardly recognize you."

"Father found a task for you even more difficult than the previous one." He replied, telling her everything that had happened in the palace.

"Don't worry. Leave it to me! It will be difficult to make a nice carpet in three weeks, but it's possible. Tell the servants to empty the small room at the back of the palace and transform it into my working room. Please order them not to enter it at any time that I may be working in there."

Every night, as soon as everyone had retired to bed, she walked into her working room, removed her frog's skin and worked on the carpet. Only mice were allowed to help her, selecting wool by its color and cutting it into pieces with which she could work comfortably. At the end of the last week, the carpet was ready. The Princess Frog rolled it up into a tight roll and in the morning she presented it to her husband. It was so heavy that Ruslan needed to call for the assistance of his servants to carry it. Working together, they managed to deliver the carpet into the palace for the King's inspection.

This time, the brothers had decided not to humiliate themselves and their wives and had simply bought two carpets, displaying them proudly. However, one thing that they did not know was that the carpets had labels on the back of them on which was stated the name of the craftsman who had made it. So, when somebody from the Court turned over a corner of it, this fact was easily discovered. When the fraud had been pointed out to King Farlaf, he became so angry that he chased the tricksters to the end of the hall, leaving them only in order to accost Ruslan. "I didn't know that I have been giving you so much money that you could afford to buy such a large carpet." He upbraided him.

"I didn't buy it. My wife worked on it for all of the last three weeks and finished it only last night." The Prince replied.

"I will find out whether or not you are being honest. Flip it around so that I can look at its underside." Ordered Farlaf. The servants unrolled Ruslan's carpet to show the reverse side and everyone could see the cotton base of it. Farlaf personally searched for the name but found none. His anger subsided and, in a calmer voice, he ordered. "Turn over the carpet so that we can see its face."

When, by the mutual effort of many people, the large carpet had been turned over, all the spectators gasped in astonishment. It revealed a picture of Arislad, including the palace on the top of the hill, surrounded by channels and bridges and bordered by a graphic Rossa pattern that was customarily used for embroidery on shirts, but not on carpets, since it was too difficult to reproduce on any carpet. The design on the border proved better than anything else that it was a local product, prompting the King to sigh. "I owe you an apology but you can see that I have had good reason to be suspicious."

Nodding in the direction of his brothers, Ruslan lifted an eyebrow and suggested. "You don't need to be angry with them, father. Now you can decorate the walls of the palace without spending your own money on it." Everyone around him laughed at this remark, including the King.

"I can now see that you have found the best wife after all." King Farlaf looked at the Prince.

"I agree, father. I just wish that she was human. All my other wishes have already been fulfilled. But please don't hold another competitive contest for a wife. You can see for yourself that it will bring nothing but embarrassment to all our family. Please accept your children for what they are."

"Ruslan, I promise you that this will be the last time. Let's go and have breakfast together and forget about the lazy women."

"Hey! Somebody! Tell my sons that I want them to join us and that they may also bring their wives. Maybe they'll be better at giving me grandchildren than in being at work in the household." He cried out to the servants, laughing loudly.

Almost a year had passed peacefully and the King had kept his word and did not disturb his sons with new ventures but, when the time came close to the anniversary of his sons' weddings, Farlaf started to talk about a big celebration. Ruslan became quiet and sad again, expecting that new trouble would accompany this event.

"Don't worry about the party, Ruslan." His wife tried to soothe his feelings.

"How can I not worry about it?" He answered. "I know my brothers and, as soon as they get drunk, their tongues will become loose and even fear of angering my father won't stop them from spoiling my evening by making jokes about you."

The Princess Frog thought for a moment and then said. "When you sit at the table, and your brothers ask you about me, just say that I will arrive later. Then, after you hear a noise like a cry of thunder, just say. 'Don't worry. It's my frog arriving in a box.' And leave the rest to me." Ruslan agreed to this and when his brothers asked why he had not brought his frog wife, he assured them that she would come later.

"She probably has had trouble choosing her dress." Ratmir remarked nastily.

The Prince ignored him, sitting closer to his father to avoid confrontation with his brothers. Closer to midnight a sudden sound of thunder scared the guests. Ruslan got up and said. "Please sit back in your seats; it's only my frog arriving in a box."

Everyone concentrated their attention on the door, waiting for what was about to happen next. A knock obliged the guards on both sides of the door to open it wide, allowing a girl of rare beauty to enter. Without fear or shyness, she proceeded to the King's table and sat next to Ruslan, showed him the ring that Farlaf had given to her as a prize for the baking contest and placed in his hand the gift that he had given to her, a tiny crown. She took a glass of sweet red wine, which was standing in front of her husband's plate, and lifted it up in greeting.

"My position as the wife of Prince Ruslan allows me to call you, the King, my father. I want to use my rights, father, to tell you that I wish to express on behalf of all of us our gratitude for this feast in our honor. For a reason that I can't reveal at this time, I have been unable to tell everyone that I was not born a frog, but forced to be one for a specific time only. During the day I require to wear a frog's skin but, when the sun goes down, I'm allowed to return to my human appearance. My name is Leubarta and I shall be grateful if you will call me by this name."

Leubarta and the Magic Dance

Following this she took a sip from the glass but poured the rest of the wine into one of the long sleeves of her dress. She then ripped a wing from the roasted swan which had been placed on the table for the guests to eat Having eaten the meat, she threw the bones into the other sleeve.

The onlookers watched her, fascinated, and waited patiently for her next move. Leubarta asked the musicians to start playing some music and she moved slowly and gracefully, almost floating, over the floor. After making a full circle, she waved with one hand and a small pond appeared right in the middle of the room. The Princess then waved with her other hand and three white swans jumped from her sleeve to land on the water and began to swim in a circle.

The assembled guests only gasped in amazement. The wives of the older brothers, jealous of the attention everyone was paying to Leubarta, decided to surprise the guests themselves. They also filled up their sleeves with wine and bones from their plates and went to dance on the floor. However, when the girls waved with their left hands, drops of red wine splattered all over the tablecloth and the guests and, with the next move of their hands, they sent bones flying everywhere. One of the bones almost flew into King Farlaf's eye, blinding him for a moment and the women who had created this commotion became very scared indeed.

When order had been restored, no one knew where the women had disappeared to. Ruslan had also mysteriously disappeared, but Farlaf didn't let Leubarta go home. "Don't worry, he has probably gone to see if these stupid women have arrived home safely."

As soon as Ruslan had returned, he was surrounded by relatives asking whether or not he had found his brothers' wives. "I helped them to go home. They were afraid that father would yell at them or even beat them." He replied.

King Farlaf was embarrassed by his son's announcement, and cried out. "I never beat a woman."

But Ruslan was not listening to him. Instead he was looking at his wife and, noticing this, Leubarta's face eventually showed a lovely flush of embarrassment, making his lips lift up in a light smile.

"Fair lady, shall we dance?" He offered her a way to escape his intense observation. Leubarta put her hand into his and they danced until the King started to yawn and spluttered that it was time to retire. Neither of them had noticed that it was almost morning until they had left the reception and had walked to their own quarters, which was surrounded by a garden.

At home, the Princess allowed herself to stretch her tired shoulders before shrinking back into the size of a small creature and started looking for her skin in the place where she had left it. At first, unable to find it, Leubarta thought that she had misplaced it before leaving home and had simply forgotten where it had rested. So she looked around but could not find the skin anywhere and then became scared.

"Ruslan." She cried out to her husband. "Have you seen my frog skin?"

"You will never wear it again." He gathered her closer.

As he spoke, Leubarta turned her head in the direction of the chimney, seeing a small pile of ashes. "What have you done?" She cried. "If you had only asked me, before burning my frog's skin, I would have told you that you would only need to wait three more days for me to become your wife forever. But now that you have broken the spell, I have no choice but to return to the person who placed the skin on me. Forget me, because you will never see me again!" She wailed. Whereupon, Leubarta's human body immediately started to fade, like a melting fog, and disappeared, leaving in Ruslan's hands only his father's ring and the tiny crown of the frog Princess.

The first beam of the sun had found an angle from which it was able to look through the window, crawling slowly to the hand of the man lying on the table. It was the only source of light at this time of day. The candle had been burned to the last inch, leaving on the table the dried design of overflowed wax. Ruslan lifted his head and rubbed his face with the hand that had served him as a pillow and realized that it was now the morning of the next day. In his dream he had just seen the chain of events and circumstances that had brought him to this place!

A small detachment of riders, followed by two covered wagons, moved along the hilly terrain with the speed of galloping horses. The bright uniforms of the soldiers showed that they belonged to a division of the King's personal guards. Some distance separated the two riders on the first line from the rest of the men, indicating that one of these officers was in charge.

"I hate this endless road." One of them shouted. He was shorter than his companion and possessed a chubby body which was dressed in rich clothes that did not meet the requirements of traveling. Unshaven, and having unkempt hair, he had an expression of irritation on his face. "We left the palace a month ago but the suffering that I have experienced since then has made the trip twice as long. I made the mistake of listening to your advice that I should not take servants with me and now I must do everything for myself. Even in my worst dreams, I could not have imagined this terrible existence into which you have forced me." Ratmir complained.

"Do not blame me! Did you forget that it was you who was appointed by our father to find a way to stop the damage to our wheat fields? I am only accompanying you to the capital of the province in order to look after your safety." His younger brother replied.

"Was it my safety that made you bypass a large town where we might have been able to at least find a bad tavern? No! You deliberately changed the itinerary to take us through side roads which would allow us to see only the edges of fields." Ratmir pulled his horse's reigns to stop it.

"Of course. I was worried about your interests. If I had not prevented you from finding a bottle, and food, you would have remained at the hotel until now."

"So what?" Ratmir closed the folds of his jacket and rode away to show that the conversation was finished.

Ruslan looked at the sun and ordered the soldiers to stop. He wanted to give a rest to both horses and people. They quickly arranged the camp and started to cook something on a fire. Two younger men removed the heavy armor and led the horses to the creek for a drink, under the protection of armed guards. The Prince, after talking for some time with the hired guide, returned to his brother, Ratmir, who was sitting on a tree trunk with a sour expression on his face.

"Our guide told me that, after another day's ride through this wild territory, we would encounter a wide stone road which will bring us to the palace of the Steward in about a week's time if we ride fast."

"Another week of this life?" Complained Ratmir, taking the plate of a simple soldier's food and showing it to Ruslan. He tried one spoon and said. "Horrible!"

"It's better than nothing." Said Ruslan, thinking about situations from his past years when he needed to forget about food for days on end. Eating his share, he thought. 'This trip will be memorable for both of us.' After the last of his men had finished their meal, he ordered them to move farther on and to ride until the sun set in the west. However, Ratmir met his order with more complaints.

"Brother, if you need to rest, lie in the wagon because I intend to ride through the night without stopping." Now he had regrets about having taken his brother with him. He paid no attention to Ratmir's threats and moans.

Next day, they increased the number of hours that they rode and eventually reached the road that made traveling easier for the horses and people. Ratmir, sitting on the seat beside one of the wagon-Masters, could see only a line of trees with fields that sometimes gleamed through the gaps that arose between the stems of white-skinned birches and old maple trees that spread their pointed leaves wide. Ratmir's happiness was genuine when the men, who were tethering a goat to a wooden peg, told him that they had arrived at the outskirts of Verisan, the capital of Roslava. Verisan was located on the left shore of a wide and deep river named the Nitar. This side of the river was lower than the opposite one which, in past years when the snow had been deep in the hills, had allowed the water to flood almost a third of the city. Eventually, the Steward had built a dam that ran like a wavy, long ribbon along the edge of the city and its flat top was now used as a bypass road. Following the advice of the guide, Ruslan took this road that allowed access to the palace courtyard through the western gate, to avoid the slow and stressful ride through the very busy streets of the town.

The detachment then rode faster, wishing to have time at the end of a hard day to properly clean up and eat. Even Ratmir mounted his horse and forgot about his sore back. The road that led them along the top of the dam was crossed by another one made from flat stone blocks that led them to the palace. When the tired soldiers had reached the town wall, the officer at the gate asked for their names and, after a short exchange of greetings, allowed them to enter the stone tunnel that led to the palace. One of the guards accompanied them to show them the way and finally brought the travelers to the porch of the Steward's residence, where he left the detachment in the care of an officer of the palace guards.

At the sounds of the commotion, created by the horses and the voices of guests, Sevran came out to see the visitors. He humbly offered a sincere welcome to the sons of his King and invited them into his palace. The rest of the men left the horses at the stables and followed an officer who showed them the way to the guards' quarters where they would be billeted.

"We were expecting you tomorrow, but I believe that everything has already been prepared for your arrival." Sevran greeted Ruslan and Ratmir. "My Bailiff will show you to your rooms and will bring water for you to wash yourselves, together with a change of clothing. I've already been advised that the food will be ready within an hour. All of my Court is impatient to see not one, but two Princes and, if I deny them the opportunity of meeting you, then I declare that some of them will probably climb the walls to look at you through your bedroom windows while you are asleep." Joked the Steward and then advised, graciously. "Remember that the sons of my old friend are precious guests in my house. Give my Court as much time as you wish and don't hesitate to let me know when you may become tired of them. You can ask for anything that you may need from the servants who are now at your command."

"Thank you for your hospitality, Sevran. But, before leaving, I want to give you a message from our father." Ruslan took a letter out of his inside pocket.

Sevran accepted it, surprised a little by the fact that King Farlaf had entrusted it to the youngest son, instead of to the elder Ratmir, but he chose not to show it. He also decided not to ask questions until he had read the letter. Sevran returned to his private quarters which contained a small room that had a nice view over the city in which the Steward liked to work and think. Taking a narrow dagger from the table drawer, he slit open the letter.

"My old Friend." Wrote King Farlaf. "I am sending to you two of my sons, Ratmir and Ruslan. I want to ask you to do me a favor to evaluate the character and talents of my elder son, Ratmir, from the point of view off his being suitable for the position of King since this is a task that I will have difficulty in achieving. I rely on your knowledge of people and your wisdom that has always served the best interests of Rossana. My youngest son, Ruslan, has difficult private business to attend to that will take him through the territory of Vanymar. Please help him as well as you would do for your own son. Your friend since childhood, Farlaf."

Sevran twisted the paper in his hands, thinking. 'Hmm, it is not an easy task to decide in a short period of time which one of the King's sons may be the more suitable for the kingship and I suspect that you, my dear friend, already know the answer but hesitate to speak it.'

Supper was served in a large room that was used for special occasions. Long tables were covered by colorful tablecloths and the food was served on silver platters. A whole fried, young pig, garnished with berries and with the traditional apple stuffed into its mouth, was placed on an oval, porcelain plate close to Ratmir who looked at it in admiration. Fried chickens, pigeons and ducks were surrounded by dishes made from vegetables and fresh fruits. Servants, carrying large mugs of wine and beer, walked around the tables serving drinks to the guests and the King's sons who, as special guests, had been placed beside Sevran. After a first toast in their honor, all the guests turned their attention to the food, loading their plates with a little bit of everything that was presented to them. None of them, however, had an appetite as greedy as that of Ratmir who had lived for the past two weeks on a soldier's diet of porridge and dried meat. Now he prepared to reward himself with an enormous amount of fried meat and intended to wash it down with equally copious amounts of red wine.

Sevran looked at him with increasing concern, becoming convinced that Ratmir would be sick later. The Steward thought up a way to divert Ratmir's attention away from his glass, by making an effort to involve him in conversation, but it didn't work.

Ruslan understood his concern and, with a spark of humor flashing in his gray eyes, he said. "Don't worry, my brother can drink a barrel of wine alone and still be perfectly fine the next day. He'll just sleep-in until late in the afternoon. No one can beat him at the drinking contests."

Sevran relaxed and turned his attention to Ruslan, trying to determine what the passions were in his being that motivated and drove him.

"According to the matter that your Highness has partaken of only one plate of food, I conclude that you don't have a very high opinion of the talents of my chef and neither may my wine be to your taste?" Queried Sevran, motioning with his eyes towards Ruslan's half full glass.

"Not at all. Your wine is perfect, and your cooks know their trade, but I serve as an officer of my father's army and have never become accustomed to spending much time at the table. As for wine, I know how much I can take of it. Also, I can be called into the saddle at any time, so it's always better for a King's son not to show weakness in the eyes of his men by dangling in the saddle half-drunk. This evening I have a special reason to be careful with wine because I plan to leave your hospitable city tomorrow and ride onward to carry out my business."

"Is this business a secret matter or can you tell me what is obliging you to travel with this small group of guards?" Sevran asked.

"My business isn't secret but I am planning to ride alone. I want to leave the guards to protect my brother until he's ready to return home." Ruslan answered.

"I would like to hear about your trouble and perhaps I can help you with my knowledge of this land and its people. However, I think that it will be better if we postpone our conversation until tomorrow."

"Gladly. This hour is for fun but for a serious conversation we'll find the time tomorrow. For this I am willing to stay one day longer."

Later, Sevran thought about the impressions that he had formed by observing the two brothers and admitted to himself. 'It looks as if Farlaf's sons have different kinds of mettle. The older one has been treated like a Prince and was never denied anything and, accordingly, he grew up selfish and spoiled. Wrapped in gold, he became imbued with the qualities of this soft metal himself; good only for women's decorations and becoming increasingly soft and weak. But the younger, on the other hand, was looked upon as a nobleman in the service of the King and his country and was treated without pity. He became a stainless steel blade, always reliable and always ready to fight. Farlaf has a difficult decision to make, since both of them are his sons but they are very different one from the other.'

Ruslan had become accustomed to getting up early in the morning and did not see the need to change this habit simply because he was in the palace of Sevran, instead of in that of his father. The Steward found him pouring out a generous portion of oats into his horse's feeding bag whilst checking its hooves.

"I didn't expect to see you up so early, Ruslan, but one of my servants told me that you were already on your feet and I came here to invite you to share breakfast with me. I intend to leave after breakfast for our distant fort on the boundary of Narymout. A pigeon sent out from here brought back a message telling us that there had been an attack on the outpost. It's not the matter of the attack itself that concerns me, since our border forts are attacked quite often, but the note stated. "The people of Narymout took the lumber.""

"The lumber?" Ruslan repeated, in surprise.

"Yes. The matter is unclear to me also." Responded Sevran. "That's why I am going to take a ship, that's already equipped and waiting for me, to investigate this affair personally."

"In that case I am going with you. I know that armed bandits usually take livestock, wheat or slaves, but not lumber! I agree that this requires you to personally look into it. During this trip I'll have plenty of time to tell you about my problem." Ruslan advised, on the way to the Palace.

After breakfast, a small boat took them to Fort Gellar. The ship was used mostly for merchant purposes but Sevran had increased the size of the sail, and also reinforced the sides of the boat, in order to turn it into a fast, patrol ship. The boat was capable of covering the distance between Verisan and the fort in a matter of days. In addition to the sail, the boat had twelve long oars, six on each side, which were used to initiate and quickly execute precise maneuvers or to be used in the absence of wind. But today the wind blew steadily and the small, brave ship forged through the body of the river pushing waves towards each shore. The head of a wooden horse, painted in red, proudly curled its head at the prow of the ship. The canvas of the sail filled with wind and the wide open eyes of the giant sun, drawn on its white fabric, gazed down on Sevran and Ruslan. The sailors were protected from arrows that could be shot at them from the shores of the river by a line of shields that had been placed along the sides of the boat.

Trusting the command of the ship to its captain, Ruslan and Sevran resumed the conversation which they had deliberately postponed from the day before. After listening to all the details of Ruslan's marriage, and his sudden separation from his wife, Sevran remarked. "I have heard stories like this before but I honestly didn't believe them. Now, in light of the things that have happened to you, in the future I will be cautious about calling them fantasy. First of all, let me express my concern about your decision to look for a Princess in Vanymar. To travel through its territory at this time is not only difficult, but dangerous. After some problems arose between Queen Aligarna and her son, Validar, small bands of riders have been searching the country for him, probably to plead with him to return home and make peace with his mother. Eventually, one of them will cross your path and, even if you change your name, it wouldn't be difficult for a smart officer to discern a great Rossana warrior within your common, Vanadian clothes. He will understand who you really are, mysterious stranger or not. Believe me, Vanadians are not stupid."

"So, what do you suggest that I do?" Ruslan asked.

"You can change your name, except that you would have to tell the real story, slightly adjusted to fit into the life of a commoner, which would also mean that you would have to say that you are looking for an Oracle. There is a Sage that lives in a far and forbidden corner of Vanymar and it will be natural for someone, who is desperately looking for his loved one, to forget about his fear and go to this dangerous place to ask for direction as to where to look for the missing woman and to seek advice on how to free her from the wizard."

"My story will sound like the tale of a disturbed man but Vanadians might believe it, especially if I tell them that I am from Beristani and a Ross like all of my ancestors. This will explain my strange behavior and they'll probably be glad to show me the shortest way to hell."

"Do not overdo it or you may make them think more deeply about it. Some of them might have heard rumors about your strange marriage and some smart officer may put all the facts together and decide to arrest you for further investigation." Sevran suggested.

"It wouldn't be that easy to do." Ruslan put a hand on the pommel of his sword.

"I'm only saying that you will need to avoid confrontation with any patrols that you may encounter. Otherwise your mission will be impossible."

Ruslan did not argue. He just looked at the water flowing behind the ship and saw only endless obstacles that he still must overcome.

The Steward's ship did not arrive unnoticed. A man hidden on a watchtower, placed on the top of a canyon, brought the news to the fort that a ship carrying Sevran's Coat of Arms had entered the narrow space between the rocky canyon walls at the point where the water ran faster towards the sea. The strongest men had taken the oars, keeping the boat at a distance from the slimy, dark-green stones, outlined by white foam, which had been smoothed by streams of water that had previously flowed over them for generations. Powerful currents of water had started to drag the boat with increasing speed, thrusting it up and down like a restless horse and making a loud noise. The chaos of sound inside the canyon completely swallowed the voices of the people who were struggling with the stream.

Ruslan was not sure how the men managed to keep the boat in the middle of the mad stream but, when it had finally passed through the narrowest part between the granite walls, the crew unfurled the sails and, within a matter of an hour, had reached the brand-new, wooden mooring post close to the fort. Armed fort soldiers helped tighten the ropes on the post and walked with the Steward and his men up to the gate of the fort. Ruslan noticed signs of a recent battle on the bodies of some men and on the land. The damaged wall of the fort was being re-constructed, as was the watchtower. New, pointed, wooden posts had been buried in the ground so that they stuck out like the spines of a hedgehog. Men, mostly without armor, greeted the visitors without stopping their tasks of hammering boards onto the gate, or sawing lumber for the new roof of the tower.

Prince Ruslan was curious about the strength of the new gate but Sevran assured him that he could trust in the skill of his people. He therefore turned his attention to the report of the attack on the fort which the Commander was anxious to relate to him.

"Are you telling me everything?" Asked Sevran, when the Commander had ended his story, patting his chest-length, gray beard with a hand.

Even Ruslan had the feeling that something was bothering this officer. The warrior had hesitated for a moment and then suddenly blurted out. "I have been a soldier for forty years and have become accustomed to saying what I have experienced and it's your business as to whether or not you believe it. Stories about strange creatures that serve under the will of Narymout's Ruler started to circulate about four months ago. Hunters, who often have mixed blood, visit the forts of Rossana freely as well as the villages of the Numats, carrying news from both sides. I thought, at first, that these mysterious servants of Cofiat were a fantasy that grew out of an alcoholic brew that the Numats had prepared for them from horses' sour milk but, when I saw one of them with my own eyes, I then had no doubt that these hunters had not lied."

"When and how did you see them?" The Prince queried.

At this, the Commander gave Ruslan a penetrating, speculative look from under his bushy eyebrows but did not question his authority.

"It happened during the attack when screaming, short-limbed devils came running towards us from every direction, to be followed by a rain of arrows flying towards us which served as a protective shield for them and which made it impossible for our archers to return fire." The old warrior paused and then continued. "He was dressed in a long, black, leather coat overlaid with gray armor. He looked more or less human but his face can only be described by me as frightening. He did not participate in the fight, only watched it from behind the fence. He never crossed the boundary between our lands, even when the Numats breached the walls of our fort and we all became involved in a hand-to-hand sword fight. Later, I realized that it was only a trick to keep us inside the walls until another group of attackers could rob us of our stored lumber. They stole all the supplies that we had prepared for trading purposes. They even stole tree trunks that we had tied into a bundle to make a raft to allow us to transfer these supplies down to the sea."

"For what reason do the Numats need so much wood, when they have been horse riders for generations?" Sevran queried.

"To build ships!" Exclaimed Ruslan, raising his eyes up from a piece of paper on which he had been busy scribbling numbers. "I have made approximate calculations and can show that the stolen lumber would be enough to build at least eleven medium boats and, if I am right, it could mean that very soon one of our cities, or an outpost of ours, could shortly become the subject of a massive attack from a river, or perhaps even from the sea."

"Ruslan, we have to return to the capital immediately and I clearly have made a mistake in taking you along with me." Then, addressing the Fort Commander, he advised. "I will leave you a cage and some new pigeons to send a message to me if the situation on the border changes for the worse or if you find out something new about that strange man."

Concerned for the Prince's safety, he ordered the men to use both the sail and the oars at the same time to propel the ship more quickly and thus to make the return trip home faster. Even Ruslan put his muscles to work, paddling with the sailors for a while in an attempt to be more useful and to show goodwill. The Steward allowed himself to relax only after seeing the riverside gardens of his city again.

"I hope that the news from your brother will be more comforting than everything we have heard so far." Sevran sighed.

Ruslan only nodded, saying nothing.

Having reached the palace, Sevran soon found out that Ratmir had not even made an attempt to do something about his father's concerns, but had spent all of his time in raiding the Steward's wine cellar instead of rescuing the wheat fields from the marauders that had been plaguing them for months. Storming through the rooms, the Steward reached the dining room where the whole company of wastrels, holding up glasses of wine, bawled out a song in stuttering, drunken voices. The enraged expression showing on Sevran's face as he entered the room scared the members of this table choir and they choked on their last words and immediately ran away like timid mice. Ratmir, who was too unsteady on his legs to run, made an attempt to lift himself up from the bench but dropped back heavily onto it.

"I did not expect you to find the people who have damaged our fields, since they are probably much too fast on their feet for you to catch, but I expected that you would at least make an attempt to honor your father's wish and find out who the perpetrators are." Sevran raised his voice as he lost his temper.

"Big deal!" Argued the drunken Ratmir. "I can catch anyone, even a witch on her broomstick. It's just that I am somehow stuck on this bench. Ruslan, give me a hand up." He ended, lamely.

Ruslan lifted Ratmir up onto his staggering feet and dragged him off to his bedroom. But Ratmir was as stubborn as any other drunken man and insisted on going off to catch "these mean-spirited vandals." Too tired to argue, Ruslan simply decided to let him go, in the company of two older soldiers who had been appointed to look after the safety of the fields, to the place where a simple cabin made from tree branches and straw stood on a strip of grass between fields. The rough road made Ratmir feel so tired that, upon their arrival at the cabin, he immediately fell down on the cloth-covered straw that served as the guards' bed and slept until late the next morning.

"Did you see anyone?" Ruslan asked his brother, after Ratmir had arrived back the next day.

"I didn't close my eyes all night since I needed to guard the field." Lied Ratmir. "I didn't even hear the slightest sound from anywhere, but when I looked at the field in the morning it had been mysteriously flattened to the ground. It must be the work of evil spirits." He finished, spreading out his hands in a gesture of helplessness.

Sevran prepared to say something, but Ruslan spoke first. "I'll go to the field this evening and try to find out what evil spirit is vandalizing our crop."

"That's right, go and see for yourself, hero!" Ratmir mocked him.

When the sun had begun to set, Ruslan and the same two soldiers went to watch one of the undisturbed fields, expecting that it would be the next target. The soldiers sat up with Ruslan until midnight and then went to sleep.

"It's pointless to wait for him, your Highness. It's better that we go to sleep. Your father has plenty of fields." A veteran, whose face showed many battle scars, suggested.

But Ruslan took his cloak and went to sit under the birch tree that grew close to the edge of the field. Around three in the morning, his eyes became heavy, as if something was deliberately trying to make him fail in his vigil. He therefore tried to counter this feeling by splashing some water from his leather bottle onto his face and continued to watch. Not long after this, a sudden wind blew along the field rustling the spikes of wheat and the Prince decided to lie on the ground under the dark cloak to await developments. Then the ground beneath him shuddered as if something heavy had suddenly dropped onto it out of the sky. Throwing a corner of the fabric from his face, he was surprised to see a large white horse, possessed of two wings, moving along the field and eating the wheat.

'Now, thanks to my brother, I know what evil spirits look like.' He said to himself, unfastening his belt to use it as a support whenever he would have a chance to get on this animal's back. The horse stopped, lowered its head, listened intently and sniffed the air with wide-open nostrils. Finding nothing that disturbed it, the horse shook its head and jumped around playfully. Suddenly it fell onto its back, tightening its wings around its body, and rolled on the wheat. If, perhaps, the horse had only eaten the wheat it would not have made Ruslan quite so angry as having to watch how the cheeky animal achieved nothing, other than doing unnecessary damage to the field. Ruslan crawled closer and, at the very moment when the horse started to get up, he jumped onto its back and closed the belt around the column of his neck like a collar.

The horse neighed in anger and turned round to see who was molesting it. Then it made a sudden jump to the side, hoping to shake this unexpected rider off its back onto the ground so that it could trample him under his feet. But Ruslan held onto the belt and to the horse's mane so strongly that it was as if he had rooted himself to the horse's back. After a few, unsuccessful attempts to free itself, the horse stopped jumping around and adopted the new strategy of trying to scare its abuser by launching into a headlong flight. It opened its white-feathered wings and, flapping them strongly, rose up high into the dark night sky. Except that Ruslan did not ease his grip.

The Prince was shocked by the experience of the flight but, after his first fear had subsided, his senses adjusted to the view of the stars flying fast towards him and his lungs were able to breathe again. His ears started to recognize other sounds, apart from the heavy sighing of moving wings, and he started to enjoy the glorious feeling of flight.

The horse, now desperate to free itself, flew downwards forcing Ruslan to grasp another handful of its silky mane. He also had to press his knee against the horse's leg to prevent his body from sliding forward along the neck of the animal, but the beast did not like the feel of this and returned to a horizontal flight. Although it kicked and jumped in the air, and spun around in one spot, the annoying burden still sat on its back. Both horse and rider were becoming equally exhausted by this confrontation of wills. Man has the will to get what he wants but the will of a horse is to be free from anyone's control and, therefore, it made a last attempt to get rid of Ruslan by making him feel dizzy from the speed. Being too tired to fly any more, the horse lowered itself to the ground and ran off so fast that Ruslan was not able to see anything at all, even close to him. The air had become compressed almost into a liquid, which prevented him from taking a deep breath.

Ruslan started to think about jumping down from the angry and scared animal the moment it became safe enough to do so but, without any warning, the horse stopped, breathing heavily. Ruslan lost hold of the mane and rolled over its head to fall on the soft mat of wheat. The horse, in its turn, stumbled and fell on its side too and both of them lay on the ground without strength for some time. When Ruslan's head had stopped spinning, he slowly turned on his side and crawled to the horse to see if it was still alive. Moving aside the long, white hair from the horse's face, he gently stroked the soft white skin on its head and neck. The horse opened its big dark eyes and glanced for a moment at the Prince, then closed them again with a sigh.

"I didn't want to bring you into a poor condition such as this. But you're stubborn, my friend, and this is the reason why we are both lying on our backs. You should have stopped kicking and running as if your life depended on it, a long time ago."

The horse made a sound like laughter and remarked. "You were dangling on my back, carried by the wind, and I thought that one more attempt by me would dislodge you."

Ruslan was not offended by this, finding it very funny. Getting up and looking around, he found that the horse had brought him back to the same wheat field from whence the incredible ride had started. His eyes noticed the straw cabin where the two lazy guards had slept throughout the whole event. The horse, walking slowly in that direction, asked Ruslan. "What are you going to do with me?"

"What can I do with you? I can't bring a winged horse home that also happens to be able to speak. I will let you go but, before I do so, you will need to give me your promise to never destroy our fields again. If you ever break that promise, I will have to catch you again. Then I would have to put you to work digging up this field to find out for yourself how much time and effort is required to grow this wheat."

The horse thought for a moment and then said. "This is fair, since I never think about the cost of my fun." It took a lungful of air and blew gently on the flattened wheat which immediately straightened up, almost as if it had been shifted under the movement of an invisible wand, and now stood perfectly straight.

"Are you a wizard?" Ruslan mocked the horse.

"I am not a wizard, but I have some talent."

"Well." Ruslan patted his strong shoulders. "I hope to see you next time in less-exhausting circumstances."

"Wait for a moment, before letting me go. You granted me the freedom that I lost in this challenge and I want to prove to you that I have good qualities too. I am the chief of all horses and my name is Windynar. I know that you are looking for a horse that will be your friend and support in difficult circumstances. Yet you have not found any animal that is suitable, so I will give you my brother, Saphir. You will not find a better horse than him for the task that you intend to complete."

"Can he talk too?" Queried Ruslan, with a wry and rather mischievous smile on his lips.

"No! Speech is the privilege of only the chief, but he will understand you very well." Windynar followed this up by hitting the ground with his hoof to send a loud call into the night. The fast wind brought an answer from another horse and, within a short time, the owner of the voice appeared in front of the Prince and his new friend. The horse was as black as night itself and stood directly in front of Ruslan to allow him to observe him critically and carefully.

"No wings, no horns, no talk. He is a normal horse that has extreme strength and speed. Saphir is the only one who can keep up with me on the ground." Windynar advised.

Ruslan touched the strong neck and shoulders of the horse. "He is perfect." He agreed, after the examination. "I think he can carry heavy armor effortlessly and ride a long distance quickly. I will treat him even better than myself." He promised Windynar.

"Good bye, Ruslan. Perhaps we may meet each other at a later date, but right now I need to return to my meadows. The sun will return soon and I do not want anyone to see us together." After these words, Windynar disappeared, leaving Ruslan and Saphir alone.

By the time that the yawning and stretching guards had left the cabin, Ruslan had already bathed and fed his new horse. He adjusted the straps of the harness to his great size and placed it over Saphir's head and then rode him back home, whilst allowing his previous horse to follow him.

Everyone who was not involved in their duties came to the stables to look at the mysterious horse that had caused so much trouble, admitting that it would be difficult to catch a black horse in the dark night. At the same time, the palace servants and guards had been laughing at the unlucky soldiers who had loved their sleep so much that they had failed to do their duty. Saphir had felt nervous in the presence of a crowd of people who stared at him and touched his neck. He had been fighting the increasing desire to bite some men to stop them from pestering him with their interest in his teeth. So Saphir had started to throw impatient looks at Ruslan, in an effort to signify to him that it was time to hurry up and leave the noisy town to return to the peace of the open fields.

"Are you relying on Lady Luck to bring you and your wife together, or do you have a definite plan?" Sevran speculated, walking him to the gate.

"Luck is a very dangerous lady and you never know where she will take you. No! I have decided to follow your advice and find the wizard who robbed me with the help of another wizard."

"I hope you are right but, anyway, I wish that your road ahead will be a smoother one." With this positive wish still ringing in his ears, Ruslan left the palace and, in due course, he found himself at a boat-mooring dock on the edge of town, looking at a small ship that was preparing to transport wheat into Arislad. Leaving Verisan, the ship reached the point where the rivers Nytar and Carnest joined together. At this place the ship needed to make a turn to enter the Carnest to continue onward to Arislad, the capital of Rossana.

A short time after they had completed the turn into the river Carnest, Ruslan requested that the Captain drop him off on the right-hand shore at the territory of Vanymar. He docked the ship long enough for Ruslan to walk his horse off the ship along a wooden gangplank and waved goodbye to his temporary friends. The Prince then took his first steps into the unknown land of Vanymar, preferring to keep close to the river, hoping that its flow would eventually bring him to the lake and to the wizard. He spent days of riding onward without see-ing anyone on the dusty and hot pathway.

The view of the grass-covered hills, and the ribbon of the river which was outlined by reeds, eventually became boring for him. The next hill was very high and blocked his view, showing only its top crowned by a white stone. He decided to make a stop under the shade of it, expecting to see only more hills from this high vantage point. But his eye had caught the movement of a single rider, appearing at the top of the hill, who had stopped to await his arrival at the summit.

The Prince resolved that he would not turn off the pathway to avoid this horseman, even if the stranger had company with him. A rider in this place could be a friend or a challenge but, because Ruslan was not a man who was afraid of challenges, he urged Saphir on to ride towards him.

CHAPTER 8:

THE GOLDEN NUT

"Tac! Tac!" The voice called. Its sound smoothly increased in volume as if it was arriving from somewhere far away. "Are you daydreaming?"

He recognized the voice of Alisa.

"Who, me?" He said the first thing that came into his mind. He could not remember how it had happened that he had frozen motionless between two briefcases containing money.

Tac himself did not care for the unpleasant, metallic smell of the banknotes. He found the strong desire of some men to acquire more of them as a very strange phenomenon.

Man has food, clothes, a place to live and everything that modern technology has to offer, yet all these things still do not satisfy Him. 'Are all humans like this?' He asked himself. 'No!' He shook his head. 'My Master is not like that, and Lana is not like that either. I am sure that I could find many other people who would never threaten an old man with a gun to rob him.' And, with this thought, Tac closed the briefcases.

"You have put yourself and others through so much danger to obtain this money." Alisa commented. "What are you going to do with it now?"

Standing up on two legs, and locking his paws behind his back, the cat swayed his body back and forth, thinking. The outcome was that he decided to share his plans with his wife. "I had a brief talk with a character named Carl who gave me an idea which I keep turning over and over in my mind."

"Another dangerous enterprise? Why? You have just returned from an adventure!" Alisa worried that he had started to enjoy the rush of adrenaline in his blood. "I am afraid that very soon you will lose interest in the quiet family life and me."

Tac decided to stop standing on two legs pretending that he was someone else and became a normal gray cat on all fours that cared very much about the mood of his wife. "Alisa." He came closer and sat beside her. "You do not need to worry. This is going to be a business venture that will not take me any farther than the nearest city. I think that you, also, can be involved in it along with other animals. As a matter of fact, all the inhabitants of the wood will be able to participate in everything that I am planning to do."

"Plan? What kind of plan?" Tac heard Carfield's squeaky voice. "Why have I not been advised about this plan?"

"You have come right in time, Carfield. I was just about to go and look for you. Without you, my plan would simply be impossible to accomplish." Said Tac.

Carfield was flattered and stretched out his neck, puffing out his chest.

"Oh, Carfield, what is this?" Alisa pretended to be concerned, looking at his tail.

"What? What has happened?" Carfield turned his head as well, trying to see what was wrong behind his back.

"It looks as if you have started to grow a peacock's tail behind you." Alisa kept a serious face.

"Alisa. You scared me half to death." Carfield touched his heart in a human gesture.

"You have missed it by a little bit." The fox pointed with her paw to indicate to him that he was looking on the wrong side of his chest.

"Thanks, Alisa." He responded, still unaware that she was joking. "I had started to think that I had lost my tail completely. My neighbor, Squirrella, asked me to babysit her kids while she was out of the nest on some business. We were playing Cowboys and Indians and, when you told me that there was something wrong with my back, I became scared that the little squirrels had pulled feathers out of my tail for their headbands. Imagine what kind of an impression I would make in the forest if I had to wander about there with a naked tail?"

"Nothing is wrong with your feathers." Tac laughed. "I think that Alisa simply wanted to warn you against the danger of allowing your ego to grow to the point that you might become difficult to deal with."

"What is this ego?" Carfield asked, puzzled.

"It is a little worm with a big opinion about itself. When it looks in the mirror it probably sees a large snake." Tac mocked him.

"Really? I had better eat it if this ego dares to crawl near me." Mused the crow.

"Carfield, let's return to my plan." Tac believed that it was a waste of time trying to explain the meaning of the word to the crow. "I want you to talk to that man named Carl."

"Yes, of course." Replied Carfield. "I remember him very well. He was the unemployed fellow who told us about the fairground, but why do you need to talk to him?"

"We cannot buy a business from the new owner of the amusement park since we are animals and it must be done by a man. You will need to find a way to talk Carl into making all the purchase transactions himself. He will buy this business in the name of our company and we will make him an employee, the Manager of it." The cat looked at the crow.

"One man cannot run the whole business himself. Even a small-headed sparrow can tell you that." Opined Carfield.

"He will not do everything himself, because we will help him. All of us, the whole wood. You, I, Alisa, Bertrond and even Alowsius! That is, if he wants to have a piece of meat every day. Running the Amusement park will be our mutual business."

"This is a stupid idea but, without trying it out, how can I say that it would not work?" Carfield added, drily.

"In that case, we need to make a phone call from my other home."

"This is a long way to fly and I think we can find a telephone much closer. Follow me." Carfield then flew ahead, waiting for Tac to keep up with him to reach the slope of the river together, and joined him in a walk through the tall stems of grass. Eventually, they saw a bright, orange tent which had been placed on open, flat ground between trees and a dusty, red car. Its back door was open displaying the usual camping equipment. Carfield stopped and listened to the voices of people enjoying themselves in the water and then crept directly to the car. Tac realized his intentions but it was too late to stop him, so he stayed under the cover of a bush nervously awaiting his return. After what seemed to be an eternity, the figure of Carfield reappeared, holding a cell phone in his beak.

"Carfield, you cannot steal a cell phone, it's not right." Tac whispered.

"I am not stealing it. I am borrowing it. Where is the note with Carl's telephone number?"

"Here it is."

"Ta Ta Ta Ta Ta." Mumbled the crow, pressing the numbers. "Hello, am I speaking to Mr. Mayer? Carl, do you remember old Joe whom you met near the antique store. We had a conversation about your deceased friend and his nephew who would like to sell the traveling amusement park which he has inherited. So, you remember very well? Good! Did your new boss find a buyer? No? No one has even called to inquire about it, you say, and he is now willing to sell it at a reduced price? Yes, I agree that he may not get too much for the business in this situation.

Well, I have good news for you. I have talked to my friend who may be interested in investing money in this business, but his proposition has a down-side to it. He has no time to deal with the transaction himself, because he is out of the country and will not be here for some time." Carfield stopped, listening to the man on the other side, and then answered him thus. "I agree with you. Believe me, money is not the problem it's just that he is on a long expedition somewhere in Africa. He likes the idea mainly because he was born into a family of circus acrobats and has a taste for a lifestyle that is connected with entertainment. He has even bought a small group of circus animals that now relies on his care. His name is Tacker J. Holmes. I am sure that you must have heard of his name. He is quite a famous explorer and traveler. I called him only yesterday and he has a proposition for you. Are you able to take on the respon-sibility of being the manager over his animals and the amusement park until he comes back, or have you already found some work? Unfortunately, my health is not good enough to put such a burden on my old shoulders." Carfield spread his wings wide. "I have to spend a lot of time at the hospital and cannot be in two places at once. As a matter of fact, I would be glad if you could take care of all his animals yourself. Carl, please think about my proposition until the end of the week and I will call you again at that time." He closed the phone.

Checking on the people at the river again, he put the phone back where he had found it. "I am too old for the role of a thief of small electronics and I think it's time for you to get a cell phone, Tac."

"I can use the cell phone of my older Mistress, Natalie, who is always at home and uses the house phone instead. But I am afraid to go home because Lana will be mad at me for some time to come after what has happened at Willie's place. She called out my name and that means that she saw me with you." He looked concerned.

"Relax." Said Carfield, in a carefree way. "You are a cat. She cannot be angry with you for a long time. Just say 'meow, meow' and she will forget her anger."

"It's easy for you to say." Tac admitted to himself that he could not be apart from the family for too long and, consequently, the tension between him and Lana must be eased in order to allow this to happen. So, one evening, he cau-tiously entered the living room of his human family, at the same time watching out for Lana. He found, with a sigh of relief, that she was not there and only his

Master and Natalie called out to him to join them. Jumping onto the couch, he put his paws on Natalie's knee, relying on her protection in case Lana would yell at him.

When, eventually, she had left her bedroom to go to the kitchen to get something to eat, she treated him sarcastically rather than in anger, saying to him. "Here he is, our new, well-known Mafioso." This made Tac pull his head into his shoulders and shrink back a little.

"What are you talking about Lana?" Natalie stroked Tac's head, seeing that he was licking his nose nervously.

"Ahh! I forgot to tell you that the other day I met our innocent, darling cat in the company of some very strange-looking characters. A stray dog that looked like a wolf, a skunk and a very suspicious crow that bribed a witness to their crime with money so that he would keep quiet about it. I wouldn't be surprised if one day a squad of police were to come to search our house to arrest Tacker, this Godfather of a criminal gang, in connection with a bank robbery. Otherwise, where did the crow get the money from? Is he an office clerk?"

After hearing Lana's story about the incident on Willie's driveway, Nicholas and Natalie exchanged puzzled looks and laughed themselves to tears. "I was worried for a moment that something bad had really happened, but thank goodness you are just joking at Tac's expense." Natalie cried out.

"I didn't know that you had such a good imagination." Nicholas, in his turn, added. "The story sounds very real. Ridiculous, but real."

Lana chose not to disturb her parents by trying to prove the reality of everything she had told them, knowing that it would not work in her favor but would only increase their concern. However, after everyone had left the living room, she gave the cat a hard stare, saying. "I can't prove anything but I will watch you, Mr. Gangsterito."

Running home to the wood with Natalie's cell phone hanging around his neck, Tac thought over Lana's words and admitted to himself that they had hurt him. 'I am not a gangster. The tie of a business man is more in keeping with the natural white collar around my neck. And, eventually, I will have a chance to prove it to Lana.'

When it was time to make the phone call to Carl, he held his paws crossed for luck. "Yes, yes!" He said excitedly, when Carl told Carfield that he had no choice but to accept the offer of becoming the Manager, taking the burden of management off Tac's shoulders.

The next step was to lease the piece of land from the city and legalize the company, which he decided to call The Amusing Golden Nut Ltd.

Carfield, carefully moving the pen, completed an application to the local business license office for the new operation, giving the address of Tac's Master, Nicholas, as the company's home office location. Then they needed to wait patiently for the answer to come from the licensing department. The crow spent several days sitting on a lamp post, waiting for the post lady to put the family mail in the mail box so that he could search through it for Tac's correspondence. Finally, the letter arrived. He pulled the envelope from the pile of flyers and shouted. "Got you!"

Tac now had a company with a legal name but, to operate the business, he needed to open a bank account. Arranging this was a very difficult and risky business which therefore necessitated the re-appearance of Old Joe once more.

Constantly coughing and sneezing at the bank, Carfield apologized for having a bad cold that prompted him to use a big, striped handkerchief that was held by Tac's gloved paw. The lady who was opening the account for him kept her distance, mostly looking at her computer screen instead of at a strange-looking old man. But, after Tac had presented two cases filled with newly-printed money, she had become scared.

"I don't think that I can take cash without knowing the source of it." She said, honestly.

Carfield pretended that her mistrust irritated him deeply. "Do you think that I have robbed a bank and then escaped on my scooter? Or do I look like a drug dealer? I sold an old treasure which I had received from my grandparents, discovering unexpectedly that it was worth a considerable amount of money. Now I want to start a business with it, because money must be spent to make money, instead of merely being left lying untouched in the bank doing nothing for me. If you do not believe me, then you may call the antique store on Sunbluff Street and ask the owner about his recent business with Mr. Holmes. Go ahead, make the call, you can find the number in the telephone book."

After some hesitation, the middle-aged-woman, who had a small plastic card pinned to her blouse with the name Monica written on it, decided that it would be better to be safe than sorry and went to talk to the manager. Common sense told her that, since the client was already angry, her cautious action could not damage their relationship any more than it already was. When the voice of Jeff Tompkins on the 'phone reassured her boss that the deal was legal, and that the money was "clean", Monica received his permission to complete all the required procedures to allow her to quickly get rid of this unpleasant old man.

After leaving the bank, Tac became worried about the possibility of the attractions being sold off to someone else and persuaded Carfield to call Carl as soon as Old Joe had safely returned to Willie's shed. But the windows in Willie's house were closed and the crow used the telephone on the street instead.

"Hullo, Carl." He said. "Is there anything new? You say that the new owner gave you only three days to vacate the trailer? Well, that is short notice, I must say. However, you do not need to worry because I have received all the necessary papers from the licensing office and my friend has deposited the money into a bank account in name of the company. Buy everything that you think we will need for a small, but successful, fairground. I have already found a piece of land and tomorrow I will call the City Hall to find out how I can lease it. A year ago, someone tried to establish a camping business there but failed and closed it down but I think that some basic amenities, such as a sewer and a phone line, are still there. It will not hurt if someone could check it out more thoroughly and I think I will take on this task myself. I am going to give you my telephone number. Since I am in poor health I may not answer the phone right away and this will mean that I have gone to see a doctor. If this happens, please leave a message and I will return your call shortly afterwards.

As far as the purchase of the equipment and electrical items is concerned, I will send you a cheque to cover the costs as soon as you tell me the total amount. Finally, please try to finish this business with Leo as fast as possible so that we can concentrate our attention on putting the park on the ground. Talk to you later, Carl."

A day later, back at his home, Tac was putting the final touches to a map. Holding a marker in a paw was not easy for him so the work moved very slowly. "Alisa, is there something wrong?" He asked. "You have been staring at me for almost an hour without saying anything."

"I was thinking about the changes that have happened since you came to live in our wood." Alisa approached him to look at the map.

"Do you think these changes are good or bad?" Tac queried, humorously.

"I do not know everyone's opinion, but you have definitely brought changes into our lives. Look at Carfield, for example. Not so long ago I could not have imagined that a friendship between him and Woo would have been possible. And Roxal, the raccoon, has always growled at me but now he is willing to help me any time that I ask him. Even Stewy, the skunk who, before your arrival, was usually ignored and excluded from any activities, has now become part of the forest team and acknowledged. You have broken the wall between the animal clans and blended them together. But probably not everyone is happy about bringing humans into our forest. There is no line of separation between our two worlds anymore; people and animals are starting to occupy the same space and unfortunately it is we who need to change in order to survive."

"A species that does not change is doomed to perish." Tac muttered sadly.

"Aah! All this smart talk has made me tired." She sighed. "Let us have a peaceful lunch before this noisy bird, Carfield, visits us again to talk into your new cell phone."

As soon as they had finished eating, the well-known voice of Carfield was heard as he entered the house. "Hullo Tac, did you call for me? Hullo Alisa."

"Sit down with us, Carfield, and have a piece of bread and cheese." Tac moved his plate to give space to the guest.

"Good food." Carfield admitted, after a few quick bites. "You are lucky to have a generous family that still supports you after you have moved out."

"Yes, but very soon we will not have to depend on anyone." Replied Tac, handing the cell-phone to him. "Carl Mayer called. I think he has news for us!"

The crow was curious himself. "Hi Carl, how is our business doing?" A long pause followed this question, ending in an excited shout from the crow. "You have managed to get Leo to cut the price almost in half? What was his reaction? I suppose that he was not really happy but did not have a choice? Yes, I agree, he is not a good businessman. I will send you a cheque tomorrow morning by courier. Carl, I can trust you. Being a manager of a fairground with a steady and secure income will appeal to you more than being constantly chased around like a thief. Before I forget, I talked to a city engineer and he told me that the sewer, the telephone and the electrical lines have already been installed at this location, but we need to put in another electrical cable for our rides. Can you handle this? Yes! Perfect! Tell me how much it will cost and I will send you another cheque. As soon as all this work has been completed you can start to transfer everything that relates to the fairground from storage to the property which we have rented in the woods. The animals' compound will be finished by the time you have completed this move. At least that's what the builder has promised me.

I will be busy myself with advertising. Putting an advertisement in the local paper is the best way to attract the attention of our potential customers but this, alone, is not enough and I will need to come up with something really original to accomplish that. If you can think of a good idea, give me a call. Yes, keep me informed about progress. Goodbye, Carl."

"Carfield, did you tell Carl that you had hired a contractor?" Asked Tac.

"Yes, but I did not tell him who it was. A family of beavers, with the help of all of us, can build a spacious cabin better than any human contractor. I will ask the Council to encourage the members of their families to participate in the project. And why wait for tomorrow to look for a place? It's only noon, so we have plenty of time to do it today."

After considerable discussion and arguments, Tac and Carfield prepared a proposal for the members of the Council to approve. The Council was waiting for them, sitting on their stones on Council Hill. They listened to Tac with interest since the animals expected something unusual from him, but the current project exceeded all their expectations. The Council members needed some time to think about the proposal before expressing their opinions.

The rabbit, Shustin, was against the idea to bring humans into the woods and immediately said so. "They will bring their children and their dogs into the fairground and they will run around everywhere, disturbing and chasing birds and small animals like me."

"Yes! They will throw garbage and leftovers everywhere and collect our berries to leave us with nothing." Brown Bob, the bear, supported him.

"We plan to put the fairground in a separate area away from the part of the woods which we, the animals, inhabit so that we can maintain our privacy." Responded Tac.

"What if some of the humans come with guns to hunt us?" Asked Rainar.

"We will put up a sign that will read. "Private Zoo, Hunting of Rare and Valuable Animals is Forbidden." And, in addition to this, we will ask the police to protect the area from armed people, advising them that we have great concern for the safety of children. The police would not leave their own children without protection, would they?" Carfield explained.

"What if the animals and the birds do not agree to work in the park as employees?" Galibur chipped-in.

"We already have a list of volunteers and I think that this list will triple when the business starts to prove its value. I am only asking for help with the construction of the building of the animal compound, to put small bridges over the two creeks and make benches for visitors. Finally, we will need to place garbage containers in different locations to keep our woods clean." Tac stopped for a moment to take a breath, allowing Galibur the chance to say.

"Enough! Enough! Tac. First we need to discuss whether or not we can all agree to turn our wood into a zoo and, after that, we may talk about details."

"Has everyone had enough time to make a decision? Can we vote now?" Rainar received their nods of agreement.

"Galibur?" he started… "Agreed."

"I myself agree." Said Rainar.

"Mixie?"…   "I disagree."

"Shustin?"…   "Against."

"Woo?"…   "I disagree."

"Brown Bob?"..."I agree."

"Carfield?"…   "Of course I agree."

Then everyone looked at the last Council member. If he were to say "I disagree" then the number of positive and negative votes would be equal and the Council would need to look for additional opinions. However the Boar, named Proff, did not rush in to vote and kept everyone waiting for his decision. 'Dogs are not good.' Mumbled Proff, to himself. 'And I do not know what to think about food leftovers being thrown everywhere.' He looked at Tac and asked. "What kind of food do they eat?"

Tac, knowing that the correct answer would be important, selected his words carefully. "Popcorn, potato chips, salted peanuts, for example. But the favorite food would be chocolate bars." Proff, immediately imagining the pathways in the wood piled up with human food, stated. "I agree!"

Upon hearing this, Mixie and Shustin tried to argue, but Rainar hit a rock with his hoof and rendered his judgment. "By the decision of the Council of Pokerweild Wood, Tac will be allowed to build his fairground and employ any animal whom he needs to do the work in his project."

During the remaining time left for Carl to bring the 'attractions' into the woods, Tac had been busy trying to be in more than one place at a time and generally exhausting himself by trying to do too much work himself.

A team of beavers had started to cut down trees for building the cabin whilst others already worked on bridges. Their helpers soaked thin branches of willows in the water to braid them into boxes to contain garbage and for the backs of benches that would later be attached to large tree trunks.

Eventually every piece of the project had been properly placed and secured on the ground.

Carl had just as much interest as Tac in making sure that the show was put on the road as quickly as possible. He had spent most of his life in the entertainment business and he was lonely without a crowd of people around him. He missed the bright colors of flashing lights, the smell of hot dogs coming from the little booth and the roaring sound of the rollercoaster as it tore down the slopes of its track. It pleased him when the metallic sound of the runners was all mixed in with the laughter and screams of excitement from many mouths together with the loud music. Carl's heart ached for movement, children's voices talking loudly, young couples glowing with happiness whilst they held each other's hands and walked around smiling at each other. Just looking at them alone was enough to light up a warm smile on his face.

Driving his trailer ahead of the rented trucks containing the purchased equipment, he turned into the wood. Bright, orange arrows attached to the bushes led a chain of vehicles in the direction of the abandoned campground, hidden inside the wood. It had been agreed that the fairground would be placed close to the lake, surrounded by a narrow strip of gray, sandy beach. The trucks had almost reached the shore when a directional arrow guided the convoy to the right side of the lake where the plot of land had been cleared of vegetation. The drivers jumped out of their vehicles, disconnected the trailers, and then departed.

Carl was left to wait for another hired crew to arrive who would help him put all of these pieces together to create a little village of brightly-painted amusement booths which would, in the future, generate many happy memories for his customers. Wasting no time while he awaited his help, Carl made a simple sketch of the future amusement park. Then he used another side of the page to mark the boxes that would need to be opened first and looked around to see if the space available here was sufficient for his plan. The clearing was located very close to the rocky bed of the small river and the view of the shore suggested the idea to him of placing the rails of the roller coaster just under the surface of the water. As the carriages crossed it they would splash water out to each side. He only needed to ensure that the people inside the carriages did not get soaking wet.

Upon hearing an unexpected sound, Carl turned in that direction and walked along the pathway to search for its source. What he saw stopped him in his tracks and his mouth fell open in astonishment. A large brown bear, dressed in the orange coverall of a road worker, with gray and yellow reflective stripes over it, shoveled some relatively-dry straw by working with a pitchfork as if it was weightless. Only one strap covered his furry shoulder, leaving the other one hanging down. The bear scowled at the man but did not make any aggressive moves towards him, merely continuing on with his work. He carried the last pile of hay up to the door of the building and put it into a straw container fixed to the inner wall at an angle. After the bear had finished the work, he returned the fork to the general tool box and disappeared behind the door of the building which had the word "Zoo" painted on a wooden sign above the door.

Carl read the sign above the first level, puzzled by its meaning. He looked upward at the second level that appeared to be of similar proportions and design. It had a balcony along the front with two sets of staircases, one on the left side and one on the right side of the building. The left staircase served not only for walking but had a storage area under it for a large barrow and boxes with garden tools.

A sudden ring of his cell phone stopped Carl from looking inside the compound and the familiar voice of Joe greeted him.

"Hi Joe." He replied. "I have just arrived on the site and am standing in front of the two-story building carrying the sign "Zoo" on it. It's written in uneven letters which are shaded in different colors. Do you know anything about this?" Having listened carefully to Old Joe's reply, Carl went on: "Oh! So this compound is the place where your friend has placed his animals? I must say that it's very close to the fairground and I don't see any cages that will keep the animals inside this area. What do you mean by telling me that they will live here free to move around as they please? I saw a bear in coveralls that, from what I can determine, lives on the first level. All of the inhabitants of your Zoo may be harmless, but they are still animals and there is no guarantee that some of them may not attack a person one day. You insist that they won't? Can you guarantee this? That's crazy! Listen, my crew will arrive in less than five minutes so I don't have time to talk. Do you have a trainer, or guard, who can watch over the animals and make sure that they don't go into the assembly site? You are saying that you have already attended to this? I hope that everything will be fine. Talk to you soon, Joe. I hear a sound of a car coming. Yes, I'll call you later."

Carl returned to the line of abandoned platforms and big rectangular boxes and, walking towards a group of the chatting men, he held out his hand to greet a strongly-built fellow.

"Hullo Carl." Don greeted him. "Please give me a moment." He looked at his watch and said to his crew. "It's a quarter to ten and, looking at the clear blue sky, I assume that it will be very hot later. Let's get started." Then, turning to Carl, he asked. "Have you decided where you want to put each item?"

As Carl nodded, Don again addressed his crewmen. "Perfect, hurry up boys. Kevin, drop your cigarette and start to work. Do you see those three containers? Measure them and mark their position with pegs. Do you see those stones on the ground? Well, this is the place where Carl wants to put them. Make sure that the containers fit into the markings. You two can start to dismantle this truck and, Mark, take the rest of the men and start to remove the sections of the rollercoaster and watch that you don't lose any of the screws."

Seeing that all of his men had started to work, he returned to Carl saying. "Putting up a rollercoaster is a tricky business. It must be secured, balanced and made safe for the children. It's not very high, but it's still very important that we do not make any mistakes. I think that your Ferris wheel would be better placed in the right corner, instead of in the middle of the park, because it will open up a fine view of part of the lake and the mountains. I think it will be a very interesting sight for the people on top of the circle."

"I think you're right."

"Next, just move the Merry-Go-Round into the middle." Don adjusted Carl's plan and walked to the shore to take a good look around. "The river is quite low and has wide shores. It will allow us to secure the base to the deep concrete posts that we'll put into the ground. Carl, this site is not a bad choice for your business and, if you work hard, you should be able to make a lot of money here. It may be far away from the city but, look, you can have a few horses here for people to ride and the lake and the river have fish in them. I myself caught a trout as big as this one." And Don spread his hands showing the size of a small shark.

"Are you sure?" Carl smiled.

"Ah, well, perhaps it was little smaller, but it didn't make the fun of catching fish any less for me." Don Laughed.

So, it took Carl three days to assemble all the pieces of equipment and to do a test run of each attraction.

During this period, Tac had spent his time thinking about better ways to advertise the fairground. "I have put an advertisement in a local newspaper, as I was advised, but from my point of view it will not be enough. We need to do something else. Something that will make everyone talk about the park." He informed Carfield.

"I do not know what else we can do. Maybe dress me up as a clown and parade me through the streets with an advertising sign pinned to me." Carfield was desperate for ideas.

Roxal and Woo chuckled.

But Tac's eyes flashed. "A parade? Yes, of course! We need a parade of costumed animals, followed by a big sign. 'Amusing Golden Nut, the best place for a weekend of family fun, will shortly open its doors!' Carfield, you are a genius. We need to ask Carl to print a simple booklet and spread it amongst the onlookers at the parade. A monkey, we need a monkey for this business!"

"A squirrel could do it, easily." The crow reminded everyone.

"I guess we need to use local talent." Tac agreed. "Carfield, can you arrange that anyone who knows how to hold a needle and can make a stitch should come to my home tomorrow, bringing any scrap of fabric that they can find. Anyone who has an idea for a costume is welcome too."

"This I can do, but please do not ask me to wear a clown's costume." The crow pleaded.

"We need to forget about our personal pride for the sake of our business." The cat gave the crow a direct look. "If it will help, I will dress up in a costume myself to bring customers in to view the opening of the park. We have spent all of our money on the park and now we need to make it work to make a profit. I now expect you to call City Hall to get permission for a Sunday parade on Sunbluff Street for the animals of a private Zoo which is owned by a Mr. Holmes. The street is closed to cars anyway and we will therefore not be interrupting the activities of the humans. Please try to be as charming as you can because we need to get this permission. If deer horns placed on the head of a dog can amuse men, we can do something better than that." Finally, addressing all his friends, he ended. "Animals, lets prove that we are creative too!"

By the end of the week, the level of the inspiration of the inhabitants of the wood had slowly risen to its highest point. Everyone was working at something connected with the future event, or just talking about it and keeping the flames of interest in the coming parade burning steadily.

On Saturday morning all the members of the parade gathered in front of the animal building, waiting for Carl to take them to the city on one of the wheeled platforms decorated with the Park's logo. As he hurriedly finished his coffee and sandwich, he looked at the clock and became more and more impatient. "Where's Joe?" He eventually asked, but a sudden telephone call startled him. 'Oh, no!' He sighed. 'Don't tell me that you're going to put more responsibilities on my shoulders?' He took the 'phone and prepared to speak to Joe whom he had not yet seen in person.

"Hi Joe, where are you? It's time to leave if we want to arrive at the city in time. I can't drive straight to Sunbluff Street because the city officials have told me to park the truck three blocks away from there and walk my animals to Sunbluff. However, they have agreed to send a couple of police cars that will watch over the safety of the animals and the people. Everything is looking very good and I feel that many spectators will be attracted to the show for sure. What? You can't come? You have high blood pressure? I will have high blood pressure too if no one comes to help me. What do you want me to do now? Do you want me to talk to the animals as if they are normal actors? You must be kidding me, Joe? What can I do if they all start to run in different directions? I know that all the money has been spent and I am willing to do everything that I can to help you. I'll leave now because I don't want to be blamed for the failure of your enterprise before it can even get started. However, if I lose your pets through no fault of mine, then please do not complain."

Carl turned off the cell phone and lit a cigarette, holding it with shaking fingers. 'Perfect, just perfect! Joe has chosen a great time to get sick.' He inwardly moaned. 'Ten o'clock.' He said to himself, looking at his watch. 'It's time to leave.' He pressed what remained of his cigarette into the ash tray and picked up the keys.

Animal Parade in Murraydale

The animals were all waiting for him. They formed a half circle, some sitting and some standing. Carl opened the back of the platform and said to them. "O.K. fellows, come inside. Your boss is sick and you must listen to me. I don't know how to work with you, so please co-operate." He then paused, searching for words, feeling like a fool.

Tac decided that it was a good time to interrupt and gave an ordering "Meow." Two deer were the first animals to move towards the truck, taking up positions along the insides. The bear was next, followed by the raccoons and four wolves who sat on the floor, leaving the space in the middle of the platform for a group of mice, squirrels and rabbits. However, the birds had decided to fly by themselves and had followed the truck. Entering the driver's cabin, Carl found a cat dressed in a graduation hat, adorned with a silken tassel dangling from its left side, sitting in the passenger's seat. A black collar finished off his sharp appearance.

Next to him sat a crow with a pointed clown's hat on his head which tinkled with bells at every movement. A winged collar, matching his hat, highlighted his neck.

"What's this then?" Carl expressed his surprise, but gave up asking questions and started the engine. Remembering about the vulnerability of his cargo, he tried to drive at a steady speed and ignored the impatient horns of the vehicles behind him. It took him a little more than an hour to reach the point where he needed to leave his truck and thereafter walk his brightly-dressed crew through the streets. A police officer looked at his driver's license and, after talking on the phone with his partner in the car, resumed their discussion about the procession. The animals had been left without supervision for only a moment but, after Carl and the officer had turned their attention back to the parade, they found that all the participants had already formed a correct square of their own initiative.

The cat was standing at the head of the throng of animals like the conductor of an orchestra, followed by a deer dressed in a collar from a man's shirt and wearing a tie which matched a gray, velvety hat which he wore sportingly between his horns.

Roxal, the raccoon, dressed in a skirt made from dry straw, accented with a garland of flowers around his neck, was sitting on the back of the deer and held one side of a stretched fabric sign, which had been Tac's idea but had been created by Carfield. The other side of the sign was held by Alisa, the fox, who wore a lacy decoration around her neck and tail and sat on the back of another male deer whose horns had been adorned with bows made out of different-colored ribbons. A necklace made from strips of the same ribbons enhanced his neck.

Bertrond, who was the only performer who occupied the third line, wore a fashionable, sleeveless coverall of a road worker and had a large pipe in his mouth which he pretended to smoke, albeit with a twinkle in his eye.

The fourth line comprised three wolves dressed in vests that imitated the coverlets which would normally adorn the backs of valiant knights' horses. The bright feathers were somehow attached to the heads of the wolves as if they, the wolves, were the brave steeds. The wolf on the left carried three mice, dressed as musketeers, on his back and a squirrel sat on the back of the wolf in the middle, wearing on her head an ice cream cone which had been painted in gold and decorated with a piece of valance to match her dress. She held up a large branch, with gold-colored hazel nuts attached to it, to reflect the park logo.

The wolf on the right side was ridden by a rabbit, powdered all over his person with white flour that served as a good background for a bright-red bow which had been fastened around his neck. His costume was completed by a silver Prince's crown on his head which had been borrowed from Carfield's collection.

All of Roxal's family of raccoons, decorated in pink, feathery scarves, and with golden threads attached to their tails, took up the next line followed by a group of four herons in white tutus with matching silky bows on their skinny legs.

Last, but by no means least, came Woo who was dressed like a Viking invader and wore a horned helmet upon his head. The second rabbit, who wore a similar helmet, was sitting on Woo's back next to a crow dressed as a clown who made everyone laugh at his bored expression.

Carl and the smiling police officer took up the position in front of Tac so that they could ask people to stand back from the parade to make space for the performers and to advise the crowd not to feed the animals or to pet them. The second officer, positioned at the rear of the parade, controlled the security of the back line and kept the curious and excited spectators at some distance from the animals.

Carl, being on the first line, had already started to give-out booklets containing pictures of the Amazing Golden Nut Park to all who wished to take them. This event did not have any music, but one of the admiring onlookers had agreed to accompany Carl and his Zoo and turn up the volume on his portable radio Thus, accompanied by heavy rock, the parade moved towards Sunbluff, pulling many patrons out of the adjoining cafes and shops like iron-filings to a magnet.

It was not long before the street was packed with laughing spectators of all ages. Parents pointed-out the funny and brightly-colored costumes to their excited children who were very surprised that the animals were not afraid of people. Walking slowly to the end of the street, the parade then turned round and wended its way back to the truck in the same formation, collecting more and more people on the way.

Two hours spent under the great pressure of being surrounded by so many people had completely exhausted the animals and they slept peacefully in the truck until they had arrived home. When Carl finally opened the back of the truck, he saw the unusual picture of a variety of different animals all sleeping peacefully in one tight group. The funniest scene was probably that of the view of the three musketeers having fallen asleep on the belly of the rough road-worker who still had his pipe in the corner of his mouth.

Early next morning, Carl's nephews, and their friends who had volunteered to help until Carl could find regular staff, arrived at the fairground. They parked their vehicles next to Carl's old truck and knocked on the door of the trailer, laughing at being presented with the opportunity to do something unusual, as they had once done when they were children.

"Hullo, Uncle Carl." Said the youngest.

"Hullo, Jason. How is your dad? I see that you are growing up." Carl examined him shrewdly with his eyes. "Thanks for helping out."

He then addressed the rest of the young men. "I am short of staff right now and I am grateful for your positive response to my call. Please follow me and I will show you how to operate the attractions. Believe me, it's very simple to do. Even a person who knows nothing about mechanics can handle these jobs, after some training."

As the group of men walked through the narrow passageway between two grounded trailers, they stopped in disbelief. All the booths and attractions had already been prepared for work. The bear, dressed in his favorite coverall, was sweeping the concrete with a broom. Two raccoons were busy chopping lettuce and tomato on the table for hamburgers and hotdogs and two large, open barbecues were standing at the table, ready to start grilling. Squirrels continued to arrange the line of stuffed toys that had been selected as prizes for the winners of different games and the cat, in the company of the crow, was walking from station to station checking the readiness of all the equipment.

"Carl, you did not tell us that you had hired animals. Look, they've already prepared the park for work. They have even decorated the gate with clusters of golden nuts. How are you going to pay them?" Jason laughed.

"We still need a man to operate the park's equipment when the customers arrive because animals cannot talk or count money." Feeling awkward, Carl turned away from the animals and went on to explain how each piece of equipment worked, sometimes looking curiously at the illegal helpers who did not seem to be afraid of the humans that had invaded their small collective.

The bear finished sweeping the area around the rides and, after hiding his broom behind the tent, rejoined the raccoons at the barbeque who were busy putting brushes, forks and spatulas onto the side table. He looked inside the cooler, growled something, and immediately disappeared to get another cooler.

"Carl." Shawn, his older nephew, spoke up. "If the bear is going to be in charge of the barbeque, then this part of the show alone would make it worthwhile for anyone to make the journey from the city to see it."

"The only unique barbequing bear chef in town!" He announced loudly to his friends.

Bertrond growled a short, sarcastic phrase in their direction and put seven wieners on the grill. Cuffy's elegant fingers gently opened the same amount of buns and lined them up on a tray like soldiers on parade. The bear dropped a hot, steamy wiener into each bun and another raccoon filled the sides of the bun with the usual mixture of vegetables, sprinkled on top with generous portions of mustard and ketchup. Bertrond took the tray and walked in the direction of the men who nervously started to back away from him. Eventually, all the men were hiding behind Carl. The bear gave the tray to Carl and returned to his barbeque, swaying as if he was walking on the deck of a ship. Curiosity pushed even the most cautious of them to come forward and pick up one of the hotdogs.

"They are good." Shawn tried one.

"Mmm! Very good." Agreed the rest of the jury and decided to give the bear the highest grade for his cooking skills.

The day was bright and warm and the music made a nice background for a happy Sunday outing. The vegetation, still fresh and green, appealed to the eyes but no patron came along to appreciate their efforts until eleven a.m. The lack of people in the park was a disappointment to Carl after all the hard work that had been completed and it almost made him cry. What else could he do to make this place popular to a family, he wondered? Eventually, somebody high above decided to reward Carl for all his efforts and one single family, consisting of two adults and two children, entered the gate. Understandably, not seeing any other people in the park, they were cautious and thought. 'Where are the others? What is wrong with this place?' They considered turning round and leaving the fairground altogether.

This would probably have happened, if it was not for the presence of Bertrond. Like a magician, he pulled out a long, white chef's hat from somewhere and placed it on his head, then put four sausages on the grill and turned them from side to side. In short order, four hot dogs were ready and had been served up on a tray by the chef himself. The ridiculous combination of a coverall and a chef's hat, which covered only one of his ears, was so amusing to the children that they timidly stepped forward to take the food from the tray rather than running to their suddenly-anxious parents for protection.

"Don't worry." Carl tried to allay their suspicions about the bear's possible aggression. "He is a circus bear and grew up around children."

The parents squeezed out a wan smile and then each tried a hotdog for themselves. At the next moment the attention of the first customer was drawn to Carfield who had landed on top of the counter and pecked vigorously at the metal body of the small cash register whilst crying out. "Money, money, money." Pretending that this was all the English that he could speak.

"They have a talking crow!" The boy screamed in excitement. "Dad, can I pay?"

"Ok." His father, still a bit nervous about the whole situation, gave a banknote to his son.

Carfield pecked out the numbers on the cash register and picked out the change to drop coins into the lad's small palm. With a radiant smile on his face, the child ran to his parents to present the change to them.

"Look, dad, he gave me change!"

"Then, let's see if the crow is correct?" His father replied. "How much does a hotdog cost?" He asked the crow, to which Carfield responded by pecking three times.

"He wanted to say three dollars." Carl explained to his first customer.

"I don't know how he calculated this, but he gave me the correct change!" The man answered, in some astonishment.

"Dad, dad, may I invite Tim?" His daughter pulled his shirt sleeve.

"Yes, Sweetie, you can call him." He handed his daughter the cell phone to share the details of their experience with friends.

After this, all the family decided to try the rollercoaster that they had first seen upon entry to the fairground. Inspired by the excited screams, their mother called up friends and within half an hour over twenty more people had arrived, all agog to see the show of the barbeque bear chef. To their surprise, they saw that the fairground was full of specially-trained animals that served as hosts at many of the games and personally delivered prizes to the winners, which made the stuffed toys more desirable in the eyes of the younger children. Meanwhile, the parents who had just arrived watched the happy faces of their children, inevitably leading to more 'phone calls being made to more friends and neighbors in order to invite them to witness this unusual fairground for themselves.

Bertrond, the bear chef, worked as if he was operating a small restaurant, producing burgers and hotdogs with maximum speed and efficiency, but without compromising the taste. He used up the supplies in two coolers, then brought in two more.

All the attractions were now operating without any empty seats. The excited screams that came from the people in the rollercoaster, when it was going through the river, quickly led to a line-up of people waiting for their turn to go on the ride and kept a steady stream of customers at this station until closing time.

By the end of the day, Carl was exhausted and postponed the counting of the money until the next day. He felt that with a fresh head he would be able to do it more accurately. Meanwhile, two wolves took up guard around the trailer to protect the hard-earned income.

The next day was Monday, the official day-off, and Carl did not need to get up early. But the question of how much they had made in cash receipts consumed his mind, even before he had opened his eyes. Wearing only his pajamas, he brought the heavy bags to the table and sorted out all of the bank notes according to their value, counted them and arrived at the princely sum of $2,689. The little, metal soft-drink can that Carl had put out to collect tips for his hard-working employees brought-in another $60 and Carl thought to himself. 'I'll spend this money on food for my non-human employees.'

It also occurred to him that it would be a very good idea in the future to dress the bear and the raccoons in white uniforms. He made himself a cup of coffee and picked up the phone to call Old Joe.

"Hullo Joe, it was unfortunate that you couldn't come yesterday. I must admit that I was scared at first that no one would come to the fairground, even after our colorful parade, but the first day was a success after all. All of my first customers' friends showed up at the gate, so I gave my first family a special gift, a stuffed squirrel holding a golden nut which is the logo of the fairground."

"That's fine. You can order another and, by the way, we can start to sell stuffed animals as souvenirs. A crow, for example, or a bear in a white hat with his cooking tools."

"That's a good idea." Carl agreed. "This can be another source of money and free advertising. Meantime, I want to tell you how much we have made."

Before he could finish speaking, the telephone suddenly disconnected. "What's the problem with this phone?" Carl pressed the number again, but the phone at the other end was silent. "Joe, Joe, pick up the phone. Don't tell me that you have had a heart attack from happiness." But there was no answer so he tried the number again.

"Hi Carl." Once again he heard Joe's voice, but this time it sounded like it wasn't coming from the phone but from somewhere close. Then the voice went on. "My phone is dying. Tell me quickly how much we made?"

"$2,689." Carl answered, looking around inside his trailer for the source of the sound.

"That's great!" Joe's happy voice came through one of the trailer's open windows.

Carl stood with his back to the wall and, hiding behind the short curtain, he looked outside only to see a cat with a cell phone who was trying to calm-down a crow that seemed to be dancing some wild Native Indian dance.

"Joe, don't go away, I want to discuss some other business with you." Carl tried to get over his shock.

Hearing this, Carfield stopped dancing and said. "I am sorry, but the batteries in my phone are dying so I will have to call you back tomorrow after I fix this useless piece of equipment." And he pecked at the little cell phone case to relieve his frustration.

"And what is the meaning of this, then?" The calm, but angry, voice of Carl interrupted his action."

Tac and Carfield immediately turned their heads in the direction of the voice and saw Carl's tense face looking at them steadily.

"Carl, please don't be angry with us. We can explain everything." Both tricksters had exchanged startled looks with each other.

Tac was afraid that Carl would quit his job as Manager if he were to discover that his boss was actually a cat and he tried to stop Carfield from saying anything more.

However, the crow hastily said to Tac. "Carl has found out that Joe is in fact you and I and we owe him an honest explanation." Then, addressing the manager, he continued." May we enter your house to talk about this?"

Carl's face immediately disappeared from the window and in a moment the door flew open. Tac and Carfield went inside and sat down on seats opposite Carl, who took out a cigarette, knowing no other way to calm down his feelings.

"Carl, we used you, that's true. And for this we both must apologize to you sincerely. In a situation like this we did not have any other choice. The problem is that Mr. Holmes is sitting right in front of you." The crow nodded in the direction of the Cat. "He was the one who found the two golden coins in the forest." He then related the whole story to Carl about the treasure and its transformation into a business.

"Who are you?" Carl demanded, blowing out a cloud of smoke from his pursed lips.

"At one time I was a regular crow, the same as many millions of my relatives, until I became a victim of an experiment that I cannot understand myself and therefore am unable to explain to others. Now, if someone were to make it public, then I would probably end my life as an experimental crow in a laboratory cage, tested and pinched with a needle so that smart doctors in white robes could understand how I managed to start talking."

"Is there any other animal in this wood that can talk?"

"No, I am the only freak." Carfield replied. "I am a scientific accident, but the rest of the inhabitants are one hundred per cent normal and communicate only in the way in which their species are supposed to. Carl, if you tell someone about me, I will not be the only one who will suffer because the rest of the animals may be put into cages as well and, for all we know, perhaps even your own normality may be questioned. On the other hand, if we keep this matter a secret, then no one needs to get hurt. We will provide an honest service and charge a competitive price and we intend to pay taxes and operate a genuine business. Unfortunately, being animals, we cannot register it as a regular human business and that is why we created Joe, the disabled old man who has a habit of annoying everyone which, incidentally, is also part of his disguise. The proof of this is that even you did not bother to look at his face, otherwise you would have noted that he was a fraud a long time ago. So, the disguise and the personality work very well together don't they?"

Carl silently puffed at his cigarette, deep in thought, until the acrid taste of its filter obliged him to make a decision about his employment. He had two choices available to him: declare the fraud and return to the same homeless situation that he had been in almost a month ago, or continue the game as if nothing had happened and try to save as much money as he could in the hope that the fraud would not be discovered for some time.

"Carl, what will you gain by exposing us? Since the company does not belong to you, it will be taken over by someone who is brutal and strong enough to keep it. Please remember that we have started to like you so why would you want to break our hearts?"

After having being shocked by their exposure, Carl did not want to give these two charmers a sense of his forgiveness too soon since he knew that things that have been given out too freely often have little value to the receiver.

So, pretending to be still angry and casually removing another cigarette from its packet, he asked them. "Is there anything else that you are keeping a secret from me?"

Tac and Carfield exchanged swift looks. The cat lifted an eyebrow as a warning to the crow who, therefore, carefully said. "There are many secrets in this wood and the mountains are the guardians of them also. Believe me, Carl, knowledge of them is dangerous and, no matter where you may go, that danger will follow you like my tail is always following me. It will be best to leave secrets to rest where they are."

"I need to think more about what you have told me to allow me to make a correct decision." Carl replied, cautiously. "Right now, I need to go to the bank and put the money into our account."

"Woo will go with you."

"Are you afraid that I will run away with the money?" Carl laughed, rising from his chair.

"No, it is not that, it's just that I want to make sure that nothing happens to you. We have a selfish interest in your safety because we need your help." Carfield admitted.

Carl was not offended by this statement. As a matter of fact he was pleased. He had not heard the words that somebody needed him for a long time and had almost forgotten how it felt to be important to someone. Another reason why Carl was sympathetic to these two liars was because he had a sneaking liking for anything mysterious himself and he was intrigued and anxious to find out what else was hidden underneath this animal business operation. Carl understood that he would never find out the truth if he walked away, so he decided to stay and carefully watch what kind of game they were all playing.

Woodan, the wolf, was waiting for him by the car but, unlike an adoring dog, he did not start to wag his tail. Instead, the wolf used his eyes alone to direct Carl's attention to the door, clearly requesting him to open it. Once the door had been opened, he jumped onto the front passenger seat beside him and remained silent all the way to the city. When they arrived at the bank, the manager left the car and asked Woo to stay inside it. However, Woo ignored this request and immediately jumped out and took up a position at his side in order to guard the case. After they had walked towards the building, Woo sat silently next to the bank entrance showing that he intended to wait for the manager to come out again. Carl removed his deposit book from the case and stood in the small queue to await his turn to talk to the cashier.

Noticing the amount of cash that he intended to deposit, the cashier gave him a respectful look and said. "Sir, you'll be served by my manager. Please walk into his office." The bank manager, who was casually dressed in pants and a shirt with an open collar, shook hands with him. He checked the figures on the deposit slip and completed the transaction.

"Mr. Mayer, I would like you to ask for me the next time you come in to deposit money. If your profits increase, which I hope will happen very soon, we will need to send a bank truck to your office for security reasons to pick up your cash. I would also like to suggest that you should consider hiring guards in the near future to protect the cash receipts on the days when you have been very busy. Your business is on the outskirts of the city and may attract people who prefer to get rich without working hard for it."

"Thanks for your advice." Carl shook the Manager's hand before leaving. After depositing the cash, he felt like someone who had suddenly lost forty pounds of weight.

"Woo, let's go shopping." He called out to the wolf, walking to the truck.

The first stop was at the wholesale store to load coolers packed with wieners and burgers for Bertrond's next cooking show. Then they parked at the general store to buy vegetables, buns and dry cat's food that the raccoons liked very much, together with bags of seeds for the birds and a carton of fresh cream for Tac.

All this time Woo waited for him patiently outside the door. People tried to converse with him, impressed by his size and wolf's appearance, but Woo only followed them with a contemptuous look on his face, smelling fear all over them. Dogs barked at him, recognizing his wild breed, but it didn't bother him. But when a little Chihuahua jumped out of its Mistress's bag and barked into his face with an annoying little voice and showed him its small, useless teeth, Woo lazily lifted his upper lip then wrinkled the velvety skin of his face and growled low, displaying the white daggers of his fangs accentuated by the line of a red tongue between them. His cold glance of hatred hit the poor little yelper like a fist, completely undermined its confidence and made it run for the protection of its Mistress hiding its funny, shaking excuse for a tail between its legs.

Eventually, Carl appeared in the opening of the door, rolling the loaded shopping cart in front of him. "Sorry Woo, it took longer than I expected. Just one more stop and we're done." He remarked to the wolf.

The next stop compensated Woo for all his good behavior by tickling his senses with the pleasant scent of fresh meat which came from the numerous packages and boxes that Carl and the shop employee had brought from the butcher's shop and loaded onto the truck. Woo followed them with appreciative eyes and licked his lips with a dreamy expression on his face. He slept all the way back home, having decided that sleep would help to reduce the long wait before he would be allowed to eat the contents of the packages.

Carl drove to the compound, shouting loudly out of the car window. "Breakfast!" Then he quickly arranged the food on plastic plates that would satisfy the appetites of his employees. For some time each of them concentrated their attention only on their own plates, biting, chewing and swallowing loudly. After everything had been eaten, noses licked clean and the plates of their closest neighbor checked for uneaten leftovers, they settled down for a nap.

"Enjoy your day off, my friends." He remarked, before leaving his staff. They only answered him with sleepy looks and lazy stretches.

The words of the bank manager were fulfilled with accuracy as if he was a medium and had looked into a crystal ball. Everyday brought more and more people into the fairground who wanted to see the hit of the season, the bear chef, and the amount of cash that the Golden Nut Amusement park made in a day became significant enough to oblige Carl to look for security guards.

Bertrond was now dressed in a white, embroidered uniform and the longest hat that Carl could find. The raccoons were dressed in shirts and small round hats, chopping vegetables with big knives for the entertainment of the public and, in the process, collecting their own share of fans.

Tac was always full of ideas. He suggested that the business should buy canoes and rent them out to visitors who were fond of fishing but were not rich enough to have their own boat. This would allow families to spend quality time at the lake together. The children and their mother could look at the animals whilst their father could enjoy himself by staring at the fishing string.

Two wolves, dressed in jackets which proudly displayed "Golden Nut Security," walked between the customers, swaying their large bodies. Sometimes they watched that nobody fell underneath the rolling wheels of the low-slung carriage. Full of yelling and laughing children, it was drawn by Boran, the boar, who was collecting snacks from the parents of his customers and eating them on the move. In fact, the business became so busy that Carl eventually decided to put an advertisement in a local newspaper about hiring more staff for the fairground. He filled available positions mostly with high-school youngsters from nearby villages, except for one young man whom he had met when he stopped to fill-up his car with gas on his trip back from the bank in Murraydale. When the teenager approached him to ask for change, Carl did not call for an attendant to escort the beggar behind the line of gas stations, but asked. "Why are you begging? You look healthy enough to work. Why do you humiliate yourself asking for a dollar?"

"I have no place to live and that is why no one wants to employ me. Without money I can't even rent a bed and, without a home, I can't get a job." The young man sadly shrugged his shoulders.

"It sounds like you are running round in circles." Carl admitted. "What would you say if I were to offer you a job in the fairground?"

"I would take it, sir. I promise that you won't regret hiring me." He nervously rubbed his hands.

Carl looked at his narrow, sharp-cornered face with the slight blue circles of fatigue around the eyes. This was evidence enough to him that the boy probably had not had food for days. It was not only the sign of hunger on the stranger's face that made Carl's heart skip a beat, but the pleading and hopeful expression in his eyes that made him realize that he could not leave him alone at this dirty gas station. If he were to do this, then he would be constantly dogged by feelings of guilt.

"Are you using any drugs?" Carl knew that even if the boy answered 'Yes' it wouldn't change anything.

"No sir." He rolled up the sleeves of his shirt to show his arms to Carl.

"Sit down in the car." Carl ended his own, and the boy's, doubts. "I can't promise you comfort but you'll have a shower, food, and a bed on my couch. The starting wage for my employees is nine dollars per hour, but I will have to charge you some rent until you save enough money to allow you to find your-self a room or an apartment. If we are in agreement then you can tell me your name."

The boy answered with a nod and a smile. "I'm Rick, sir."

Rick was rubbing himself with Carl's sponge in the washroom without any idea that his soapy, skinny body had brought out an argument between Carl and Carfield.

"Carl, did you pick him up under a trash can? You basically know nothing about him. He can even be a criminal wanted by police. We do not need any trouble." Carfield complained.

"He is just a kid in trouble. If somebody does not help the lad, instead of calling him names, he may very well end up becoming a criminal. I was myself in a similar situation at one point in my life and now I want to use this chance to keep goodness in balance. I want to give him a home and care, in the same way that I was treated many years ago by a man who befriended me. I was a drunken scruff at the time but he saw something good in me."

"If you have so much faith in him, then I prefer to say nothing more. Are we going to have supper?" Carfield decided to change the subject to something a little less irritating.

"I completely forgot about supper, arguing with you. Let's prepare the table." Carl brought food from the fridge.

"Wow." Said Rick, rubbing his wet, dark-blonde hair with a towel. The only time that I have seen so much food was in the window of a store. Are we going to eat all of this?"

"Of course! Sit down, Rick."

Carfield flew over to his plate at the corner of the small table which was covered by cups, cans, plates and plastic containers. The close proximity of the bird, possessed of a strong beak, scared Rick and made him move further away to the other side of the table.

"Ahh, you haven't met him yet. This is Carfield, my bird secretary, who is very smart and is probably a hundred years old which, of course, is the reason that he is not easy to live with. He has the habits of an old bachelor, is grumpy and dislikes new faces." This last phrase stayed Rick's hand from petting the crow. Carfield only gave Carl a short, sharp look and took a piece of cheese to put it on his plate.

"Here, buddy." Carl poured out some milk into the crow's cup. Then, addressing Rick, he said. "Carfield does not like tea, but what about you, Rick, would you like a cup?"

"Yes sir."

"Do not "sir" me. Just call me Carl." With these words Carl put a cardboard box, containing purchased Chinese food, onto his plate.

"Thanks, Carl." Rick responded in a hesitant voice.

"I need your social insurance number and your full name to fill-in the application form."

Rick looked at his plate and said. "I don't have any documents with me."

"I was right!" Carfield exclaimed, but realizing his mistake, he swallowed the rest of his words.

"He can talk?" Rick was astonished.

"Yes, Rick, he can speak some words. But, right now, you interest me more than Carfield's talents." He threw out an angry look in Carfield's direction.

Rick chewed his lips. "I should have told you about it, but I was too tired and hungry to risk losing a supper. I ran away from my foster parents when I was fifteen because I couldn't stand them anymore. My foster mother was not a bad woman, even nice to me, but my foster father was not. If he had just insulted me it would not have been so difficult to take, but listening to how this man exercised his dirty tongue on my mother, I mean my real mother, was impossible to bear. I don't know why she gave me away but I want to believe that she wanted me, just got herself into trouble and was not able to keep me. I was able to find a job on a small farm as a general helper and I spent three years there, working for only food and shelter, until some good citizen reported to social services that my farmer was keeping an illegal worker. Then I had to leave in a hurry with just one small bag and twenty dollars in my pocket, which just happened to be the whole contents of the farmer's wallet. The money ran out quickly and I started to beg to survive. A couple of days ago someone stole my bag when I was sleeping in the park so now I have nothing again, just like the day I left home."

"We need to get your birth certificate to apply for your Social Insurance card. Because of this I can't hire you as an employee right now but you may stay at my house, just as a guest, for the time being. You can help around the park, but you won't receive any money." Carl awaited his reaction.

"That's fine, if you'll help me to dig myself out of this situation I'll be in your debt."

"I have a place on the river where I rent-out boats to people who like to do Sunday fishing and I need someone to replace an old friend who is running it right now. Do you think you can handle it?" Carl queried.

"I am used to working with cows and horses, but…" Rick's face showed a dubious expression.

"So you have experience with animals?" Carl mused. "Well, I know what you can do. We harness a deer or a boar to a carriage which we use to give rides to children around the park and I need someone to look after these animals and watch out for the safety of the children. Rick, you are not hired yet but are definitely welcome to become a member of the family."

Tac was proud of himself because the business had started to make a profit. Even after the payment of expenses on park improvements, there still remained a large sum of money in the bank account in name of Mr. T. J. Holmes. The cat recognized that this name had now started to attract the attention of people but some things were still hidden from him. He did not suspect that some of the eyes of those who were watching the growth of his project were not all friendly. Some were critical and some were jealous but one particular person was looking at all the activity with deep envy.

"Vultures!" Repeated the owner of these eyes, hitting the table with his fist. "They have stolen all my ideas." Complaining to the drunken company of friends, he conveniently omitted to tell them that he had gone bankrupt long before Tac had leased that part of the wood that he had owned.

"The owner of the Amusement Park is making huge money on entertainment and probably even more on food and drinks. Last Sunday the place was packed with cars. I know that he is somewhere traveling right now and I can see how he can afford to do this since he has expanded his business by adding horse-riding around the lake." Said one of the men who sat around the table.

"How do you know that?" Roger Hawk, the former owner of the unsuccessful campground, asked.

"I took my family to the amusement park last weekend. My daughter, Jessie, didn't give me five minutes peace after her friend had told her the story about her family weekend spent in the woods. I must say that this Mr. Holmes is a shrewd businessman. He has not only put together a zoo and a fairground but he has also added something to do for every member of a visiting family. From my point of view, there is only one thing he has overlooked."

"What's that, then?" Roger was happy to hear that his business opponent might have a vulnerable spot.

"I did not see any security guards or a police station close to the park. The amount of money that all the separate divisions of his new business bring in by the end of the day must be huge, especially on Sunday. Since all banks close for the weekend, where does he keep all this money? I haven't seen any suitable structure, except a barn for the animals and the manager's trailer, in which the takings could be stored safely. No one seems to be guarding all of these large sums of money and I only saw teenagers operating the equipment and some older, retired folks doing casual work to make a few extra dollars?"

"How much do you think he is making?" Roger moistened his dry mouth with a sip of beer, trying to hide the greedy shine of his eyes from his mates by looking inside the mug.

"I would say it could be up to ten thousand dollars on a sunny weekend, easily."

"Next month it may be even more." Added someone's voice from the side.

"Yes! The sign outside the amusement park is advertising special rates for spending a long weekend at the lake." Remarked the man with a daughter.

"Thief!" Shouted Roger, standing up. "It was my idea." His face turning red from anger and alcohol.

"Sit down, Roger. You blew your chance to achieve success by making the mistake of having a fight with one of the customers while you were drunk. Be thankful that he didn't take you to Court." The man nearest to him pushed him back down onto the chair.

But not all of Roger's friends who were sitting at this table agreed with the thoughts of the man who had just spoken...

"Let's go and burn the place to the ground!" Someone shouted.

"Vandalizing someone else's property can be costly fun." Opined the man with a family at home. Even in his drunken state he realized that the evening could turn bad and, consequently, he left the pub shortly afterwards. One by one, other men started to leave too, each using a different excuse. Only two of Roger's closest friends stayed with him and continued to discuss different plans of revenge. However, Roger already had his own plan of attack prepared in his mind. This plan did not involve gasoline or matches but required the use of a gun. He grasped the shoulders of the men sitting on each side of him and, pulling them closer, he whispered. "Holmes stole something of mine and now I want to take something from him. What can the manager and his employee do to stop a man with a gun in the absence of proper security?"

"Roger, don't tell me that you want to hurt somebody? There are many women and children at the fair and, in a situation like this, anything can happen. Personally I don't want to spend the rest of my life in jail." Sam, one of his remaining companions, shook his head.

"What are you talking about? I don't want to shoot anyone." Cried Roger. "We'll go there at night when the customers will be in their beds and the park will be empty and quiet. All that we need to do is to open the trailer and ask the old manager nicely to show us where he keeps the safe. Surely it can't be too big? Then we'll take the safe away with us to open it in a secure place, share the money and next day we will peacefully drink a beer and watch T.V."

The picture that Roger drew, to convince his future partners in crime that the robbery would not end in violence, did not completely remove their lingering doubts about the outcome.

"What if the manager won't tell us where the safe is?" Asked the skinny man called Nick, rubbing his chin reflectively.

"His trailer is not large enough to hide a safe and we'll find it!"

"I agree to this plan only on the condition that no one gets shot." Repeated Nick, stubbornly.

"What are you talking about, my friend?" Roger laughed. "We have never been killers in the past. We only wanted to have some money in our pockets."

Trusting no one, Roger made the trip to the Golden Nut Amusement park by himself to survey the location. He arrived at the park about closing time, sneaked around the trailer and was pleased to find that there were no fences around the target and that it was far away from the camping round. He waited, hidden in the bushes, until the last employee had left the park and, checking the time, he then left as well.

Carl looked through the last bag containing money and then locked everything up in the portable safe. He was not afraid to have money in his trailer since he knew that the twin-brother wolves, Rowal and Growal, had taken up their positions at two corners of the trailer in readiness to guard the safe through the night. The wolves lay quietly on the ground, hidden in the shade of maples. Only their large, triangular-shaped ears moved as they turned in the direction of any suspicious scratch and rustle. They were still wild and this was the reason why Carl did not like to leave the trailer at night and did not allow Rick to wander around the campers' trailers at the lake, advising him. "These twins will not hesitate to bite your skinny bottom and the fact that you are a park employee will not stop them doing this. So, if you disregard this advice, do not complain if one day you end up being unable to sit down for six weeks! And, by the way, that girl that you flirted with this morning has an elephant-sized daddy and, if they don't get to you, then he surely will. I suggest you forget about night walks and just go to sleep. We will have to get up early in the morning to buy food for the animals and do the banking. Once the money is in the bank then we can enjoy the rest of the day."

"The bank will open at nine. So we don't need to get up very early, do we?"

"Rick, I am an old man and like to be in bed before midnight. Now, look at the clock. It's almost ten minutes past my time limit. I hope that we'll receive your documents soon so that I can start to pay you for your work and can boot you out of my home after you have saved enough money to rent your own place."

"Ok! Ok!" Rick started to make the bed. He was used to listening to this speech about his living separately since Carl had a habit of repeating those words again and again, like a broken record.

"You will never boot me out, Carl." Rick teased his boss as he slid under the blanket.

"And why do you think I won't hesitate to do it?" Carl looked at him, curiously.

"Because you like me. You nag and order me around as if I am your own child. Why would you waste your time teaching me everything you know if you didn't like me? All this makes me believe that you wouldn't kick me out." Rick replied, with a smile.

"Aah! I can see that you are smart. This is in addition to your other talents, such as romancing girls and having a healthy appetite for ice cream." Joked Carl, going off to the washroom.

There was only one washroom in the trailer and, consequently, Carl and Rick needed to take turns to get ready for the night.

A sudden scream from outside made Carl run from the washroom, wiping toothpaste from his mouth onto the towel.

"One of our wolves is attacking somebody!" He shouted, on the way to the door and then cried out. "Stay inside." As he left the trailer and slammed the door behind him.

Five hours prior to this incident, an old, blue Ford pick-up, driven by a scruffy-looking man named Sam, turned into the road that led to a bungalow which was set deep inside the property. The shadow on Sam's cheeks had passed six o'clock probably four times over and had turned into gray stubble. His hair, that had lost its color, had been left to grow uncut until it had become long enough to tie into a pony tail. The man slowly passed Roger's silvery-gray Dodge truck that had been deliberately parked in a manner that would not allow anyone else to park alongside. As a result, other drivers had to park at the side of the house or on the grass.

Sam had always admired his friend's taste in cars but this truck was special. Light, silvery flames had been painted on both sides of it and the large head of a Ram had been layered onto the rear window. Its large size and accessories emphasized the great need of its owner to appear manlier. Roger hoped that girls, after looking at the truck, would overlook the fact that the man inside the vehicle was not Prince Charming. Although he was in good shape from frequent exercise, nevertheless he was short, bald and had an unfriendly expression on his face. The look of his blue eyes was generally heavy, cold and stubborn and people usually avoided him because of the disagreeable expression on his face and, in any challenging situation, they fully expected to hear an insult from him.

Leaving the Ford pick-up truck, Sam checked to see if anyone else had noticed him and then opened the front door of the house. The interior was set-up in the way that one might expect from a bachelor. It had a large T.V. set which was augmented by surround-sound, two comfortable, dark blue couches and an old, gray chair which had lost most of its color. The remains of the afternoon meal lay in an open box on a coffee table, surrounded by potato chips and empty beer cans. An ash tray full of cigarette butts had been placed in the middle of the table. This living space was a man's world and had been decorated accordingly. Calendars, showing smiling girls in bathing suits, hung on the walls instead of paintings. Broken electronics filled up a corner of the room beside fitness equipment used for working-out. This unsavory picture was completed by the presence of dirty clothes which had been cast aside onto the floor.

The windows were covered solely by Venetian blinds and the green rug under the coffee table did not match the light gray color of the walls. The distinct impression left by all of this chaos was that Roger did not care about having beauty in his life. It was enough for him that the things that he owned were functional and easy to find.

"Hullo Roger, hullo Nick, what's up? Are we going to the fairground?" Sam sat in the chair next to Roger.

Roger lifted his heavy gaze towards him but did not bother to reply. Finally, he muttered. "So, Sam, it seems that you've decided to prove that you are a man after all? In that case, move closer to me. Now that we are all here I can tell you the plan, which is not complicated. We are going to go to the park after all the employees have left and the manager will have retired to his trailer." Then, placing a jimmy on the table, he instructed. "Nick will disconnect the phone and, using this tool, will open the door in order to tie-up the old man. I am going to look for the safe as soon as he is lying on the floor. After that, Nick and I will transfer it to Sam's truck and we will then all disappear before someone stumbles upon our scheme."

"What do you want me to do?" Sam asked.

"Your job will be to remain outside to warn us if, by any chance, someone from the camping area happens to come by to see the manager."

"And then what?"

"We'll then drive back here to open the safe in my barn to share out the money. After that you, Sam, will dump the safe in the river on the way back to your home."

The idea of his fiddling around with the safe on his own did not appeal to Sam but he did not dare argue the point with Roger. He decided that alcohol would take care of his fear and wipe it from his mind completely.

"Can I have a beer, Roger?" He asked.

"In the fridge."

Sam went to the kitchen and opened the fridge to take out a can of beer from the shelf, but changed his mind after he spotted an almost-full bottle of whisky sitting in the corner of the tray in the door. Sam only wanted one small glass to drown out his negative premonitions about this operation, but one glass proved to be insufficient to achieve this state and he continued to drink until he had completely finished the bottle. By the time that Roger and Nick had realized that almost fifteen minutes had passed since Sam had gone to get a beer, it was too late to do anything about his state of inebriation. He was found by them peacefully asleep with a happy smile on his face, holding an empty bottle like a child would tightly clutch its teddy bear.

"The dirty skunk, he has drunk the whole bottle and now he'll sleep until the morning even if we shoot a gun over his head." A frustrated Nick kicked Sam to try to wake him up but he only gathered himself into a ball like a cat.

"Leave him alone. We don't have time to wake him up." Roger took the key for Sam's truck from his pocket and, pulling a black skiing mask over his face, left the house. As they approached their destination, he turned into a side road and proceeded to hide the truck amongst tall bushes at the bottom of a small ridge. They crept along the pathway, keeping undercover of the shadow produced by the bushes.

The manager's trailer was only ten steps ahead of them when they heard a low, threatening growl. They did not understand what was going on until a wolf came closer, continuing to growl at them. His eyes glowed in the darkness, frightening the intruders, and forcing Nick to remove the gun from the pocket of his jeans to point it at the wolf. He was so scared that he completely forgot about the danger of attracting the attention of people from the camping ground located at the river. However, the wolf did not wait to be shot and jumped up at Nick to grasp his hand with his teeth before he even had a chance to make a move. Dropping the weapon, Nick screamed in pain, making Carl run from the washroom with a mouth full of toothpaste.

Meanwhile, another wolf approached Roger from the opposite side of the trailer. He tried to shoot the wolf, but missed him because the wolf adroitly evaded it. As a coward, he left his partner to fight alone on the ground with his assailant and ran away without even thinking about where he was going.

The sound of the shot interrupted Bertrond's peaceful observation of the moon – the bear was in a good mood after supper and had gone out for a short stroll before going to bed. He thought at first that the man running towards him was Carl. But his nose detected a foreign smell and he saw a glimpse of silver metal in the hand of the stranger. 'He's a hunter!' He realized. Bertrond rose up to his full length to try to scare the man with his size. His intention was to push the intruder back to the trailer where he and Carl could disarm him. Roger pulled off his mask and backed-up slowly to reach the open space where he had left his partner. Turning round, he found Carl kneeling beside Nick and dressing the wounds on his hand and hip with bandages.

"Give me the money." Roger hissed, pointing the gun at Carl.

"What are you talking about? There is a wounded man lying here who needs help." Carl looked at him, incredulously.

"I want all the money that you've made this weekend. And call off your pets before I shoot them!" He pointed the gun at the wolves.

At this, Carl lifted his hand to calm down the scared robber and to persuade him to put down his gun, but the sudden appearance of Rick changed the situation for the worse. Roger's fear completely overcame his senses and he turned the gun in his direction. Being close to the robber, Bertrond could see that the man was insane and would not hesitate to pull the trigger, and possibly kill the boy, so he jumped forward to prevent the disaster. For a second he shielded Rick with his body and took the two bullets intended for him.

Roger did not have time to take any more shots because Carl's fist knocked him unconscious with one fierce blow. Rick dropped on his knees beside Bertrond, trying to press the emergency number on his cell phone with shaking fingers. He was unable to talk but mumbled something, forcing Carl to take the phone from his grasp to explain the situation to the operator and to ask her to immediately send an ambulance to the wood. Carl was worried that the thief would die before help reached the fairground. Approximately ten minutes after Carl's call, the screaming sirens of the police and the ambulance cut through the night and a team of paramedics divided their attention between the two wounded parties, one attending to the man and the other to the bear.

"Take Bertrond to the hospital!" Carl demanded.

"He is a bear!" Exclaimed the Paramedic. "We can't even fit him into our truck!"

But Carl refused to accept this, stating menacingly. "I won't let you leave this place until you've treated the bear that has saved the boy."

The timely arrival of a fire truck prevented a confrontation between the park manager and the scared paramedic. The firefighters were braver, or perhaps they simply had more compassionate feelings towards animals but, in any event, one of them dressed the bear's wounds and, with the help of the rest of the available men, they managed to put him into Carl's truck.

Meanwhile, the driver of the ambulance made a call to an animal hospital, where he personally knew the Veterinary surgeon, and asked him to be ready to receive a patient. A convoy of emergency vehicles, headed by a police car, drove to the city at high speed.

Bertrond was unconscious by the time the firefighters were able to take him into the surgery room. Carl wanted to go inside with the bear but the paramedic, who had agreed to assist the Doctor, turned him back saying that in this situation it would be best if he simply waited outside the surgery room.

The door closed behind the hospital trolley, leaving Carl to anxiously wait for the outcome as he held a weeping Rick.

CHAPTER 9:

"IT'S A BOY"

T he frenetic business of lunch had passed and the café had started to empty slowly. The customers who liked to take time to eat their meals often combined it with reading the newspaper, or had a conversation with someone sitting next to them, then paid their bill and left. The later time, about 2p.m., was favored by older folks who preferred to have their lunch without being disturbed by the loud chatter of multiple conversations.

A small group of them chose to sit near the window to enjoy the view of the sunny street. They still wanted to be connected to the fast flow of life but to do this without being distracted by the noise, heat and dust on the outside.

Lana kept an eye on them to refill their coffee cups and clean the tables which had been abandoned by their patrons, putting the tips into the pocket of her lacy apron. The friendly smile that she had on her lips didn't reflect her inner feelings. It wasn't the work that made her feel tense but the waiting for the end of her shift that slowly ate away at her patience. She stretched her tired back and looked at her watch for the umpteenth time.

"Another hour to go!" Lana bit her lip, wanting to push the lazy watch hands forward. She worried that leaving her mother in the house alone in her current state of health wasn't safe. Lifting the tray stacked with used dishes, she looked around for more work to keep herself occupied.

The Sunnyside Café was popular. The soft, dim lighting inside of it gave the impression that it was much cooler to be in here than on the street. This feeling of comfort was created by the tastefully decorated interior and the carefully selected and well-prepared food.

It did not take long for the clients of "Sunny Side" to discover that the apricot porcelain shakers contained salt and the green ones were filled with pepper. Dark, cherry counters and narrow cabinets looked dramatic against a background of light-colored walls. Framed paintings of flowers occupied the walls that were free of furniture.

The most intriguing focal point for the eyes of the customers was a collection of salt and pepper shakers which had been displayed on the shelves of cabinets. The owner's collection included almost a hundred items of different shapes and sizes, from vegetables and fruits to amusing figures of animals and people, all of which had been purchased by him mostly at flea markets and thrift stores. Lana's gaze slid along the shelves but she had no interest in being amused by the different varieties of the ornaments. She merely wanted to make sure that everything was clean.

"Excuse me, may I have my bill?" Said a voice behind Lana's back. She approached the group of older women that came here from time to time to gossip together.

"Of course." She smiled at them, and quickly returned with the bill.

"It's my turn to pay." Said one of the ladies she called the 'White Queen.' Her tiny, barely-five-foot body moved with grace and was complimented by the elegance of her short, white hair. It was difficult to overlook her and the name which Lana had given to her had come into her mind naturally.

"Thanks, my dear." Her voice was always soft and had intimate notes in it as if she had known the person for a long time. "We were just talking about a shooting in the Golden Nut fairground. My friend called me this morning to talk about this incident. Her son is a paramedic and, apparently, he had told her that somebody had been shot last night, but maybe she was just exaggerating for all I know. I have known her for a long time and, unfortunately, she has a habit of doing this. Have you heard anything about what may have happened in the fairground last night?" She asked Lana.

"No, Ma'am, I know nothing. I think that if something had really happened there then we should be able to find out all about it in the local newspaper or on the television."

"Thanks darling." The woman got up from her chair and, putting her bag in the crook of her hand, commented. "I think you are right, we cannot trust gossip. We will need to find a local newspaper." She used her credit card to pay the bill and led her companions towards the door.

"Goodbye. Have a nice day." Replied Lana, returning to her previous mood and moving between tables automatically, without any real thought about what she was doing.

"Lana, what is wrong with you?" Stephany asked her, after Lana had finished removing the dirty dishes from a table that had been served by another waitress. You run about all day, reminding me of a clockwork toy that is unable to stop. Have you decided to replace all of us and prove to the boss that you can run the café all by yourself?" She joked.

"I am sorry. I don't do it on purpose. I have half an hour left until the end of my shift and I need something to do to keep me from worrying about my mother." Lana again anxiously glanced at her watch.

Stephany came to Lana to hug her shoulders. "Everything will be fine. Women have been delivering babies since the beginning of time."

"Stephany, I have good reason to worry since my mother is not feeling well. Dad talked to the doctor about her tests and told me that she was very concerned and had even advised that mom is not healthy enough to have a child. Her kidneys are barely working under the double pressure. The doctor put her on medication and has sent her to the laboratory for more tests. Her treatment will cost us a lot of money but do we have a choice? Actually, the doctor did mention a choice." Lana's body shuddered as if she was about to cry. "She said that if the situation becomes worse then she would suggest that we terminate the pregnancy."

"What?" Exclaimed Stephany. "Kill the baby?"

"The doctor has advised that dad must start thinking about this possibility, otherwise we may lose them both. Even if the treatment helps, and mom's condition stabilizes, she probably won't be able to carry the baby to full term. She has already scheduled my mother for an operation to take the baby as soon as possible without causing damage to it."

"Lana, this is terrible. I didn't ask questions because I was afraid to appear nosey. Honestly, I thought that you were still upset about losing your boyfriend and I could not have imagined that it was Natalie's health that made you look so depressed. You know! Just go home. I can replace you for this last half hour and I will tell Sunny everything about your situation. He is a good man and I am sure that he will not mind."

"Thanks Stephany." Lana rushed to the door right from the spot where she was standing, removing her apron on the way. "Oh! Money!" She gasped, feeling it in her pocket, and quickly handed the tips over to Stephany. Then, not even bothering to change her clothes, she jumped on her bike and rode home. Making an attempt to control her breathing, Lana opened the door of the house, trying to be silent. She congratulated herself for being cautious, seeing that Natalie had fallen asleep in the living room. An open book had slid from her mother's hand and was hanging on the very edge of the couch.

Lana tiptoed over to her and gently removed the novel before it could fall onto the floor. Noticing the small pill that was lying on the top of the coffee table, Lana immediately looked at the clock, thinking. 'Mother should have taken her pill fifteen minutes ago!' She froze, trying to make the right decision in the dilemma now presented to her; either to wake-up her mother in order to administer the pill and destroy her nap or just let her rest. After calculating the possible amount of damage that might occur in either situation, she decided that a good sleep would have more value than a slight skip in the schedule for taking the medication. She therefore crept into the kitchen and closed the door behind her tightly.

Natalie was woken up by a strange feeling that she needed to do something. Her dreamy eyes lost their sleepiness when she looked at the clock and realized that she had missed the time for her medication. After a short struggle with her rounded body, Natalie managed to get up and, holding a pill in her hand, went into the kitchen. "Hi Sweetie. Why didn't you wake me up?" She asked, while accepting a glass of water from her.

"Dad had told me in the morning that you hadn't slept last night and I thought that you would benefit more from taking this rest than the pill." Replied Lana.

"How was your day?" Asked Natalie, sitting down at the table to watch her daughter cooking something on the stove. She thought about helping Lana, but a spasm of nausea stopped her immediately and, instead, she took two deep breaths to return herself to a normal condition.

"I am cooking a special sauce from the recipe that I received from our chef." She answered her mother. "He even wrote it out on a piece of paper for me in case I forgot it. Are you hungry?"

Natalie did not have much of an appetite but decided not to show it to avoid upsetting her daughter, who had obviously worked hard to cook the dinner. "Let's wait for dad and we can all have it together."

Lana studied her mother's face for a moment, pretending that she had not noticed the sudden paleness that had come over it. She was concerned that Natalie had not been eating enough, had lost a lot of weight and felt constantly tired.

"Today, I served one of my favorite customers. You know, the one I call the Queen, actually the 'White Queen'. She told me that some trouble had happened in the fairground and someone had been hurt. Maybe we can find out something about this in the local news?"

Lana told her this in an effort to take her attention away from her own sickness to something else and, to entertain her, she turned on the T.V. It showed a scene with a camera sliding alongside a building showing "Kirkland Animal Hospital" on it and a reporter relating the gripping story of an attack.

"As a result of this attempted robbery one man has been arrested and the other intruder, who sustained serious injuries, has been taken to hospital and is now under police supervision. But the victim of the attack, a 'star' at the new, local fairground, who is loved by many children and known as Bertrond the Chef, has been shot twice, as he tried to protect Mr. Carl Mayer, his trainer and the manager of the fairground. Right now, the bear is behind the door of this animal hospital in very serious condition. One bullet went through his shoulder but the other went into the chest, close to the heart. Although the fairground star has undergone an operation, his condition is still unstable. I see that the manager of the amusement park is now walking through the parking lot. He can probably tell us more about any changes in the bear's condition."

"Mr. Mayer, I hear you have been talking to the Sheriff. Are the police going to do something to ensure that this incident doesn't happen again?"

"Yes, I have had a conversation with the Sheriff and we have discussed a variety of ways of trying to prevent a serious incident such as this from ever happening again. For our part, the Administration of the Golden Nut Amusement Park will do everything we can to protect the guests and the staff of the park from any future attack from armed robbers. I am sorry, but I can't say anything more right now."

"Do you have any news about the condition of the bear?" Queried the reporter.

"I am going over to see the doctor right now to discuss his progress. As a matter of fact, a couple of his good friends want to see him too and they are with me now." Carl turned to look behind him and the camera followed his movement to show the strange duet.

"Lana, the cat on the T.V. looks just like Tac! Doesn't he?" Natalie cried out.

"Yes, indeed he does." Replied Lana, looking mostly at the crow. She was not sure if it was the same bird that she had encountered at Willie's place some time ago and was waiting for a sign to confirm her suspicions.

The crow stopped, turned to Carl and gave him a familiar nod of his head. Lana was ready to jump from the couch but managed to stop herself in time to avoid scaring her mother.

Pretending that nothing had happened, Lana got up slowly. "I'll go to check if there is any mail for us, but I'll be back soon."

'I've suspected that something was not right with Tac.' Lana thought. 'He has changed since he disappeared into that forest.'

"Heh! Merry! Wait for me" Lana shouted and waved to the post lady who was looking through piles of letters in her hands. "Do you have anything for us?"

"As a matter of fact I do." She selected three envelopes from the collection in her hand and handed them to her. Looking through them, Lana thought. 'This is probably a telephone bill and this is a letter for Dad, but what's this? T. J. Holmes? But the address is ours so it must be a mistake?'

She looked along the street for Merry, wanting to return the letter to her, but the post lady had disappeared. Since it didn't look important, she thought about writing a note on the envelope and sending it back.

Lana's mind had been busy analyzing strange things that had been happening to her recently and had not noticed that Nicholas's car had turned the corner and rolled into their driveway.

"Heh, Princess." Nicholas greeted her, hugging her shoulder with his arm and bringing her closer. "What's the reason for such deep thoughts, or who?" He joked.

"Dad." Said Lana, embarrassed that he suspected a heart involvement. "Do you know who T.J. Holmes is?"

"No." Nicholas looked at the letter. "It's from the bank and somebody might be waiting for it. I'll send it back with a note. How is mom?" He asked on the way to the door.

"She's been sleeping."

"That's good news." Nicholas dropped the mail onto the table in the foyer. "Do we have anything to eat? I feel hungry."

After dinner, Nicholas took his turn at entertaining Natalie with stories. Being involved in conversation, the family did not see Tod creeping towards the table. He stood up, then pulled the envelope addressed to T. J. Holmes from the pile and took it outside the house. The dog waited with the envelope for Carfield to take the letter from him and fly away with it to the wood.

Lana later searched for the letter but could not find it and decided that Nicholas had already sent it back. In fact, being very happy about Natalie's sudden progress, he had completely forgotten about it.

Even an evening spent peacefully was not sufficient to wipe out Lana's worry about Tac. She saw just one way to get rid of these disturbing thoughts and that was to go to the hospital in order to do her own investigations.

She found the one-story building of the hospital without any difficulty. The portable stand, displaying paintings of the bear which had been done by the young fans of the local star, drew her attention. The ground around the stand was packed with boxes of biscuits and jars containing jam and honey. She smiled as she looked at the unusual display. 'Bringing sweets is more reasonable than flowers if your star is a bear.' She thought, as she parked her bike at the next free parking spot, still having two hours free until the beginning of her shift at the café.

She had been unable to find the telephone number of the manager of the park but hoped to obtain it from the doctor or from the nurse. Apart from this,

Lana also wanted to know what had actually happened during that unfortunate night when the bear had been shot. But, most of all, she wanted to find out what kind of role Tac had played in this event. She put on her dark glasses and introduced herself as a reporter of the Pokerweild News and was pleased to learn from the receptionist that Mr. Mayer was already in the hospital, visiting Bertrond.

The receptionist promised that she would arrange a meeting for her with Carl after he had finished his conversation with the Veterinarian.

"You don't give him too much of a chance, doctor?" Lana overheard Carl's voice.

"The second bullet is lodged dangerously close to the heart. I will tell you honestly that if he was a man he would be dead already. But he is a wild animal and his body has much more resilience and the ability to recover than that of a human being. But it is still difficult to say what is going to happen. Nevertheless, I'll do everything that veterinary science can achieve to help Bertrond to stay alive. This I will guarantee. But I am not a prophet and I don't make predictions." The doctor spread his hands wide, indicating a measure of uncertainty in his diagnosis. She decided not to interfere and pretended to be interested in a picture on the wall.

Carl returned to the room which had been occupied by Bertrond since he had been brought there after the operation. It was big enough to allow the bed to fit in it and also all of the machines that sustained the life of the unconscious bear, a small cabinet for medical supplies and two chairs for visitors.

Poor Bertrond was so ill that he did not need to be caged. He was deep in some other world and could not even hurt a fly. Machines which made clicking and whistling noises kept alive a small spark of life deep within his large, brown body. His chest rose and fell weakly, but rhythmically. When Carl slowly walked into the room, Tac was already sitting on a chair close to Carfield who had landed on the edge of the bed. None of them knew what to say or do in this sad situation.

Carl had heard that people, even when unconscious, were able to hear their relatives but he did not know if this applied to a bear. He shifted indecisively from one foot to the other and tried to reach him. "Hi, Bertrond. How are you doing? I have come with your friends to see you. Will you please come back to us, we need you. Find your way back Bertrond. Fight! And, by the way, children have brought honey for you. Can you smell it?" He opened a plastic jar to bring it up to the dry nose of the bear and added. "You can't leave these goods for someone else to eat, can you?" From Carl's point of view this was reason enough for Bertrond to regain his interest in living again.

"I saw Bertrond's favorite biscuits on the stand outside. If I bring them in here, and start to peck at them, perhaps he will become jealous and quickly wake up." With these words, Carfield flew through the open window. He found a package of biscuits and was about to carry it off to Bertrond's room when he suddenly spotted Lana's motor bike. The crow walked around it to confirm that it was indeed hers and then became so scared that he forgot about the biscuits and immediately flew back to warn Tac.

"Tac! Tac! Your Mistress is here." He cawed in a human voice, panicking so much that he forgot to speak in his own language. Then, addressing Carl, he shouted. "Since we cannot give her any explanation for our being here, maybe we need to run?"

The scared cat jumped onto the window ledge and disappeared out of sight, thinking, 'She has probably seen me on the TV.'

Carfield had no choice but to follow his friend through the window to search for him on the ground, leaving Carl in the room alone. The manager felt a desire to jump through the window himself but, instead, he answered a light knock on the door.

"Mr. Mayer, the reporter of the local news wants to talk to you. Will you see her now?" The receptionist asked.

"Yes I will." Carl turned to Bertrond and murmured to him. "Keep on breathing, buddy, I'll be back."

Carl did not need to search for Lana. She was standing at the reception desk so he decided to approach her with a question. "Are you the reporter who is looking for me? If so, I am Carl Mayer, the manager of the Golden Nut Amusement Park."

Pretending that she had shaken many hands in her professional life, Lana grasped Carl's hand casually.

But the manager did not miss the slight shaking of her fingers. "Do you want to go outside?" He invited her, whilst thinking. 'She's very nervous but is prepared to play the game with me. I wonder what kind of need is prompting her to do this. Hmm!'

Walking towards the door, she offered. "I think it'll be a good idea to avoid being in the way of the pet owners." Since there were no benches outside the hospital entrance, they both sat on the edge of a concrete planter which was full of bright impatiens and pansies which surrounded tall, bushy grass in its center.

Lana wanted to start the conversation as she had planned but, after some conflict within herself, she said firmly. "I am not a reporter. My name is Lana and I came to talk about the cat. I saw him on the evening news on T.V. in the company of a crow when both of them were on their way to visit the injured bear."

"Have you found it strange that such different animals have built a friend-ship with each other?" Asked Carl. "I agree, it is a rare case, but it sometimes happens. We know of many instances where a cat has lived peacefully with a mouse or a bird and the story about Mowgli is a classic example of an unusual friendship."

"That is a novel, but I'm talking about real life." She took a deep breath to keep her temper even.

"I can mention more examples from real life. Have you seen the article in the newspaper about a snake that lived in a glass cage at a Japanese Zoo with a hamster that had been placed there as food for it but, instead, became a companion. The snake stubbornly refused to eat the rodent, preferring frozen mice for its dinner. You don't need to worry about the cat just because he is friendly with a crow."

"It's not Tac's mental condition that worries me, but his safety."

"Why do you think that he's not safe with the crow?" Carl asked, in mild surprise.

Lana didn't want to continue this argument and simply told him the story about Tac, and the strange company with him, involved in some game with money and dressing-up as an old man. "You probably don't believe me." Her eyes were sharp as she examined the expression on Carl's face.

"I must say, this is unusual." Mumbled Carl, trying to find a way out of this conversation without exposing his involvement in the secret. "Lana, I promise to look more closely at this pair to determine if there is anything in their relationship about which you need to worry."

"I'll give you the telephone number of the café where I am working." Lana dug in her bag for a piece of paper. "I just don't know which shift I am going to be working next week. You will just need to ask for me at the front desk." She wrote and talked at the same time. "My mom is going into the hospital soon and I want to be with her in the late afternoon when my dad is still at work. She feels worse close to the end of the day and needs someone to be around her at that time for support."

The word 'hospital', mentioned by Lana, changed Carl from being a distant observer of her problems to a more sympathetic and attentive listener. "I hope your mother will feel better soon. Hospital bills can eat up all your savings." He added, thinking about his own situation.

"We will be fine. I hope you will understand my unwillingness to discuss sensitive family matters with a stranger. I'm sorry, but I need to leave. I have only fifteen minutes before my shift begins." They shook hands and parted company.

Since Carl had his own business to attend to, he did not allow his thoughts to dwell on her concerns and quickly resumed his search for Carfield.

Suddenly, the crow obliged him by landing on his shoulder. "Thank goodness she has left. Why doesn't she leave Tac alone? After all, he is an adult."

"Why can't you try to be more friendly towards her? And, by the way, you may tell your 'adult' friend that his Mistress's mother is going into the hospital.

Perhaps he would be interested to learn this." Replied Carl, as he walked back to the hospital.

Bertrond could not understand what had happened to him. The last thing that he remembered was people carrying him somewhere. The bear's sensitive nose had detected the smell of smoke which oozed from their clothing and, although it had faded, it was still recognizable to his senses. He had then sunk deep into a dream, seeing how the smoke transformed itself into different shapes and flowed all around him. At one point it had become a solid wall which rose up directly in front of him. Suddenly the middle of it had opened and he saw himself surrounded by the excited fans of his barbecuing talent.

"Bertrond." Whispered a voice from far away, blowing his pleasant picture completely away. He tried to turn his head while he wondered what was going on. Then all the lights and the voices disappeared, leaving him alone in the all-enveloping darkness.

'Is it night?' He asked himself.

But, for him, it seemed to be a very unusual night. He did not remember the night ever to have been as absolutely dark as it appeared to him at that moment. Usually, he was able to see at least the shapes of the objects around him, even if the light of the moon was dull. Bertrond made an attempt to open his eyes and tried to catch at least some distant sounds in this total silence. Eventually, he got a measure of response in the shape of a dull pain in his shoulder and chest but, to his surprise, it brought him happiness. 'At least something feels in this body.' He sighed. Bertrond did not know that the doctor had given him a very slim chance of staying alive and therefore he concentrated on clawing his way back to consciousness, recognizing the importance of it. He had treasured his own plans for at least twenty years and did not intend to abandon them, no matter what anyone's opinion was about his condition.

Shifting his body to become more comfortable, he was satisfied to know that he was injured because it would give him some advantage over his friends. 'I am not so stupid as to show them that I am feeling better. I am going to look at everyone through half-closed eyes brimming with pain and I intend to enjoy the fuss that the doctor and my friends will create around me. After all, I am the hero who disarmed the bandits and therefore I deserve recognition!'

The room was silent, which encouraged the bear to slightly open his small, black eyes to confirm that he was indeed alone and, using this opportunity, he took a good look around. Bertrond had never been treated by a doctor in a real animal hospital before. He examined the ceiling and walls with increasing curiosity, finding that they were too smooth for his taste and the smell of the medications also did not appeal to him.

In addition, lying on his back with an arm tied to the bed felt like a violation of his freedom and this was something that he would not allow, even for the biggest reward. So, forgetting about his decision to lie quietly, the bear made an attempt to free his arm despite the pain that his injury caused him. He only succeeded in knocking down a tall metal stand to which was attached a clear plastic bottle, half-full of liquid. The signal in the machine changed to 'flash' and brought both Carl and the doctor rushing into the room. Another person, a female, looked through the opening of the door without entering the room, since she was afraid of the growling bear.

"Bertrond, lie still!" Carl ordered, with a stern expression on his face. "Look at what you have done to yourself. Do you want to start bleeding again?" The injured bear breathed heavily and looked suspiciously at the drip-stand that had been returned by the doctor to its place. But soon his attention was drawn to Tac who wiggled his body between the door and the nurse's legs and had climbed onto the bed.

"Bertrond, I am glad that you have found your way back from the dark forest." He purred, rubbing his head against the bear's good hand.

"If I had known that somebody was going to take advantage of me, by shaving my chest, I would not have allowed myself to faint." Complained Bertrond.

"Ugh! Don't get upset for nothing." Remarked Tac. "The fur will grow back soon."

"But what am I going to do right now? I cannot show myself to the public looking like this." Retorted Bertrond, grumpily.

"What has happened?" The newly-arrived crow realized that Bertrond was upset but did not yet know why.

"This happened!" The bear pointed to his shaved chest covered by a bandage.

Carfield closely examined the patch on the skin, looking at it from different angles. "This can be covered. But, personally speaking, I would just leave it the way it is. When the children will see how badly you look, they will bring you twice as many cookies and honey than they already have."

"Someone has brought me honey?" The bear's eyes lit-up with interest.

"Bertrond, I have already loaded up a bag with their heartfelt gifts and have sent it to your home but I will need to load another one, with the snacks that I have found, right now. The offerings are under the watchful eye of your assistants, Cuffy and Muffy, who will ensure that no one removes anything." But, instead of comforting Bertrond with this news, Carfield only succeeded in making him more restless.

"I want to go home!!" The wounded bear cried, shaking his head from one shoulder to another. "I do not want to stay in this room any longer. I will start dreaming that someone is stealing food from my room every night if I have to remain here"

Carfield did not know what to say and went to look for Carl, eventually finding him discussing something with the doctor.

"You can't put Bertrond in a cage." Carfield heard Carl's voice. "He will die from fear because this will be the first time in his life that he has been caged."

"But I can't keep him here. It is dangerous for my staff." The Vet argued. "He is not as weak as before and his course of medication is finished. He just needs to rest and keep his bandages clean and in place. I have a large cage in a back-room. It will be tight for him, but he will only be there for a short while."

"If Bertrond doesn't require any special treatment, I'll take him back home to the park. Tell me how much I owe you and I'll write you a cheque."

"The bear can't walk by himself. Although he does look better, his wounds may open if he moves and that could create complications in his treatment." The doctor argued.

"So he will not move!" Carl interrupted the doctor, angrily.

"How are you going to get the bear into the truck?" The doctor had become more concerned about the outcome of this proposed trip.

"I will ask the firefighters who brought Bertrond to the hospital to assist me to take him back home."

The Veterinary surgeon thought for a moment and then agreed to this suggestion. "I can't stop you from taking the bear but I want to give him some sedatives to keep him asleep on his way home just to ensure that he does not injure himself or, possibly, someone else. I will also give you some pills to give to him every day to prevent the development of complications and some antibiotics to help in healing his wounds. When do you plan to take him?"

"I can't do it today since I am not ready, but I will probably take him the day after tomorrow." Carl was happy that the argument had ended well.

The Friday then became a memorable day. A team of firefighters arrived to help with the difficult task of transferring the bear from the hospital bed to the back of Carl's truck. A new mattress had been placed on the floor of the truck to smooth out the effect of the road bumps on Bertrond. Being really stubborn, he had refused to be sedated but had promised that he would not open his eyes nor make any growling sounds that might scare the men. Carl had visualized the picture of his wrestling with the bear while having a needle in his hand and admitted to himself that administering the injection would be an impossible task to achieve. So he had agreed to go along with this ruse.

Bertrond was carried on the backs of the men, with his shaved shoulder wrapped in a white towel, as if he was a Roman Senator from days long gone by. As soon as he was put on the mattress, with four pillows pushed under his head and shoulders for support, the anesthetic in his system immediately wore off and the now fully-awake bear demanded that Carfield open the backpack and give him some honey. The crow looked at Tac with a questioning glance.

"Give him his treat." Tac laughed.

Trusting no one to hold his treasure, Bertrond placed the can inside the folds of a towel, dug his paw into the plastic can and licked it with a smacking sound. It was fortunate that it was dark and no one was around to witness his lack of manners.

The hospital where Natalie had spent the last few days to strengthen her fading health, and complete the necessary tests for her pending operation, was a complex of three buildings connected by a glass gallery. From Lana's point of view, it was a modern version of an ancient labyrinth. She had lost her way a few times and wished that she had a spindle of thread in her hands to assist her to find her way out. The narrow corridors all looked the same and, after several turns, she was lost again. She stopped to wait to ask someone for directions. 'Who would build a place like this?' She wondered, frustrated by her mistake.

"I hope that this will be the last time that I will need to stay here." Natalie wiggled in her wheelchair in order to find a more comfortable position for her back. Do you think, daughter, that it is ridiculous to ask me to leave the hospital in this way? I can walk for myself."

"Mom, after three weeks, you will need to come back here again so you had better comply with their rules." She checked to see if Natalie was ready to continue the ride. "Did you manage to get rest Mom?"

"Very little. Every time that I came close to falling asleep, something happened to spoil it. Either it was noise coming from the corridor or it was the nurse coming in to check on my room-mate or visitors. At night I was listening to an old lady snoring and whistling as if she was playing in a band."

"I'm sorry." Lana stroked her mother's shoulder gently. "At home you will have all the peace that you need and, if dad happens to snore too, then we will send him to sleep on the couch." She smiled and resumed their progress towards the exit. "Ah! All roads lead to Rome anyway." She sighed.

"My frequent stay in the hospital concerned me but your dad refused to discuss the money issue with me. He said that this is his problem since I have my own worries to deal with." She probed to get what information she could from her daughter. "Did he tell you something?"

Lana was old enough to sense a trap and answered in a casual manner. "Mom, I think that we are fine with money." Distracted, she took the wrong turn and was surprised to find that, instead of the main door, she had reached the emergency entrance. After a second's hesitation, she pushed the door with her hip and carefully rolled out the chair.

"Are you sure, Lana, that we are going in the right direction?" Natalie looked around for her husband.

"I've made a mistake but I see a positive side to it. Instead of going home though the enclosed space of the hospital we are going to make our way to the main entrance in the fresh air." Lana had stopped to give way to an approaching white car and remarked. "I just need to watch out for the traffic." She then continued to roll the wheelchair along the pathway around the building, pausing for a moment to murmur. "Mom, you are already looking better and it doesn't surprise me. These corridors make me feel as if I am travelling inside the intestines of a fish that has swallowed me. Dad is here."

She waved to the man who had been focusing all his attention on the main door. "Dad!" she called out, prompting Nicholas to walk towards them and to take the handle of the wheelchair, softly moving Lana aside.

"I didn't know that you girls were having a party and I had started to worry about your whereabouts." He smiled, but Lana did not appreciate his joke. She turned her head and took a last look at the hospital, relieved that her mother was going home.

Tac had been waiting for Natalie to arrive home for some time. He bothered Tod with the same question again and again. "Are you sure that she is coming home today?" He had taken time off from his fairground business and was thinking about the work that would be piling up for him back at the office.

"I know that it will happen today because Master and Lana have been talking about her return all morning. We just have to wait patiently for them to arrive." Todd lay down on the grass and, putting an ear on his paw, demonstrated how to do this. The cat got up, took two soft steps on his padded feet and lay down on the grass also. But, at the sound of the car coming from behind the corner of the street, they both sat up excitedly, anticipating the sight of their Mistress.

Tod started to jump around Natalie as soon as she had left the car but Tac waited calmly for Tod to finish expressing his feelings. He expected to be invited inside which would give him the privilege of escorting his Mistress to the couch and did not want to fight with his friend, Tod, for her affection.

"Look at him." Lana towered above Tac with her hands on her hips. "I haven't seen him for four days because he has been hiding from me but, as soon as you come home, he appears immediately. How did he know that you were coming back, I wonder?"

Tac listened to her with some amusement and, with his tail proudly standing up, he followed Natalie into the house to comfort his Mistress and drive away her worries. Half closing his eyes, and purring under Natalie's hand, he watched Lana running back and forth with the dishes from the kitchen to the table. She didn't pay attention to anything else and almost crashed into Nicholas who had come in from the outside carrying a pile of mail.

"Is there something for me?" Lana pretended that she had not noticed that he had nervously folded one of the envelopes and put it into his pocket.

"No darling, only the usual stuff; bills, flyers and a letter addressed to Mr. T. J. Holmes."

"Again? I am wondering who this T.J. Holmes is. This time I will definitely have to call the post office to enquire about it."

The determination in her voice made Tac swallow hard. His eyes followed the official-looking envelope which Lana had placed on top of the T.V. stand before she had gone to the kitchen to look for her cell phone. Tac was in a dilemma - how could he get the letter without attracting the attention of Natalie? Nicholas resolved the challenge by picking it up to look at the name of the sender.

"This is from the bank." He exclaimed. "Somebody must have made a mistake, or it was a glitch in the computer. I am sure that Lana will be able to sort it out. In the meantime, we need to discuss more important things, like how do you feel now?" With this, Nicholas dropped the letter onto the coffee table.

'Bingo!' Tac jumped from the couch to make a circle in the living room and pretended that he had no interest in anything except stretching his legs. His Master was not paying any attention to him, since he was fully occupied in discussing the lay-out of the baby room, and this gave Tac an opportunity to take the letter and quietly reach the entrance. The rescue of his own correspondence in fact turned out to be more difficult than he had anticipated. He needed to wait until Lana had finished talking on her cell phone and had left the kitchen, allowing him to walk some distance along the corridor to sneak out onto the porch, unnoticed.

Tac stopped for a moment to grasp the envelope more firmly, thinking. 'Tomorrow I will have to ask Carfield to change my mailing address to that of the fairground. Tod has forgotten to pick-up the letter from the mailbox and, if it were to happen again, Lana would go to look for this Mr. Holmes. We need to keep away anything that could hurt the fragile well-being of my Mistress.' He didn't care if it was someone's prayers, or Natalie's cooperation with the doctor's instructions, or the mutual determination of the family to keep her happy that allowed this to be achieved. The most important thing for him was that she continued to feel reasonably well until the 7th of November, the day of her operation.

"I've nothing to worry about." She said to her reflection in the mirror. "Another three or four hours and everything will be finished and I will be able to see you." She stroked the baby through the stretched, thin layer of muscle and skin that separated the child from the world. All of the family members were waiting for her in the living room, looking nervous. Natalie picked up a plastic bag with the things that she wanted to take with her and looked around for the last time. She was the only one who talked about the operation in the car whilst Lana and Nicholas listened silently, but attentively.

After Natalie had been taken by the nurse behind the door that marked the point beyond which visitors were not allowed to go, Lana's optimism dropped to the point where she was on the verge of tears. Nicholas, realizing that he needed to take her quickly from the hospital to prevent an emotional break-down on her part, gently urged. "Let's go for breakfast far away from here, to Murraydale."

"I can't eat." Lana nervously rubbed her fingers as if they had lost their sensitivity.

"We need to do something for two hours and you need to eat because, if you collapse from exhaustion, Mom will not forgive me. Let's go darling." Nicholas softly turned her towards the way-out. "We are unable to help and the best we can do now is to not disturb the nurse with questions."

"When you are waiting for something important to happen, time always stands still and it is frustrating." Lana sat at the table in the restaurant and drew a face in the middle of the omelet with her fork.

"Did you find an egg shell?" Joked Nicholas, trying to turn her attention away from sad thoughts.

"No." She took a piece of the omelet and swallowed it without enjoyment.

"Everything will be fine. Mom is in the hands of professional people. Do you know how many years they have been studying to do their job?"

"I know. But I'm still scared."

Seeing that Lana did not have an appetite, Nicholas decided not to push her, satisfied that at least she had drunk a cup of coffee. He chose to return to the hospital by a country road, hoping that Nature's scenery would take her mind away from disturbing thoughts.

Lana looked through the window with indifference. Only one thing was important to her - time. She looked at her watch again and again.

Nicholas gave up on his attempts to distract her and turned onto the main road in an effort to reach the hospital more quickly so that he could obtain some information about Natalie's condition.

"Mrs. Vladner's operation is finished." The receptionist answered his queries. "I will tell the doctor that you are here and are waiting for him. He will come to see you as soon as he can take a moment."

"How is my wife and the baby?"

"I am sorry, but I can't say anything more. Please wait for the surgeon." Replied the receptionist, turning back to the papers spread in front of her.

Lana grabbed her father's hand. "Why did the nurse not say that she is fine? She could at least have done that. Maybe there is trouble with mom and the receptionist does not want to tell us!?"

"Lana, please calm down, it can't be more trouble." He took her hand, worried that she might run through the door to look for her mother. "Surely one problem is enough for us or it will be unfair?"

"Dad, to what trouble are you referring?"

Immediately Nicholas realized that worry had made his mind slip and he had said more than he should have done. Right now he was too exhausted emotionally to lie and nothing came to his mind except the truth which he had hidden from his daughter and his wife for some time. 'Maybe this will take her attention off her mother and stop her from imagining scary things.' He reasoned to himself and then blurted out. "We owe a large sum of money to the bank."

She didn't show surprise. "I know this."

"Did you look at my bank statements?" Nicholas didn't look very pleased.

"No. For what? I just know how many times mother has been in the hospital and I can imagine how costly it has been. I saved my money, knowing that we will need it to pay our bills. My co-workers also wanted to help me after my boss, Sunny, managed to extract the news from Stephany. One of the girls is going to give us a baby bed and a stroller. She said that both of them are in good condition." Lana spoke fast, seeing that her father was taking a deep breath prior to refusing the gifts.

"Lana, we are not beggars..." He started.

"These people want to help us not because they think we are beggars but because they feel that I am a friend and I can't say 'no' to them just to save your pride. Excited, they even decided to hold a 'shower' for our newborn baby on Sunday. Try to understand that I can't reject their kindness."

Nicholas thought for a second and said. "O.K., do as you think fit, but I will return to you all the money that you now intend to spend on the family."

"Of course, Dad." Continued Lana, as innocent as could be. "I expect that it will be you who will pay for my wedding."

"Are you getting married?" His face changed color instantly.

"No dad, I am talking about the distant future." Nicholas did not have a chance to reply, noticing that a doctor had appeared in the corridor and was walking towards them.

"Doctor, how are they?" He asked, with concern.

"Your wife and son are in good condition. Natalie's blood pressure has been rather low but perhaps this is only because she is very tired. But don't worry, now she is resting. I suggest that you allow Natalie at least a couple of hours of rest before talking to her. In the meantime, I can show you the baby. He is in a special protective environment so you can't lift him, but you can see your son. He is probably sleeping too." The doctor smiled. "Please follow me."

Lana and Nicholas, barely holding back their tears, looked at the tiny body wrapped in a bandage and sleeping with a peaceful expression on his face. The little fingers of his hands were tied in fists. Nicholas and Lana exchanged looks of adoration, unable to step away from the panel of glass that separated them from the baby boy. All their worries and fears were replaced by feelings of joy.

By the time that Natalie's health had improved enough to allow her to be released from the hospital, Nicholas and Lana, assisted by their close friends, had put a fresh coat of light blue paint on the walls of the baby room and had found the right spot for the changing-table which had been made by Nicholas.

Sunny, Lana's boss, was not joking when he said that he would hold a baby-shower for Lana's brother. The day after the baby had been born he had made a special display on the wall of his restaurant. This consisted of a picture of the baby pasted on a welcoming sign. The gifts which had been brought by all of Lana's co-workers were quite an interesting collection. Chewable and noisy toys were mixed in with shirts, pants, and socks that looked as if they had been made for a doll. Stephany had even brought a tiny pair of blue shoes that had been matched to a pair of toy jeans. Everyone wanted to hold them to compare their size to their own hands. Sunny had added a small boy's bicycle, making everyone laugh.

"Sunny, is your present not a little premature?" Someone asked.

"No." Sunny proudly looked at his gift. "Children grow fast. You will hardly have the time to count the fingers on your hands before he rolls into the Sunny Side Cafe on this bike. I'll see how you'll laugh at me then."

Lana needed to borrow a car from Sunny to deliver the gifts to their home. She had prepared the shelf with toys, the diapers, the baby oil and the soft flannel wraps colored in blue-green and highlighted by pink and yellow stars and moons, thinking that very soon this showroom would be inhabited and brought into livable disorder by the new arrival. Natalie approved of everything that they had done and had purchased. She liked the curtains that Lana had made from the same fabric used for the wraps and noticed that the border of the wallpaper had the same design of the stars and moons as everything else in this room.

Natalie touched the toys which hung above the bed and stroked a white teddy bear with a blue bow around its neck and remarked sadly. "I am so sorry that our baby is still in the hospital and that the doctor didn't allow us to take him home. I miss him so much."

"Mom. You'll need to get better before Troy arrives home and creates a lot of extra work for you."

"You're right, I'll go and lie down; I suddenly feel very tired." Natalie was enjoying her last two days of lazily lying on the couch, in the company of Tac, watching Lana and thinking how lucky she was to have a grown-up daughter.

The arrival of little Troy had brought together the whole family. Even Natalie's aunt from Canada had arrived to see the new addition to the Vladners' household. Lana was surprised to see how quickly her family had dropped what they were doing and had gathered around the baby. They looked inside the carrier in admiration and made noises to attract Troy's attention. Despite being just a fraction of a human being, he was the most important person in the room.

"He's the lucky one." Said Lana, without jealousy. "No one even looks at me anymore." Worried that her mother was tired from the noise produced by people talking all at once, she took on the task of caring for Troy herself. She went to the kitchen to find a bottle of baby milk to heat it. Entering the living room, she found her mother in the middle of a conversation with her noisy aunt, Sue, who was instructing her about the importance of making the correct choice of Godmother for Troy.

"Do you have someone on your mind?"

"A cow." Lana took the baby from her and sat on the couch to feed him. Ignoring the laughter of the guests, she explained that her mother's milk had disappeared before Troy even had a chance to try it. This, then, was the reason why his 'mother' for now would have to be a cow.

"Oh, that's not good." Aunty Sue shook her head. "You are a poor thing."

But Troy apparently did not feel that he was at a disadvantage since milk flowed easily to quench his appetite, without any hard work on his part, and he filled his small stomach without a problem. He pushed the rubber nipple of his bottle out of his mouth and blew out frothy bubbles. Lana waited until Troy had burped loudly and then promptly took the sleeping prince to his room.

Nicholas opened the bedroom door to ask if she needed help.

"He's sleeping." Lana studied her father's face knowing him well enough to detect that something was spoiling his happiness. "Dad, would it not be smart to talk to me about things that are bothering you? Two heads are better than one and, together, maybe we can find a solution to the problem that you may have? You can't discuss your problems with mom since her health is still fragile but you can do it with me. Talking about her, I think that it is time to diplomatically suggest to our family that their visit has now ran its course. It looks as if mother needs to take a nap."

"What a smart girl I have. Let's talk tomorrow but, for now, let's go and kick out the relatives. However, we will do it tactfully." Laughing, they left Troy to sleep.

'I wonder what kind of dreams he has.' Thought Lana, looking down at her brother next day. The baby made convulsive movements with his hands, pulled his neck into his shoulders while he turned it from side to side and wrinkled-up the bridge of his nose. 'Someone once told me that babies don't have dreams. Therefore, why is he making these faces?' She pulled on the soft, fleecy blanket and covered the small, pink fingers before rushing over to the window, attracted by the sound of a car turning into their driveway. "Dad!" She whispered, running downstairs to meet him. "Dad, why are you so late?" Her questioning was halted by the gloomy expression on his face which scared her.

"I have bad news, Lana!" Nicholas paused and leaned back to support himself against the car while he massaged his temples with spread fingers to ease a headache.

The length of the pause became unbearable for Lana. "Are we up to our neck in debt and is this the reason why you have been hiding the bills and bank statements from mother?"

Nicholas met his daughter's eyes, hating himself for putting the weight of his problems on her shoulders. At the same time, he knew that he had not done anything wrong. However, it did not ease his feelings of guilt for failing to protect his family from financial disaster.

"The matter is even worse." He eventually said. "When I had received all the medical bills from the hospital, their total exceeded our ability to pay on time. The bank wants me to sell the house and pay off our debts or they will do it for me."

"Will they take our house?" Lana was shocked.

"Yes! They will. I am afraid to talk to Natalie because I don't know how to put the words together to make it less painful. Since I am a man I can pack my things and go somewhere else but she is a different matter. She cares about our home so much that I am afraid she might start to feel insecure, or depressed, and then become sick again?"

"Dad, I do not know what to say. Honestly, I feel like I have been hit by a train. Do we have at least some time to find a new place to live? And what about all the things we have? Do we need to sell them or give them away?" Lana had become very fearful as to what the future held for her family. Since Nicholas had been experiencing the same feelings for weeks already, he understood very well what was going on inside her mind.

"It will be a big change for us but we will survive, won't we?" He sighed.

"Yes." She nodded, her throat still tight.

Nicholas added. "The bank manager doesn't feel happy about evicting a long- term customer from his home and he has decided to give us two months to sort through our belongings and then find a place to live."

Lana wanted to say something but Nicholas interrupted her. "There is no way that we can find more than two hundred thousand dollars to pay to the bank. We now need to start thinking about losing the house and moving on and

I would appreciate your opinion on what you feel will be the least stressful way of telling mother about this painful truth."

Lana cleared her throat and remarked dryly. "May I suggest that the money that will be left over after the bank has been paid be put into an education fund which will help Troy greatly in the future? In addition, we'll save the costs of running the house, including taxes and the money which otherwise would be spent on repairs, and this will allow us to go on a vacation to a tropical island."

"What would I do without you? This way, instead of thinking about the loss, mom will think about the benefits." He joked. "Let's go inside the house before she starts to look for us."

The unpleasant feelings created by the bad news had receded from Lana's mind; but it was too early to say that she accepted the situation. She excused herself for her lack of appetite and went upstairs. Very soon she would be leaving this home. Up to this time she had not really paid much attention to her own bedroom but now looked more closely at everything that had surrounded her. 'If something doesn't hurt then we don't think about it.' Lana admitted to herself, lying down on her bed.

She smiled at the memory that, at one time, the light, apple-green walls of her bedroom had been bright pink, the same as everything else in her room. She was happy that she had passed through this "pink" period quickly and had not become addicted to it like her friend, Maggie, had done. She had decorated her bedroom with three pictures of hydrangeas in bloom painted in antique bronze. Then she found an ivory-shaded lamp with a collage of bronze birds' feathers neatly clustered on the base. Her bedding was edged with an apple-green border accented by a bouquet of hydrangeas in the center of it, brightening the room with shades of lavender tinged with purple. All the colors in Lana's bedroom were coordinated and even the artificial orchids in a vase were selected in the same ivory color, detailed by spots and stripes of purple and cherry red. Lana felt sorry that all the energy that she had spent to create this space would be wasted.

Following an impulse, she put her hand under the pillow and pulled out her secret, a gift from the stranger whom she had seen only once in her life. She liked to watch the changing shades of color on the stones as she turned the cross to make it sparkle in the light of the bedside lamp. On its reverse side the cross had a design of spirals running in different directions. She noticed that one of the sections looked a little different from the rest and, to determine this, she got up and took a magnifying glass. To her surprise, the surface of the spiral had been formed by a sign in an unknown language which ended with the numbers 1123. 'What does this mean?' She knew only one man who could help her to find the answer to this riddle and maybe even read the sign. Lana lifted her cell phone and dialed Maggie's number.

"Hi Maggie, how are you?" She would rather have not asked this question because it might take an hour to listen to the answer but, if she did this, Maggie might think that Lana was ignoring her well-being. She waited for the opportunity to say. "Maggie, I think that everything that you have told me is too important to discuss on the phone. You can tell me all this when we meet today. I want to ask your dad to translate some text for me. I think it's Swedish. Do you think he will help me? I am leaving right now."

She put the cross into her backpack, picked up her jacket and ran down the staircase.

"Mom, dad." Lana shouted, on the way out of the house. "I am going to see Maggie, so somebody will need to feed Troy." Then she rolled out her motor bicycle and rode off in the direction of Murraydale where Maggie lived.

The first thing that Lana heard from Maggie was unexpected. "Lana, you shouldn't allow your parents to turn you into a nanny. When was the last time that we went out and how will you be able to date someone if you are busy changing diapers? Do you intend to do this until Troy is ready to attend school? By that time all the good men will have been taken. Do you want to be married to some loser?"

Lana kept her answer short. "Hullo, Maggie. I intend to do this for two more months until my mother recovers from her operation and will be able to take care of Troy herself. Then I'll be able to go back to my dance school and perhaps even start to see someone."

Maggie wanted to object but her cell phone rang. "Hullo." Her voice had suddenly turned sweet, which told Lana that there must be a man on the other end. This offered Lana a chance to leave. She made a sign with her fingers and waited for Maggie's reaction.

"Do what you want, I am busy right now." She dismissed Lana with a wave of her hand.

Mr. O'Donnell was in his office as usual and was pleased to greet her. "Hullo, Lana. I haven't seen you for a long time but I hear that you have had a good reason to disappear. How is your family? And how is the little one?"

"Mom is still recovering from her operation. But my new brother, Troy, is a healthy baby with a good appetite and this keeps me busy. Maggie has given me a lecture about my neglect of her. I hope you don't feel the same way. I have no choice but to help my family."

"We always have choices. Maggie told me that you had buried yourself in diapers. Instead of this, you should go with her to London to live with my relatives for a month. She is planning to return home engaged to a Lord."

"Oh." Lana gasped. "These Lords in movies look so cold and snobbish. I think that Maggie doesn't deserve such a terrible fate."

"Do you think that she will allow a man to spoil her life?"

"I don't know." She sat down in the chair. "She is pretending to be independent but, in reality, thinks the same way as her mother does and is still wearing pink, Barbie glasses. But one day she'll probably grow up and take them off."

"I hope so. Maggie told me that you have a problem with some text."

"Yes, I do." She removed the cross from the bag and showed him the sign.

"Hmm!" He took the cross to weigh it in his hand and then looked back at Lana. The expression on his face became suspicious. "Where did you get this?"

Lana had known him since she was a little girl and told him the real story. "I know it sounds strange, but my neighbors, Stephany and her brothers, are witnesses to what happened. The horseman, Validar, who wore a cloak and carried a sword, was as real as this gift."

"Why do you think that this is a gift?" He looked at the sign through a magnifying glass and made a copy of it. "I don't want you to show this to anyone else, especially to Maggie because she can't keep a secret."

"Why are you worried about it, anyway? It's only a cheap, fifteen-dollar imitation isn't it?" Lana still didn't understand the reason for his concern.

"I can tell the difference between painted glass and real stones and these stones are real!" At this, a heavy silence filled the space between them. "Have you shown it to anyone?" He asked.

"No, only to Stephany and her brothers. They were the first people to tell me that it is a worthless object. I don't think that they know anything about the value of precious stones though."

"Lana, this cross can be very dangerous for you. You have come into my house carrying this trouble in your bag and now I can't let you go home alone. If something were to happen to you on the way home, then I would never forgive myself for being careless. I am a parent too, after all. I'll take you home myself and you can pick up your bike later. Of course, after I have brought you home, it will be your father's responsibility to look after your safety. I think it would be better if we leave through the back door. Later, I will tell my daughter that your mother called and you had to leave in a hurry."

Lana was so scared by this secrecy that she didn't think about arguing. They left the house without saying goodbye to anyone and remained silent for the first couple of miles. Slowly Lana recovered from the fright and adjusted her feelings to the gift. "Mr. O'Donnell, is there any possibility that you may be wrong and that this is not real jewelry?"

"No, this object is worth a small fortune. I just can't tell you exactly how much it is worth."

"So, if we sell it, we could pay off all our debts to the bank?"

"If you had found it hidden somewhere for centuries, then selling it would be exactly what I would suggest. But it does have a mysterious owner and presently you don't know whether or not you are at liberty to sell it. Maybe you are only the keeper of the cross for some time. And there is another question that is bothering me. If it had been Validar's intention to give you this cross for only a short time, then who will come back for it? Him, or someone else? This is the reason why I am driving you because I don't want you to be attacked on your way home."

"But how can this imagined person know that I have the cross with me?"

"He may arrange a car accident to allow him the chance of searching you before someone else finds your body."

"This sounds like a scene from a movie and it makes me feel strange somehow."

"Let's see what your father says." He turned the corner leading to Lana's home. The gravel of the driveway crackled under the wheels of his car and attracted the attention of Tod who started to bark at the stranger. But, after recognizing Lana, he only jumped around, beating the dust from his coat with his tail, and rolled himself almost into a circle.

Lana opened the door and invited him into her home. Having seen the light in the kitchen, and hearing the sound of dishes, she went there to find her father making himself a cup of tea.

"Ah, Lana, you are home."

"I'm with Maggie's father."

"Hullo Brian, please come in." Then he turned to Lana, immediately forgetting about his tea. "What has happened? Did you get into an accident?"

"Dad, I am fine. Mr. O'Donnell will explain everything."

"Nicholas, I think we may need something stronger than tea because this will be quite a story. May we sit down please?"

"Of course." Nicholas showed the way to the living room. "Will a beer suffice?"

"Splendid." They sat on the couch. "Lana, show your dad what you have."

Lana put the cross on the coffee table, worried about the outcome of their conversation. Since she had learned the true value of the cross, her adventure did not look as romantic as it had before.

"I've seen this cross in Lana's hands a few times." Nicholas lifted an eyebrow in surprise. "I was wondering about it because it does not accord with her usual style and it is too large for her to wear. But, since teenagers wear weirdthings, I decided not to ask questions."

"Nicholas, I would not have bothered you this late in the evening merely because the style of this cross has disturbed me. But the value of it is so high that I have serious concerns. I am not an expert but I know something about jewelry. I can assure you that the cross is made of real gold and precious stones and this means that your daughter has received a treasure. There is something else that I want to bring to your attention. There is a sign on it together with the date1123. If this is the year when the jewelry was made, then only a very noble person was able to own such a thing at that time. If I can find the name of its owner, this cross could be priceless."

He looked at Nicholas to observe his reaction. "I hope that you can now understand how dangerous it is for Lana to have this thing in her possession. It is very fortunate that she has been too busy recently to talk about her adventure to her friends just to make all the other girls turn green with envy. The existence of the cross is still a secret. Lana has told me that she wants to sell the cross and I have already advised her that this is not necessarily the best thing to do, except in a situation where your family may have a very serious financial problem. From my point of view, you have two choices: you can sell this dangerous thing or you may keep it. But, before you make a decision on this, I want Lana to tell you the circumstances under which she came into possession of the cross."

Nicholas listened to her intently and his face changed its expressions from disbelief to worry and anger. "And you didn't tell me anything?"

"I didn't think that it was so important to discuss it with you because I was not hurt."

He rested his head on his locked fingers, thinking. 'What if Validar were to return, and demand his precious possession back? I am not trained to fight back with a sword and we can't rely on the protection of the police since they will intervene only in the event of someone becoming seriously hurt.' Finally, he remarked. "I have made my decision. We will hide it and wait until the owner comes back for it."

"Dad, if this dangerous man comes back to retrieve his cross, then he will expect it to be returned to him immediately. To avoid the possibility of his becoming angry, I should have it close to me at all times so that this story will end without violence."

"Nicholas, she is talking sense. He will not deal with anyone but the girl."

"Lana, I don't like the idea of your becoming a target but you are right. He will try to approach you alone and, if this happens, I must beg you to just give it to him and then run away from him as fast as you can."

"Yes, dad, I will." Lana was pleased that her opinion was valued. She knew the personality of the stranger sufficiently well to feel no fear for herself, but did not want to discuss it with her father.

O'Donnell rose up from his chair. "In this case, I'll forget that I have ever seen the cross and won't make any further enquiries to avoid attracting attention. Nicholas, I will see you later." They shook hands and he added. "I haven't had a chance to see Mrs. Vladner so could you please say 'Hullo' to her for me and give her my congratulations. Goodbye, Lana."

"Brian, thank you for your concern for my girl." Replied Nicholas. "And you, young lady, you should go to sleep because it's late."

Tod was keeping a close watch on his Master, curious as to why he had suddenly started to collect different things from the garage and around the house, obviously cleaning out the place. 'Are we going to have a big party?' He asked himself.

A party is a good thing in a dog's life because it brings many tasty bones to him. Tod had started to feel happy but the sad expression on his Master's face spoiled this feeling for him. Being just a dog, Tod had trouble understanding complicated human feelings and behavior and thought. 'Without Tac I am unable to understand anything. I am like a cat without whiskers who cannot catch a mouse, having no senses. But who knows when Tac will return from the forest, so I had better go and look for him myself.' He jumped over the fence and ran to Pokerweild forest. It was not difficult for him to find it since any dog knew its location, but he was not sure how to find Tac's home in the woods. He decided to follow the road and very soon he had reached the fairground. He sniffed around, trying to find the cat's footprints, but it was impossible to detect them in the terrible mix of smells that had been left by so many people. Tod, disappointed and frustrated by his failure, lifted up his face and howled the song of a lonely dog.

"Why are you howling and frightening the hard working animals?" A voice spoke behind him. Tod turned round quickly to face the stranger. Spreading his legs wide, in case he needed to jump aside quickly, he saw the cheeky raccoon that always accompanied Tac on his late trips from the forest to his doghouse.

"I am looking for Tac." He gave Roxal an unfriendly look.

"I do not like you either. But he is also my friend and that is why I will lead you to his home."

Tod gave a short bark and followed him eagerly.

"What has happened and why are you here?" The cat asked, finding Tod and Roxal on his doorstep.

"Tac, I suspect that something strange is going on in our family. I am unable to understand if it is good or bad and this feeling makes me restless. I could not take it anymore and came to ask for your help."

"Can this not wait until tomorrow?" Tac replied, seemingly annoyed.

"Maybe. But can you sleep peacefully knowing that I cannot rest and that something unusual has happened to your family?"

"You are right." Tac thoughtfully replied. "Alisa." He shouted to the inside of his home. "I am going out to see the family because my brother, Tod, thinks that there is something worthy of my attention. I will see if I can clarify this situation and will probably be back tomorrow."

"That's fine. Off you go."

Addressing the raccoon, he said. "Thanks, Roxal, but now I will take care of him." Then, turning to Tod, he remarked. "I will show you the shortest way home."

"She is a good female, your wife." Tod made an attempt to adapt his speed to the cat's pace. "She did not growl at you."

"She is smart." Replied Tac, jumping over a tree trunk. "That's why I married her."

They didn't run along the road that had earlier brought Tod to Tac's home because the cat was a slower runner than Tod and it would have taken them twice as long to return home by the same route. Tac chose pathways that only he recognized and led Tod without hesitation, as if he was a natural inhabitant of this wood. This 'new' Tac moved silently between very tall trees with self-confidence and sparks of excitement in his eyes. He did not resemble the fat cat who had, in an earlier time, stumbled in front of the open gate with a paw held in the air indecisively and with eyes round from fear. Surprised by the change in his friend's personality, Tod missed the obvious signs that the wood was ending. He even looked back in disbelieve when he realized that he had passed through its mass.

The rest of their way lay through the small fields that were familiar to both of them, eventually bringing them to the river at the stone bridge. Crossing it, they ran along the reeds and then turned onto the pathway that took them up to the top of the slope. There it merged into a small fruit orchard at the back of the house.

"Look, dad! Tod has brought us a helper!" Yelled Lana, as soon as she saw Tac.

Nicholas had collected together all the rusty metal junk that had slowly accumulated at the side of his property since he had bought the house. He stretched his tired back and removed his gloves, calling the cat to come closer. Naturally, the cat received a generous share of patting from both Lana and Nicholas after which he sat on the stone wall and enjoyed the coolness of the shade. Half closing his eyes, and pretending to be drowsy, he listened to the conversation between them.

"Thank goodness this is the last pile of junk. We will have to deliver the metal to the truck and dispose of it later. I am too tired to do it now." Lana sat next to Tac on the wall. "I think that tonight I will sleep like a log. Troy can cry as much as he wants but he will not wake me up. Are we done with cleaning dad?"

"I think so. There are some things in the garage that I still want to sort out to see which ones I want to keep. After that, we are going to put a coat of paint on the garage walls and put the house on the market."

"How much do you think we may be able to get for the house?" Queried Lana, speculatively.

"I don't know yet. We need to make an enquiry from a broker to find out what price a buyer would offer for a house of our size."

"Dad, when we move, what will happen to Tac? He won't understand why we have been replaced by strangers. What if they hurt him?" She stroked his head.

"We will have to explain to the new owners about him and ask them not to scare him. Or, alternatively, you'll need to lock him in the house and take him with us in a cage. Eventually, when he gets used to living with us in our new place, either he'll forget about the wood or he will run away and never come back."

"No." Lana lifted the cat onto her lap and buried her nose in his fur. "Tac, you won't leave me."

Tac did not like this turn of events but did not show his concern. He needed to find out why his Masters had suddenly decided to move, in view of the fact that they now had the responsibility of a newborn baby on their hands.

"It will be difficult to find a place where pets are allowed." Continued Lana, as she put him back on the top of the wall and watched her father pushing a barrow, filled with metal junk, towards the truck.

"I know. I have already started to look, Sweetie. Don't worry. We'll find something."

"Wherever it is, it will not be as nice as our house." Lana's mood once more became sad.

"If we didn't need to pay money to the bank then I would never sell our home." Remarked Nicholas.

'Money!' In a flash the dreamy expression disappeared from Tac's face. 'My family owes a large sum of money to the bank and that is why they have to sell our place!' He silently slapped his forehead with a paw and sighed. 'I heard my Master talking on the phone about some problem that had left him with a money loss, some time ago. If he already had money problems, then the additional expenses connected with the birth of the baby only increased this. Now I am not surprised that the bank has demanded payment of the loan in full!' He jumped softly from the fence and ran to the house, stopping for a moment to exchange a few words with Tod who had been lying under the car.

"Tod, can you find a way back to my home by yourself?"

"I think I can, I am a dog after all." He fluffed up his ear.

"Good! Please now run and tell Alisa that I want to meet Carfield tomorrow. She knows where he lives and will find a way to contact him. I need to stay here to find out the name of the bank that is pressing our Master and the important detail called the account number. I think I know where to look for it."

Tod barked agreeably and jumped over the neighbor's fence, cutting the corner to the road.

Tac Steals his Master's Bank Statement & Lana

Tac, on the other hand, did not need to hurry so he straightened his fur and muttered to himself, ironically. 'It looks like stealing bank papers has become a specialty of mine.' Then, hearing Lana calling him, he followed her into the house. The first thing that the cat did was to greet Natalie and was glad to see that her face had regained its former healthy color. He rubbed his cheek against her hand, purring, and then went to look at Troy who was sleeping in a carrier.

'All small creatures start their lives in exactly the same way; they just eat and sleep.' He mused to himself, as he stared at Troy. 'I wonder if he is blind like I was at his age.'

Right now, Tac had an advantage over Troy because his eyes were as sharp as a tack and did not miss any movement inside the house. So he was aware that his Master kept his important papers in his office, including his bank statements. If he could find a way to get inside this room he would be able to remove it. In the summer he could climb in through an open window. But now the window was closed and he needed to forget about obtaining access to the room from outside the house. 'It looks as if I will need to find a way to stop the door from being closed.'

This version looked promising and therefore he concentrated upon it. Bringing two small rubber balls, he put one against the wall close to the opening of the door. When Nicholas finished checking his mail and had left the room, Tac kicked the second ball to make it roll along the wall until it pushed the first one forward. It rolled too fast to block the door open and bounced off the edge of the closing door, but the second one blocked it. Nicholas didn't notice it and walked away without fixing the problem. He sank his claws into the ball and pulled it to open the door wider, allowing him entry to the study. Reaching the top of the table with one jump he started to study the pile of folders. After opening the third, he did see something that looked close to what he was searching for. Grasping the first page, he bent it in half and took it down onto the floor. Outside the room, he pressed the side of his face against the wall to look across the space in front of him. No one was around and all that he needed to do was to bring the bank statement to the wood to read it with Carfield.

Two days later, Lana was coming home from school and, as soon as she opened the door of the house, she heard the voice of her mother crying out "Nicholas, is that you?"

"No mom, it's me." She went inside the house and found both her mother and Troy in the kitchen. Troy looked unhappy, impatiently waiting for his milk. He showed, with the movements of his body, that if mother wouldn't hurry up with his dinner he would start to complain loudly.

"Look at this cranky little guy!" Lana touched his hands, trying to attract his attention with the soft animals which were attached to his carrier. But Troy's attention was concentrated on his empty stomach and he was not in the mood to play with his sister. He started to make coughing sounds and his face was beginning to turn deep pink.

"Here!" Natalie gave a bottle to Lana. "This will make his good mood return. Troy had quickly learned the feeding procedure and did not need any instructions. He grabbed the bottle as soon as it was close to his nose, making both women laugh. They were so involved with Troy that they didn't hear Nicholas as he entered the kitchen.

"Ahh! Here you are." He observed.

Troy was busy drinking milk and didn't pay attention to his father, stroking the glass bottle with his hand as he examined its shape. However, he didn't mind replacing the bottle with one of his dad's fingers, holding it tightly with all of his own.

"He has a strong hand." Nicholas smiled as he tried to gently free his finger.

"Nicholas, I almost forgot. The bank manager has called you several times. I think he needs to talk to you urgently."

The soft, relaxed lines of Nicholas's face tightened visibly. He left the kitchen to make the 'phone call from the living room, worried about how he could soften the expected bad news for the ears of his family. Shortly afterwards he returned to the kitchen, holding a jacket in his hands, and briefly said. "I'm going to the bank."

"But it's late." Natalie looked at him in surprise.

"Dad, what's going on?" Added Lana.

"I'm not sure." Nicholas shrugged, still thinking about the conversation he had just had. "The bank manager is waiting to speak to me in person so that he can explain something very important. He didn't want to do it on the telephone."

After his return, Nicholas was greeted by the impatient looks from the women. However, his face reflected only puzzlement, instead of anger or concern.

"Please sit down on the couch and I'll start from the beginning. The bank was already closed by the time I arrived there, but the manager let me in. He looked confused and his attitude towards me was extremely friendly, as if he was receiving a movie star in his office. He surprised me right away by saying that I should have told him that I have a very wealthy relative who is willing to help us. I told the banker that I had no idea what he was talking about. He gave me a strange look and said that he always treated all information that he learned from any source, whether it be business or private, as strictly confidential. Then he told me that the manager of an amusement park had called him this afternoon to make an immediate appointment to discuss important business. Then he added. 'Of course, Mr. Vladner, you will understand that I could not refuse to meet my wealthiest client. The manager of the Golden Nut Amusement Park came with instructions from his boss, Mr. Holmes, to pay off all your debts. Mr. Carl Mayer signed the cheque in my presence and said that Mr. Holmes was very upset that his relative had been a victim of unfair circumstances and he wanted to make things right for the family. Money is not a problem for him, Mr. Vladner.' He then shook my hand and gave me a new bank statement which showed that we owed nothing to the bank." To prove the point, Nicholas showed it to the stunned women.

Natalie had known nothing about the problem with repayment of the loan and asked Nicholas for an explanation.

Meanwhile, Lana had run away upstairs to her bedroom, not wishing to show how deeply she had been affected by the news. Nervous tremors shook her body and forced her to look for a blanket to wrap around herself. She felt the interference of a mysterious stranger in her life again. At least she did not need to wonder about the identity of the benefactor. By putting together many small clues that had come to her recently, she felt that she knew him. The first clue was her meeting with the stranger, the second was his very expensive gift, then a letter that came into her house addressed to Mr. Holmes and, finally, his generous gesture. She fully realized that people do such things for others only if they consider them to be very special.

'I don't know why he is doing this.' She thought. 'But no one else fits into this pattern of behavior other than Validar. I will need to find him to clarify my curiosity about the meaning of the connection between us, before it blows me apart.'

And a plan of action started to slowly form in her mind...

CHAPTER 10:

THE ROBBED DRAGON

April had waited long enough, watching how her sister, March, had vented her frequently-changing moods upon the land and its inhabitants. At first, March had shown her goodwill by allowing a few warm days to occur, then, suddenly becoming sad, she had again soaked the plants and animals in a cold rain. But her worst trick was to step aside allowing her older brother, February, to invoke his playful pet, the Northern Wind, to distribute a late, swirling handful of snow into the nearly-awoken fields and forests.

The trees, the insects and the animals had grown tired of this game and called for the protection of blue-skied April. "April, please come and bring steady weather so that we can start to open our buds, stretch our wings and legs in the warm sun and start to scratch off our winter coats."

Answering their calls, April duly stepped forward to push away the petty rains and look around to make sure that the inhabitants of the mountains and the woods were ready to receive rejuvenating spring.

April felt pleased with her progress. She had helped to melt the last patches of snow which still lodged in some deep ridges and had started to prepare the ground for the first flowers. Following this, she moved higher up the mountains to see if they, also, had received the message about the approach of spring.

Before her departure, she melted the ice crust around the opening of the cave, close to the top of the mountain, and looked inside. But there was no occupant to wake up after the winter season. She only saw a large pile of gray rocks lying on the floor of the cave.

But April had playfully blown a warm breath of air into the cave, merely as a joke, and left without noticing that the pile of stones on the floor had shuddered and thrown out a long tail. The movement had revealed that the heap of stones was in fact a giant reptile, deep in sleep. Even the monster, who was wearing a suit of hard armor, was unable to ignore her call. His dreaming began to fade.

The dragon was still half asleep when he stretched his legs and slowly lifted up his wings. The deep wounds that he had sustained in his last battle had healed completely and he needed only time for his burning heart to awaken his dormant energy. Breathing out the stale air, he rose up on massive, slightly-bent legs. Slowly, he remembered the past events that had brought him into this cave and this refreshed his anger. The dragon checked that part of the cave where he had previously found a source of energy but, to his disappointment, the stone cup was almost empty but he licked up what was left of the oil. The realization that this would only sustain him for a short time made him think about whether widening the tiny cracks in the walls would be sufficient to refill the empty reservoir.

He breathed his fire directly onto the wall, which forced the trapped air to expand and hit the opposite side of the cave. Deep down inside, the bowels of the mountain answered with a distant rumble and part of the wall behind the dragon slid away, turned into dust and brought more destruction. The dragon became scared by the falling rocks and rushed to the entrance. Then, hovering at some distance from the cave and flapping his large wings, he watched as a massive cloud of dust ejected from the mouth of the cave. Suddenly a deep crack ran along the wall starting the destruction of the side of the mountain. After the dust had settled, he discovered that his cave had disappeared completely, together with a large part of the mountain. The new wall sparkled with freshly-exposed minerals but did not have any large caverns in it which he could use for shelter. With his temporary home lost, he was now homeless. Of course, the dragon blamed the two creatures that had brought him here for this catastrophe and for all the other troubles that had happened to him recently.

'I will make them pay dearly for this.' He vowed and then moved away to look for a new place for his nest. Making a wide circle above the mountain, the valley and the forest he did not find a spot that appealed to him. The unusual green color of the trees had an alien appearance. 'What a cursed land. I would love to blow it into ashes but to use my fire on it would surely be a waste of my energy.' He thought, as he returned to the slope of the mountain, hoping to find a suitable cave.

"Tac. I have something to tell you. A horrible-looking bird flew over my tree and nearly frightened me to death." Carfield screamed out as he stormed into the cat's home.

"What kind of a bird? An eagle?" Tac was just able to catch Alisa's favorite vase from falling to the floor.

"An eagle!" Exclaimed Carfield, sarcastically. "It was like the one I saw in the orange woods and inside the black box in your house."

"You mean the dragon we saw on T.V?" Asked Tac, the proud owner of the first T.V. and satellite dish in the wood.

"Yes." Carfield was glad that the cat was not laughing at him. "To be correct, this creature had a different appearance but resembled the one on the screen in size. If it was not so early for the event I would have thought that someone had dressed-up for Halloween. However, its skin looked too perfect to be artificial. Do you think that I have lost my mind?"

"Do not worry, Carfield. I don't think that anything has happened to your head. No matter what kind of shape the beast has, it is still a dragon. Before we start to panic, we need to make sure that the creature that you saw is actually him. I suggest we now go to the kitchen to see if Alisa has something to eat for you. It's early in the morning and maybe you are just hungry and have decided that your dream about a dragon came to life."

Carfield had spent only a few minutes in the kitchen before another visitor rushed through the door, talking just as quickly and nervously as the crow.

"Tac I need to tell you what I have seen."

"You saw a dragon? Right?" Tac replied, calmly.

"How did you know?" Galibur looked at him in surprise, but the presence of the crow had given him a hint. "Carfield told you about the dragon, did he not?" He reflected.

"At least we have clarified the first part of our agenda. Two witnesses are enough to confirm that we have a problem."

"Unfortunately, I need to admit that it was us who invited this dragon here by showing it the way. The shadow which we both saw on the night of our arrival was a large reptile from another world. We, alone, are responsible for all future troubles." Sighed Galibur.

"I know that it may become a worse problem than a cloud. But why are you talking so dramatically?" Tac queried.

"Because, when humans discover this aggressive animal, they and the dragon will battle each other and will bring much destruction upon the land." Galibur speculated. "Of course, if the dragon eats us before any of this can happen, then we shall have nothing to worry about and they can destroy this world together at their mutual pleasure."

"After all the hard work we have put-in to make our lives better, we cannot allow this creature to destroy everything. We are going to fight." The crow ruffled his feathers angrily.

"Carfield." Replied a very somber Tac. "I think the matter is serious enough to disturb the Council. Galibur, I also have business for you to attend to. Place watch-posts to observe every movement of the enemy. Can you show me the place on the map where you last saw him?" He enquired.

"I can even show you the place where the dragon is building a nest."

"Perfect. Let's go and have a look at the map."

Galibur pointed to a spot. "Here is where my cousin saw it."

Tac made a mark with a pen and prepared to listen to the eagle.

"The collapse of the side of the mountain attracted the attention of my cousin, Seran. He was searching for injured animals. But, instead of food, he found a beast and was lucky to escape undetected to relate this story to me. For him it was just amusement, but for me it was a real concern. Therefore, I flew to the mountain myself but I could not find the dragon in the western part of the mountains. As I was circling above the area, another member of my family crossed my path and, during our greetings, he mentioned that he had noticed a strange structure that resembled a tower. The dragon had built his new home on the northern mountain of the chain, where two sharp peaks with poorly vegetated slopes have created a deep valley. The patches of grass which grow here are only sufficient to provide food for families of snow goats.

The western mountain, Aran, has a glacier on its side that gives birth to a small and talkative river which rolls its water through the valley and forest to feed the lake. Faststream is what we call the river, although humans give it another name. This river has provided fresh water for the woods that grow along the valley and climb up the slopes of the mountain in some places.

The northern mountain, Tavren, has never liked to wear a green coat like his twin brother, Aran, standing as a naked rock, gloomy, inaccessible and crowned by gray clouds. It has a quite large, flat platform on one side and it is here, high above and separate from the rest of the world, that the dragon has made a nest using chunks of rock ripped from the body of Tavren. It has a perfect view of the valley and the animals that roam along it. Perhaps this place reminds the dragon of his own world and he will stay here until he has eaten all the animals.

Allow me to tell you what will happen after he finishes-off every living creature in the valley. He will move to Pokerweild in order to feed on the people who are coming to the fairground, bringing the police and then the army here. If the soldiers do not blow this place to bits it will be the dragon that will burn it to the ground and, in both cases, we will be dead."

Galibur's Search for the Dragon's Tower

"This is completely unacceptable to us and to our plans! Galibur, we will need to scare the dragon away or kill him." The cat cried out, aghast.

"It's easier said than done." The eagle sighed.

"Let's both think about it." Tac replied. "Maybe by the time that a meeting can be arranged we will be able to come up with some idea."

"The meeting is appointed for tomorrow morning. I heard it from a messenger sent by the Council." Alisa brought this news to their attention.

"This means that the members of the Council have also heard the news and are so scared that they have rushed to do something, or already have a plan." Commented Galibur, preparing to leave.

Tac got up early the next morning, thinking about what he was going to say at the meeting but, instead of preparing his speech, he spent most of his time trying to talk Alisa out of going with him to Council Hill. He reminded her that she was not a member and would not be allowed to be present unless she had been invited. He tried to deter her by saying that the rain could catch them on the way and, to convince her to stay at home, pointing out that he would never leave the bed to go outside on a cold spring morning unless the circumstance was one of great urgency and need. But all his arguments were to no avail since Alisa had made-up her mind and was not prepared to change it. Tac agreed that she could accompany him on the understanding that she must stay down at the foot of the hill no matter how long the meeting would last.

"Alisa. Tell me honestly, why do you want to go so far without needing to do it?"

She smiled shyly and fluffed-up her neck. "I would die from curiosity if I did not hear the outcome of the discussion immediately."

Her confession made him roll his eyes. "I have heard from my family that 'curiosity killed the cat', but I did not know that it could be deadly for a fox too. Let's run faster. I do not want to be late."

He was glad that they were both still wearing their winter coats because morning was cold. Their warm breath froze into white clouds as soon as it had left their mouths. Last year's dry leaves, whitened by frost, cracked under their paws and lost their beauty after they had been mixed in with the dirt. They did not stop to sniff at anything, or look around at the wonders of the morning, because it was not a run for pleasure. So, all interesting details, such as the amusing design of the ice on the surface of a puddle at the bottom of the ridge, the family of snowdrops with the narrow green leaves stretching upwards to the sky, the willow branches covered with puffy, gray bunny tails and many other things, were passed-by unchecked. The branches of shrubs, which had been stripped of all their leaves, stood on both sides of their way with nothing to stop prying eyes from seeing through them.

Consequently, Council Hill could be seen before Tac and Alisa had reached the edge of the forest and stepped out onto an open space covered by dry grass, colored in shades of brown and beige. Tac changed the angle of their passage, moving more to the left towards a group of animals standing at the foot of Council Hill, soon finding that the dark silhouettes belonged to the relatives of Council members. Alisa stopped feeling bad about her own stubbornness, seeing that she was not the only one who was guilty of curiosity and impatience.

"Good morning, Tac." The Elk greeted him, coming down the hill. "I see that you have brought a spare tail too." He looked at Alisa.

Embarrassed, Tac only shrugged. "You can stay with Rainar's family, Alisa."

"The discussion will start as soon as Galibur has returned with fresh news about the dragon. He has promised to reconnoiter the area and check on him." Rainar advised, before they took their respective places, the elk at his stone and the cat on the round platform designated for a speaker.

To Tac's surprise, he found that Bertrond and Alowsius were also present. Ignoring a variety of friendly and unfriendly looks, he related the stories of his adventures again.

"I did not have any doubts that it was you who has brought this trouble down on our heads." Alowsius came closer and walked around Tac with his eyes full of hatred. "I knew from the first time I met you that I should kill you before you became a pest for us." Then he growled to the assembled throng of forest animals. "We need to send him to the mountain to talk to his good friend, the dragon."

"Alowsius, return to your place." Brown Bob rose up from his stone seat.

"Blaming somebody for this calamity will not improve the situation." Carfield reminded him. "Look! I see an eagle in the sky coming towards us. I hope that he will tell us that the dragon has now flown away."

Just as he finished speaking, Galibur landed, bringing with him a strong current of air. The eagle braked with his wings and made two hops to complete his landing. "I am unable to comfort you with good news. I found that the dragon had completed the building of his fortress on the top of the slope. There is no way for anyone to reach his nest from the ground, or get closer to this place without his knowledge, except by sneaking up on him from above. It will be very difficult to fight him and, unfortunately, there is very little we can do to persuade him to leave our mountains and move somewhere else." Upon completing his report, Galibur jumped onto his stone.

"I am appointed by the Council to express our decision and I hope that our friend, Galibur, will agree with it." Shustin sent a glance in his direction. "We have three candidates for the position of King of Pokerweild forest and those are: Tac, Bertrond, and Alowsius. The one who finds a way to kill the dragon, and save our woods from destruction, will be crowned as King with all the power and the respect of the inhabitants of the forest."

"I do not intend to participate in this hopeless contest even for the greatest reward because my mind is still intact, thank you." Alowsius walked out of the circle, adding. "There are many woods around here for me to live in." Upon hearing this, everyone looked at the remaining candidates.

"I am King of a grill already and I am pretty happy with it." Bertrond stood up and moved to the edge of the stone circle. This now left only Tac to stand under the intense stare of the cross-examining looks.

"I'd like to walk away too but it would leave no one to complete the task. I will try to find a way to kill the dragon and free the forest of him, but I will need all your help to do this. If I need to engage this monster in war then I need an army to do it. Will you help me Bertrond? "

"You can rely on me, Tackie." Bertrond chuckled. "My injured shoulder still aches with pain sometimes, but my healthy arm is yours." And he saluted Tac with his paw.

"You will get all the help that you need, Tac. Only free us from this horror. I think that everyone here shares my opinion." The crow looked around, seeing nods of approval from his colleagues.

"In this case." Tac sat down so that he could think in comfort. "We will need to send messengers in all directions to carry our call for help to all who may wish to assist us. The more claws and teeth that we can have in this business, the better for the successful outcome of our cause."

"Tac, claw and tooth will not work against an enemy armed with fire." Galibur reminded him. "The worst damage that we can do to him would be to bombard his head with stones. This would not harm a dragon protected by armor, only make him more angry."

"So we need to find another way." Responded the cat.

"Tac, no one can produce a solution in a minute and, after you have thought about the strengths and weaknesses of our enemy, the right decision will come to you, as it always does." Shustin advised.

"Thoughts! I need thoughts. Please come to me!" Tac sent his plea up to the blue sky, both humorously and seriously.

"I think we already have one good thought." Said Carfield. "I will send my family to carry your call for help in every direction and to ask all volunteers to arrive by noon this Sunday. Let us see what happens."

"We will close the meeting on this positive note." Rainar stamped the ground with a hoof. "If anyone comes up with their own idea or proposition, we will be happy to listen to it at the next meeting."

The Council members got up from their places and, gathering in small groups, continued to exchange their views and concerns.

"Galibur." Tac approached the eagle. "You told me that when you went fishing you saw a dragon swallowing some black stones."

"Yes, that is true. I found it strange."

"Do you know what kind of stones they were?" The cat went on.

"Tac, I am a bird and know nothing about things that lie on the ground, unless they are about to become my food. You will need to ask someone who lives on the surface, or under it, about these stones." The eagle spread his wings and lifted his body upwards.

Tac was left to think about why any dragon would need to stuff himself with stones? The cat's legs worked on their own, without being controlled by his busy mind. They brought him to the bottom of the hill towards Alisa and then automatically turned him in the direction of home. Alisa wanted to ask him something, but was left behind with an open mouth. This was not her husband's normal behavior and it scared her.

"Tac! Tac!" she yelled, chasing after him.

"What has happened Alisa, did I say something wrong?" He asked, stopping and turning to face her.

"You are not talking at all and it seems as if your mind is far away from here. If it were night time I would say that you were possessed by the moon." His wife replied.

"I am sorry for scaring you. I was thinking about the stones." Tac apologized.

"What kind of stones? What do they look like?"

"They are black and shiny and are edged with silver sparks."

"I know someone who knows everything about dirt and stones." Alisa stopped to sniff the ground, searching for something. Her movements became more and more excited and, eventually, she found a large pile of earth. "Mister Mole!!" She shouted into the hole. "I have a question for you from the Council."

"What kind of question?" Asked a voice from under the ground, prompting Alisa to push Tac closer to the hole.

"I am Tac." The cat looked lost. "I need information about a stone." He told everything that he knew about the subject of his enquiry to the unknown owner of the voice.

"I know this stone that you are looking for. Give me some time to locate it because there is only one place close to the mountains where I can find it." answered Mr. Mole.

"I will be at Council Hill tomorrow afternoon. Is it enough time for you to deliver the small sample to our meeting?" He shouted down the hole in the ground.

"I am an old mole, Mr. Tac, and not as fast as when I was young. It is a good thing that my tunnels lie under the whole forest up to the mountains. I will bring you the stone by that time, but it will be a very small sample."

"That is fine. I only need it to show to my friend who will be able to identify it. Thanks, Mr. Mole, I am looking forward to seeing you on Sunday. Have a nice…" Tac paused, wondering what kind of a 'day' could be in the darkness of underground tunnels and then finished. "Have a nice time."

"The same to you." The voice faded.

Next morning Alisa was getting ready for her work at the Golden Nut Park. "Tac, if you do not finish brushing your coat right now, you will have to go to the amusement park by yourself!" She warned him, a cat who did not like to start his mornings in the fast lane.

"I am almost done. Why are you so worried? You will not be fired if you arrive at work a little late." The cat joked.

"You try it." Alisa pretended to be angry. She admitted only to herself that she liked being the wife of a boss.

They ran fast to keep their bodies warm, happy that the cool morning was dry. Most of the way to the Golden Nut Amusement Park, they traveled on their own. However, as they came closer to it, more and more animals that worked in the same place joined them coming from the side pathways, or following them by jumping from branch to branch.

"See you at lunch time." Alisa licked Tac's neck, turning to her booth.

"Make me a lot of money!" Tac yelled after her, then shouted. "Hullo fellows." as he greeted two security guards who were patrolling the perimeter of the park.

The human guard ignored him but the wolf acknowledged him with a short "woof", keeping their relationship professional. Tac slid under the animal door of the trailer, abandoned by the manager since winter. He and Rick had celebrated Christmas in their new two-story log house which had been built on the side of the river, not far from the campground.

"Morning, Carfield, did you find out any information that could be useful?" He asked the crow who was sitting on a post in front of the computer. A black telephone was attached to a table on his right side, accompanied by a large notebook and a pen in a holder. Carfield had another telephone on the left side that was connected only to stations inside the Golden Nut Park. "I see that you have made yourself a good nest here."

"What is this?" Tac pointed at a woolly scarf, rolled up in a ball and tucked into the corner of the couch.

"It belongs to Squirrella. She has left her babies under my watchful eye while she is at work. Her twins were jumping around like rubber balls only five minutes ago but a good bottle of warm milk has put them to sleep better than sleeping pills." Laughed Carfield. "Look at what I have found out about the dragon." Knowing that Tac could not read, Carfield took upon himself the task of reading out the text on the screen.

Tac listened with interest to all the tales about the ways that heroes had used to kill dragons, but unfortunately it didn't work for him. "I do not want to look ridiculous. Imagine my standing on the battlefield with a lance or a sword in my paw." The attempt to visualize this picture made him chuckle.

"What's so funny?" The voice of the crow was strict. "We have a war on our doorstep, don't we?"

"It's a bitter laugh, Carfield. I am laughing at my stupid promise to kill the dragon?" Replied Tac. "What if we could find a way to domesticate the dragon instead of killing him? To be honest, I would feel petty and mean if I were to kill the last dragon in our world because he is a very rare and mysterious animal. To kill him would be the equivalent of wiping out the last bit of fantasy from our world and turning it into a place of little more than a boring, business existence."

"How are you going to win his favor? Are you going to give him a cookie?" The crow smirked.

"You had better look into your computer instead of being sarcastic." Replied the cat, firmly.

At his request, the crow scanned for information that would allow him to understand the nature of dragons, but could not find any situation where somebody had actually tamed one. "It's impossible." He concluded, after his study. "A dragon is a short- tempered, nasty creature that is hungry for gold and is cruel and dangerous. In addition to this, he likes to burn-up everything and has no interest in anything other than destruction. Trying to talk him into changing his ways would be a suicide mission."

"At the very least, I need to try to save him so that my conscience will be clear of guilt later." The cat remarked.

"Help yourself." Carfield flapped his wing in the direction of the screen.

As a result of this disagreement, Tac and Carfield stopped talking to each other during the time that was left prior to the next meeting. Even after the meeting had started, they still directed frowns at each other, giving Tac the reason to think that Carfield was prepared to undermine his plan to make peace with the dragon. He understood very well that his idea would collapse under the weight of opposing arguments, but still wanted to present the plan as an alternative to killing the intruder.

The first group of volunteers appeared at the time when the sandstone clock almost showed noon. Their arrival was so unexpected that no one dared to start a conversation with them. Three women, in the company of a boy of approximately ten years, walked slowly to the middle of the circle, followed by astonished looks.

Animals can sense things better than people, perhaps because they have a closer connection to nature, and this was the reason why the Council members knew that the guests were not ordinary humans. One of the women looked like a typical grandmother, dressed in an old-fashioned, long dress with ruffles and a lacy, white, embroidered apron. A white hat, made from fine cotton and lace, covered her grayish hair that was tied into a knot. An expression of kindness on her face suited her softly-rounded form, the same as the smiling wrinkles around her brown eyes looked quite natural. She had a bag hanging from her crooked elbow, made from an upholstered fabric.

The woman to her right was close to her age, but of a completely different type. She was skinny and slightly stooped and it was a wonder that her sharp elbows had not worn holes through the dark fabric of her dress which was decorated with large buttons on its front. Her hat was black to match the color of her hair. This made the skin of the woman look even paler than it already was and her long, narrow nose served as a good landing place for her small round glasses. Without these glasses, everyone viewed by her would have been knocked out by the piercing, angry looks of her black eyes.

The last woman was young and beautiful. Her blond hair flowed down her back like a river of curls and her blue eyes looked with excitement and approval at everything around her. The form of her bright, red mouth gave the impression that she was about to laugh out loud at any minute and the expression of happiness which radiated from her spread quickly along the line of stone seats. She was dressed in a pale, violet dress accented by a flower design. Darker-colored, silky ribbons outlined the dress along the chest with ends falling down freely.

She was the only one who wore jewelry and whose shoes had high heels. A fine amethyst necklace and earrings enhanced the lines of her slim neck, a bracelet imbedded with the same stone dressed her wrist and a ring inset with a beautiful, large stone sparkled on the middle finger of her hand to complete the set.

The boy was a normal child of his age, skinny and clumsy in his body. His long, dark hair was in slight disorder as if somebody had run fingers through it. He looked at the world through large, luminous, gray eyes and his slightly-open mouth completed the expression of wonder which seemed to emanate from him. The boy was dressed in a blue shirt, half-length gray pants and sandals without socks. He was holding the hand of the younger woman as if she was a caring sister. This strange group stopped in the middle of the circle and greeted the company.

Rainar, who usually introduced the guests and subjects of discussion to the Council, stepped forward to say. "We sent out crows to spread our plea for help to fight the dragon but I do not see how three women can help us."

"We don't know anything about your call. We were invited by him." The older lady looked at Tac.

"Me?" The cat showed surprise.

"Of course, is it not you who called for thoughts? We are the sisters Thought. We live behind the mountain, but no distance can separate us from someone who is calling for us. We came to help you in your task."

"How can you help me?" He was puzzled and in some wonderment.

"I am Candice, the kind Thought." Continued the older woman. "If you intend to start a war then you are going to sustain casualties and have frightened people as the outcome. No one can take care of wounded warriors, and comfort the weak and the scared, better than I."

"I am Nasty, the angry Thought." Stated the woman dressed in black, stepping forward. "If you need to learn how to harm someone without damaging yourself, or to build traps and spread problems, then you need me."

"I am Funny." Said the lady bedecked in gems. "I am a happy Thought and I bring news about victory and wipe away tears from sad eyes. When the war is over, and it is time to celebrate the end of suffering, you will need me."

"Who is this boy?" Asked Tac, allowing the young stranger to scratch him under his chin.

"This is our younger brother, Ides, the strange Thought. He has not decided what he is going to do with his gift yet but I feel that, when he finds his destiny, we will witness unusual events." The kind Thought advised.

"Are you willing to accept these guests, Tac?" Asked Rainar.

"Welcome. Stay with us. I hope you know much more about dragons than we do and will be good advisors." The sisters were well-mannered and they bowed to the assembled company in acknowledgement of their acceptance.

The sudden sound of many bagpipes made everyone turn their heads in the direction of the music. As the stirring noise increased, the pipers approached the place which had just been vacated by the sisters Thought. Now stopped, in plain view of everyone, a band of Scottish Collies dressed in the tartan of their clan, and playing their instruments in perfect unison, had formed up in four straight lines. They were led by a sheep jauntily sporting a round Scottish Toorie on his head, adorned with a high grouse feather.

A scarf, made from the same tartan fabric as the Collies' kilts, was wrapped around the neck of the leader who introduced himself thus: "I am Rory MacBa-a-a and this is my ba-a-nd. We have arrived from the Isle of Sky-y-e on a tour. Your messenger, the crow, told us about your problem and we decided to come over to help you. You will need a ba-a-a-nd to keep the spirits of your army high."

Tac shrugged and said. "I guess you are welcome too. Now we have advisers to help with the plan and a band. So all we need now is to find an army to do the fighting!" He watched with interest as the band took their place on the opposite side of the sisters Thought.

Suddenly, a third guest appeared in the middle of the circle out of nowhere, scaring even Tac who promised himself that he would not be surprised by the selection of guests made by his destiny.

"Who are you?" Tac looked at the stranger. He was short with thin, slightly-bent legs and was dressed in huge, green shoes with buckles on the front of them. The little man's clothing was entirely in the color of green, including his jacket, pants and his tall hat with beveled edges. The silky, dark green ribbon on the hat held a buckle matching that on his shoes. Even his socks were striped green.

"Were you invited by crows and now want to help us?" Someone asked.

"I have no interest in talking to crows and I help no one. I am Brian O'Greedy, the Leprechaun."

"In that case, what brought you here?" Tac felt antipathy towards the man and hoped that he would not stay for a long time.

"I have heard from a reliable source that a dragon has appeared in your mountains, meaning that you have gold here. It's common knowledge that their caves are full of treasure." O'Greedy rubbed his hands with crooked fingers and the lines of his face took on an expression that made his features even more unpleasant than before.

Tac had started to feel scared but tried not to show it. "You have made your way here for nothing. The dragon came to our mountains from far away and did not bring any gold with him. He is a penniless refugee and the best you can do for yourself is to return to the place from whence you came."

The Leprechaun lifted his eyes to his bony forehead, twisted his eyeballs to the corners of his eyes and then bent his head to the side as if he was listening to some sound that was coming from a long distance. "Incredible." He declared. "I can't sense any gold around this dragon, although he is growling and crashing rocks on the slope of the mountain." Then he turned his color-less eyes onto Tac. "It was you who robbed him and took all the gold from the dragon."

"If you have such sharp senses, then you can clearly see that I do not have any gold." Tac spread his arms to the side, inviting the visitor to search him and be done with this conversation.

O'Greedy, narrowing his eyes, walked towards Tac with his fists tightly clenched. "Do you think that I can't sense that you have touched gold recently? You are a smart eater of rats. I even know that you are hiding some of it in this forest and I won't leave this place without this gold. If I have to, I will turn you into a meowing grasshopper in order to make your friends co-operate." He raised a hand with the fingers now bent into a frightening claw.

"You do not need to harm anyone since I will bring you gold." Carfield cried out. The crow covered the distance to the house and back in record time. On arrival, he found that the atmosphere inside the circle had become heavy and tense.

"Here is your gold!" Carfield threw the box at O'Greedy's feet.

"Is that all?" Yelled the Leprechaun, his face slowly turning dark red. "You mean to tell me that I have left all my businesses at home for this?" He shook the box, producing a rattling noise. The sound made him open the box to reveal a pin which he angrily threw far away. "I am giving you three days to give me a thousand golden coins as compensation for my trouble in coming here. If I don't receive this payment on time, I promise that the threat from the dragon will be nothing compared to the damage that I may do to you." He then turned on his green, high-heeled shoes and walked away, mumbling the rest of the threats under his breath. Witnesses at the scene were unable to even sigh, being too frightened to draw their breath.

"I thought that the dragon was the nastiest creature that we have encoun-tered to date." Carfield shook his head. "But, apparently, I was wrong. Now what are we going to do? We were being consumed by flames but now we have exchanged it for fire."

"What are you going to do, Tac?" Asked the kind Thought. During the inci-dent, she had been studying the faces of everyone involved without making any attempt to stop the cheeky stranger.

"I think we need to find the pin. I know that you prized it highly, Carfield." Tac's calm voice surprised everyone. He then walked to the side of the hill and looked down. It was not necessary for him to spend much time searching for it between the stems of grass since the pin lay in full view on the top of a big stone. It was almost as if someone had deliberately put it there to be found.

"What a mystery!" Exclaimed the crow, after exchanging surprised looks with Tac. "I have never seen this stone here before, although I have flown over this hill many times."

"Interesting!" Tac walked around the stone, sniffed it and scratched it with his paw. "Stone is stone, it's nothing unusual. Carfield can you give me the pin? I am not very skilled in climbing rocks."

Carfield jumped down from the top of the rocks, carrying the pin. "Here it is."

"What has happened?" Asked the voices from the top of the hill.

"I do not know yet, so it's better if you stay at a distance." Tac warned the Council members who wanted to come down to look at the stone for themselves. Then he examined the pin and gave comment to his thoughts. "One of the birds engraved on the pin is sleeping which means that it is resting and the other is dancing which means that it is active. When the pin fell here it hit a rock that was not here before, or it was not a rock before the pin hit it. No one move!" He cried out. "I am going to do an experiment." Then he touched the rock with the dancing bird and it started to grow into a giant boulder that almost reached the top of the hill. "Now I will try the sleeping bird." He ended.

"Maybe you should leave the bird alone." Said a scared Carfield, who was hiding behind Tac's back.

"No. I need to know the secret of the second bird. The active bird makes things larger and it is logical that the second bird, the sleeping one, will make them smaller." The touch of the sleeping bird on the rock returned it to the original size that Tac and Carfield had seen before they had started the experiment. After the second attempt, it turned into a small stone that was now covered by grass and barely visible. Only the circle of broken grass served as living proof that everything they had witnessed had really happened and was not some mind-game or delusion.

"Carfield, you are the owner of a real treasure whilst O'Greedy chose a worthless piece of metal." The cat addressed the crow, giving him the pin.

"I have had this pin in my home for years and did not even think that it had an important use. I cannot call myself a wise crow anymore."

"We do not have time for self- blame, Carfield. We need to find gold to get rid of the Leprechaun so that we can spend our time thinking about how to fight the dragon." The wolf, Woo, reminded them.

"Yes, you are right. Let's go back to the stone circle to cool down our emotions and think over our problems more calmly."

The members of the Council took their places again and listened carefully to the elk. "The time is almost three o'clock and I think that we can stop expecting more guests. Our agenda has changed unexpectedly. Now we need to not only fight the dragon but also to find gold for the Leprechaun. Do any of you have any idea as to how we may accomplish all that?"

Tac stepped into the middle to speak. "I know of only one place where I can find enough gold to meet his demand. It's the homeland of the sisters Thought and the dragon. When I left the orange forest, I took only two coins and left the rest of the treasure on the ground. I am thinking about going back to collect the rest, hoping that it will be enough to satisfy O'Greedy. A larger group is more likely to attract undesirable attention and I would prefer that only my friends, who visited the land of the monsters before, will join me in this quest."

"Galibur, Carfield, will you go with Tac to the orange woods?" Asked Rainar.

"I will." Answered Galibur. "I am afraid of that place, but I will go to help my friend." The crow only nodded in agreement, but without enthusiasm.

"Do we all agree that we should send an expedition to the other side of the mountain?" Rainar looked at everyone. "Then, the decision is made."

"What are we going to do about the dragon?"

"I can help you with this. Some time ago I had a problem falling asleep. It happens when you have too many happy thoughts." Laughed Funny. "Our closest neighbor, Shmata, made a sleeping powder for me. He told me to use only a tiny portion of it because the substance is so powerful that it can even put a dragon to sleep. I do not know for how long the medicine could be effective but I think that we can expect that the dragon will not give us any trouble for at least three or four days and Tac will have enough time to finish his business with his unpleasant green man."

"How are we going to give the powder to the dragon?" Asked Brown Bob.

"I will do this and please don't worry about me." Happy Thought smiled at him. "I am not a person so I cannot be harmed. I can even be invisible if I choose to approach the dragon in the form of a thought."

"If you are as light as a happy thought should be, then I can deliver you to the dragon's nest." Galibur proposed.

"That is very thoughtful of you. I do not want to destroy my shoes walking to the mountain." She laughed. This did not surprise anyone because the animals had started to get used to the fact that she was always ready to laugh for any reason. Funny removed something from a small purple bag attached to her waist and showed the company a delicate box, made from an unknown material which looked like a spider's web, that somehow held a sparkling white powder inside of it. Then she turned the ring on her finger and her body shrank to a size which was small enough to fly on the eagle's back. "I'm ready to go with you."

Galibur froze for a moment, surprised, and then spread out one of his wings to help the little figure climb up onto his back. When she took hold of his feathers, he lifted them both up and soon they had disappeared from the Council's view.

"It will take them at least two hours to fly in both directions." Rainar pointed out. "I have asked my secretary, Roxal, to serve lunch to the guests down the hill. All of us have had a stressful morning and we need to renew our strength."

The guests and the Council members were hungry and welcomed this proposition, happily. The food was of different kinds, for meat eaters and vegetarians alike, and was served on two separate tablecloths spread out on the ground. It allowed everyone to choose whatever they wanted, without spoiling the appetite of someone else. The sisters Thought did not eat ordinary food but, instead, removed from their handbags something that looked like sliced cheese, from which they took only small pieces at a time. "It's enough for us to feel full." The kind Thought answered Tac's questioning look.

After the animals had finished lunch, Carfield and Brown Bob took the first watch of the sky. The rest of them lay on the grass and watched Woo playing with the strange Thought, chasing him and trying to knock him down on the grass as if he was just a little boy. The eldest Thought, together with Rory, Tac and a few Council members, discussed the living arrangements for the guests.

"My family would be happy if Rory would like to stay the night with us. We will show him a wonderful grass field that looks fantastic in the moonlight." Said Rainar.

"I have no objections because I would rather spend the night under the stars than in a barn." The sheep replied.

"Bertrond, how do you feel about offering the rooms on the first level of your zoo to the other members of the band?"

"Of course. The wolves and I can sleep on the straw or on the floor in the office."

"Perfect! Now all we need to do is to find a place for our special guests, the Thoughts, to stay." Rainar commented.

"I know where they can stay." The cat exclaimed. "The log house of our manager of the Golden Nut Amusement Park has three bedrooms on the second floor. I think that Carfield will be able to talk Carl and Rick into willingly giving them up to our guests and to sleep on the living room couches themselves. It will only be a temporary arrangement, in any event."

"It looks like a good idea to me." Agreed Rainar. "That is, if the ladies have nothing against it, of course. We have never lived so close to humans and it could well be a very interesting experience. Isn't this right, sisters?"

The kind Thought turned to the rest of the family. "Yes! And I will have the opportunity to see how they react when I put a cockroach, or a dead fly, onto their plates." The angry Thought giggled as if she had said something quite funny.

"Sister, you are going to be well-mannered and grateful for their hospitality and you must forget about that idea." The voice of the kind Thought was not angry, but firm.

"The fact that you are the eldest in the family does not give you the right to make my life boring." Angry Thought pulled her hat down almost to her eyes and placed her sharp elbows in a way that made them stick out from both sides of her body like prickly thorns. The rising quarrel between the two sisters was ended by the return of Galibur, carrying the happy Thought on his back.

Funny jumped down onto the grass then turned the ring on her finger in the opposite direction and returned her body to its previous size. "The dragon is in a deep sleep." She sang, as she danced around her sisters.

The kind Thought looked at her with a smile but the angry sister pulled her head into her shoulders to show her disapproval. The Council members and the guests surrounded the happy Thought, wishing to hear the details.

But Tac was looking steadily at Galibur who seemed to be disturbed by something. Using the excuse that he needed to discuss tomorrow's events, he left his gossiping companions and went to speak to the eagle.

"I am glad that everyone is gathered around the happy Thought and left me alone." Galibur admitted to Tac.

"And what is it that you do not want to tell them?" Tac queried.

"When we came close to the mountain, on which the dragon had built his stone fortress, Funny told me to land on the top of an old tree. She jumped from my back onto a branch then undid the spell that had made her body tiny and grew a pair of large wings right in front of my eyes. Then she flew off to the mountain."

"Flew?" Asked Tac, thinking that he had not heard correctly.

"Yes! She reached the slope of the mountain with the help of her own strong and beautiful wings. The girl left me sitting with my eyes wide open in amazement, wondering why she pretended to need my help."

"I cannot answer your question and I think it would be better if you will not tell anyone about this important matter."

"Knowing that this expedition was successful is enough for everyone else, but to you I will tell what happened next." Remarked Galibur. "When she reached the dragon, he did not make the slightest move of aggression towards her and appeared to be extremely pleased by her visit. The lady Thought offered the dragon her magical powder which he took trustfully and then fell heavily to the ground in a deep sleep. The girl came back to me in an unaltered mood of happiness, as if nothing special had happened at all, and once again returned to her smaller size. Climbing onto my back, she requested that I bring her back here."

"Let's not jump to conclusions and give her a chance to explain everything herself." Answered an equally-mystified cat.

Next day, everything was ready for Tac's trip for the gold. He had arranged for Rainar, Roxal, Carfield and the happy Thought to meet Galibur and him at the shore of the River Woblar. This time he was prepared to fly in a more comfortable mode of travel, since Alisa had taken all of his requirements and suggestions into consideration and had adjusted the famous pillow by modernizing it into a newer model. Now he did not need to hold on to it with his claws anymore but was attached to it by means of straps, which left his paws free for self-protection.

"Now I can scratch my nose if it gets itchy." He joked, tightening something that looked like a backpack.

"Fair wind." Alisa cried out.

Tac had been frightened by previous flights, but this time he unexpectedly found it enjoyable. He lacked Galibur's sharp eyes so, when the eagle suddenly slowed down, he wondered why he was descending in wide circles. Eventually, he noticed that dots on the ground were his friends, accompanied by sister Thought, walking on the terrain below. He had arranged the meeting with them at the river because the fact that the sisters Thought had hidden their talents had made him suspicious and careful. But he shared his concern only with Galibur.

To make a successful landing, the eagle flew steadily along the river then glided down to the level of the hill and smoothly stopped almost under the feet of their assembled companions. Tac greeted everyone without leaving Galibur's back and reminded them about the need to leave immediately.

Funny shrunk herself to a size that allowed her to fly on Carfield's back, whilst Rainar and Roxal waved goodbye before turning around to go home.

Galibur's powerful wings soon reached a comfortable level of flight that gave the cat the opportunity to have a wide view of the forest, which triggered past memories and awoke complicated feelings within him. On the one hand, he wanted to see the Orange Woods where his previous adventures had happened but, at the same time, he was afraid that he would not find them in the same condition in which he had left them. He was reminded of the phrase, heard some time ago, that you cannot step twice in the same river because the water that you see when you stand on the bank of the river is the first that is arriving to meet you and is the last that you see before the water flows away.

'It would be a pity if the Orange Woods were to disappear.' He thought. Tired from contemplation about different matters, he fell asleep and was woken up later by the sound of a shout from Galibur to Carfield. "Follow me to the wall." Tac opened his eyes with a start and found that Funny was no longer on Carfield's back but was leading them to the gate. She looked more like a bird herself, with her wings spread wide and sparkling with millions of tiny points of light like snow crusts under the bright light of a winter's day.

With a graceful move of her hand, she pointed downward. "Do you see the chunks of rock lying at the foot of the mountain? I think that a long time ago the gate was accessible from the ground but, after a part of the sloping mountain wall had collapsed, we were only able to enter the gate from the air." She then moved her hand along the wall to search for any way to engage its opening and in one place her hand went through the wall as if the surface was just an illusion, masking an opening behind it. She called them to follow and disappeared inside.

Galibur and Carfield worried that the magic would end and they might crash straight into the hard rock. But the entrance didn't collapse. Familiar lines of running lights transferred them through the body of the mountain and released the travelers on the other side of it. To Tac's delight, the misty lake and the sandy-beige fields of grass were unchanged and spring here was warmer than the weather that they had left behind. The wind was playing with the threads of grass as it had done before, moving them wave over wave, and the sound of water lapping against the sand of the lakeshore left a soothing impression of the complete peacefulness of this place.

"Our ways will now part here for some time." Funny advised. "You have been here before, Tac, and know all about the dangers that you can meet here, but I still want to remind you to keep away from the lake. It is often visited by the dragons that fish here. The fish is not important to them as a source of food and they look upon fishing merely as a sport. A dragon has trouble concentrating the vision of both of its eyes on a small object and very often loses small prey. The several hours of futile attempts makes him really angry and willing to attack anyone who is unlucky enough to be around. Like anyone else, he does not like to lose. Remember this and avoid crossing his path."

"I thought that you would be assisting us in the search for the treasure." The cat was starting to feel very small in this world and was now afraid of losing their guide.

"I cannot stay with you because my presence will betray the secrecy of your arrival. I will wait for you tomorrow at this place to take you back home."

The triplet of friends followed her with their eyes until the body of the happy Thought had turned into a faded silhouette and had disappeared from sight. Both birds turned their heads towards Tac, waiting for instructions, but he only replied. "Do not look at me as if I know what to do. I remember that we need to go along the left side of the lake until we see a small cottage and then search for an opening where the boar had dug out the treasure."

"We cannot stay here any longer. The dark color of our feathers can be viewed from a long distance away."

"In that case, let's fly as fast as we can." Tac replied, making himself ready for the journey.

Galibur opened his wings like large fans and threw his body into the air. A strong wind freed him from the necessity of working his muscles too hard and allowed the eagle to glide smoothly to save his strength. He turned his head from side to side, watching for danger, but Carfield could not match his gliding skill and was busy flapping his wings in order to stay close to the eagle whilst keeping a position just slightly below him. The unusual trio of adventurers now flew along the shore of the lake, simulating a low-flying arrow which had been shot into the heart of the forest, and used the narrow road that led to the cottage as a guideline.

The tree which Tac had once climbed to escape the attack of the boar was the main subject of his nightmares and was, accordingly, strongly imprinted on his memory. However, the details that he remembered about this place did not match what he now saw. On the contrary, the broken stems of trees suggested that some terrible event had happened here not so long ago.

"Your treasure has disappeared." Carfield remarked.

"I think that several dragons found the gold and fought for it here." Tac pointed to a piece of broken dragon scale that he had found impaled on the trunk of one of the trees. "But we cannot go back empty handed can we? We will have to steal at least one piece from the dragon that won the struggle and removed my gold."

"Once we get back home, we can then multiply it with the help of Carfield's pin." Galibur added.

"It's a very risky business, indeed, to rob a dragon." Carfield sighed. "Maybe it would be a better idea for us to check the cave where I found my pin. Perhaps the other dragons have not yet found the entrance. If we find even one forgotten coin, then it will complete our mission and remove the necessity of engaging in a conflict with a live beast."

"Do you still remember how to reach it, Carfield?" Galibur asked.

"I wish I had forgotten or, even better, never to have found it in the first place. But what is done is now impossible to undo. First we need to cross the lake and then go into the valley that will take us to the foot of the mountain with a flat top and the cave below."

Tac looked up at the sky and commented. "Since we have not seen any dragons around the lake so far, then perhaps we will be lucky to avoid meeting any of them. It is now close to lunchtime, so would anyone like to have some of the crackers that Alisa has put into the pocket of my pillow?" He queried.

"Crackers? I do not eat them." Said Galibur. "And I think it's best if we finish this business before we have lunch. I can always get a fresh fish for us, instead of these hard, dry biscuits. Get on my back Tac!" This time Galibur followed Carfield, maneuvering his heavy body between the stems of giant trees and rising almost to the top of them to avoid lower branches that left him very little space for movement.

Tac did not complain about the sudden ups and downs. He was prepared to bravely meet any danger except that which he was now seeing below him. Even a dragon frightened him less than the sudden expanse of the lake that lazily lapped the edge of the forest with gentle tongues of waves. The future King of Pokerweild forest had hidden his greatest weakness from his friends. He hadn't told them that he was afraid of water, especially a large amount. He was afraid to humiliate himself by screaming out in panic and firmly ordered himself. "Do not look at the water but search the sky for dragons instead."

To his relief, Galibur rose higher above the lake. The eagle did not want to scare his friends by mentioning that he had seen a large, dark body moving under the surface of the water, which had followed them from the moment that they had started to cross the lake. He increased his speed, but the underwater body followed him just as fast. However, Carfield, who was much older than Galibur, had trouble keeping up with the pace and the distance between him and the eagle started to increase significantly. By the time that the predator, following Galibur underwater, had realized that the eagle had no plans to land and rest on the surface of the water, and was therefore about to escape his jaws, Galibur had already flown out of his reach and had landed on top of a large rock that stood alone on the beach.

Carfield's Narrow Escape

Angry and frustrated by his loss, the creature then made an attempt to attack the poor, old crow by jumping high out of the water and barely missed Carfield's legs. The beast fell back with a splash of water that almost knocked Carfield into its wide-open jaws. Fear, and a desperate desire to stay alive, made him forget all about his tiredness and his age and made him work miracles with his wet wings. Screaming hysterically, the crow made it to the shore, followed by the living submarine while Tac and Galibur only watched, terrified, but unable to help.

Exhausted by his efforts to escape, Carfield simply fell on top of them. Tac managed to catch his shaking body and held onto him while Galibur untied the straps of the pillow and spread Carfield's trembling body on top of it.

"Stay with Carfield while I make a circle to see if the attacker has now left us alone." A few minutes later Galibur returned to them with the good news that the creature had left, no doubt to look for an easier prey. A big fish that he had brought with him restored their strength, but Tac decided to stay there for at least another hour to give the crow a chance to recover completely. They both took a nap on the pillow under the protection of Galibur who shaded them with wings spread out. After an hour had passed, he shook his friends to get them up. "Half a day has gone but we still do not have a coin."

"Do we have any of that fish left?" Asked Carfield.

Tac laughed and gave him one of the crackers instead. "I see your appetite has recovered and this is the signal for us to resume our search for the treasure." The crow had finished the cracker before he had even managed to get ready for the flight.

Looking down at the valley, the cat wondered how Carfield was able to find his way in the featureless, rocky landscape. He started to look with greater respect at their leader. Very soon even he was able to see the entrance to the cave. It looked abandoned. No single footprint disturbed the dusty ground inside the cave, illuminated along only a quarter of its length. Tac couldn't see any sign of a dragon's attempts to improve the work of nature to make the cave more comfortable. He muttered. "What a strange creature."

"The gold has not been stored here." Carfield interrupted Tac's observations. "I found it in the other room that is connected to this place by a narrow corridor." They reached an opening in the wall and turned into a tunnel. It was lit by an unnaturally pink light, the source of which revealed itself as soon as they had entered the second room. The deep indentation in the middle of the cave was full of an orange-red fire that was rising high and spreading a circle of glowing light around it.

Tac was curious as to why the fire was still alive in this forgotten place and found the answer only when a drop of oil fell from somewhere above. He looked up and saw a narrow stone gutter dripping oil sufficiently to keep the fire burning. Scratches on the wall suggested that the gutter was specifically made by the dragon. A big, flat platform in front of them was empty. No single piece of gold was left for the disappointed treasure hunters.

"Unfortunately, someone has been here before us." Observed Carfield. "I am sure that the gold was here before, because I recognize this channel around it. At that time it was full of fire but now it's empty. The fire in the channel was probably fed in the same way as the cup but, as time passed, the end of the channel became blocked by falling rocks and, without a fresh source of fuel, the fire died out."

The air inside the room had an unpleasant smell to it and was so low in oxygen that the party of friends decided to run outside to get a breath of fresh air.

"Does anyone know how to rob a dragon?" Tac asked, after they had recovered from the effects of the poisoned air.

"We will need to return to the lake again to find the dragon and follow him to his nest. But, to stay out of his sight, we should camouflage ourselves with the dry lake weeds." The crow suggested.

"Personally, I am agreeing to participate in this only because I am afraid of that Leprechaun even more than the dragon." The cat confessed, as he climbed onto the pillow.

Carfield was about to ask Tac why, but the eagle was already on the way up. The previous attack from the creature had proved to him that the lake was not a safe place and, when something caught his attention, Galibur suddenly returned to the line of rocks and called the crow to follow him.

"What has happened?" Asked Tac, as they landed on top of the biggest stone, bleached and cracked by the sun.

"I saw the creature, which wanted Carfield for its meal, hiding in a deep hole under the water. It may just be an old log that is lying on the bottom of the lake but I will need to check." Galibur pulled a loose stone out of one of the wide cracks and carried it to the place which had aroused his suspicions, then dropped it into the water.

At this, the creature jumped out of the water with a long, whistling yell, frustrated that his plan had been revealed. For a moment they were all able to see a strange hybrid of a crocodile and a whale with a long, narrow jaw attached to a chubby body ending in a flat tail. The creature made quick moves from side to side, hoping to hit Galibur with water splashes, but the eagle was familiar with its tactics and turned away. The crocodile-whale threatened the eagle for the last time and then disappeared beneath the water. His departure did not make the adventurers feel safer on this shore.

By mutual effort, they gathered up a large pile of lake weeds. The crow became a watcher whilst Galibur and Tac built the shelter. Bored from the endless waiting, they started to chase the small crabs that hid under the wet stones and waved aggressively with their pincers when they were exposed. Moving quickly sideways, the crabs ran to find another stone that could afford them a safe place to wait until the water of the lake had returned with the new tide. Their fun was stopped by the voice of Galibur calling them up to the stone.

Reaching the stone, they were able to see that the flying creature had landed on the sandy shore by braking with his massive legs and, at the same time, rolling a mountain of sand ahead of him. He was not a fully-grown adult and probably, like all youngsters, he liked to play. However, his game was quite dangerous for everyone who was around him. The young beast showed his strength by flattening the mountain of sand with his feet, shaking the ground. Then he decided that throwing a stone into the water would also be a good game so he grabbed a large rock and threw it into the lake. The splash that he created soaked his body and he collapsed on his side to roll around to dry out his scales, shaking his body afterwards as if he was a dog. The pieces of wet sand flew off in all directions and made the three friends worry about their cover.

"I hope he does not discover that we are hiding here and blows fire in our direction. If so, we will resemble the three little pigs from the fairytale which ran for their lives." Whispered Tac, smiling apprehensively.

His friends were too scared to appreciate his humor, and were too busy watching the dragon, to pay much attention to his remark. The beast looked at his back and roared, seeing that his tail was still covered with sand, and then shook himself again.

Tac was fed up with the sand bath and started to move deeper under the cover of the weeds but was stopped by the sound of metal hitting stone. His body tensed when he saw a coin half-buried in the sand. Probably it had been stuck under a scale when the beast had been sleeping and became dislodged by the shaking.

The dragon moved fast to his treasure, swaying his body from side to side like a big lizard, and grabbed it from the sand. Since he did not plan to go home quite yet, and didn't have pockets to hide it, he simply placed it on the rocks.

Tac showed silently to his friends that he was going to take the coin.

By this time, the animal was busy making a trench in the sand and blew fire in the direction of the waves that dared to flow inside his tunnel. Hissing like a very large snake, he turned the water into clouds of steam that made a nice cover for Tac's disappearance. But, no matter how deeply he was involved in his own game, he was still aware of every sound and movement around him. In addition to this, the wind betrayed the cat's plan by turning the mist in the opposite direction and stretching it along the shore.

The dragon didn't need to wonder who had taken his treasure since he saw two bodies fleeing in the direction of the mountains. Red sparks of anger flashed in his eyes and he decided to eat the cheeky birds. When Carfield looked back, disturbed by a strange feeling that they were being followed, he saw only a huge, wide-open mouth closely following behind them.

"Try to lose him in the labyrinth of rocks." Galibur shouted, turning into the valley. He forced his follower to maneuver between the narrow and sharp blades of rock rising from the ground, but the dragon was still attached to their tails. However, he was not as good a flyer as the small birds.

"This chase reminds me of something from another time." Tac screamed at Galibur. "And it did not finish too well for me."

For his part, Galibur was concerned only with the fact that the dragon was close enough to turn them into flying torches.

"Be careful." He yelled to Carfield. "Go down if you feel the slightest movement of the air, or a change in its temperature." His warning was timely.

The dragon lost patience, irritated by the resentment he bore towards his prey, and changed his mind from wanting to catch them to burning the thieves with his fiery breath. Both birds dropped down like heavy stones, saving themselves. Only the cat sustained some minor damage, losing one side of his whiskers. "Why is it always me who gets hurt?" He complained, rubbing his face to get rid of the burnt smell. "Now I definitely want him to get lost, but this smell is spreading behind us like an invitation to dinner."

The dragon moved closer and Galibur was afraid that his next attempt would be more accurate, so he shouted out to Carfield. "Do you see the narrow side of the mountain that is coming towards us?"

"Yes." Answered the crow, trying to stay on the same flight line as the eagle.

"Well, when we reach the edge of it, we will go around each side and eventually meet each other on the other side. I hope that this will slow him down by forcing him to make a choice - which one of us should he follow?"

Before they had reached the point of separation, the two of them needed to execute another maneuver to avoid the second blast of the dragon's fire. This time they managed to escape only because a large block of snow fell from the side of the mountain and deflected the fire away from them. Despite the fact that, by now, both of the birds were scared and tired, they managed to increase their speed in an attempt to reach the dark mass of weathered rock directly in front of them. The wall, stained by patches of snow pressed into its body, appeared to move faster and faster towards them until they had reached the point where they had to take opposite paths around the mountain to allow them to disappear out of sight of the dragon. The beast was confused by the maneuver and slowed down, then changed the angle of his wings and turned in the direction of the pathway chosen by Galibur.

"Cheaters!" Growled the dragon, increasing his speed to catch up with the eagle. The dragon could not see anything in front of himself, being blinded by the dance of the snowflakes that were being disturbed by the movement of his wings. He again sent a narrow stream of fire along the side of the mountain, in the hope of catching his enemies, but this only melted the snow from the side of the mountain and turned it into small streams of dirty water.

The eagle had suspected that something like this would happen and had lowered his flight path almost to the middle of the mountain, thereby being able to dodge the flame. Stretching his wings almost into a straight line and tightening them more closely to his body, the dragon went down after Galibur, cutting through the air like a missile. Tac hung on for dear life and closed his eyes, scared by the thought that he was about to become the first victim of the dragon's attack. His supposition was not far from the truth since the beast's eyes were fixated on the eagle's back.

Suddenly, Galibur, who was searching the slope of the mountain for anything at all that could hide them from death, saw the possibility of escape. The wall below him looked too flat for a natural formation, having symmetrical black holes in it, so, gathering all his strength, he rushed in that direction. Soon he was able to see the four columns which, although damaged by time, still stood as the guardians of the door to the cave entrance that was open just enough for him to pass through it.

The eagle contrived to squeeze himself and Tac through the narrow opening. Both found that they were undamaged by the frantic pursuit, but the dragon would need to open the door much wider if he wanted to enter but it hadn't been used for a long time. Carvings above eight symmetrical bays had cracked and fallen onto the floor in front of the door and the figures that had stood in each of them had become unrecognizable. Only parts of their bodies were still on display. Neither Tac nor Galibur saw any sign of trespassing in the cave, or had time to wonder what kind of a God had been worshipped here. They rushed farther into the chapel, followed by the burning hatred of the dragon's breath hurled at their backs. Trying to enter the cave, he could not fit into the hole of the doorway, no matter which way he turned, and finally accepted defeat. Enraged, the beast let out a terrible roar and smashed at the door with one last blow which closed it tightly and also succeeded in crashing down some of the columns. This meant that they were now trapped inside the chapel, which was guarded on the outside by a very angry, frustrated dragon that continued to attack the door again and again.

The walls of the room vibrated from his assaults on the door and, although small stones and dust dropped down from the ceiling, it held firm. So the prisoners turned their attention to the inside of the cave, in an effort to understand where they were. At this moment the dragon realized that it was pointless to bang himself against the door any longer and, instead, decided to fry his enemies through the cracks above the door by directing another red-hot blast of fire at them. This did not harm them but made it clear that they could not stay there much longer.

Luckily for them, the dragon's breath lit up the oil in the big brass lamp and gave the trapped friends enough light to look around. They found that the cave was at least partially man-made and was a foyer that led into another larger space. The room at one time had contained some furniture which had now decayed into grayish, rotten wood and only a massive staircase, with one tall, brass lamp standing on each side of it, remained intact. The size and craftsmanship of the structure served as proof that it had been a magnificent place at some time in the past. The ceiling, separated into sections, had been decorated with images that were now partially destroyed by cracks. Large objects, the significance of which was unknown to Galibur and Tac, still stood along the walls of this inner chamber.

Another powerful crash on the outside of the door rudely ended Galibur's deliberations. He quickly flew to the first step and allowed Tac to get out of the pouch on his back.

"We have to forget about the front door. Even if the dragon left this place, we could never open the door ourselves."

"I agree." Galibur replied. "We need to go deeper and look for another exit."

"This place must have several exits. Many people would have been needed to build and service a temple of this stature. I cannot imagine that all the priests and servants who inhabited it used only one door." He started to climb the staircase but Galibur outstripped him by simply flying to the top of the staircase where he waited for Tac to come up.

The big room behind the foyer was partially-hidden by two screens with a gate between them and was supported by a column on each side. It was so large that both of the explorers instantaneously moved closer to each other, feeling small and vulnerable. Two lines of fire illuminated the chapel, running along the walls and ending under the feet of a giant figure that was sitting on the podium at the far end of the room.

Nature undertook most of the job of decorating this part of the cave by enhancing it with twinkling flows of alabaster waterfalls, accented by shades of orange, red and aqua. In some places, spirals of stone became a bed for crystals pushed up in the shape of perfect prisms. Clear crystals of quartz reflected the red colors of the burning fire and returned to their natural appearance only at the times when the wind, coming through the cracks in the walls, subdued the fires almost to the level of the floor. Thin, flat plates of stone, with images created by a mixture of different minerals imbued in them, were present in places that lacked natural beauty.

The builders of the temple had strengthened the ceiling with columns and had placed colorful tiles on the floor. Part of the wall had been used to carve out the figure of their Goddess. Her size dominated everything else in the cavern and the shadows thrown by her bulk hid the beveled openings of other rooms which were situated on either side of her.

The attention of both of them was, however, riveted on the beam of bright light that crossed the space in front of the Goddess. Following it with their eyes, they discovered that the light was entering this temple through some window or opening.

"Tac, take your place on my back." Urged Galibur. "We are going to fly to the source of it."

Losing interest in further exploration of the temple, they flew straight upward to find themselves in a narrow tunnel with a mirror placed in it so that it could catch the sunbeam reflected from another mirror, farther along it, to transfer it into the cave. After entering a few tunnels like this, Tac admitted. "These builders were clever, but I do not understand why they did this in a place already brightened by artificial light."

"I do not know, Tac. To be honest, I do not care why, or how, they did it. I only care about finding an end to these tunnels and being free from this temple and the cursed dragon so that we can find Carfield and return home."

"I want to be far away from this place too." The cat gasped. "When we were flying up to the ceiling, I looked down at the figure of a Goddess staring down at her empty world and I almost understood the wisp of a smile upon her attractive face. It was sarcasm. The object that she held on her knee was not a cup, as I first thought, but a mask. The view of the mask from high above revealed that its appearance contradicted the beautiful features of the Goddess. It was frightfully ugly."

"What you have just said supports my opinion that this place is creepy." Said the eagle, taking another turn. "I think this is the last tunnel, thank goodness. I feel the flow of fresh air coming in my direction."

The sun was suddenly bright in their eyes, even as it was setting to the side of the distant chain of mountains.

"I hope the crow is waiting for us at the appointed place by the side of the mountain." Murmured Tac, gravely. "If we do not find him, then we will have to fly alone over the lake to the Portal and look for him there. We cannot circle above the mountain to draw attention to ourselves again. I do not want to bring this kind of company to our dear dragon that presently sleeps in Pokerweild wood."

The sun may have been setting but the crown of it still painted the sky in wide stripes of pink and violet. The sides of the mountain, wrapped in dark blue and purple shawls, had already surrendered to the evening by gently settling and falling asleep.

Galibur had reached the agreed meeting point with Carfield, and had even made a circle above the ground, but was unable to find him. So, he rose again and turned towards the lake to reach the Portal, expecting to make the whole journey before nightfall.

Tac fell asleep, having nothing else to do, but his sleep was not peaceful. Worries disturbed his mind. He was finally jolted awake by the sudden shift of his pillow that was produced by a change in the angle of Galibur's wings as he began to prepare his descent.

"Have we reached the Portal gateway?" He asked.

"No." The eagle answered. "I have lost my direction in the approaching darkness and turned too far to the right. However, the place we are approaching is familiar and we are going to land on the tree which hid us when you met the daughter of the wizard. Do you remember?"

"Yes. It means that we are close to our destination." Tac replied.

"This will not change anything. We still need to wait until morning or we will become even more lost than we already are." Galibur pointed out, decisively.

Warmed under the wing of the eagle, Tac fell asleep for a second time and dreamt that he was back home with Alisa and, when the morning cold pinched him slightly, he whispered. "Alisa, you have pulled the blanket off me again." A strange, bubbling sound transformed the smiling face of his fox-wife into the face of the mask, which breathed with cold rage. He suddenly jumped up, risking falling down from the tree, and was greatly relieved to realize that the laugh belonged to Galibur.

"I assume that you expect me to serve you breakfast in bed." Galibur teased his friend.

"No, we had better fly to the Portal to see if the happy Thought will be waiting for us. I hope to find her there to end my worry about Carfield."

The land beneath them had already been woken up by the spring and brightened by a mat of flowers which was new to Tac who had last seen this place close to the end of the season.

"I see even more beautiful pictures ahead of me!" Galibur cried out.

When they came closer to the mountain, the figure of the happy Thought, in the company of Carfield, came into view.

"Ohhhh!" The cat exclaimed, pleased. He was fiddling impatiently on the back of eagle until Galibur suggested dropping him down onto the ground, to give him the opportunity to run to the gate on his own four legs. Tac stopped moving, but jumped down as soon as it was safe. His reunion with Funny was accompanied by his loud and happy purring whilst he rubbed his head against her hand, buffeting it with his wet nose.

Carfield was not impressed by the cat's custom of greeting and hopped away as soon as his wet nose landed on his beak. "You had better tell us how you managed to escape the dragon." He huffed, from behind Funny's skirt.

"We were lucky to find the entrance into an old temple. Once inside, we flew through connected rooms and found the way out whilst the dragon was crashing against the entrance door. Shortly after this, we arrived on the other side of the mountain and approached the point where we expected to see you. Where were you?"

"I watched and watched for you by circling above the same area but, the longer I waited, the more scared I became." Sighed Carfield. "I started to think that I had overlooked you somehow and decided to fly to the opposite side of the mountain, hoping to meet you there. When I saw the dragon scratching the slope of the mountain, I understood that you were in trouble and all that I was able to do was to watch him helplessly. When the sun started to set, he decided to end his unsuccessful attempt to get you and went away, leaving behind piles of burned rubble. The door had been cracked in many places and was missing slabs of stone, but was still standing and, after examining every window above the door, I found that they were all blocked by rocks. It would have been impossible for me to open the heavy door by myself and the only one person to whom I could turn to for help was Funny. I flew to the Portal and barely closed my eyes all night, waiting for the morning. I was very glad indeed to see the first rays of light on the horizon and her appearance out of the mist of the lake."

"He was on the edge of panic when I found him." Said Funny. We immediately started to make plans for a rescue of you and Galibur, thinking to ask for assistance from the wizard. Luckily you appeared in time to avoid disturbing him."

"We had better not involve ourselves in any business with wizards." Said Tac. "You never know what way it could end. We have managed to get the gold coin and will transform it into many more coins, with the help of the magic pin. We should return home immediately."

After the company went through the Portal, Funny asked the cat. "Where do you want me to take you to? I assume that you probably want to fly home?"

"I would like to go home but this will be a selfish thing to do. Only after I see that the pile of coins is large enough to pay off the Leprechaun, will I finally be able to see the dragon in my dreams instead of being chased by him in the company of the Leprechaun."

"You are right. Let's finish our business connected with the gold." The happy Thought supported him.

The rest of the team agreed with this plan also, no matter how tired and hungry they were, and turned towards Carfield's abode on the two-headed tree.

"Home, sweet nest." Carfield sang out, leaving his friends to sit and lie between the protruding roots of his fir tree whilst he went up into his home to get the pin. He did not keep them waiting for long and returned with his treasure. Tac took the pin and touched the coin with the dancing bird. They all expected to see a large pile of coins but the result scared everyone. The coin started to grow and grow; finally turning into a huge plate which reminded Tac of the one that he had seen lying on the top of a sewer shaft in the city.

"What are we going to do with this?" The cat asked, scratching his forehead.

Carfield walked around, pecked at the coin and stated. "Gold." And Funny tried to lift it up, but without success due to its weight.

Galibur, with his reasonable judgment, concluded. "The pin did not work in the way we expected it to, after all."

"My sister, Candice, is very smart. Let's seek her advice." Suggested the happy Thought.

"But she is far away..." Tac started to speak but, before he had a chance to finish, the figures of all the sisters Thought suddenly appeared on the ground as if they were mushrooms jumping up after the rain.

"What is happening, sister?" Asked the kind Thought. "Why did you call us?"

"We tried to multiply the coin that Tac had managed to obtain, but look what has happened!"

"Wow." Exclaimed the strange Thought, running closer and trying to lift the coin.

"That's not a very good idea, darling." The kind Thought stopped her younger brother, then took the pin from Tac to look at it carefully. "I saw this thing a long time ago and I must say that its magic is not always perfect. How can one explain to the pin that it is not just the material that is important to you, but quantity as well?"

"We could melt this giant coin and make many small ones." Proposed the strange Thought, kicking the coin with his feet.

"That is a clever idea and I am surprised that it did not occur to me but, anyway, I know that there are the ruins of an old settlement somewhere close to the mountains. The old barn, which was once used by a blacksmith, is now buried under the ground but it is probably still functional." The kind Thought advised.

Responding to her words, Tac called out to the crow. "Carfield, can you do me a favor and send someone to find Rainar and the rest of the Council? We will need the help of many animals to accomplish this task because, personally speaking, I am completely exhausted."

"Don't worry." Candice stroked his head gently. "We will find helpers to do the work. But, first, we need to return the coin to its previous size so that we can travel with it to the settlement."

Obeying her advice, Tac touched the coin with the sleeping bird and returned it once again to its former, small size. Without any warning, the landscape in the eyes of the group shuddered and moved aside. A second later Tac found himself and his friends standing on the top of a hill and looking down upon an empty village. It was the same village that he had found when he and Galibur had been looking for the Cloud. This unpleasant memory made Tac arch his back and hiss.

"Forgive me. I had forgotten how much trouble had happened to you in this place once before. You can have breakfast with my sister, Funny, whilst leaving me with angry Thought and our little brother, Ides, to reopen the forge. I do not think that there is any need for us to bother the Council. Look, help is already on its way and now we can start the job." Candice watched a family of bears climbing the side of a dry creek and shouted to them. "The forge is hidden beneath the opposite hill that is covered by blackberry bushes."

"Start to clean off all the vegetation and remove the layers of soil from the roof and the walls." The largest bear growled instructions to his family.

Tac had not had anything to eat since yesterday and went off to get some food that was being served on a blanket. He decided to lie down to rest after his meal and unexpectedly fell asleep next to his bowl. Wandering in a dream for some time, he was abruptly woken up by a noise. Unclear to him at first, it slowly focused into a metallic, clanging sound. 'I had better check out what this is.' He slowly opened his eyes and stretched his back. From the top of the hill he was able to see the forge and the working team perfectly. By now the bears had exposed the remains of an old stone wall which had previously formed the main structure of the forge.

The father bear, wearing a leather apron, was working hard smelting chunks of gold and pouring the hot metal into forms. Tac ran down to join the sisters Thought and Carfield who were watching the coin-making process. A pile of them was already lying on the ground to allow them to cool down whilst other, newly-minted, coins had been left in their forms since they were too soft to remove.

"Do we have enough gold?" Asked Tac

"We started with your coin, transformed it into a large chunk of gold with the help of a pin and just cut pieces from the warm metal to smelt into the forms." The bear informed him.

"I am glad that the Leprechaun found my pin to be useless and threw it out. It proved to be useful for us." Carfield spoke.

"It's almost noon, Tac, we have no time to carry all the gold to Council Hill in the usual way." Said the kind Thought. "We are going to do it with magic. If you are still afraid, then you can close your eyes."

"It's not necessary since I have become accustomed to it. Is the entire stack of gold ready?" He asked, hiding his concern about the need to trust her with his life and the well-being of his friends.

"It's ready." Growled the bear, shaking the last few coins out of the forms onto the large heap on the ground.

"Tac, I am sensing some resentment in you. Are you afraid of me or you do not trust me? If so, what have we done to scare you?" Queried Candice.

"Yes, I am very much alert when somebody from your family is in my presence." He replied. "If you had come to us with honorable intentions, why did your sister, Funny, hide her ability to fly?"

"Aaahh!" Laughed Candice. "The magical world has its own rules which we need to follow and, according to these laws, the happy Thought may reveal that she has wings only when the victory has been achieved and the spirits of the onlookers have been uplifted. Otherwise it would bring confusion and mistrust. Believe me, Tac, one day you will see her flying openly but, before this can happen, even a happy Thought must hide her gift. Do you now trust me enough to take you to the Council Hill?" She asked, looking at the cat with a gentle smile.

"I am glad that this has only been a misunderstanding." Tac sighed with relief and moved closer to her.

For Tac, the magical method of transportation felt like a soft wing that had closed around him for a second and then had dissolved, leaving him together with his friends and a pile of gold right in the middle of Council Hill.

Expressions of fright on the faces of the Council members and Rory's band almost made him laugh. But he managed to control himself by remembering how often he, too, had been frightened by magic.

The Leprechaun appeared exactly at noon. The expression on his face had become sour when he saw that no one was surprised to see him. He simply did not realize that his method of arrival was no longer original and his plan to scare everyone no longer worked either. He wanted to say something but the sight of the coins captured his whole attention. Observing the treasure, he moved his bushy eyebrows into an angry, straight line.

"Do you think that I'm a fool?" He screamed, in an unpleasant voice. "These coins are still warm. You didn't find them, you made them. There must be more gold which you've hidden from me." Turning to the company, he fixed his piercing eyes upon them. "I can be the richest member of my family if I can get my hands on all the gold but, instead, you give me only this pitiful portion. You'll have to give me more gold or I'll bring tornadoes, invasions of spiders and snakes to this accursed place." He spun around in some kind of demonic dance, spreading his hands wide whilst he gradually lowered his body to the ground. The vile expression on his face made everyone move farther away from the center of the hill.

"So much work! And for what?" Tac was about to exclaim.

But the angry Thought, who had not participated in anything so far and had stood with tight lips, suddenly stepped forward and moved towards the Leprechaun. No one heard what she whispered to him, but suddenly the Leprechaun's face turned white and he pulled his head into his shoulders, becoming nothing more than a rather pathetic and very small man. He touched the top of his hat and disappeared, together with all the gold. The angry Thought turned to the spectators and laughed out loud with a strangely-cruel happiness. "He has become accustomed to scaring helpless animals and people but did not like it at all when he was forced to experience it himself. This trip was not a complete waste of my time after all."

"We had to pay a heavy price. But the result was worth the effort because we have finally got rid of that horrible Leprechaun. Now we can all breathe more easily, without constantly looking over our shoulder to see if he is about to jump upon us from behind."

Tac's ironic remark satisfied everyone present.

CHAPTER 11:

THE DOMESTICATED BEAST

Tac didn't mind staying in bed for the whole day after his expedition into the orange woods, but he had other very important business to do.

'The dragon will not sleep forever.' He reminded himself, climbing out of bed. 'However, I am willing to learn whether or not anyone else is leaving a warm bed behind so early in the morning, after returning from such a dangerous adventure. Or is it only me?' Leaving this question unanswered, Tac straightened the bed covers and went to look for Alisa in the kitchen, interrupting her manipulations to his backpack.

"If you don't hurry up, you are going to be late" She gave him a glass of milk and opened a can of cat food for his breakfast.

"Canned meat…?" He wrinkled up his nose in displeasure. "I had better run to the creek and catch some fish for us."

"You do not have time for this." She pushed him back into his seat. "Do not be picky and eat your breakfast. We need to leave soon if we want to be at Carfield's house on time and I hope that I do not need to remind you that this is not going to be a short trip."

"Why did I agree to meet with my friends at his house?" Mumbled Tac, with a full mouth.

"Because Carfield had earlier complained that it was not fair that all the meetings took place at our place and, therefore, you agreed to discuss all future plans for action against the dragon under Carfield's tree." She reminded him.

"That was a mistake." Tac licked his lips clean and put the dirty dishes into a large bowl to wash later. The backpack that he slung onto his shoulders was quite heavy so he asked Alisa. "What is in it?"

"Some snacks in case the discussion carries on past lunchtime. You will all need to take a break to avoid your heads exploding."

"Yes! It may be a very long discussion." Tac agreed. "Our adversary is very strong and I can see only one good thing about our current situation, which is that it's only a couple of days until the start of May. Look around, everything is green, uplifting the spirit." They made their way along a pathway that wended through a narrow grove standing between two low-lying hills. Leaving them behind, they turned in the direction of Carfield's home.

Most of Tac's friends had already arrived. Galibur was having a conversation with Carfield on a branch, whilst Roxal lay on the ground watching Proff trying to kill time by rooting around in a dry mat of needles. Rainar stepped from behind the tree almost at the same time as Tac and both of them observed Bertrond approaching the hill.

"We can start the meeting." The bear shouted from a distance. "The sisters Thought will not come today because the strange Thought became sick. He developed a kind of allergy from human food and his sisters, Candice and Funny, took him to a local wizard for a healing." Bertrond chuckled into his paw and passed his opinion. "I hear that the strange Thought has emptied Carl's fridge and I think that he simply over-ate himself and needs to only flush out his stomach. However, the sisters fussed around him, saying. "This child is only a thousand years old and needs to be examined by a specialist." Then they departed, leaving the angry Thought to attend our meeting in their stead, but Nasty told me that she already had plans for today and, consequently, does not intend to change them for us."

"I am glad that she will not be coming because I cannot stand this grumpy, black apparition." Said Carfield.

"We must not call anyone names, even if we do not like the person." Rainar gave the crow a stern glance. "We should look for a means of persuading the dragon to leave our neighborhood, ourselves. Personally, I support Tac's opinion that killing the dragon would not be the best thing to do and this should be considered only if we don't have any other options. But everyone here is entitled to express an opinion." He then stepped back, to allow space for the next speaker.

"I have never seen the dragon." Proff spoke-up, unexpectedly, because he usually stayed silent at meetings. "But, if I was a beast and someone promised me a nice place to stay, with lots of food thrown in, I would be interested in going there."

"We can use food as a lure. Maybe if we can find out what the dragon's favorite snack is, then we can make him follow it like a donkey that is trying to reach a carrot hanging on the end of a stick." The cat nodded.

"I have something to suggest, as well." Galibur jumped softly onto the ground. "Before the dragon had started to chase Tac and me, he had engaged in a fight with another, more aggressive dragon and sustained an injury which forced him to retreat. If we can produce a dragon larger than he is, then perhaps our beast would be scared enough to return back to his homeland."

"Where are we going to find this larger dragon and what if they became friends and, together, started to chase us?" Tac lifted his eyebrow. "I think that this plan is too dangerous!"

"What if we use my pin to turn the dragon into a small bird?" Carfield asked.

"Well, we have never tried using the pin on living objects so we do not know what could happen, but it could be an interesting experiment." Tac responded, cautiously.

"When I was very small." The voice of Roxal chimed in. "My family lived on the outskirts of the city and we had a nice plot of land alongside a small creek. The backyards of humans' homes were located only a short distance from the den where we lived and the residents of these homes provided much food for us. To get a dinner we only needed to knock down their garbage cans and open the top. One night we went to check our territory and found that a meal had been laid-out for us on the ground. For some reason my mother became suspicious and pushed us away from the temptation but dad did not listen to her. He did not come back home that evening and we eventually found his body lying close to the creek. He was dead, having been poisoned. Mother was so scared for us that she left her den at the creek and returned to her family in the woods. If nothing else works to get rid of this dragon, then we can try to do the same to the dragon as those humans did to my father."

Tac looked at the raccoon in sympathy. "I am sorry about your loss, Roxal, and I will keep your story in my mind. To mete out such a fate to a dragon would be difficult to achieve because we do not know exactly what a dragon eats, apart from live animals." He wanted to say something else, but stopped and stared down at a spot on the ground that had started to shake and rise up to form a small crater.

A curious Alisa stepped forward to look inside it and heard a weak voice from under the ground. "I sense the smell of a fox. Alisa, is that you?"

"Yes it is me, Mr. Mole." She quickly replied.

"Is your husband around?" He queried.

"Yes he is."

"Good! I promised to bring this stone to the Council meeting but it took me longer to find it than I had anticipated and I was late. Here is the stone which interests him." The small hand of the mole pushed a shiny, black piece of coal out of his tunnel.

"Thanks, Mr. Mole." Tac shouted, urgently searching for his backpack, thinking to give something from it to him. But the backpack at this moment was being examined by Carfield who suddenly pulled an apple from one of its pockets and looked at it longingly. Tac, afraid that the mole would disappear before he could get a chance to reward him, grabbed the apple from Carfield and lowered it into the hole, saying. "This is for you Mr. Mole and I hope you enjoy it."

"An apple!" The mole sounded pleased. "I like apples but, as you know, it is impossible for me to get one from a tree." At that, the mole and the apple disappeared and the last words that the cat heard were. "Thanks, if you need anything from me in the future, just shout into my tunnel."

The crow felt robbed. He had opened his beak and was about to scream, but Alisa prevented an argument by sticking another apple right into Carfield's beak. Tac acknowledged her help with a smile and then turned to Galibur. "Is this the same stone that the dragon ate?"

The eagle bent his head and looked at the piece of coal. "I think so. It certainly looks very much like it."

"That's interesting." An idea flashed into Tac's mind. "Bertrond, could you take a look at it also, please?"

The bear not only looked at the stone but sniffed at it and then said. "Well, it smells exactly the same as the ones that I use for my large grill."

"Congratulations! I think we have just found the source of the energy for the dragon's fiery breath."

"So why does he eat flesh?" Rainar looked puzzled.

"I do not know." Tac admitted. "Carfield, I need to borrow your pin again to try out its magic power on the dragon."

"I will go with you!" Carfield cried out, as he dropped the unfinished apple onto the ground. "Someone will need to be a witness to an experiment and I will be able to describe the outcome much better if I can see everything with my own eyes. Wait a moment, I am going for the pin."

Having returned, Carfield wanted to try out its powers right away. However, Alisa insisted that the famous team of the two birds and a cat take their lunch first and then fly off to wherever their business might take them. They left immediately after lunch.

The wind ruffled the fur on Tac's face and rocked him from side to side, whispering lilting songs to him. He relaxed and lowered his eyelids to protect his eyes from the bright sun. The sky was so clear-blue that it seemed to him he was being carried towards the mountains by a boundless stream of air, instead of on the wings of an eagle.

Tac looked down. He suddenly realized how strongly he had become attached to this forest and its inhabitants and, if the dragon were to burn this place, it would seem to him as if he had lost his own family. These past acquaintances of his, or even complete strangers not so long ago, had now become his close friends. He would fight for them and for Carfield whose squawking voice sometimes gave him a headache. 'Keeping all of my forest family alive is worth dying for.' He admitted to himself.

Tac turned his attention from the forest onto the still distant mountains where his opponent was held as a prisoner of a magical dream. A gentle glow of light outlined the tops of the twin mountains, making the chain of hills at their feet look dark by contrast. The sharp tops of the fir trees that covered them were drowned in a smoky mist but the head of the left mountain, named Aran, was shiny white with blue shades along its sides.

Tac's eyes were drawn to Tavren, the black Mountain, which only had strips of snow in the deep cracks. The cat craned his neck forward over Galibur's shoulder in an effort to see the figure of the sleeping dragon, but all that he could see was rocks. After Galibur had brought him closer to the mountain, Tac suddenly realized that the heap of stones that was lying on the ground was part of an animal whose scales were moving slightly as he breathed 'This dragon is well-camouflaged and blends in with the rocks perfectly.' He thought.

Galibur chose a spot on which to land and waited for Tac to slide down from his perch to the flat slope outlined by the large boulders. Tac imagined personal combat with an animal of this size and strength and cold fear slid along his back.

"Where is the pin? Let me try it out and then we can run from here before he wakes up."

Carfield, shaking himself, pulled the pin from the big wallet attached to his chest and gave it to Tac. The cat touched a scale on the dragon's leg and waited for a moment but, seeing no change in him, touched the scale again and again.

"That's enough." Galibur interrupted his attempts. "It's clear that the pin does not work on the beast and we had better leave now!"

Reluctantly agreeing with this opinion, Tac returned to his previous position on top of the eagle. Being extremely frustrated by this failure, he was quiet all the way home and, after his arrival, he allowed Alisa to unfasten the straps of the pillow. "Please come to my home tomorrow to discuss what our next steps should be to resolve the problem. Meantime, tell everyone that our endeavor did not work." He said to his friends, before entering his home.

"I will do that, Tac." Carfield was unusually stingy with words, understanding that his friend was too upset to listen to a long speech. Alisa also avoided asking any questions, allowing Tac to just lie down with his legs tucked underneath him and quietly drift into deep thoughts.

The next day did not improve his mood and Alisa wisely decided to leave him alone to allow it to fade away. She warned the crow, who had just arrived, to be sympathetic to his condition.

Carfield didn't even have a minute alone with him, almost bumping against the angry Thought who asked, with an unpleasant smile. "Was your visit successful?"

"You know that we got nothing positive out of it, so why are you grilling him?" Groaned Carfield.

"Because he should not make decisions on things he knows nothing about. Instead, he should ask for my advice. In this case I have to tell you that this magical thing does not work on live objects and this has been well known since the beginning of our world."

"You sent a messenger to us saying that you were too busy to attend our meeting at Carfield's home." Tac lost his temper.

"Yes! I said that because I had expected you to come to me yourself and ask me nicely. But no! You relied on your own judgment and decided that you could conquer the dragon all by yourself, using only your primitive cat's mind. You thought that you had found a solution on your own." She laughed, sarcastically.

"Yes, I did make an unsuccessful attempt. But at least I did something more than just stand aside, criticizing anyone who tried to do something."

Angry Thought didn't let him finish. "Did you even consider the fact that it was not only your own life that you were putting at risk by your foolish actions but the lives of your similarly irresponsible friends?"

The cat was ready to jump up to scratch her, but he managed to control himself. Although the fur on his back was still standing up, his voice was calm.

"You talk to us as if you have no interest in helping, but only to distract us with anger so that we make more mistakes. Do you really care about our well-being?" He asked.

"Do I care for YOU?" Screamed the angry Thought. "Is it not enough that my sister is doing everything to protect you at a time when no one appears to be worried about my darling, malicious dragon?"

"So what are you doing here?" Carfield jumped in front of Tac. "Why do you not go and help this dragon, then?"

"Thanks for the advice! That is exactly what I am going to do." She retorted and instantly disappeared.

"What has happened?" Alisa came out of the house. "I heard your angry voices."

"I think that we have spoiled our relationship with the angry Thought and created a new problem." Tac felt that he had gone too far in this argument. When everyone who had missed the incident between them had gathered together, Carfield explained what had happened twenty minute before. He didn't try to hide that it was he who was responsible for the incident. The real extent of the damage that had been done to their current situation was fully revealed only when they saw the worry on the faces of the other sisters Thought.

"Oh!No!" Funny cried out. "If our sister is helping the dragon it means that all the plans that we have made together must now be abandoned. Yesterday the dragon was only an angry and scared animal but now, armed with the ideas from our sister, Nasty, he will be a clever and cruel enemy. She will change his agenda from being generally troublesome to all the inhabitants of these woods, simply searching for food, to become your personal enemy. This may involve destroying everything and killing everyone who is important to you, Tac. And do not forget that our sister can read your thoughts and even people who are not living in the forest are now in danger also. I mean your human family, Tac."

"I created all this mess and this means that I must now answer for it. I will go and surrender myself to the dragon. After that, you will need to ask your sister to take the beast with you and forever close that Portal that started this disaster." He was too upset to worry about himself.

"You are allowing your guilt to influence your decision, Tac! If you were dead, how would you stop the dragon if my sister does not change her plans for your loved ones?" The sad expression on his face softened her next words. "My sister, Nasty, took advantage of both Carfield and you very skillfully, leading the conversation in a way that achieved her desired outcome. Manipulating both of you, she made you say exactly what she wanted, so you will be blamed for what has happened. She has wanted to have her own dragon for a long time but could not get the beast. Both my sister and I forbade this because we knew the very real danger of their union. Now our sister can say that she has only followed your advice and is not responsible for upsetting us."

"Nasty will never catch me in a cheap trap like that." The strange Thought boasted.

"Am I hearing the voice of a young man who spent last evening, and part of the night, suffering because of the dangerous advice that he accepted from his sister, Nasty?" Remarked the kind Thought, flashing him a scornful look which forced Ides to disappear behind his older sister, Funny.

"So, even a strange Thought can get caught on a fishing hook if it has the right lure on it?" Tac's joke made everyone laugh.

"Nasty told me that if I wanted to learn about this world I would need to try things that it produces." His voice mumbled from behind Funny.

"To have knowledge, you need to read books given to you by the wizard, Shmata, and do not try to make experiments on yourself because it can hurt." Candice continued.

"Sister, you are too hard on him." Funny brought him forward with an arm round his shoulder. "He is just a child. I can now see that Nasty's plan to have a dragon started with her advice to Ides that made our little brother sick. She knew that, because of his illness, we would take him back to our home, conveniently leaving her in charge of the situation here. However, our sister doesn't know that we have brought a special spell with us. Using it, we have built an invisible barrier around the valley between the mountains Tavren and Aran that includes the strip of forest that leads to the gate. It prevents the dragon from wandering around and, later, we will transport him back to where he came from.

"We are lucky that you have restricted his movements in time." Said Rainar. "But what about the different animals that presently live inside the secured area but have now become locked in there by the spell? Can they escape this trap?"

"Yes! Unfortunately, they are trapped as well." The happy Thought admitted, ruefully.

"I know that a large family of foxes lives under the hill. Generations of them have dug into the hill and made their dens all over it. Inhabitants of this area can negotiate with the elder of this family to obtain refuge from the dragon in the cool tunnels, but they cannot stay there for a long time. They need food and water." Alisa advised them.

"My mice can dig a tunnel under the barrier to deliver supplies to the trapped animals and this area has many creeks so water should not be a problem for them. This temporary measure will buy them some time until we can find a way to rescue them from the trap." Mixie offered.

"We are too far from the place of our interest and have no idea what is going on there right now. Therefore, to make our decisions accord with changing situations, I suggest that we all move closer to the twin Mountains." The cat suggested.

"I know a hill that would give a perfect view of the Valley and I am quite willing to ask my family to deliver there everything that we need." Replied Galibur.

"Yes! And we can move there with the speed of thought." Funny flapped her hands excitedly.

"Wait for a second. Where will we get the mice that we need to dig the tunnel? It will take time to transport them from the forest." The cat's question stopped the spread of excitement amongst his friends.

"Don't worry, Tac, I think that the population of local mice is sufficient to complete this task. I need only a few hours to organize the working team." Mixie reassured him.

"In that case, let's move to the new location."

"Everyone come closer to me." Beckoned Funny, spreading her hands. The long sleeves of her pale lavender dress fell down like the petals of an exotic flower. The intricate drawings on the fabric hypnotized their eyes and made everyone relax. Tac closed his heavy eyelids for a moment and, without warning, found himself on the top of a high hill that was free from trees, having only separate groups of shrubs scattered along its edges. Galibur had not exaggerated when he had said that they would be able to view the entire area where the dragon had been imprisoned by a magical spell.

"Galibur, look there, your eyes are better than mine. Tell me what the dragon is doing."

After a few minutes of intense staring, the eagle answered. "I cannot explain his actions. He is backing up slowly without any rational purpose."

"Unfortunately, his actions do have rational explanations." Remarked the kind Thought. "He is digging a long trench in the exact place where we were planning to make a tunnel. Now he is breaking off scales from his back to block the openings of the creek. I think that he is planning to leave all the animals of our interest without water and we have no way of stopping him."

"I am wondering how the dragon learned about our project if we only finished discussing it ten minutes ago? I assume that he must have found the underground springs by himself. But, how can you explain that he started to dig in the exact place where we wanted to be connected to the hill? Do not tell me that he is a mind reader." Galibur wondered.

"He is not, but our sister is. And look who is riding the beast, poking him with a black umbrella." Candice pointed, obliging everyone to look in the direction of the mountain.

Tac obeyed, rather sheepishly, feeling guilty for creating this strange alliance between Nasty and the dragon, at least partially.

"You need to avoid any angry thoughts." Candice advised him. "Being angry will simply open a door for our sister into your mind and she will not hesitate to invade your thoughts."

"How can I fight the war, and look at the destruction and death of my friends, with only kind thoughts in my mind? I cannot plan the murder of my enemy with laughter on my lips, even for the purpose of hiding our plans from your sister. Perhaps I should hit the dragon between the eyes with something extremely unexpected." He shrugged.

The voice of Ides made the cat turn in his direction. "You can hit a dragon with strange things if you want. That is, of course, if you are not afraid to go to the orange woods again to look for blackberries."

"And what am I going to do with these berries when I find them? Feed the dragon?" asked Tac, sarcastically.

"Exactly!" The boy put his hands in the pockets of his pants and kicked the stone carelessly. "There are many plants and animals that have been changed under the influence of the magical lake and the blackberry is one of them. They have power over things. Sometimes they can transform big into small, young can become old and smart can start acting foolishly."

"Do they work on living beings?" Tac narrowed his eyes, with interest.

"Yes they do." Replied Ides. "To make the berries work you need to feed them to the subject, regardless of its diet."

"How many berries do I need to collect to transform the dragon?"

"I think one basket should be enough." Ides answered, after some deliberation. "I am positive about it."

"I hope that the dragon will shrink to the size of a bug so that I can peck it and make Nasty blow out all of her anger." Carfield muttered. "Without the dragon I think that she will be as powerless as a boiled, black mushroom and unable to do any further harm, at least for some time."

"Carfield, did you feel angry during this speech?" Asked Tac.

The fear written on Carfield's face answered this question better than any words could.

"Congratulations! We need to go for the berries right now before the angry Thought can stop us. Galibur, will you please carry me to the Portal."

"You cannot go through the gate. Our sister has already prepared a trap for you this way. Let me transport you, though, by means of a happy thought." Funny took both Carfield and Tac under her arms and disappeared, carried away by her own laughter.

They were immediately transferred to the orange woods in the blink of an eye. Tac looked around, lost, but Carfield recognized the alley of giant trees covered with paper-thin bark that he had seen many years ago. The yellow leaves, etched in apple-green along their edges, moved gently in the fresh breeze. Their unusual shape intrigued Tac sufficiently that he slowed down, fascinated by the game of light coming through their thin skins.

The crow interrupted his inquiry by calling him. Running to catch up with his friends, Tac almost banged against them. He wanted to ask why they had stopped, but discovered the answer for himself. It was the figure of a tall, savage-looking man, dressed in a helmet with horns protruding from the sides. The man blocked their way, grinning at them and playing with a heavy club.

"The First Astrou"

"Do not be scared." The happy Thought advised them. "He is an Astrou and is dangerous only if you are afraid of him but, if you start to laugh, he will be disarmed." Seeing that her friends were too frightened to understand the meaning of her words, Funny laughed and flapped with her hands like a child. At this, the savage man made a fast turn and transformed himself into a grotesque figure dressed only in a pink tutu and a helmet with a large, pink bow on each horn. Instead of a club, he was holding a stick with a sparkling star on the end of it. The man looked at the star in astonishment and then lifted the tutu to discover that his leather pants had disappeared, leaving his fat, hairy legs exposed. Now it was his turn to get scared and the expression of fright on his face made even the most fearful burst into laughter. Terrified, the man ran away to leave the way clear and the company of friends continued to walk along the pathway that, in some places, had disappeared under the bushes.

The cat and the crow chatted excitedly about their victory, laughing at the man and their own fears, until Funny reminded them that it was still too early to relax because danger awaited them everywhere. The proof of her words did not make them wait for very long. Another monster jumped out at the company from the branches of a tree.

Astrou and Happy Thought

"Let me try to surprise him." Tac closed one of his eyes to concentrate his thoughts on the figure of the clay beast. The creature moved towards the group with a low growl but suddenly stopped, blinded by a large white flower that suddenly grew out of his forehead. The monster hit it with his heavy fist, but the cheeky flower was sucked inside his body before its petals were crushed. Teasing the monster again, the flower opened itself on his shoulder and then on his knee. Growling in anger, the clay monster forgot about Tac and his friends in order to chase the annoying plant all around his body.

Leaving him busy with the flower, the friends tip-toed farther to the opening that was occupied by a large clump of rare berries. Tac discovered, to his disappointment, that they had arrived too late. At first, he heard Nasty's unpleasant giggle and then saw her jumping on top of the silvery bushes. She turned to face them with a gloating smile and disappeared.

"She has destroyed all of the plants." Tac looked at the disaster in dismay.

Carfield walked between the piles of dead plants, looking for fruit that had survived the rampage. "Nothing!"

"I have found one undamaged bush." Shouted Funny, from the far, shaded corner of the opening. Tac and Carfield ran in that direction but their hopes evaporated after they saw the plant. It was hidden under the branches of the tree and, lacking light, its berries were the same color as the leaves. This lack of maturity had saved them from being noticed, but green berries were of no use to Tac.

"Don't be upset. I can speed up the development of the berries." Funny rubbed one hand against the other to produce a narrow disk of blue light which she then rolled into a sphere that changed its color to orange-yellow. She hung this miniature sun above the bush and sat on her knees to watch them mature. It looked as if the plant was sucking the sphere inside itself because, the smaller the ball of light became, the bigger and darker the berries grew. When the last particle of light had flashed brightly and disappeared, the bush had been covered with ripe, black berries tinged with blue. The cat and the crow carefully collected all the berries and placed them into a wooden basket. Funny removed a ribbon from her hair to tie back the branches of the tree and, by this means, gave the rare plant a chance to be exposed to the light.

"It will spread its roots underground and replenish this area with new bushes." She explained her actions to them. "But it would not be wise to rely on only one plant to do the job." She took five or six big berries from the top of the basket. "We need to plant these berries in different corners of the opening, to keep this magical plant available to all good people." After Tac and Carfield had finished watering the newly-planted berries, she queried. "Do you want me to return you home in the same way that you came, or would you prefer to go through the gate?"

"I appreciate your magic, Funny, but I am not fond of it. I prefer to go through the gate. It feels a little more natural than disintegrating into nothing, hoping that you will reappear on the other side without being adorned with horns to frighten your family and friends with your new appearance." Tac admitted, with a shy smile.

The happy Thought only laughed and then took Tac, along with his basket, and carried him back to the gate.

Both animals had, by now, crossed through the Portal so many times that it had become an almost boring procedure. "Only, do not let the Force throw me on top of the tree that has thorns." Tac pleaded, as he entered the gray vortex of energy. When the travelers had reached their destination on the other side of the mountain, Funny asked the crow to watch out that no one had followed them. However, Carfield was bored just from thinking about sitting alone on the tree, looking at the granite walls while great actions could be happening elsewhere. "There is no point in sitting here since we did not meet any men or animals on our way towards the Portal. So, if we did not see anyone, no one could have followed us."

Funny saw the logic in this and allowed all of the company to fly to the temporary post on the hill in northern Pokerweild. But, if Tac had waited at least fifteen minutes, instead of flying off right away, then he would have seen something unexpected. The body of a tall man had landed right on the tree previously mentioned by Tac. He was lucky to find any support to break his fall, even if it was a prickly tree. The stranger rubbed his hurt elbow and back, pulled the chip of wood from his palm and, carefully choosing his way, lowered himself to the ground. Coincidentally, he moved in the same direction as Funny with her friends.

Arriving on the top of the hill, Tac found that the camp was almost ready. A line of tents, covered with camouflage, had been set-up in a straight line together with storage for food and water. Alisa had even brought a map and a medical box from their house to Tac's tent. While his advisors gathered for a meeting, he quickly checked everything out and listened to a brief report about the dragon. His tent was too small for all the assembled company to sit down so Ides was asked to sit on the lap of his sister and Funny next to Candice who was holding Shustin and Mixie. Bertrond sat on the floor, comfortably spreading his legs and allowing enough space for Roxal to squeeze in. The Owl took a seat on the back of the chair occupied by Alisa. The last available spot was taken by Rainar.

Tac jumped on top of the table to enable him to see everyone and to spread out the map. "First of all, I will explain the meaning of this strange object that's hanging around my neck. I see that you are very curious about it. This is an amulet that is protecting me from the penetration of the angry Thought into my mind. Since Carfield does not possess one, I have asked him to temporarily withdraw from the discussion of our plans and sit at home. Believe me, it was not easy to convince him to do this." Tac's words were met by understanding smiles.

"Our little group has managed to bring the required amount of berries from the orange woods but we all understand that this is only part of our task. Somehow I need to find a way to feed the berries to the dragon, except that I have no idea how to do this."

"Intruder, spy!" A scream from Carfield and a crashing noise interrupted his speech. Everyone jumped from their seats to run outside. They saw a man, clad in a cloak, who was surrounded by growling animals. A long sword in the stranger's hands outlined the circle that the guards were unwilling to cross. Instead, they awaited Tac's order.

The man turned to face the newly-approaching enemies. Despite the fact that only a part of his face was showing under his helmet, Funny recognized him and cried out. "I know him. He is Ruslan, the Prince of Rossana."

"Prince? What is he doing here?" Tac, looked at the warrior with suspicion.

"We need to invite him into the tent to give him food and water and then ask him questions. It's an old Rossa custom to meet strangers from distant places. If we treat him with courtesy and respect he will be our friend."

"Let him go." Tac ordered his guards. "It will be better if we follow Funny's advice and treat the stranger as a guest." Then, turning to the crow, he asked him. "Carfield, can you speak his language?"

"I am a smart crow and I can speak any language."

"We have not yet received any royal persons in Pokerweild and, to date, we have not yet had an opportunity to meet guests of a high position. So, I think we need somebody for the position of Ambassador to look after them properly. Carfield, you are now an Ambassador under my administration and your duty is to receive the guest."

"Me?" Asked Carfield, scared. "I do not know how to do this."

"Ambassador, you are an educated bird and remember that you have been in a worse situation than this." Tac encouraged him. "I think you will discharge your duties in an excellent manner."

"Ambassador!" Mumbled the crow, as he walked towards the warrior.

Ruslan was standing calmly and supporting himself with his long sword as he gazed at the assembled company of adventurers with great interest.

"Prince Ruslan." Carfield cleared his throat. "Your Highness, forgive us for not recognizing your person. Please follow me into the tent to share our simple supper." Carfield showed the direction with his wing.

"What a strange world." Thought Ruslan. "It looks like animals and people live here as equals." His face didn't show surprise, no matter how amused he was by everything he saw around him. He only touched his forehead with his fingers and bowed, following the crow into the tent. Choosing a strong barrel as a seat, he took a glass of water and lifted a biscuit from the plate offered to him.

"We are at war at this time." Carfield apologized. "And our food is not really suitable for a royal person, but we are honored to share what little we have with you." The crow took a deep breath and looked at Tac with the silent question "How am I doing?"

"Perfect." Answered Tac, with the same silent sign of approval.

"Thank you for your hospitality." Said Ruslan. "I would appreciate being introduced to everyone in your party and please explain the circumstances of your war to me."

"The dragon from the land behind the mountain invaded our forest, killing animals and burning everything around. Our ally, Candice, the kind Thought, with her family Funny, the happy Thought and Ides, the strange Thought, came to help us protect our world. We decided to transform the dragon into a smaller version of himself and, instead of killing him, make practical use of him. For example, he can work as a grill-assistant to our bear to cook the hamburgers with his fiery breath."

"How do you plan to decrease the dragon's size to prevent him from eating his boss?"

"Well, we have decided to do it with the help of magic berries that need to be placed directly into the dragon's mouth." The crow explained.

"And who's this crazy hero who has agreed to do that?" The Prince looked around.

"The hero that will save our forest from the dragon is right in front of you and his name is Tac." Said Carfield. "By the decision of the Council he will be awarded the crown of a King if he succeeds."

"You mean, if he stays alive after challenging the dragon." Ruslan corrected the speaker. "I can hardly believe it. You need a warrior to slay a dragon but I don't see any of these fighters amongst you."

At this point Tac decided to join in the conversation using Carfield as a translator. "I am just a cat, but under these circumstances I have no choice. I am going to be a warrior."

Ruslan only lifted his eyebrow, thinking over these words. Then he said, reflectively. "A cat versus a dragon doesn't sound like a fair fight."

"My friend, Carfield, was just a crow only minutes ago but now he is an Ambassador. We all have to make a choice of who we want to be. So I have made mine."

"I understand what you mean and, believe me, my heart is bursting to help you but my mind is telling me to mind my own business."

"What kind of business brought you to our wood?" Asked Tac.

"I'm looking for my wife. She disappeared under very strange circumstances, but I was given good advice to ask about her from the wizard that lives in the Valley of the Star. When I came close to the place where the two lakes almost touch each other, a strange creature attacked me and scared my horse away. Searching for him, I found this place. I was surprised to see life on the other side of the mountains because everyone in my country has always believed that there was nothing here except uninhabited desert. I'm now hoping to find Leubarta in this new world."

"Leubarta? Did you say Leubarta?" Exclaimed Tac.

"Yes! Do you know her?" Ruslan's voice became emotional.

"I met a Princess at the lake which was situated very close to the place where you searched for your horse. We exchanged our stories about the reasons that had brought us to this empty shore and I know for certain that she still lives somewhere in your world. So, I advise you not to waste your time looking for her in these woods since you will not find her here. Now my heart longs to show you the place where she swam in the waters of a magical lake to restore her ability to transform herself into a bird. She comes here every year and you just need to wait for an opportunity to see her once more. At least it is better than having no hope in your heart at all."

"Did she mention any danger to her well-being?"

"No." Replied Tac. "The Princess only mentioned that she was missing you."

"I have a proposition. You will give me all the details of your conversation with my wife and, in return, I will help you in your difficult mission to feed the berries to the dragon."

"It's a deal." Tac agreed, happily. Then he jumped onto the table again to point out the dragon's whereabouts on the map. "The dragon is trapped in this area and this hill is the center of his interest right now. He is guarding an unknown number of our friends in the fox tunnels under the hill and has dug a wide trench along the northern side of it to prevent our rescue operation. Before he had formed an alliance with the angry Thought we had a plan to move him closer to the gate and transfer him back home. The problem was that Nasty found out about this scheme and we had to abandon it. Now we are looking for an alternative way to deal with the problem."

Ruslan thoughtfully listened to the crow's translation and pointed out. "To my knowledge, the dragon has only two vulnerable places, his eyes and his mouth. The rest of his body is hard as stone."

"He will not open his mouth for you, Tac, so you will need to catch him by surprise and jump on top of him from some cover." Insisted Galibur.

"How wide and deep is the dragon's trench?" Ruslan queried.

"It's quite wide." Tac answered. "The dragon has not found any difficulty in walking inside it and, if I remember, the edge of the trench is approximately on the level of his elbow."

"This isn't deep enough." Exclaimed Ruslan. "We need to build up one side of it high enough for Tac to be on the same level as the head of the beast."

"To be able to achieve this, we will need to persuade the dragon to leave the top of the hill and, by the time he returns, we will have raised the level of the ground high enough for Tac to throw the bucket of berries into his mouth. Then we shall see what happens to the dragon." Remarked Galibur.

"I think it's a good plan." Tac looked at his friends. "It is still in a raw state but, together, we will find a way to make it work."

Carfield interjected, thoughtfully. "The easiest way to increase the height of the trench is to place a flat stone next to it and then use my magic pin to magnify its size."

"Do you think that the predator will let us do it? Do you actually think that he will just sit there and watch you without interfering?" Mixie questioned his plan.

"You are right! We need to divert him. Let's make a lot of noise as we are preparing to attack him, let's say, here." Galibur touched the map with his claw at a spot close to the black mountain. "The beast still has a nest on the slope of the mountain and he will not allow us to build a position close to his home."

However, Rainar disagreed with Galibur. "The grass field on the slope of the mountain is too open for this purpose and it will not be difficult for him to discover that the threat carries no real force. You can hardly expect the dragon to be scared by a group of screaming animals."

"But what if another monster invades his space?" Asked the eagle.

"That would be another matter. He will run to the mountain quickly to protect his territory." Brown Bob replied.

"I think we have a plan." The cat wanted to finish the meeting to get some rest before nightfall.

"We have not discussed the last, important matter that no one has mentioned yet." Ruslan spoke up. "I hope that everyone realizes that this desperate action may cost Tac his life. Even if he is lucky enough to escape the fire at the moment when his basket reaches the target, he can still be burned. There may not be enough time for him to find a place to hide."

"It will be a painful but fast death." The cat joked bravely, but unconvincingly. The pity written on the faces around him made him lower his eyes and fight the churning in his stomach.

"Even if I had my shield with me, I do not think that it would be able to withstand the fire and I'm sure that its metal would melt like a piece of ice." The Prince added, ruefully.

"We cannot send Tac to his death without any protection whatsoever. When I was working on the computer I saw a figure dressed in silver clothing that was walking through a fire, unharmed. If we could find the same material, would you be able to save Tac?" Carfield asked Ruslan.

348

"I could make a shield from it to protect both of us." Ruslan's response restored the positive mood of the company.

"Right now it's too late to make any preparations for the coming battle." Murmured Candice, who was only listening to the discussion but had not chosen to participate in the arguments. "We are all tired from the pressure of the daily events. I feel that the best thing for us to do now is to break up for the day and then return to the discussion of our plans tomorrow. I only want to suggest, Tac, that you divide up the whole operation into several small portions and appoint a different person to be in charge of each."

"I should call you smart Thought." Tac answered, with a relieved smile. "The noisy part will be under the management of Bertrond."

"In that event we shall have to call it "Come Fool." Carfield interrupted.

Tac considered these words and then agreed with his friend. "The dragon is probably not bright enough to crack the puzzle but he does have a second head, that belonging to Nasty, and I do not expect that you will be able to fool her for a long time. I also suggest that you recruit Carfield for this job. He is ideal for this since his ideas are usually so crazy that they can fool anyone."

"Thanks." Said Carfield, sarcastically. "I am flattered and I will be glad to test out my ideas on that simple fellow."

Tac only chuckled and then continued. "The second part is to build up the side of the trench, as we have discussed already, and this is my responsibility. The third part is to arrange for the appropriate protections and this matter will be handled by Ruslan. Before I forget, Carfield, it looks as if you are going to be very busy, searching for a silvery costume or the material that would have been used to make it. Be on the telephone from first thing in the morning and find everything that Ruslan will need. Do not be cheap, just pay any money that is asked. This matter is completely in your hands and the money in my bank account is at your disposal."

"Hands?" Asked Carfield, looking at his legs in some surprise.

"Never mind." Said Tac. "And last, but by no means least, Rainar, I charge you with the responsibility of making sure that all the supplies that will be needed, either in the camp or for the future battle, will be available in time. Will someone please wake me up early, even if you need to pour cold water on me?"

The next day flashed through Tac's life like a comet that was dragging a long tail of worries, conversations, enquiries and adjustments to the original plan. He was very glad indeed when all the supervisors, whom he had appointed, reported back to him that their teams had completed their tasks fully. "If, for any reason, something does not work the way we expect it to, then we will need to improvise." He said to them.

Turning to Ruslan and Bertrond he observed. "Our allies, the sisters Thought, have used up the last bit of magical powder that has held the dragon inside the trap. The northern wall of our invisible prison will collapse first but, fortunately, it's also the starting point for all the events that will follow. The beast must be transformed before he discovers that nothing can stop him from crossing the boundary and walking into the middle part of the forest, or to reach the city of man. Since I cannot be in two places at once, I choose to be close to the hill to meet the enemy at the second point in our plan and complete my destiny."

"Do not doubt us." Said Carfield. "You will see our best performance tomorrow."

Ruslan and the bear only nodded in agreement.

The dragon had managed to fall asleep after long hours of tossing and turning on the flat top of the hill. Hunger was the reason for his restlessness and inability to sleep. He tried to block the squeaky voice of the old witch, who was calling him back to the misery of famine, and growled while covering his ears with his massive claw.

"Get up! You lazy ancestor of chickens." She yelled at the beast, poking him with an umbrella. Seeing no response from the side of her overgrown pet, Nasty removed a small flute from a bag and blew an annoying sound into the dragon's ear.

He rose up reluctantly, wishing to flatten her with a heavy foot but, after crossing eyes with his Mistress, he lost his will. Bending his large head to the ground, he assisted her to sit in the improvised saddle between two, protruding thorns on his back.

"Go, go!" Nasty ordered, kicking him with her foot. The large eyes of the beast caught a glimpse of silver far away almost on the edge of the valley and mountains and, ignoring the impatience of his Mistress, he moved forward cautiously. Unable to recognize from this distance whether it was simply an object, or a large animal wagging its tail at high speed, the dragon steered the flight towards the subject of his curiosity. The closer he got to the target, the angrier he became, having a good reason to be upset. A small, cheeky and ugly dragon dared to challenge him and annoyed him with a wide grin. It didn't retreat, making a low, whispering sound by the swishing of its small, silvery tail.

Puzzled by the strange tactics of the intruder, the dragon decided to provoke it into action by approaching his smaller opponent from behind but this did not make the enemy answer in the way that he expected. He simply paid no attention. The dragon moved even closer, thinking. 'I can take it easily. Its legs are too thin to fight me successfully and its type does not have claws. Without wings, this dragon is just a sad ground-runner.' He made the decision to jump onto the smooth, flat head of the enemy that was looking at him with large, stupid, wide-open eyes. However, he was thrown back by a cracking noise and ribbons of fire which came from under his feet. The sky above the smaller dragon exploded into thousands of bright sparks which continued to fall down amidst loud, frightful, screeching noises. In addition, the body of the wingless beast exploded from inside and threw pieces of burning debris outward. That was too much to witness for the ordinary dragon. He panicked, then turned away and fled on foot from this place, leaving his pride and bravery buried under bits of burning metal.

"Stop! Turn back! The way out is free." Screamed his rider, mercilessly hitting him to make him pay attention to her message. But the dragon was completely deaf to any sound, except the comforting beat of his feet against the soil. The angry Thought left the saddle to move along the dragon's neck towards his eyes, hoping to get him back under her control, but the dragon shook his head violently. This dislodged her body and she fell to the ground. Losing her hissing steed, the powerless Nasty could do nothing else but cry out in frustration whilst she hit the ground with her fists.

"No doubt you had imagined that you were the only one who could make excellent tricks." Laughed Tac, looking at her through a pair of military binoculars.

"Hurry up and let me look." The Crow impatiently hopped up and down on his thin legs then, grabbing the instrument, added his own impression. "She looks like an old black cat which has been rescued from a muddy ditch."

"You have stared at her enough." Tac took the binoculars back. "I need to find out the exact whereabouts of this dragon."

"I can tell you this without looking through the binoculars." Commented Galibur, dryly. "He has returned to his nest on the side of the mountain."

Carfield broke into the conversation to remark. "I scared him so badly that the ground of the valley no longer appealed to him. I feel sorry for blowing-up that old army helicopter, but I burned up your money for a good cause."

"Now, Carfield, my smart friend, tell us how you are going to persuade the dragon to come back to the hill. If I understood you correctly, without a victory Tac will never receive the crown." The animals heard the calm voice of Ruslan behind them. This decreased Carfield's excitement considerably.

"We will ask Candice what to do." The crow looked self-satisfied.

"She's left." Ruslan's voice remained even.

"What do you mean?" Carfield shouted.

"She said that she needed to take care of her sister and then drew a sign in the air with her finger and promptly disappeared." The expression on Ruslan's face was unreadable, but his gray eyes had lost their usual spark of humor. This told Tac that the matter was very serious.

"In this situation we need to do the same as we did before. We need to turn the dragon's attention towards us." Tac exclaimed, and then shouted over the head of the crow to the leader of the Scottish band in the distance. "Rory! Is your band brave enough to parade along the hill to draw the dragon's attention to yourselves?"

"I am un-a-a-ble to promise that the whole ba-a-a-nd will agree to do this, Tac, but some musicians will definitely pl-a-a-ay their pipes for you." The ram answered.

"Good! Please dress them in very bright clothing and make a terrible noise."

Then, turning to the bear, Tac ordered. "Bertrond, make sure that everyone is hidden as soon as the dragon comes close to our position. When the dragon appears on the top of the hill, I want the musicians to drop their instruments and run for cover. There are still plenty of these in the store and we can easily replace their losses."

The small army of animals silently followed their leader between the shrubs and boulders that lay along their way to the burned hill until its vandalized body suddenly appeared, surrounded by green meadows that proudly displayed their richness. Poppies and white daisies of different sizes grew between the fields of bluebells. Their stems, topped with tiny blue flowers, stood so tightly together that no other plant was able to find space between them. But the beauty of nature was forgotten when the adventurers caught sight of the severely burnt land and realized the extent of the damage. Suddenly, the animals that had ran in front of Tac slowed down and then stopped completely. Tac was already close to the first line, maneuvering between band members, when he saw the reason for the delay. Supported by her sisters, the angry Thought was limping slowly towards the camp.

"Nasty has broken her leg!" Shouted the strange Thought, running towards them.

"Not broken, but badly twisted." Candice corrected him.

The injured Nasty had lost her hat and her dress was dirty and wrinkled. Her small face took on an earthy shape, becoming even smaller.

Tac, feeling pity for her, turned to the boar. "Boran, please take the woman to the camp. There is a sleeping bag in my tent and plenty of water with which she can clean herself up."

With this act of kindness, Tac made peace between them. The lips of the old woman started to tremble as if she was about to cry but, instead, she looked at her feet and said. "The dragon is hungry, so use food to trap him. He will forget about his fear and I can give you a spell that will allow the Prince to understand you long enough to complete your task." From her pocket she removed a crooked dry root and gave it to the cat.

"Quickly, run to the hill, I know what to do." Tac shouted, resuming his progress. Half an hour of steady running brought them to the edge of the burnt ground. "I cannot imagine how anyone could survive here." He looked at the complete destruction of the place. "Even a mining company could not make as much damage as this one dragon has achieved."

"Yes! You are right!" Bertrond supported him. "Before the dragon had arrived in this valley the hill had been a nice place to live. The sandy ground that created it had been brought here by the fast currents of the river but, after it had disappeared, the hill was left lying like a narrow ship that had been thrown onto the shore by a storm and then forgotten by its crew. Foxes built their dens at the foot of the hill whilst small birds chose the hard-to-reach parts closer to the top and marked the territory of their colony with the black circles of the entrances to their nests. Then families of rabbits built their homes between the roots of the trees that grew on the top. Neighbors do not always live peacefully on the same soil but, somehow, they all got used to the presence of each other."

"Now it's a sad place." Galibur added to the bear's remarks. "We transferred all of the survivors to safe ground but I must say that there appears to be less of them than I expected."

"Well." Tac responded. "We can't start to count our losses quite yet because the enemy is still free to go where it wants and to do more damage, which means that we need to finish him off now."

"Bertrond, I need you and Rory to take care of the noise and Carfield, could you please stay with me. Ruslan, may I ask you to crack the piece of coal into smaller fragments? I want to lay a pathway from the beginning of the trench to the platform where I am going to wait for the dragon. Once I get there, I will burn coal nuggets to spread the smell of the dragon's favorite food to whet his appetite. Let's see for how long he can withstand the temptation." Tac did not need to remind his helpers about the importance of working fast. Rushing around, they had just finished off the last preparations when the voices of the watching guards warned Tac that the dragon had entered the territory.

"Hide, everyone!" Ruslan grabbed the light shield which had been made from the protective silver fabric. Carrying a bucket of berries in another hand, he ran to hide under the camouflaged netting where Tac was already waiting for him. The busy place suddenly became silent. Tac and Ruslan were able to see through the holes in the netting as the dragon swallowed the first black stone prepared for it and then slowly walked to another, turning his head from side to side and hissing like a large, angry lizard. His yellow eyes watched for the slightest movement and the skin on his throat trembled, showing that he was ready to blow fire at any second.

The dragon was so huge that Tac's body started to shake nervously even if his desire to attack the beast had not changed. Trembling like a leaf in the autumn wind, Tac waited until the head of the dragon had reached the same level as his hiding place.

"Now!" He ordered his stiff body and, ignoring its plea to stay out of danger, he rushed out to take advantage of the element of surprise. The dragon pulled his long neck into his shoulders to throw it forward, like a heavy rebounding fist. He would probably have succeeded in swallowing-up the bucket of berries and Tac, if Ruslan had not left his hiding place to stop the cat from falling over the slippery edge of the stone platform right into the dragon's mouth.

Fuflow's Last Attack on Ruslan

Tac was tossed onto the Prince's shoulder and dug his claws into the metal section of his chain mail to hold himself in place. Ruslan's own hands were fully tied-up keeping the shield up in front of both of them. The impact of the fire that the dragon shot their way was so strong that both of them were pushed from the smooth surface of the stone platform onto the burnt soil which surrounded the trench. Ruslan looked for his shield, but it was too late to reach it because the head of the dragon was poised directly above them. The dragon opened his mouth to turn both enemies into ashes, but suddenly realized that something very strange had happened to him and the expression on his face turned to one of complete surprise. The beast tried to breathe fire again, but the tiny cloud of smoke that he was able to produce only scared him and the next try made him cough. He opened his mouth wide as if he was unable to breathe and slapped his chest, producing a strong sound. Then he unexpectedly collapsed inside the trench, making the ground shake. Ruslan jumped to his feet and lifted Tac off the ground. The cat was surprised to find himself still alive.

"I must reasonably conclude that I am not in cats' heaven if I can still see you." He gasped to Prince Ruslan. "Let me see what has happened to our adversary."

To his disappointment, the dragon had not changed his size and still had his frightful appearance. He was lying flat on the ground with his neck stretched out and his eyes were closed as if he was asleep, or even unconscious.

"No, let's wait." Tac stopped Ruslan from jumping down into the trench. "I think that he may only be pretending to be dead." Without a warning, the dragon slowly opened his eyes, pulled his head closer to his body and shook it as if he was still in a state of confusion.

"I must have swallowed some kind of virus." The beast mumbled in a low, and unexpectedly pleasant, voice. "What a terrible taste I have in my mouth." And the dragon blew a stream of white steam along the trench. The last piece of coal that he was able to find on the ground was enough to bring back his good mood.

"I am Fuflow." He introduced himself. "What are your names, and where am I?" He asked them.

"I am Tac and I am a cat. My companion is a noble who is Prince Ruslan."

"Prince?" The dragon almost whispered. "Please do not kill me, I am only a poor dragon that has lost everything--my nest, my clan and something else but I just can't remember what it is right now." Then he blurted out. "Ohhh! I know what it is! I have lost my savageness and I do not feel malicious anymore. How am I going to live without my hatred and anger? I am finished." A heavy tear slid along his narrow face. "Sir Prince, it would be better if you were to kill me now and put me out of my misery and shame."

"Being kind is not shameful." Tac moved closer. He had started to suspect what kind of changes had indeed occurred within the beast. Instead of changing the dragon physically, the berries had changed his personality. Tac then started considering the rare possibilities that might flow from having a civilized dragon in his forest. However, prior to affording him refuge, he decided to clarify the details relating to his menu.

"Is it necessary for you to eat animals? Can you replace your desire to consume warm blood with something else? Let's say, warm milk? We can buy you a herd of cows if that would help."

"I will be honest with you, Tac." Fuflow answered, in a confidential tone of voice. Flesh is the worst food for a dragon that you can imagine. It's low in calories and cannot sustain the fire within my body. We only pretend that we are bloodthirsty to frighten everyone but, in reality, dragons like the creamy and rich blood of the earth, such as raw oil or coal. It fills my stomach up so much that I do not need to eat every day."

"Very well, we will find oil for you to give you a chance to be in good health when you return home." The cat responded, evenly, to find out how homesick the dragon actually was.

"I cannot return home." Fuflow sighed and then became sad again. "Without viciousness I am useless to my clan and they will kill me. My new feelings of kindness will not allow me to fight against them but, on the contrary, my family will tear me to pieces without a second thought. They are ruled by a cruel law and I cannot blame them for this since my family has always lived in a tough world where the weak had no rights to exist because they took food and space from the strong and successful members of our Fa-nag clan."

"I will ask the Council to allow you to live in our mountains." Said Tac.

"It will be impossible to keep the existence of such a large animal as Fuflow secret forever and one day somebody will kill him for money, or just out of selfish pride." Sighed Ruslan. "But I know of a place where Fuflow can live safely under the protection of the wizard."

"I think I know who you mean. Yes, I think that the wizard will be a good candidate for the position of protector and companion. Personally speaking, I would not dare to challenge the wizard's power, especially when he is in a bad mood." Chuckled Tac.

Then, addressing Fuflow, he informed him. "Even your own kind will envy you if the wizard takes you into his household."

"Do you think that he may take me in?" Fuflow asked, hopefully.

"You can guard his cornfield against thieves." Tac suggested, flashing a look in Carfield's direction, to which the crow made an unclear sound to hide his embarrassment.

"I hope that both of you will stay with us for Tac's crowning and the attendant feast tomorrow. We are going to celebrate the end of our troubles, which have been created by the careless interference of somebody into a magical world." Carfield looked sternly at the cat.

"I would like to stay for more than one day, but I need to continue my search for my wife." Ruslan reminded his new friends that time was precious for him.

"You are right, we all have busy lives." The cat agreed. "And, by the way, it's time to eat something. My stomach has been growling for quite a while now and it needs to be filled."

"I will fly to the camp to tell Alisa to start serving dinner. Otherwise, you will need to wait until the food is ready." Proposed the crow.

"I am willing to bet that, by the time we come to camp, Carfield will have stuffed himself with cheese and biscuits and will ignore us by sleeping somewhere in a high corner of the tent." Tac teased his friend.

"That is unfair. I cannot promise to wait for you without eating anything but, at the same time, I am also thinking about your welfare as well. It will take you an hour to walk to the camp so why can somebody not warn Alisa that you will be arriving soon?"

"Why are you both arguing?" Fuflow joined in the discussion. "I can take you all on my back and carry you to the camp in a matter of minutes."

"Let's arrive at the camp on the back of Fuflow and surprise everyone." Retorted Tac, starting to climb onto the shoulder offered by the dragon.

When Ruslan, and part of the troop of animals that were not afraid to travel on top of the dragon, took a comfortable position on his back by holding on to his thorns and scales, the beast jumped up into the air. In a surprisingly-gentle movement he carried them evenly, rocking his passengers only slightly. He then took a wide half-circle to arrive at his destination from the side of the hill that had been cleared of vegetation, instead of dropping his ponderous body directly between the tents. Despite his good intentions, he did manage to scare the camp dwellers very badly, much to the delight of Carfield. But, after hearing Tac's story of the victory over the dark side of the dragon, the whole camp was filled with cheering and happiness.

"I do not see the sisters Thought. Where are they?" Tac asked Alisa.

"They have left only recently." She answered. "Nasty was crying all the time and complaining that the mattress was too hard and hurt her back and that she was not able to stand the cat smell that gave her an allergy. To prove it, she started to sneeze constantly until the other two sisters agreed that it would be better for everyone if they were to take her home. I suspect that Candice and Funny were completely exhausted by their efforts to please their difficult sister. However, they promised to come back next week to see if we still needed their help."

"That is nice! How can we open the Portal without them?" Asked the cat.

"What an incredible creature the angry Thought is." Remarked Carfield. "The woman really is a pain in the neck. She has managed to spoil everyone's plans again."

"Unfortunately." Tac observed. "Ruslan is now obliged to be our guest for a much longer time than he had earlier envisaged. But we will not find a solution to the problem on an empty stomach, so let's eat and then we will think about this new complication."

CHAPTER 12:

THE RESCUE MISSION FOR THE DOG'S DIGNITY

Prince Ruslan did not deny that he was curious about the ceremony that was about to take place on the top of Council Hill. "I've participated in many special occasions at my father's palace, but I can't remember witnessing anything as unusual as this forest celebration." He remarked to Tac.

By chance, Ruslan had become an observer of the argument between Tac and Rainar about the length and the greatness of the official part of the ceremony that would transform Tac from a house cat, that was not of any special breed, into a King with all the attributes of that position. This meant that he would have a crown and obtain the power and the privilege of being able to make decisions. Rainar had wanted to have a great show, with long speeches and many guests, but Tac had refused to be a part of his plan. Favoring short and simple ceremonies, Tac was bored with most of Rainar's proposals which he viewed as a great waste of his time.

From Ruslan's point of view, matching different opinions was a very difficult business since it required a willingness to listen to opposing arguments and usually involved mutual sacrifices. The Prince had expected to learn something about the art of negotiating for his own benefit in the event that the debaters would succeed in finding a compromise. He was approached by Roxal as soon as he had climbed up to the top of the hill.

"Your Highness, I have prepared a seat for you next to the chair of the King. Please allow me to show you the way." The raccoon limped, clutching his notes in a front paw.

The decorations on Council Hill had not changed very much. Only the stone that served as a seat for the King had been covered with red velvet and had a cushion made from the same fabric with golden tassels attached to each corner. Three apple trees had been planted behind the stone with their branches having been stretched aside and bent into the shape of a mug. Delicate, pink flowers completed the decoration of the background of the ceremony.

Tac's Coronation on Council Hill

The Council members had already taken their places at their appointed stones and all wore breast plates that showed their high positions at this important gathering. Rory and his band, as special guests, were seated in a half circle next to Ruslan's chair and the native animals sat on the opposite side. The low sound of casual conversation between the animals present at the coronation hung in the air like the buzz of working bees but was replaced with loud cheers when Tac quickly crossed the open circle in the middle and jumped onto the cushion.

"Dear citizens of Pokerweild forest and precious guests." Rainar bowed his widespread antlers in the direction of Ruslan and Rory with his band. Then, turning his head to his fellow friends, he continued. "We have all come here to express our gratitude to an animal who has risked his life to save our homes and families from death and destruction. For this heroic act the Council will crown him as our King. He will become our ruler whose opinions will be respected and his orders will be obeyed." The voice of the stag was drowned out by the yelling and the whistling of the crowd. Rainar waited until some of the excitement had subsided and went on. "Our new King is modest but, nonetheless, we have prepared a present for him that he will not be able to reject."

Roxal, with an important expression on his face, stepped forward, carrying the breastplate of a king, together with a crown, on a large platter. They were made from pieces of polished wood that were connected together by bleached stems of dry grass and brightened with the red beads of dried berries. Originally it had belonged to the eagle, the fifth King Matyar, but the breastplate and the crown had been re-assembled and widened to match Tac's larger size. It had been chosen for him on the assumption that the spirit of a retired King would help him to make wise decisions in a time of need.

Accompanied by the happy cheers of the assembled throng, the crown was duly placed on Tac's head. Rainar intended to continue but forgot his speech when he was suddenly faced by the furious figure of Alowsius who had jumped from behind the first line of spectators into the open circle in front of the King.

"This coronation, together with this King, is a complete fraud and I demand that it be stopped immediately." Alowsius cried out. "The Council promised him a crown provided that he killed the dragon and we all know that the dragon is still alive. Which means that Tac has failed in his mission and deserves to be kicked out of our wood instead of crowned as a King!"

"Tac's mission, as you called it, was to save us from death and he accomplished this successfully." Protested Rainar. "There is no danger anymore, not for animals and not for our habitat. What more could you ask of him?"

"I demand that this King does his job and kills the dragon." Growled Alowsius, who, was clearly unable to accept the truth that killing the dragon was no longer necessary.

"Alowsius, you need to learn to lose with dignity and avoid looking ridiculous." Galibur suggested.

"Am I ridiculous for opening your eyes to the tricks of this city tramp? Who can guarantee that he did not invite the dragon to take over power here and usurp the land of the animals?" The wolf had barely finished this phrase when a chorus of many voices rose in disagreement with this statement.

"I can swear that the intentions and actions of King Tac were honorable and genuine." A deep voice came from the background and the large head of Fuflow slowly rose above a terrified Alowsius. "I can swear that the danger the King overcame was real and I would have eaten him at that time without a moment's hesitation. He freed me from my hunger to kill but, if he has need of my service now, I would not mind swallowing some grumpy old wolf that might be spoiling our celebration." Fuflow concentrated the stare from his narrow, snake's pupils on the shaking figure of Alowsius.

The wolf jumped up as if someone had spilt boiling water on him and promptly ran away, followed by laughter from the crowd.

"Long live the King!" Said Fuflow.

"Long live the King!" Answered the combined voices of the animals.

"I am going to spend this day helping you around the house." Said Tac to Alisa, the next day. "I told Brown Bob that today is going to be my day off from my royal duties. You have been doing everything by yourself while I was at war, but now things will change. Being a King does not mean that you should allow your house to become untidy. I need to dispose of all the branches that the wind has blown down from the top of the hill and we are going to plant flowers along the pathway and around the house like my family did at my old house." Tac then became quiet, deep in memory.

"Do you miss them?" Asked Alisa.

"Yes I do. I have not had time to visit them for three weeks. I am curious as to how the little one is doing and also Tod. Perhaps I will run over to check on them after I finish sorting my papers on the table and planting in the garden. Do you think that we need to hire a professional landscaper?" Joked Tac.

"No thanks, I do not need a human close to my den. If I need help I will hire someone from the forest." Alisa replied.

"It's fine with me." Tac walked into a small room that served him as an office.

He had barely finished collecting waste paper into a woven basket for the trash, when Alisa entered the room with a strange expression on her face.

"You wanted to see Tod? I have to tell you that you do not need to run anywhere."

"What has happened?" Tac examined her face.

"Go and look for yourself." Alisa waved with her paw in the direction of the door and went to the closet to pull out two fluffy towels from a pile on the shelf.

Tac rushed outside. From the first look he was unable to recognize the figures that were standing on the threshold. Wet fur was glued to the skin of their faces and merged into a mold of strange thorns on their foreheads and necks. Only by looking at them more closely did Tac realize that it was Roxal and Tod. A piece of rope still hung from around Tod's neck and the dog was shivering and hiccupping.

"Take them inside before they catch a cold." Said Alisa, handing a towel to Roxal and rubbing Tod with the other one. "Tod will need a cup of warm milk before you begin to question him." She moved the figure of the dog, now wrapped in a towel, inside the house.

Roxal forcefully used his towel to dry his fur and talked at the same time. "I was running along the river when I suddenly saw Tod standing on the edge of a flat rock with a stone attached to his neck. If he had not been your brother I probably would have pushed him into the river myself but, instead, I jumped into the cold water to rescue the dog. The stone pulled him right to the bottom, where he was wriggling like an orange balloon, and I had to quickly bite the rope and drag his unconscious body back to the bank. I did everything that I could to start his breathing again and after he had stopped throwing up dirty water I was able to take him to your home. Excuse me, but I need to run since I have already lost a lot of time by dealing with this burden. Now he is yours." And Roxal ran away, leaving Tac with a wet towel and a fresh problem.

Having only one source from which to obtain answers to his questions, he went inside the house to look for Tod. The soothing and comforting voice of Alisa came from the kitchen and Tac found her and Tod sitting at the table. Tod was being served with dog food that had been kept in the house for him. Warmed up by the glass of hot milk, he had stopped hiccupping and now looked much better. But the sad expression in his eyes, combined with his drooping ears, told Tac that the depression that had pushed Tod to make an attempt to drown himself was still present. Tac knew that the best way to get rid of it would be to talk it out. So he thanked Alisa for the care shown to his friend and sat on an empty chair next to him.

"I am surprised and very concerned to see you in this condition. So, please tell me what made you feel that your life is worthless and you decided to take early retirement?"

Tod lowered his head, avoiding the studying look of the green eyes of his friend. "I know that I am not perfect, but service to the family was the meaning of my life. Having failed in my duty, I decided that I could no longer stay under Master's roof and I punished myself by leaving the house. I walked to wherever my legs would take me and eventually they led me to the river. A nasty, little voice in my head reminded me of all the events in the past when I had done something wrong. My whole life was analyzed and separated into the good and bad things and each side was carefully examined and weighed. It appeared that I was a totally worthless creature and the same voice whispered to me that the pain would disappear if I were to end my life. To stop this torment I jumped into the water. I was very scared at first but soon the pain lost its sharpness and became just a sensation that slowly faded from my being. I did not ask the raccoon to rescue me." Gulped Tod, sighing heavily.

"I still do not understand why you are blaming yourself. I want to hear facts, instead of conclusions based on the opinions of some ghostly voices." Urged Tac.

Tod scratched his ear, and started slowly. "I do not know why misfortune chose me. Maybe I was off guard, having been mellowed by our happiness. This special, happy mood came into our family with the arrival of the baby and affected even me. Problems became very small, worries became only temporary and our life moved along the street of good times. Even our Master decided to start farming again and bought bags of seed and spent hours preparing the old tractor for the hard work.

That terrible evening, when the incident had happened, was not much different from any other. I had my supper, then sniffed all the places that were easy to breach for the foxes and the rats but did not detect any suspicious smell. Returning to my doghouse, I found more beef on my plate. Eating some of this was the last thing that I remembered. Next day I got up feeling unwell. Sick as I was, I nevertheless went to look at the strangers that were talking to the Master. He gave me a frowning look but the police officer knelt and patted me. 'Don't blame him. Tod is an old dog and that's why he didn't hear the robbers. Maybe it's a good thing that he didn't disturb them, otherwise you could have lost your dog as well.' The word 'robbers' stirred my senses and I ran to the barn to find that all the bags containing the seeds had disappeared. Concentrating on the smell of the thieves, I followed their tracks. When the footprints of one of them turned towards the house, I became very nervous and fearful. The door was not closed tightly and I squeezed myself inside. My investigation brought me to the second level. Here the intruder had spent some time at the door of the baby's bedroom but had turned to Lana's door instead. He had searched her backpack which had been left on the chair and had removed something that belonged to her. I was angry at myself for having allowed this to happen but redirected my fury onto the innocent bag.

'Tod what are you doing?' I heard my mistress behind me. Surprised by my aggressiveness towards her backpack, she took it from me to check that everything was in place. Her urgent search through the contents revealed that something was missing. She froze for a second, thinking, and then ran outside.

'Dad.' Her voice trembled, nervously. 'Somebody has been in the house and has stolen my notebook.'

'Maybe you left it somewhere? What is it that is so important in this notebook?' He had asked.

'Information! I'm investigating one person and all the information that I had found out about him was in this notebook. It looks like I'm not the only person who has an interest in him.'

Who is this person and why are you spying on him?' Master looked surprised.

'I was trying to find out who the mysterious Mr. Holmes is and why he has been helping us. Perhaps the robber just pretended that he'd come for the corn.'

'That's enough. I'm going to put a security system into the house. I thought that I had a dog guarding my house, but I was wrong. I have just a fly watcher that is unable to protect the family. Someone dangerous came close to us but Tod was peacefully sleeping during this incident.'

If our Master had beaten me with a stick I would have felt less pain and, frankly, he is right. I am worthless."

"Do not rush to blame yourself." Tac interrupted. "Let's go back to the part about the second supper. Who put it on your plate, if all the family members had been inside the house at that time?"

"I never gave that any thought." Admitted Tod, honestly.

"Did you eat all of this meal?"

"No, I was quite full. I ate a little bit, but some white stones that were mixed in with the meat did not taste very nice. I spat out the food which was already in my mouth and did not touch any more of it."

"It is a pity that I cannot look at your very suspicious supper.

"Unfortunately, this is not possible. In the morning my plate was clean."

"It must have been cleaned by the robbers. The family would have been too busy with the police to bother about the dish."

"Tac, why did they bother to clean my plate?" Tod felt confused.

"Because, my friend, the robbers put something in your food to make you sleep, so that you would not warn the Master with your barking. I know that Lana is desperate to find out the identity of Mr. Holmes because she has even gone to the trouble of starting to work in the Golden Nut café, hoping to run into the owner one day. She has a family to worry about and has too much personal pride to accept my help easily. But, if someone else with unclean hands has started to dig into our affairs and has frightened my family, this makes me furious. I am going to find out who the robbers are and make them think twice before coming near the Vladner home again. You know, Tod, it looks to me as if my plan to have a peaceful vacation is now only a dream." Tac said with a sad smile. "It is so inconvenient. I am still dealing with the warrior that needs to be sent home and the fate of the homeless dragon. Now, in addition to everything else, I have a complicated robbery and your nervous breakdown to contend with. Oh well, stay with me for today to let Master's anger cool down and tomorrow I will send you home with a friend."

"I cannot return home after what has happened." Cried Tod. "How can I prove that I was innocent if all the evidence has disappeared? How can I prove to Master that I am capable of protecting the women and the baby when he is not around and how can I look at his eyes if I do not have his trust and respect." He wept.

"Thanks." He took a napkin from the fox.

"Alisa, Tod needs to stay with us for some time until I can find a way to bring him back into his Master's favor."

"Of course. You must help him since he is your brother. Tod, we will use Tac's office as a guest bedroom and will make you a royal bed from the thick mattress and pillows."

"Oh, you do not need to go to all that trouble for me." He tried to hide the fact that he was very pleased at being the center of attention.

Tac closed the door and left them to their friendly debate. He ran along the pathway smiling at the thought that, with Alisa on the job, Tod would soon forget about his depression. Four short, but fast, legs carried the cat quickly onwards and eventually brought him to Carfield's hill.

'To pull Tod from a hole this deep we will need a really radical solution.' He thought, as he climbed up to the crow's home. 'That's why I need to talk to the inventor of the most bizarre ideas.'

Carfield was always attentive to Tac's problems. He started to walk in a circle with small, nervous steps with his wings crossed behind his back. "So, your Master was upset with Tod because he thought that the dog had been sleeping on the job and had left them unprotected? In this case we will need to prove that Tod is an expert fighter and could easily have overcome any serious enemy, even a wolf."

"I can do this, by talking Woo into playing the bad guy."

To which Carfield responded by making another two circles. "A good fight needs to have a good reason." He stopped, as an idea had just come into his mind. "Tod will chase the wolf that has threatened Lana or the baby and, after a fight, the dog will make his enemy run away in disgrace."

"The idea is good, but has some weak points." Tac admitted.

"I will strengthen the plan. Give me time until the end of the day and I will present it to you." The crow mused.

"All right. Then I will see you at my house to discuss it further." The cat got up. "Only remember, Master is not a fool. I need a very realistic plan or he will not believe it."

The way back down to the ground always took twice as long as when he had climbed up. Carefully going down backwards he used the branches as a ladder where possible. "Thank goodness!" He sighed, jumping onto the firm ground. However, his physical activities did not end with this since he needed to run a long distance to talk to Woo and also to invite Roxal. On the way to Woo's home, Tac fortunately met a trusted bird and sent word to Galibur.

All this running around was the reason why the cat had missed dinner, coming home quite late, tired and thirsty. "I encountered some difficulties in getting the consent of Woo and Roxal to my plan. Both of them don't like dogs but agreed to help because I asked them to do it." He confessed to Alisa and Todd, quickly cleaning the food from his plate. "I think that it will be better if we prepare the bench to sit outside, because Galibur and Woo do not feel comfortable in closed spaces."

Together, they brought a small table and two low chairs outside the house whilst Alisa spread out a mat filled with straw. He then jumped onto the chair, waiting for his guests.

Usually it was the birds that came to meetings first, but this time it was Woo and Roxal who appeared before them. Woo instantly reacted to the presence of Tod by raising the fur on his back and growling, but Tac stepped between him and Tod. "You are here not to display your dislike of dogs but to work together with my brother." Woo sniffed and lay on the mat in a way that did not oblige him to look at the dog. Roxal sat next to him and asked. "For whom are we waiting?"

"Here they are." The cat exclaimed, watching the birds land. Galibur used the back of the chair as a perch but Carfield took a seat.

"My thanks to everyone who has agreed to participate in this proposed operation to save my brother's reputation."

"Eating white stones?" Roxal clucked with his tongue, teasing Tod. "He is lucky to be alive."

"We will not discuss this." The cat intervened. "I want you to know that it is very important for me to return Tod to his home as soon as possible. Someone unfriendly to me in the role of Mr. Holmes is circling around my family and disturbing their peace. Tod needs to be there to watch out for their safety. He has learned a bitter lesson and in the future he will be cautious." And Tac looked at Tod who only nodded silently, in agreement.

Carfield's plan was dangerous but beneficial to Tod's reputation. The wolf, played by Woo, would kidnap the baby to give a chance to the dog to save him, with everything ending happily as he returned Troy to his grateful parents.

Todd was against the idea of involving the baby in this risky operation and said so openly.

"There is no danger for the baby, Tod." Carfield replied.

"I agree with Carfield. The frightening wolf is going to be Woo. He will not harm a child." Roxal was puzzled by the dog's deep concern.

"I cannot trust any wolf to touch Troy." Tod growled through his teeth. "I know perfectly well the kind of ideas he will have in his mind when he will have an innocent creature in his claws."

"Are you saying that I am such a monster that I would eat my friend's child?" Woo jumped up and exposed the sharp daggers of his teeth.

"Sit down both of you and hide your teeth! You will have a chance to punch each other out later. I want to remind you that if we do not work together then this plan will collapse and somebody will definitely get hurt. As the King of this forest, I order you to temporarily forget that you are a wolf and a dog and hate each other for being who you are. For the time being, you are both cats. I am not ordering you to meow but, if you will not stop provoking each other, I will have to consider this as a punishment." Tod and Woo docilely returned to their places and did not interrupt the work of polishing the plan. Every slight detail was taken into consideration but the plan still did not satisfy the company.

Eventually, Galibur said. "I think that it will help if we choose a place for this event and then adjust the plan accordingly. I have one in mind. It's a small, sandy beach near the fairground. A long strip of bushes outlines the shore on one side, leaving only a narrow pathway between the water and the branches of some wild roses. We can trim a narrow tunnel through the low branches wide enough for only the wolf to pass through. Finishing his performance, Woo can escape through this tunnel in the same way that he came in. Humans will only be able to follow him to the edge of the bushes. They can try to run around but, by the time the first of them has reached the opposite side of the roses, Woo will be out of sight."

"Excuse me." Carfield interrupted. "We have a small problem. How are you going to make sure that a family with a small child will be at the shore at the exact time that you want them to be there?"

"I do not know yet." The eagle admitted.

"I know!" Cried Tac. "As the owner of the Golden Nut Park I will decide to make a Sunday picnic for my employees and their families at this lake. Carfield, you will need to check the weather forecast to make sure that it will be warm enough for Troy otherwise the Vladners might refuse my invitation, worrying about his health."

"Perhaps it would be better to postpone this picnic until next weekend? The sisters Thought promised to return this Sunday to transfer the Prince and the dragon back to their homes. There is always the risk that something will go wrong if you schedule two difficult events on the same day. However, I am not saying that Ruslan will give us too much trouble because he is a fine fellow. He has fixed the gate at the campground, the doors of the horses' stables and has done much work around the fairground without expecting payment. The Prince has also learned a few words of English and has literally melted the hearts of all the ladies around here with his royal manners."

"Oh! Do not tell me that he is walking around my amusement park dressed in armor, with a huge sword dangling from his belt and attracting the attention of the public?"

"On no!" Laughed Carfield. "Carl has bought him a pair of jeans and T-shirts and has shown him, by means of signs, that it would be better if the Prince were to exchange his nice, but foreign, military uniform for something of a local design. Carl has told everyone that Ruslan is an exchange student from some far-away country which is barely known to the public and, as a result, no one is surprised when he does unusual things. Do not worry, Tac, everyone likes him. Frankly, I am more concerned about Fuflow. His size makes the business of hiding him from people's eyes very difficult. He is inside his tower on the mountain but there is no guarantee that he will not be spotted should someone fly over it in an airplane. I'll sigh with relief when he leaves our world and I can return to my normal life."

"Ah, Carfield, you sound like a grumpy, old codger." Laughed Tac. "Think what our life would be without magic? Only a boring existence!"

"I would like to have one boring day without worrying about something and having to deal with constant telephone calls." The crow complained.

The sound of a ringing cellular phone made him jump and gave everyone a chance to smile in empathy with him. He removed the telephone from his pouch and opened the panel. "Carfield, secretary of the Golden Nut Amusement Park, how may I help you? Oh, it's you Carl, what's up?" Motionless for a moment, he listened to the voice on the other side then made a sour face. "Can you read me the note please?"

Carfield became furious.

"What has happened?" Tac believed that the problem was not worth smashing the cell phone as the crow had intended to do and he took it away from him.

"You have to hear this." The crow sounded really upset. "Carl just called to advise that he has received a message from Candice. You will not believe the news."

"Carfield, stop being dramatic, just tell me what this is about?"

"They cannot come because the Portal is jammed, or blocked. It does not open." He spread his wings tragically. "She heard rumors from somewhere that a second gate exists somewhere and all of their family, along with the wizard, is sitting surrounded by books and searching for its location. They are also searching for the key to open it because each gate has its own key. Why am I not surprised?"

Roxal tried to comfort him by saying. "Carfield, you are not the only one who is upset and tired of this situation." But he only got a dirty look.

"You can schedule your kidnapping for this Sunday; there is no reason to delay it?

Perhaps we shall get lucky and at least solve the problem concerning your brother. It's not as complicated as trying to find a hidden Portal between two different worlds and we can easily handle one of our life's normal challenges. I will see you all tomorrow, at noon, at the lake." His mood concerned everyone.

"What's wrong with him?" Roxal asked, shrugging. Woo only twisted his paw at his temple.

"Goodbye, Tac. Are you coming with me, Roxal?" The wolf waited for the raccoon and together they ran along the pathway to their homes.

"I need to return to my nest too." Galibur commented. "It is getting late and I must hurry up if I don't want to fly in darkness." He launched himself upwards into the changing sky.

"Let's take everything back home, have supper and go to sleep." Addressing Alisa, Tac stretched his back.

The cat and the dog probably would have talked late into the night if Alisa had not sent them to bed. Needless to say, Tac had difficulty in getting up the next morning after his late party.

"I hear that wiping your face with a wet towel will help get rid of sleep." She suggested, standing over him.

"Please do not do this." He jumped out of bed, licking his paw and rubbing his eyes. "I am quite fresh now, thank you, without cold water."

"I am sorry to wake you up but you wanted to give out the invitations to your employees today. I am sure that Carfield will already be waiting for you in the office."

"It's easier for him. He is a bird, and gets up with the first beam of light."

He had started eating his breakfast without even looking at what had been served and did not bother to argue when Tod insisted on going to the office with him, instead of staying home and probably becoming very bored.

Meanwhile, Carfield walked back and forth in front of the office door, waiting for him impatiently. He met Tac with the remark. "Thank goodness you have come. I need help to print-out the invitations. I have prepared the text for them, which is brief but rather charming, and called a catering company. The program for the picnic will be exciting enough to ensure that everyone will want to come."

The three of them stopped working only when the piles of envelopes, carrying the accurately-printed names of all those invited, had been sorted according to the workstations.

"Hi Lana, I'm glad that you came." Rick displayed the friendliest smile that he could. "We are going to have a cool day. The management offers to the staff and their families all the food that they can eat, together with different competitions and games. By the way, in some games you may not be accepted if you don't have a partner, so may I sign you up as my partner?" Rick was talking fast and looking at Lana with a child-like excitement. Despite the fact that she didn't have any interest in playing games, and was in a strange mood, she was thoughtful enough to agree to his proposal. She didn't relish the possibility that the joyful look on his face would turn into a disturbing expression of disappointment and his mood would become a reflection of her own.

"Oh! Thank you, Lana. I'm going to run over to the table to sign us up."

'Thank goodness he's left.' She thought, with a sigh of relief, as she walked back to the red blanket stretched out on the sand. Both of her parents were busy making Troy comfortable in the carrier, but the baby did not want to stay inside and was producing short, anxious sounds that could turn into crying at any moment.

"Mom, it's warm enough to let him sit on the blanket and have the freedom to move around, instead of sitting in this box." Removing a towel from the bag, she put Troy on top of it. The baby's face became wreathed in smiles and he started to kick out with his tiny legs.

"Look, Mom, he's happy." She sat next to him and tried to catch his attention with a bright toy. The baby touched the toy with his little fingers and then concentrated his stare on Lana's coworkers who had stopped to talk to him with smiles of adoration. Troy eventually got tired of looking at the strangers and turned his interest back to his own tiny fingers, putting some of them into his mouth.

"Are all of these girls your co-workers?" Asked Natalie, looking around with her hand placed at the level of her eyes to shade them.

"I work with some of them and others I have never seen before but, if they eat the food which has been purchased by our boss, then they must be his employees."

"Lana you don't look very happy. At your age you should enjoy life." Remarked Nicholas, handing her a paper plate with food.

"I'm not hungry, dad, but thanks." She got up and walked away without any particular plan in her mind. She understood that her parents were trying to pretend that everything was perfect with them, but she didn't share their feelings. Drifting between people, she found a quiet spot and sat on a large stone to look at the waves coming towards her. The sparks of dazzling light which danced on the water had relaxed and entranced her. Daydreaming, she had missed a major part of an incident and had only started to pay attention to what was going on around her when women started to scream loudly. Worried about her family she ran back, maneuvering between strangers, to the place where she had left them. Loud screaming rent the air and no one knew what to do...

The bodies of two large animals circled each other in a fight around Troy. The baby was sitting on the sand and looked at them excitedly. Natalie and Nicholas were trying to get to their child but, every time they made a move, they were repulsed by the bare teeth of the wolf. A beige dog that looked like Tod barked furiously and jumped around, trying to force the wolf away from the baby. Suddenly, the wolf jumped aside and, dragging his tail beneath his stomach, tried to escape but was immediately chased by the barking dog. Both of them reached the edge of the bushes where the wolf dived into a narrow tunnel, leaving the dog to savor his victory. Barking for the last time, the dog returned to the baby, licked his face and wagged his tail.

Witnesses of the incident cheered the dog, glad that everything had ended well. However, when the parents rushed forward to hug their rescued son, they were knocked down by the bodies of geese plummeting from the sky. More of these birds landed on the sand, stretched out their long necks and hissed at the people who, in turn, grabbed bags and blankets and waved them at the birds in an effort to scare them off.

However, the geese didn't want to leave. While part of the flock continued to hold the parents at bay, the rest of them attacked the crowd and the dog. He was whirling around like an orange tornado, evading the beaks whilst trying to grab them with his teeth. Tod was finally able to return to his position over the baby and even managed to catch the wing of one of his attackers. But two large geese split-off from the line of those that were keeping people away from the child and attacked him. He then jumped swiftly but a stone-hard beak hit him on the head, throwing him onto his back. The dog lay on the sand without moving, his forehead becoming red with blood. The biggest Goose, who was the leader, screeched something and, with the help of other members of the flock, lifted up the child. Then, flapping their wings heavily, they carried the baby over the line of bushes farther into the forest.

Lana at first refused to believe her own eyes and stared at the disappearing shapes. She wanted to pinch herself to have proof that she was not asleep, but her arm had enough pinch marks already and was bleeding from a deep scratch that she had received when one of the birds knocked her down to the ground. This was not a dream and Troy had been taken from them. Jumping up from her knees she ran to hug the tearful Natalie whilst someone called the police.

Turning to look back, Lana saw Rick and a few ladies cleaning-up and putting bandages on, the dog's head.

"The dog has a collar and a tag." He screamed into the crowd. "Is somebody missing a dog?"

"His name is Tod." Lana cried out, hugging her mother who remained standing only because of the support of her husband. Taking her mother's hands to get her attention, she said. "Mom I need to look at Tod." Natalie said nothing and let go of Lana's hands. "This is our dog." She shouted to the people who tried to give some water to Tod.

"You must take him to the Vet. He has cuts on his head." A man dressed in a pair of jeans, and a white shirt stained with blood, advised her. Lana looked back at her family indecisively.

"Don't worry about Tod." Said Rick, understanding her dilemma. "I've already called Carl. He's coming with a car to take him to the city."

Lana bit her lip to stop it from trembling. Unable to talk, she just squeezed Rick's hand and returned to her parents who were surrounded by police constables and witnesses to the tragedy.

Almost at the same time, Tac with Alisa, Roxal and Carfield were sitting peacefully in the shade of a young tree, with no knowledge that the little play that they had prepared so perfectly had turned into such a terrible disaster.

The casual conversation taking place between Tac and Carfield had not disturbed the sleeping Roxal. Like all of them, he had risen early and had been doing a lot of running around to check if the tunnel was clear and had become exhausted.

"Stop your gossiping." Alisa said to them. "I see Woo running here at top speed. Let's listen to the news." Woo reached the shade and collapsed next to them, breathing heavily. Drops of liquid were hanging from the end of his tongue that was pulsating to the rhythm of his breath.

"Did everything go well?" Tac was desperate to hear the whole story immediately.

"I would be a liar if I were to say that it has been an easy task. I even thought for a moment that we should forget about this plan completely. But, suddenly, I saw my chance to commence the attack. Most of the young people had gathered round the older woman who was talking loudly and had diverted their attention. The baby was lying on his stomach out of his portable bed and, consequently, this made my task easy. I lifted the baby carefully and carried him to the place where I needed to wait for Tod to rescue him.

The little one probably decided that I was playing with him and giggled happily, but his parents did not see the fun in this. They became scared and wanted to take the baby back but I showed them my teeth, as had been planned. After that, most of the humans jumped up, screaming, until Tod appeared on the scene. He hit me with his shoulder and growled through his teeth. 'Move farther away from Troy so that we will not scare or scratch him accidentally.'

'I do not think that he is frightened. He thinks that we are the hired entertainment.' I growled back, although I did jump aside for the sake of the baby.

Woo and Tod Fighting Over Troy

We attacked each other, chest to chest, and pretended that we were trying to rip out each other's throats. I jumped aside, then again to pretend that I was scared and ready to give up. Seeing that somebody was running in my direction with a stick, I played the coward and ran away under the bush. I think I impressed the public on the beach." Said Woo, with a smile. "And I think that Tod right now is on a glorious high and is looked upon as a hero because he has saved the baby from the teeth of a ferocious wolf. I am surprised that I don't see Galibur here. He had a good view from his post up on the tree and should have been able to bring the story faster to you than I."

"What may have stopped him?" Mused Tac, looking upwards, but he overlooked him anyway.

"Tac, what happened at the lake is just awful!" Galibur cried out, as he walked towards them with his wings still open.

"What is awful? Did our plan fail completely?" Asked Tac, in surprise.

"No, it worked, but only for a short time. I started to follow Woo after he had disappeared under the branches, as we had agreed, ready to warn him if people with sticks and stones had decided to chase after him. Suddenly I noticed a flock of unusually large white geese. I had never seen them around before and wondered what they were doing here.

Close to the shore of the lake two of them separated from the group and attacked me but I escaped them without difficulty. Making a half-circle, I returned with the intention of finding out why they were being so aggressive and even attacking humans. The people on the shore quickly recovered from their surprise to hit the birds with towels, blankets and anything else that was available to them. I had to leave them to take care of themselves and looked for the baby who must have been in danger in the middle of this chaos.

My presence scared the geese but, before they left the shore, three of them lifted the baby up and carried him over the bushes. I could not do anything, realizing that if I attacked the kidnappers they could easily drop the baby and I was not sure that I would be fast enough to catch him before he hit the ground. Whilst he was in the air, it would be safer for him to be with the geese because I had noticed that they cared for him.

Troy and his Geese Kidnappers

Troy was sitting on the back of the largest bird and two other geese were holding him to prevent the child from slipping from the back of the leader. It was probably his first experience with birds and he appeared to be very intrigued, touching the soft feathers with his hands.

Flying for some time in a straight line, the geese eventually turned towards the mountains.

It happened that I crossed paths with one of my relatives and transferred the task of watching the geese over to him. Then I flew here to warn you about this unexpected outcome of our enterprise."

"What happened to Tod? Did you see him? Why did he fail to protect Troy?" Tac looked devastated.

"I saw him lying on the sand." Galibur responded, glumly.

The cat was about to run to the shore himself but was stopped by a call that came in on Carfield's phone. The conversation was short and, putting down the phone, the crow informed everyone. "It was Carl. He called me to say that he had taken Tod to an animal hospital. He is suffering from a slight concussion and two wounds to the head. His life is not in danger and Carl will bring him home where the family will take care of him. His Master is remaining at the shore with the Rangers and the volunteers to look for Troy. They are going to search all the woods around the lake, but we know that they are wasting their time since we have just learned that the geese have taken him to the mountains. This means that we need to organize our own rescue mission to find the child."

"I need you to take me to the mountains." Tac looked at Galibur.

"In that case, let's go to pick up your traveling pillow." Said the eagle, and the whole company immediately got up from the ground to run, and fly, in the direction of Tac's house.

Coming closer to the house, Tac saw the figure of a man who was sitting on the ground close to the entrance to his home. He recognized Ruslan, although he looked completely different in modern clothes.

"I heard about the incident at the lake. The theft of children like yours has happened in my country many times. These geese have earned a bad reputation and this is the reason why parents there guard their children closely until they reach the age of two. I don't know why the birds need children but I believe that Troy is in real danger."

"In this case we can't wait." Tac took the pillow from Alisa and helped Galibur to lock the straps around his chest. They were still fumbling with the locks when the young eagle, Sar, flew in with information that his family had found the place where the geese had made their stop.

"It's a cave on the ground level, camouflaged with vegetation. My father and I followed the flock secretly and saw them disappearing inside the cave. I brought my brothers to ensure that they were trapped there until the King decides what to do."

"You did the right thing." Tac said to Sar. "I am going to the cave to lead the rescue mission. Carfield, please show Ruslan the place where the cave is located because we may need his help." He then climbed up onto the eagle's back.

Half an hour of fast flying brought him and Galibur to the first line of mountains that looked like the high hills which were covered by a forest. The cave had been discovered five years ago when a crew of loggers had cleared the tall trees from the hillside, leaving only the young saplings to restart the forest. Galibur landed on top of a rusty-red, round platform which was all that was left of a century-old hemlock. The young firs had tried to hide the devastation done to the forest but they were not yet mature enough to hide the large stumps of the missing trees.

The black opening of the cave had been exposed and looked like a sarcastic smile on the body of the mountain. Ten or more eagles sat on branches around the cave like silent guards. Tac wanted to look inside, but Galibur stopped him.

"Your paws are not the right weapons to use against these birds and their feathers will be hard for you to penetrate. Allow the eagles' strong beaks to do the job."

Tac therefore stepped aside to let the eagles enter the cave one by one and immediately the silence within was replaced by the flapping of wings. He danced on one spot, nervously, but continued to wait outside.

"How is the fight going?" He heard the voice of Carfield from above.

"I do not know. Should I go inside?"

"Wait for Ruslan." Carfield landed next to Tac. "He is riding one of Carl's horses and by now he must be close by."

The battle inside the cave ended before the Prince had reached them. All the eagles left the cave almost simultaneously, supporting the bodies of two wounded relatives. The cat and the crow ran closer to the scene, hungry for news.

"These geese are not ordinary birds and turned out to be difficult opponents. That is why we had no choice but to retreat after two eagles from our group had sustained deep wounds. I am glad that I talked you out of going into the cave." Galibur said to Tac. "After we entered the cave we found that the geese were wearing sharp steel beaks on top of their own. Even our skill in fighting was futile in this situation."

"I know somebody who is invincible to even a steel blade. Do you think that the entrance is wide enough for a dragon to enter?" The cat queried.

"It's difficult to say. The cave is very big inside but the entrance is low. I saw only a small part of the space that's close to the entrance and could only assess the size of the cave from the reflection of sound from the opposite wall."

"Did you see Troy?" Asked Tac, with concern.

"Yes. The geese had managed to steal not only the baby but also its carrier and a bag with his stuff. The bottle for the baby food stood empty on the floor. Therefore, I assume that the geese fed Troy and kept him warm in the cold cave."

"Thank goodness for that." Tac expressed relief. "Someone needs to bring Fuflow here. We cannot just sit, waiting for the chance to retrieve Troy, knowing that every minute we delay will be unbearable for his mother."

The place where Fuflow was waiting for an opportunity to return home was a short distance from the cave and it did not take Galibur very long to reach him. The dragon tried to land softly but, despite his intentions, he still created a real storm with his wings.

Tac explained to him. "The kidnappers are trapped in the cave but they are armed with steel beaks and have wounded two of our fighters already. They still keep a little child in their possession that we are trying to rescue. I do not care about punishing the thieves but I need you to remove the baby so that we can return him to his parents."

Fuflow lay down on the ground and tried to crawl through the entrance to the cave. Eventually, his high back got stuck in the narrow hole. The dragon backed up, bit an edge off the opening to remove a large chunk of wall and then moved into the cave. Desperate to see everything with his own eyes, Tac rushed after him.

Ruslan, carrying a burning torch that was just a branch of a tree, followed him with sword in hand. To their surprise the cave was empty and even the bag, and the carrier that had been mentioned by Galibur, had disappeared. Only a rectangular print on the dusty floor and birds' feathers served as evidence that the geese, together with a child, had been present here not long ago.

"This wall is very warm." Remarked Ruslan, studying it in the dull light of the torch. I have only one explanation to what has happened here. This cave probably hides the second Portal."

"Maybe this is the gate that the sisters Thought have been trying to find in the old books?" Tac Guessed.

"In that case, we should try to open it." Ruslan returned his sword to its scabbard and, putting the torch into a convenient crack in the wall, pressed both hands to the stone wall and stood still for a few minutes. Stepping back, he said. "I can't open the gate but I did send a thought message to get help from the other side."

At this, all the company turned back towards the entrance.

"Ruslan, I will need to ask you and Fuflow to guard the gate while I go back to talk to the Council and to say goodbye to my wife."

"Do not worry, Tac, we will wait for you here." The dragon assured him.

"I am also leaving to advise Carl about all the developments and to check on Tod so that Tac can leave home with an easy heart" Carfield stated. "But, of course, I will rejoin him in this important mission."

"So, you're not afraid of dragons anymore?" Fuflow teased him.

"I am afraid of them very much, but I am going to go with Tac anyway!" Retorted the crow.

Returning a few hours later, Tac did not recognize the place. The abandoned slope was full of animals. They were not just running back and forth, but were busy making a temporary camp for the group who were about to leave. Of course, Carfield was already here, checking supplies and watching the progress of the preparations. Fuflow didn't need food or sleep but Ruslan didn't mind taking a nap in the tent while he had a chance.

"I did not find Carl to talk to him. He was somewhere in the city and I left him a detailed message on an answering machine." The crow advised Tac. "But I did see Tod. Because he is feeling better I needed to talk him out of going with us. His injuries would slow us down."

"I thought that you would have preferred to stay home to help Carl?" The cat mused.

"He did not need me. Even a squirrel can run the Amusement Park since I have installed a perfect system to operate it. I am sure that everything will be fine. How did Alisa take the news that you are possibly going to look for the child?" Asked Carfield, with interest.

"She was strangely calm and just said that she wanted us to spend together the time that was left prior to my departure."

"Well, well." Carfield had nothing more to say.

A sudden flow of air coming out of the cave abruptly ended their conversation. It felt as if the cave had taken a deep breath and then suddenly released the air to make it reverberate around the entrance. The friends prepared to run inside the cave to find out what was happening but the explanation soon became self-evident.

"Candice!" They exclaimed, simultaneously, as they looked at the woman.

"I am glad to see you too." She smiled at them. "We received a message that you had found a gate and needed our help. Are you ready, then?"

"I am ready!" Carfield cawed, excitedly.

"Not yet." Tac moved him aside. "I am waiting for the forest Council to be informed about my departure and to discuss with them the matter of my replacement since I do not know how long I am likely to be absent. Do you think the gate will stay open until tomorrow?"

"This gate does not stay open. I will wait until you are ready and then we will leave together." Being a Thought, she didn't need to ask too many questions.

The evening had not yet spilled the raspberry-colored sunset over the dark blue sky when everyone, who wanted to say their last words to the King, had gathered to share with him a last supper on this land. There was no sadness due to their knowledge that Tac had visited the orange woods many times, each time returning with intriguing stories. Tac carefully kept his personal feelings about the future trip a secret.

"I wanted to ask Roxal to escort you back home but he surprised me by saying that he was going to follow Carfield's example by joining me on this adventure." Tac confided to Woo.

"That is not strange since I am going with you too." Woo replied. "When I told my wife that you were going to reclaim the baby from the kidnappers and return the lad to his parents, she looked at our sons and said that, if I wanted to help the King, she understood my motivation and would wait for my return."

"Who is going to accompany Alisa home?" Tac shouted, looking around.

"No one!" The fox said firmly. "Instead, I will go with you too. You have been traveling alone at least twice and this time we will go together."

"Alisa this is not a tourist trip." He reminded her.

"And that is exactly why I want to be close to you. I have asked my cousin to look after our house." She responded, with a crafty smile. "I have also advised her that I do not know exactly when I might be back."

"Has anyone else made a decision to follow me without advising me first?" Asked Tac, looking at his friends with suspicion.

"I will go." Shustin suddenly volunteered. "In some situations you may need someone who is weak and looks harmless." Tac only lifted his eyebrows, thinking over this statement.

Bertrond expressed his decision almost as a joke. "In this case I will go with you too, Tac. After all, you will need someone large and strong to ensure that all the harmless and weak participants will be protected and will return home safely."

"I am glad that I will have good company with me." Tac admitted.

The last thing that he did before going to sleep was to make the elk, Rainar, the Steward for the time being. In the morning, he found that most of the animals had already left to avoid attracting attention to this place with their numbers. Only the bear, who had remained behind to dismantle the tent and return it to storage, greeted Tac and the rest of his group.

After a short breakfast, all of them crossed the entrance to the cave. All the walls of the cave looked exactly the same to Bertrond and Shustin. They looked at each other with ironic smiles that hid an underlying question; is this a joke? But, when Candice used a key to open the gate, revealing a dark space which carried a line of dots of light, they lost their smiles. Instead, their eyes opened wide and their hearts beat faster. The same thing happened with the hearts of the rest of their team, with the exception of Candice, whose anatomy was different.

Shustin asked Candice to pick him up, complaining. "My feet have gone to sleep and I do not think that I can take another step, not even a small one."

"Everyone is afraid of the darkness." She said, in an understanding tone, as she lifted him up.

"I will go first." Fuflow volunteered himself. Candice, carrying Shustin, was next and then Bertrond, followed by the flying Galibur and Carfield.

Alisa, Tac and Roxal were the last to step behind the edge of the cave.

The surface of the Portal started to bubble and then visibly shrank, as if a rope had been attached to the middle of the opening to move the edges closer together. Before the gate had closed completely, a lone figure stepped from behind a large stone and approached the gate in small, careful steps. The coward was shaken but hatred, and the hope of being able to get revenge, made Alowsius jump through the Portal. The air became slightly disturbed, then everything returned to stillness and the gate closed.

After the disappearance of Troy, the Vladners had locked themselves in their house, mourning the loss of their child, and refused to talk to anyone except the police.

"Why don't they leave us alone?" Lana looked outside through a small slit that she had made in the Venetian blind. "Isn't the pain and anguish enough without our suffering additional discomfort? No matter where you go they're under our feet." She sighed and said to her father. "I called the office to inform them that I wanted to take a vacation but no one answered. Dad, can you distract the man who is sitting outside in a truck so that I can sneak out through the garden gate?"

"You're too nervous and suspect the worst in everything." Nicholas replied. "He is probably waiting for his girlfriend." But he still put on a light jacket and went outside to open the gate for her and to talk to a young man in a dark-gray truck parked near their house.

Lana took her backpack and looked around for the key to her father's truck. As she crossed the living room, she almost tripped over the hem of her yellow, graduation dress lying on the chair. 'Mother has cried twice, seeing it.' She reminded herself. 'Perhaps this dress brought back happy memories about the days when she was waiting for Troy to be born.' The irritation that she felt towards the dress morphed into a decision to get rid of it. She folded and pushed it roughly into a bag to take with her.

Trying not to make noise with her high-heeled shoes, she tip-toed to the foyer and found Tod standing in front of the door, apparently calculating his chances of opening it by just staring at the doorknob steadfastly.

"Tod what are you doing here?" She lowered herself down so that she could see his stitches better. The edges of the cuts looked inflamed but did not show any signs of infection, prompting Lana to tell the dog. "O.K., I'll let you go outside if you promise to cancel you're digging activities for at least three days." Then, scratching Tod's neck, she opened the door for him and walked towards Nicholas's old truck with him by her side.

Lana opened the door of the car and looked to see if the gate was open. When she was ready to sit inside, she noticed that the dog had disappeared. Using the brief period during which her attention had been concentrated on something else, he had jumped inside the cargo space to hide himself behind Nicholas's tool box. 'That's strange. Where's Tod?' She mused as she checked the mirror and pressed the accelerator.

"Goodbye Dad." She waved to Nicholas, who was still standing at the door of the gray truck talking to the man, and thought. 'He was probably right and the man was simply waiting for somebody.' She felt relieved that her fears appeared to have been groundless.

Leaving the car in the parking lot, she knocked on the door of the office of the fairground but no one answered. However, the door was open and she entered the trailer. The clock showed a quarter to nine. She leant against the table, wondering whether or not she should wait for the secretary until her gaze fell upon the answering machine, tempting her to press the button. 'This is not the White House.' Was her first thought. 'What kind of secrets could I possibly reveal or disturb? Perhaps I'll find out at what time Carl will be back?' Without further concern, she pressed the replay button.

After the greeting message, she heard the recorded voice. "Hullo Carl, it's me, Carfield. I have no time to wait for you to come back to the office. Please listen to this message carefully. We almost caught the kidnappers who took Troy. But they have a friend who is knowledgeable in magic and this person had opened the gate to allow the geese to enter the world from whence the warrior and the dragon came to us. Tomorrow Tac, Bertrond, I and the rest of our group, together with the Prince and the dragon, will open the gate with the help of our friend, the kind Thought. I have no doubt that Tac will turn this land upside down to find the child, with the help of the Prince who has promised to give him passage through his country, but it may take some time. I know you will not be pleased to hear this, but you will need to roll the Golden Nut by yourself until we can return with Troy. I do not think that I will have a chance to see you tomorrow because the cave on the Bold Mountain, where the gate is hidden, is too far from the amusement park. You will find my instructions on how to successfully run the Nut in the safe. Carl, wish us smooth roads."

Lana nervously pressed the button again. This time she listened to the message even more carefully, her mind separating out the information that was the most important to her. 'Tac, with the help of my mysterious savior, has led the rescue mission to find Troy from the place that is called Bold Mountain? Where is this place?' Her fingers glided over the computer keyboard as if they were composing a symphony from the words. "Finally!" She exclaimed, when a web page showing a picture of a mountain side appeared on the screen. The accompanying text told a story of a cave hidden in the forest which was recently discovered by loggers, with its location marked on the map by a bright dot.

'You're right, Carfield, it's far away from here.' Lana admitted to herself. 'It will take me half a day to walk through the forest but, if I take my truck and go along the old logging road, then I'll surely cut the time significantly. This way, perhaps, I'll be lucky enough to catch up with you and your entire group, Sir Prince.'

"Good morning, Lana!" The voice of Rick behind her back startled her. "What are you doing here so early? Your shift doesn't start until noon."

Lana blew a stream of air through her teeth to hide her irritation. She quickly turned to face Rick who, by now, had already got a good idea of what she was doing by simply looking at the monitor.

Cursing himself for not clearing the tape after Carl had listened to the message, he said. "I can explain everything." In his turmoil, he babbled words like a child, afraid that Lana would go to the gate alone. "It's just a stupid joke from a friend of mine. I'm very sorry that you heard it."

"Joke? I don't think so." She frowned at him.

But Rick deliberately stepped forward to block her path, stating firmly "The road to this place is old and dangerous and, in places, has been destroyed by floods."

"How do you know if you've never been there?" Asked Lana, pointedly.

Rick didn't know what to say so he paused, searching for an answer.

"Is there something in this cave that you and Carl are hiding from everyone? Now, let me go!" She demanded.

"I can't, because Carl would kill me if something bad were to happen to you." Rick tried to stop her by holding firmly onto her hand. The warning growl of the dog made them both look behind at Tod who was standing in the doorway and ready to protect his Mistress.

"How did you get here, Tod?" Lana was both pleased and, at the same time, displeased, to see him. "Let's go boy." She called him, leaving Rick to stand with his hands up as if he was being held-up by a gunman.

Rick was in a panic. He called Carl on the 'phone to ask for his advice but the manager didn't answer. Having no other options, he decided to stop the girl, even if the dog attacked him. It was too late. They had already jumped into the truck and had rolled away at a slow speed. This forced him to run after her vehicle and grab onto its side to throw his body into the back of the pickup. Despite the fact that he was pounding on the back window, Lana stubbornly continued to drive towards the old logging site. Now it had become apparent that she was very determined to get there. The imprints of the wheels of her vehicle bit deeply into the soft, muddy surface of the forest road as it bounced over rocks and weaved around fallen tree trunks, or crossed depressions in the road surface which had filled up with water.

It was not difficult to track her, so the man who had secretly followed her for several miles allowed a cruel smile to flicker around his lips. After he had read her diary, he had been waiting for a chance to find her alone for weeks and now was sure that he was going to have her exactly where he wanted her-- almost alone and out of the protection of her father.

Roger had heard the argument between Lana and Rick about some secret and this had increased his suspicions that some dirty trick had been used to make this amusement park successful. He had been the first owner of this part of the wood and felt that he had the right to receive a significant piece of this success. But, before he was going to approach this Mr. Holmes, he wanted to know what kind of a man he might attempt to blackmail. 'I will not step back if Holmes is a dangerous type.' He thought, with a self-satisfied grin. 'He will meet his twin.'

The road in front of Roger turned to the right and crawled uphill to a small square platform where the old truck was parked at the edge of the slope. Roger looked downhill to see the figures of the teenagers and a dog crossing the clearing. They needed to climb up between the remains of logged trees to reach the blackness of the cave where the secret was located. Having little time, Roger ran to his car to remove a gun and a ski hat with two holes cut in it for the eyes. He did not want to show his face to them so that he could avoid any problems with the police later.

'Shooting the chef-bear is not the same thing as killing kids and it will be a shame to kill Lana. She is such a cute chick.' He thought, pulling his mask down over his face and adjusting the holes. Jumping down from the slope, he ran towards the people from whom he intended to get all the necessary information.

"Look, this place has no significance. No one has visited it recently and it has been abandoned completely." Rick put Lana's bags on the ground.

"Really?" Lana was studying the markings on the ground. "Then how can you explain these holes? Someone obviously had a tent here and this was probably yesterday. Look at these fresh footprints."

"But most of these prints belong to animals. Perhaps some crazy animal-lover decided to feed some wildlife here." Rick argued.

"An animal lover like Carl?" Asked Lana, ironically, not really expecting an answer. "I have a flashlight in the bag so let's check out the cave."

"O.K., but promise me that after we check the cave we will immediately go back to the office. Frankly, this place gives me a chill. I feel that someone is looking at my back but, when I turn round, there is nobody there or I only see a waving branch."

Lana shook her head, smiling, as if to say. 'Don't even try to scare me.' She searched her backpack for a flashlight and, asked him. "Why did you drag all my bags here? I told you to bring only the backpack. You have carried my dress for nothing. Oh! I have an idea. Why don't we just leave it in the cave so that someone may find it centuries later and will wonder about the mystery of the yellow dress?" She laughed, but the smile left her face as soon as she had entered the cave. "This place is very suspicious."

"Is something wrong?" Rick looked at her, trying to understand the source of her concern.

"Don't you have the feeling that the cave inside looks much taller than it should be?" Lana asked Rick and then stepped into the sunlight to take another look at the outside of the cave before going back in. "Very strange!"

Rick didn't make any comment, thinking that if he didn't show any interest in exploring the cave then Lana would lose interest in it much faster.

"Those footprints definitely belong to a man who wore heavy boots." She sat down and pointed the light towards the floor. "The smaller print with the narrow end could have been made by a woman or a child, but the rest of the footprints definitely belong to animals and, for some reason, they were all dragging a heavy log behind them. Let's go deeper into the cave to see how far they actually penetrated."

"What's this?" He pointed.

"It looks like the remains of a fire torch and it's still warm." She replied, cleaning her fingers from the black ash after she had touched the ground. "Here's another one." Using her flashlight, she circled the top of the stone which still had a black deposit of ash upon it.

Suddenly, Tod flashed past them deeper into the cave and disappeared into the darkness.

"Tod!" She called after him, but heard only barking. Lana and Rick followed him inside until the dancing circle of light from her flashlight caught Tod standing beside the wall, looking upward.

"What's there Tod?" Lana sat down at his level. "Look, Rick, they stood here too!"

"Okay Lana, that's enough!" Rick was irritated. "This man with a child, or a woman with a pack of dogs, made a fire at this spot from a log that had been dragged all the way up here from the forest. Then they cooked dinner, ate it and left. And it's now time for us to leave too."

"But there are no footprints to indicate that they left the cave!" Lana protested.

Before they started to argue again, something scared her. The figure of a heavily-built man, dressed in a mask and holding a gun, stepped out of the shadows and into the light.

"Hands up!" He ordered, whereupon Rick dropped the bags and raised his hands but Tod took a step forward and growled angrily. This immediately made the gunman point his weapon at the dog.

"Please, don't shoot him." Pleaded Lana. "Tod, lie down, down." She lowered him with her hand and Tod obeyed, slowly.

"What do you want from us? We have nothing."

"I don't know yet." The man came closer. "Perhaps you'll have something that will interest me after all."

Rick caught Lana's hand and pulled her closer to hide her behind his back. The result of this was that the button on Lana's jacket slid out from the buttonhole and exposed part of the cross that she had decided to wear today to give her comfort.

"What's this thing? Give it to me!" The attacker demanded.

Lana slid her fingers under the jacket to touch the sharp edges of the stones embedded in the cross and realized that she didn't want to take it off. She couldn't lose it under any circumstances. Shrinking back in fear, she felt the hard, but warm, surface of the wall press up against her body.

"Give it to me, or shall I shoot your boyfriend first?" The stranger threatened her.

Lana raised her hand to remove the chain from her neck but, at that moment, the wall behind her moved, losing its solid structure. The texture of the air also changed and became like a stream of water that swept her up, together with the other occupants of the cave, in a rushing movement. The stripes and dots of colored lights streaming away from her forced her eyes to close. She tried to overcome her fear by thinking. 'It must come to an end!'

Gradually, the firm cushion of air that had supported her softened and she opened her eyes to see a mountain wall that was moving away from her. Lana fell down on her back and quickly caught Tod who fell on top of her. They both rolled aside before Rick landed on his face on the same spot they had occupied only seconds earlier. As he tried to get up, Lana's bags hit him on the back and knocked him down again.

"Are you okay?" Rick gathered up his body and shook sand from his chest, hands and clothes. "Where are we?" He looked around in wonder.

"I believe that we are in the same place where your friends, Carfield, Tac, Bertrond and the rest of the group, including the Prince and the Dragon, went to look for my brother." She replied with a teasing, but nervous, smile as she pulled a T-shirt, jeans and a pair of runners from her backpack and then a compass, a pair of binoculars and a bottle of water from the side pocket.
"Have an energy bar while I change my clothes." Handing him one of the chocolate bars, she shared another one with Tod.

"Do you take a change of clothes with you every time you go to work, or because you knew we would get into trouble?" Asked Rick, with his back turned to her.

"No, I can't predict the future. But I thought of asking Carl to allow me to take a short vacation. I wanted to look for my brother in the place where the trouble arose. It's a strip of forest in the north-west, close to the mountains. Now I'm ready to go." Lana lifted up her binoculars and looked at the orange woods which were separated from them by a narrow channel of water.

"Where do you plan to go?" Rick looked in the same direction.

"Right there!" She gave the binoculars to him and pointed to the cabin which was standing beside the water on an open strip of grass, free from yellow trees…

Made in the USA
Charleston, SC
23 September 2012